THE MARCH OF THE BLOOD RED KING

THE MARCH OF THE BLOOD RED KING

ANTON JONES

PAGE + PLOT PRESS

Published in the United States of America by Page + Plot Press, an imprint of the Empowered Press, LLC, Orlando, FL.

ISBN: 978-1-957430-33-1 (paperback)

ISBN: 978-1-957430-34-8 (hardcover)

Library of Congress Cataloging Publication Data is available.

http://theempoweredpress.com

publish@theempoweredpress.com

Cover Art: Caleb Egland

Map Art + Design: Caleb Egland

www.calebeglanddesign.com

Cover Title Design: www.ongraphica.com

Layout Design: Jill Carlyle

The Empowered Press can bring authors to your live event. For more information or to book an event, please email: publish@thempoweredpress.com

Shatter Rock

Wilheim
Academy

Rodrick the
Merchant's
Palace

Wilheim

The Warring
Nations

Canyon L

Lake
Verdín

Oros
Pass

Trayhaz River

Andhataz
Platuea

The Bloody
River

Highland
Pits

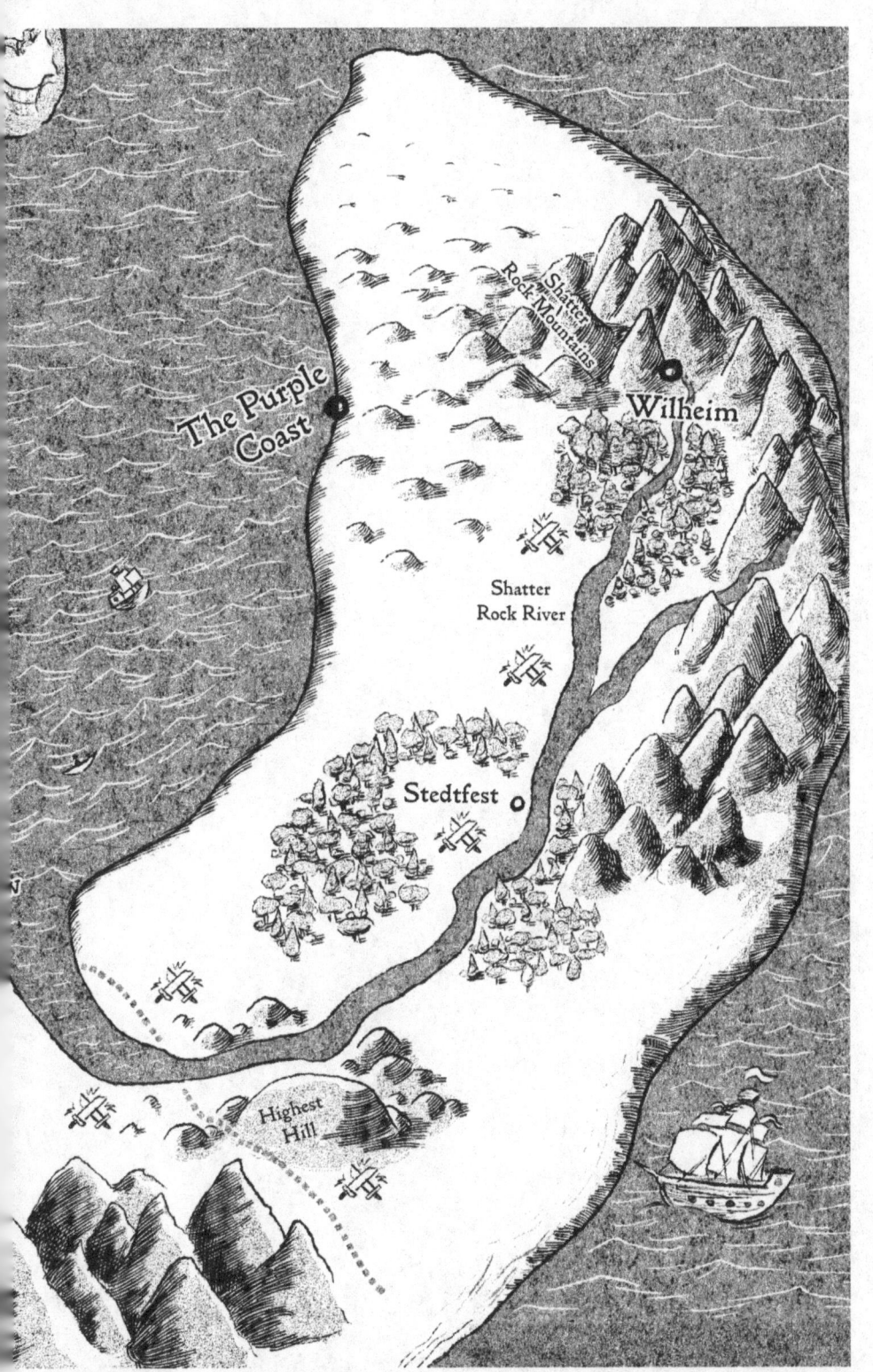

CONTENTS

PART THREE
EVEN IF THERE'S NOTHING LEFT TO
PROTECT

AUTHOR'S NOTE AND DEDICATION

For a long time, I was turned off by the notion of escaping into fantasy worlds. To me, that seemed like surrender, like I accepted that I couldn't make my immediate world good enough. Why would I need a cause to escape otherwise? But then I was struck by a rogue letter *s* traveling one hundred and forty years into the future concealed in the first lines of the hymn "How Great Thou Art."

> *Oh,* Lord, my God, when I in awesome wonder
> Consider all the worlds thy hands have made...

Worlds. Plural. Never have I been so dumbstruck by the placement of an *s*. I now see all worlds, including the fantasy ones, as domains we have been charged to safeguard. After all, I hope my own fantasy world can change the outcome of the physical one in spectacular ways.

My lyric memoir, *This is Not a Death Sentence,* was dedicated to my family and helped me work through my past. *The March of the Blood-Red King,* and the series that will come from it, is for the future. It is for my students, many of whom took part in making this book possible.

From the classes I've taught and the conversations I've had, I know that my greatest challenge as an educator is to do battle with the hopelessness that gives way to apathy. Many students give me a blank look when I ask them what they dream of doing, and that concerns me. Some of my students seem to have forgotten the purpose of dreams, that they are what keep us growing ever more and striving ever higher.

I wanted to write a fantasy series that wrestles with the questions, "How do we keep living when it seems that the world exists to kill our dreams? How do we keep living when our dreams are no longer attainable? What happens to a person who tries to live without a dream?" This is for the students who haven't found dreams or their reason to strive. But it is also for my students who gratefully welcome challenges and see them as opportunities to test their resolve, to demonstrate how much their dreams are worth.

I personally fluctuate between both mentalities, but one thing is certain: the more strivers I see, the more I am encouraged to keep striving. To paraphrase one of my character's, apathy and hope are equally infectious. Some people take comfort in their lack of agency, that the world has already ended on a planetary scale a dozen times before we were even born and will continue to end over and over again until all becomes dust. This attitude removes accountability for personal action. But a hopeful person could hear that same factoid, that we should have gone extinct a dozen times, and be amazed that somehow we persist. That hopeful person will take action to make sure we keep persisting. If we decide not to care, we just made it easier for those around us to give up, too. But if we hope and dream and strive, there's no telling how many worlds we will save. Worlds. Plural. Thank you for your resilience.

PART ONE
THE PROTECTORS ARE GONE

CHAPTER I
LIFE AND LIMB

THIS WAS NOT the sound of hammer on anvil that echoed around the walls of the dark prison cell. It was a muted, repeated thudding and crunching, skin-tearing and knuckles crunching on unforgiving stone. Roran continued beating his hands bloody against the walls, too dark to distinguish what kind of stone it was. Not that he cared. All he cared about was making himself bleed. Any stone would do.

His sweat and blood dripped down off his face and elbows. Exhausted, Roran slumped toward the red-stained wall. The slick stone greased his dirty shirt as he slid down to the floor, until he sat facing the center of the cell. Everything was red: not just the walls, but his hair, his hands, the corners of his eyes—eyes that focused on the only piece of furniture in the room, a long table doubling as a bed. And on that table was a glass jar. Its contents were tempting, offered by national law to all prisoners—the believed "Way Out" of suffering. It was considered a mercy. Roran saw it as a taunting curse. He would not allow himself to die because somewhere else in the castle his eight-year-old brother Arno was on his stomach, his back raw from being branded. Again. Arno's tender, thin skin was seared from the flat of a red-hot sword, a sword Roran had just finished making.

Though it hurt his aching, bloody knuckles, Roran gripped and balled up the worn fabric of his simple trousers. He wore clothing of a prisoner, various degrees of beige stains, and dishrags stitched together by an apathetic hand. His dark red hair was matted with sweat and cell dust. Even though Roran was large, even compared to trained fighters, there was little he could do in a case of stone, except for beating his hands.

He breathed in sharply, set his jaw, and looked down to assess the damage. Though it was hard to see—light only came in from under the crack in the heavy, iron door and the small, barred opening near the ceiling of the cell—the crimson of blood was unmistakable. His hands bled from multiple cuts along his fingers and knuckles; other parts were bruised and swollen. He couldn't move his fingers very well. Perfect.

Other than the table, he had a waste bucket in one corner, which was emptied every other day. Comfort was never really necessary for the weaponsmith. All comfort did was induce stagnation and dull once-fine swords. But he'd never wish discomfort on anyone else, least of all Arno. Or his sister, who was still a shadow, carried around in Roran's mind like a boulder. Her whereabouts were unknown. He didn't know what had happened to her in the chaos surrounding the seizing of the family forge, and that was worse.

He had responsibilities as the eldest child. Failing those had kept Roran awake for days. But having punched the wall until he was breathing heavy, until his hands were shaking, until his knuckles had possible fractures and breaks, he let his eyes close.

Bloodying his own hands served multiple purposes. The least of them to drift in exhaustion toward something like sleep, where the empty—the starless sky—waited . . .

Roran floated above
Watching events unfold
Powerless
In this night, Roran watched
Over a massive lake
As a man in academic robes
Washed up on the shore
Roran noted details despite the gloom
A golden sun emblazoned on the back of his robes
His hood up to conceal his face
Ripples, then waves as
A massive hand emerged from the lake
Semi-translucent, tinted with tiny stars
It smacked the man's back
And he coughed up water, breathing
Gluttonously, as if for the first time
The hand shrunk though it was still holding the man's shoulder
It helped him up
The man raised his hand
Fire from the sky
Came down in a line
And blazed the trees in front of him
Making a bright path
A road of flame pulled taut
From the academic past the horizon
Where he could walk to his destination
The fire grew tall
And Roran was pulled in
He tried to fly away
But a lick of flame
Grabbed his foot
While another
Seared his back

Roran was startled awake by the metal slit in the door sliding open. He jumped up from his slumped posture against the wall, his hands up defensively. Roran had learned to fight from a young age, partly to defend his siblings from neighbor bullies, and partly because he itched for the thrill in testing himself against struggle, hammer against ingot.

"It's okay, Roran," a women's voice said. "It's just your food."

Her eyes were the only things of hers he had seen in these past weeks: flecks of green. They belonged to Henrietta. The slit in the door was large enough for her to peer through and offer a plate of food.

"It's corn and bread, but I hope it keeps up your strength." She paused and her eyes darted somewhere else away from Roran. "We need you to be strong, for our kingdom's sake."

Roran grunted at the irony. The ancient city of Wilheim, from which the kingdom and the whole peninsula were world-renowned for its scientific progress and technical advancements. All of that relied on him, and he was no longer sure if he wanted to save it, even if he could.

Roran reached toward the slit to take his tray.

"Your hands!" Henrietta let go of the tray, which clattered to the floor in Roran's cell. "I'm so sorry! I'll go get you some more." She closed the slit. Roran could hear her footsteps hurry away to then immediately hurry back and once again open the slit. "And I'll get bandages. The prince needs . . . we need those hands."

Roran looked blankly at his pile of corn mush and stale bread at the foot of his door. He sat on the small table. The jar pressed up against his leg.

He wondered when they'd make him try again and if beating up his hands would buy him time. Would Prince Zerebril still demand another sword with his hands bloodied? Roran raised them to his face. Or would the prince just take it out on Arno?

He knew the plan was ill-tempered and somewhat moronic, but Roran couldn't think of any other option. Griselda probably could have, but she was missing. All Roran knew how to do was be a force. He could bend metal with will, he could shape it with pressure, he could harden it with heat. It's what they wanted from him after all, to make his father's weapons, weapons capable of burning entire cities to the ground. But Roran couldn't, so he'd used force to break himself since they wouldn't listen to reason.

Even still, the plan would likely not work, might make things worse, but he had to try *something*. Trying something, even if it failed, was better than doing nothing and waiting for suffering. Otherwise, they were going to keep hurting Arno, keep making Roran watch as they burned his younger brother with metal made by Roran's own hands.

He gritted his teeth. If Roran died in this cell, he would find a way to make them pay, even in death. He would haunt everyone in the castle, everyone complicit for the suffering of an eight-year-old boy.

Roran adjusted his weight on the table, and the table creaked under the pressure.

Yes, that was his purpose now; more than just force—be rage. Rage could pass the time, could keep him breathing, could give him purpose in the dark of the cell. It was the only thing he had, and the only thing that could protect Arno.

But sometimes, even the fires of hatred would fizzle out. Roran, during his weeks in the darkness, would oscillate between exploding rage and crushing grief. As he exhausted himself thinking of all the ways to kill those who hurt children, the grief would come. Even if Roran and Arno were set free, everything he would do from that day forward would be tainted with the knowledge of vanity, that each time he helped Arno, a child somewhere else was being tortured. Grief would follow him for the rest of his life, which he assumed would be very short. And with the grief, the temptation to give in completely to despair—to lose hope and stop breathing, stop striving for a life beyond the cell reunited with his siblings—a life where he could fight for glory and bolster those he loved. Even daydreaming became hard in such darkness.

The jar intruded on his thoughts—cold glass felt through his trousers, touching the side of his knee. Roran picked it up and examined it. A viscous, dark-green liquid moved side to side as Roran stared through the glass, barely able to see the color in the dulled light. He set it down farther away on the table, to the edge opposite him.

Why did the poison have to be green? It just reminded him of Arno: green, his favorite color. Arno loved to climb in the trees that dotted the edges of their home. He collected leaves that were oddly shaped, and even though they would wither in his room, it was an excuse to collect more as the seasons passed, green turning to reds and oranges as nature appeared to light itself on fire.

Roran tried to push back the memory of fire, but it was too late. He was looking into his brother's terrified eyes as Prince Zerebril examined Roran's most recent sword. It was not like his father's, and so Arno was punished. Zerebril had looked repulsed by the weapon, like he couldn't touch it himself. The prince gave it to a soldier who, in turn, gave it to Arno's back. Roran hit his head with the palm of his hand, trying to beat his brother's screams out of his mind. It didn't work. Instead, he closed his eyes and tried to find a different memory.

Arno pulled Roran out of the forge after working long into the night with their father, Cormac. Though they were on the outskirts of Wilheim City, outside the tall stone wall, the bonfires in the city squares gave off enough light to make the sky faintly glow. The glowing could be seen for miles around, even, Cormac said, from Lake Verdin. Not to mention the fires of their own forge and how much light streamed out from the windows. The windows on the stone building were massive to let out heat in the summers, but they were not entirely open so that Cormac could board the windows and keep working in the winter.

"Wait here!" Arno said, giggling.

"Alright," Roran only pretended to be exhausted, though he should have been after moving all that metal and swinging the hammer countless times. But it was hard to be tired around Arno. His curly hair bounced around his head as he ran, no, *bounded,* away. Arno was small for his age, but his enthusiasm sometimes made him seem larger and stronger than Roran. Roran looked at the dirty back of Arno's trousers and shirt, evidence that he had been climbing and falling out of trees.

Giggling still, Arno pulled their sister Griselda out of the house, separate from the forge. She had just finished cleaning up after supper, the scent of rosemary and potato stew still clinging about her. Cormac liked a tidy house, so Griselda took time to wash and store the iron-cast plates and utensils, wash the table, and sweep the floor of any crumbs. Until Arno interrupted her and dragged her out into the chilled evening air, of course. Despite Griselda's best effort to tame her auburn hair into a bun, stray strands stuck stubbornly to her sweaty face. The forge made everything hot, even their separate cottage next to the forge, where they all slept. The sixteen-year-old Griselda was every bit as saturated with life as Arno. She, too, was giggling as she let herself be pulled by Arno outside. Joy clung to her like her freckles clung to her cheeks and nose.

Arno grabbed Roran's waiting hand as he took them both to the far edges of their property near the trees, where the air was much more humid and colder away from the forge. The three of them stood there under the stars and irregularly shaped moons, moons that swept across the sky far more quickly than the sun.

The siblings barely contained their goofy grins like a trio of chuckling fools with the world's best joke that only other fools could understand.

Arno let go of Roran's hand, turned around, and waited, his tiny fist pulled up to his chest in excitement. He would get to see his siblings "steam." Thin wisps of vapor rose from Roran and Griselda's damp skin, mingling with the cold air like mist curling off the Shatter Rock River at dawn. Though any laborer in Wilheim would recognize it as the mark of hard work during a chilly autumn day, fascination gripped Arno as he imagined all the things he didn't yet know were possible.

"There it is! There it is!" Arno said, jumping up and down. "There's the steam!"

This was the second day in a row he had intentionally pulled Roran and Griselda out into the night to see it. Arno saw it first by chance when Roran wandered outside of the forge to fetch some supplies.

Roran and Griselda looked at each other and couldn't help but smile at their brother's amusement. The three freckled faces had all been infected with a burning need to enjoy life, evidenced by smile lines, dimples, and rosy cheeks.

"You know I smell really bad and I'm sticky with sweat," Griselda said.

"I don't care," Arno replied. "Even if you're gross, you must be doing something right to steam! You're the right kind of gross. You both work hard enough to steam. That's what I want to do when I grow up."

"Steam?" Roran chuckled. "You want to steam?"

"Sure do!"

Roran smiled. He wanted to say, *This is nothing special, it happens all the time for people working hard in the cooling air as the season changed.* But this was Arno, and Roran refused to step on a child's ability to make meaning and magic out of the mundane. However, this was a teaching moment, and for once,

Roran was on the other side of it instead of listening to Cormac's weapon-smithing wisdom.

"Well, you'll need to work to steam. You have to earn it. So, what do you want to do for work? You want to help in the forge?"

"I don't know. But whatever I do, I want to steam—oh no!" Arno shouted. "It's fading away!"

Griselda shrugged her shoulders. "Oh well, guess that means we'll have to keep working so that we start steaming again." Her free hand, the one not holding Arno's, was concealed behind her back. She pulled it out to reveal two wooden practice swords.

Arno's eyes lit up brighter than Wilheim's bonfires as Griselda tossed Roran a sword, rolled up her dress to knee-height, and assumed a springlike stance, crouching, sword arm outstretched and pointed at Roran.

Roran laughed and caught the sword. Growing up around their father, a famous weaponsmith, had no doubt inspired his children to play with wooden versions of the weapons their father made.

Roran had little time to assume a stance, as Griselda pounced out of hers and thrust the tip of her wooden sword toward Roran's chest.

"Corpse caller!" Roran shouted as he jumped back to safety. "You're not wasting any time."

"Watch your language." Griselda smiled wryly and nodded at Arno. "We have an audience." She was more like a fencer, quick and precise. Doing so, she learned, would counter Roran's raw strength and stamina. Roran beat her often enough at swordplay that she had to learn to adapt in order to stand a chance. Roran's wide frame, built by years alongside Cormac in the forge, was fearsome to look at even without him holding a weapon and bearing down.

At one point, Roran had gone easy on her, but she scolded him for doing so. So, he didn't hold back. He gathered his footing and swung his sword to the side, knocking Griselda's far off the center line. Calm and clearheaded, she seemed to be expecting this and moved to the left behind where her sword wanted to go. Roran frowned. Knocking her weapon to the side usually created an opening where he could strike and force her off balance while she backed away. She was learning very quickly how to flow *with* rather than *resist* Roran's strength. She moved forward and Roran stepped back to assess but stumbled as he did.

The footing was hazardous; exposed roots, piles of leaves, and stray fallen branches seemingly arranged themselves to try and trip Roran.

No, the yard debris isn't arranging itself to trip me, Roran thought, *Griselda is forcing me to backpedal into hazards herself.*

Griselda lunged again and Roran batted the sword away reflexively. Griselda gathered herself where Roran forced her sword and then flowed into another attack. Roran was being pushed back out of the open yard and toward the trees.

Griselda laughed, Roran panted, and all the while Arno jumped up and down and offered his commentary. "Ooh, that was a close one! Get him good, Griselda! Roran, what are you doing? Push her back!" He giggled while cheering for both sides.

Roran batted her sword away again. Swinging a sword, even a wooden one, would get tiring, which is usually how Roran found an opening on his sister. However, because she was flowing, she wasn't spending nearly as much energy as she usually did.

Lunge. Lunge. Lunge. Roran tried to maneuver himself so that she would lunge into his own attack, but she saw it coming and feinted. Roran bit too hard on the feint, and Griselda brought her sword crashing down onto his knuckle.

Roran smiled despite himself. Though he lost by getting hit on the hand, which seemed trivial, he knew all too well how crippling an injury to the hands could be from experience in the forge and how defenseless he would be without them. Roran dropped his sword and raised his hands above his head in surrender.

"Well done, you're getting good. Do you really spend all day cooking in the kitchen, or are you actually practicing your swordplay?"

Griselda scoffed, "It doesn't take all day to—" her voice was lost as Arno tackled her to the ground.

"Winner! Winner! Ellie beat Woe-Woe!"

"Get off me, No-No! You'll get my dress dirty! I just washed this!" She tried not to laugh as she scolded him. It didn't work.

Roran didn't even try to contain his laughter. When Arno was a toddler, he had trouble pronouncing the *r* sounds in Roran's name, and Griselda's name was just too long. So, he shortened them to Ellie and Woe-Woe. Ironically, Arno couldn't pronounce the *r* in his own name for a long time either, and so Roran and Griselda took to calling him No-No as a joke even after Arno learned to pronounce their given names.

"Alright, you dirty, rolling dogs," Roran chuckled as he pulled Arno off Griselda.

"It worked!" Arno yelled, pointing to the sweat misting away from Griselda's forehead. Both brothers then helped Griselda to her feet.

Griselda brushed the leaves, twigs, and dirt clumps off her clothes and frowned at the places where they were stained green and brown. She shrugged and sighed. "We can't stay out here sweating all night just for you, Arno."

"But I'm not ready to go inside," Arno mumbled, looking at his feet.

"How about we make a deal?" Roran asked, hoping to keep up his brother's good spirits.

"Ooh! What kind of deal?"

"You're almost old enough to start helping out in the forge;

carrying small ingots and learning the names of tools will come first. But soon, you'll be working hard too, alongside us. If you go to bed now without complaining, I'll teach you how to work hard enough to steam."

"Deal!" Arno offered his hand, which Roran took. Arno shook his hand rapidly up and down, threatening to yank Roran's arm out of his shoulder.

"It's important to have dreams, Arno, even if it is to steam. Soon, you'll be like Oros from Griselda's bedtime stories!"

Arno ran in a circle, waving his arms about like he had the fabled flaming wings of the beast from *The March Through the Mountain Pass*.

"But right now, you're more like a duck," Roran teased.

Arno stopped and frowned at his brother. "Hey! I'm not a duck. I don't quack!"

"Well, you don't have wings of fire, either," Griselda said.

"Just you wait, Ellie. I'm going to steam hotter than the forge. I'll be what Oros is scared of!"

Griselda smiled at the exchange before picking Arno up from behind, hoisting him over her shoulder, and walking back to the house, both giggling yet again.

Roran noticed that Cormac's pounding hammer swings had stopped. He looked over at the forge to see his father leaning against the wall with his arms folded, muffling a cough. His bald head glistened, and his red beard mirrored the flames used to create his swords. A smile tugged at the corner of his lips.

And from those lips escaped Cormac's singsong but hearty Ardhatazian accent, "Well, if it ain't da angriest man in da world caught in da act of having fun, eh?"

Roran walked up to him and chuckled at his second familial nickname. It was a low effort nickname—and corny—but it was accurate. Roran had been scolded for his temper many, many times in the shop. His lack of patience had ruined several blades. Once, he went outside and beat a badly quenched bent blade against a tree until it snapped. Roran thought it was such a stupid nickname that he couldn't help but laugh whenever someone broke it out, cooling him before he started kicking tree trunks.

"Tink ya could hold dat smile for a bit longer?" Cormac said.

"Is it done, Pops?"

Cormac coughed up an "Aye" before waving Roran into the forge. Cormac, though strong of body, had weak lungs. More and more, he had coughing fits after a day in the forge. He sometimes had to eat pain-killing poppy extract from the Wilheim Academies for the pain after making one of his signature weapons.

"Dese are me last two," Cormac said sitting on the anvil at the center of the forge.

Roran looked at the twin swords on the table and took in the light that streamed from the flame-like blades. Before Arno pulled him out, Roran had fitted the pommel to one sword while his father did the other. But now the two great swords were glowing. They weren't when he left.

"Dis un's commissioned for da crown prince, da eldest son, Gunter the Gallant," Cormac said, pulling up one of the great swords. The weapons were identical, though it would be impossible to wield both weapons at once. These swords were massive, meant to intimidate as well as to cleave. They each had an ornate pear-shaped pommel; long, pointed quillons for murder strokes; two ring guards on either side extending to cover the hands near the hilt; a ricasso for half-swording; parrying hooks at the top of the ricasso shaped like Oros' heads mid-roar; and an undulating blade that made it resemble a long, wicked flame like the fires it came from. From pommel to blade tip, the weapons were nearly as long as Roran was tall.

"And this one?" Roran said, picking up the other sword. The long but thin flamberge blade almost seemed to vibrate in the air as it glowed. "Weren't they both for the princes? One for Gunter and the other—"

"For ya."

Roran stared, mouth agape, at his father. Cormac smiled broadly, though it was hard to tell through his dense beard. Cormac's smiles manifested in the creases around his eyes.

"But Pops, what am I meant to do with it?"

Cormac coughed some more but finally managed, "What ya will. It's yers, don't matter what ya do wit it."

Roran looked back at the glowing sword in his hands and lowered himself into a stance. He ran his hand over the face of the flamberge blade, which was both hot to the touch yet somehow cold and wet, as if the ever-warm blade was secreting a chilled oil. Roran flourished the blade from left to right, keeping in mind of his surroundings so that he didn't accidentally hit it against the ceiling or anvil.

"Woah now! Don't ya go swinging dat in da forge!"

Roran chuckled and set it back down on the table. He didn't need to be told not to swing it. Cormac's swords were legendary and dangerous to enemies and users alike. For reasons not even Roran knew, Cormac could imbue his weapons with power. Swinging his swords fast enough would ignite the blade and air, causing massive waves and lashes of flame to trail in their wake. They were weapons designed for solo bounty hunters, elite guards, Lichtfangrs, and men who would face large forces alone, as allies would only get in the way. The wealthy paid especially well for a skilled mercenary guard who they would then equip with Cormac's weaponry. Only one was needed, as a single well-armored warrior with a Cormac weapon could burn down dozens of bandits and the forest they rode out of. For the past eight years, his blades have been some of the most sought-after in all of Verdin.

"Truth is Roran, I know ya've got bigger plans dan dis forge."

Roran looked down at his feet.

"Aww, don't ya feel bad 'bout it. Yer like me. Least before

yer mom had ya. Back then, I was ridin' the sea. I know yer heart's gold. Dat ya don't want to let me legacy die, but only I can do what I do. Best ya do someting else, someting ya want." Cormac's chest convulsed as a fit of coughing seized him, forcing him to set the sword clattering onto the table beside the twin sword made for his son. His breaths came in ragged gasps, each cough shaking his frame as he gripped the table's edge, his knuckles whitening under the strain of keeping himself upright.

When he coughed, Roran sensed that the air trembled and the forge seemed almost fainter, like his father's illness was threatening to snuff out the hearth that kept their family thriving. Tools rattled on the shelves as Cormac roughly shook the table and everything around it in his fit. Even the soot in the room seemed to vibrate in response.

Roran walked over and placed his hand on Cormac's back, partially covered by his smithing apron, and softly patted. He didn't think it would help, nothing helped the coughing fits, but it seemed like all his hands could do. Roran whistled the Anvil Tune. He only knew two songs, the "Wilheim Lullaby" that Griselda would sing to put Arno to sleep when he was younger and what the family called the "Anvil Tune," Cormac's fluttering whistle, just as trilling as bird song but with the urgency of hammer against steel. Roran whistled it now, almost unconsciously, as he steadily patted Cormac's back like it was any other day in the forge, hammering away on an ingot.

Finally, the fit subsided and Cormac used his apron to dab at the blood mixed into his beard. "Like I said . . . dese are me last two," he coughed again. "Wit what Zerebril is paying for dis present to Gunter, all kinds of seas will open demselves up to ya, Griselda, and Arno. It's time to do whatcha want."

Roran had nothing to say. Both he and his father spoke little. Even this much talk was unusual for Cormac. They couldn't hear each other talk in the forge anyway, with hammer and flames and bellows. Roran, though impulsive and thickheaded, was not stupid. He knew the implications behind his father telling him this, by finally making Roran his own sword. Cormac could see the end of the March and it was time to get his affairs in order.

Unable to find the right words, Roran let his actions speak instead. He clamped onto his father long, despite the occasional coughs. His father suppressed the fit as best he could and embraced Roran in return.

Three weeks later, Roran missed Cormac's burial.

The grating slide of the iron latch echoed through the chamber, drawing Roran's attention to the door. Henrietta, no doubt, returning with his meal. But when the door creaked open, it revealed not just the chambermaid, eyes fixed on the floor, balancing a fresh tray of food in her trembling hands, but also Prince Zerebril, his presence grim. In one hand, he gripped a roll of bandages; in the other, a thin sword that caught the little light the torches had to offer and swallowed it up. Anger flared up in Roran's chest as his heartbeat quickened in reaction to seeing the man who had ordered the searing of his brother's back. Roran spat on the ground and fixed Zerebril with a fierce stare, the whites of his eyes only partially visible under his thick, furrowed brow.

Zerebril stood in steel plate armor with bulky pauldrons meant to present the shorter prince as considerably larger. The plate was painted by the prince himself, as the armor was more for decoration. He was not wearing his helmet, revealing his short blonde hair and shadowed blue eyes. His face was still boyish but had a seriousness that betrayed his youthful appearance. He had almost no lips to speak of, his mouth almost always appearing like a hard, straight line.

Roran had imagined that face on each stone brick he

punched. He imagined his hand punching through the stone, through the bone, and caving into the prince's skull.

Roran, who stood about a foot taller than Henrietta and the prince, leaned forward and drew up his shoulders to force his shadow upon them. As a precaution, Zerebril had his rapier drawn and pointed at Roran before the door fully opened. They were out of sight, but Roran could hear the clanking armor of other guards positioned on either side of the open door. Zerebril was someone who did not take chances. However, the more Roran interacted with the prince, the more it seemed like the prince was changing, becoming less sure of himself, sometimes even appearing woozy, dazed, or out of it—his pupils enormous, glazed, and looking far off into the distance.

"Hold up your hands," Zerebril said.

Roran held them above his head.

"Not . . . not quite what I meant. I mean, hold out your hands so I can see them."

Roran moved his hands in front of him, torchlight from the hallway finally revealing just how much damage he had done. His hands were shaking, partially from the pain and partially from fury.

Henrietta covered her mouth with the hand not holding the tray.

Zerebril winced. "I told my father that it was foolish to not bind you. At the very least, I'm glad to see you do this rather than take the Way Out. It was more foolish to offer you the custom." Zerebril spoke with barely masked bitterness, though it didn't seem like the aggression was directed at Roran. His voice even cracked now and then. "Forced to die as the fool." He said, seemingly to himself.

Roran stepped closer. "I'm no coward. I wouldn't choose death while you torture my brother. Just let him go."

Zerebril ignored the comment. "With Gunter dead, I am to lead, and learn to lead I must. Guards."

As Roran had expected, two royal guards, clad in articulated steel of the highest quality, some of which came from Cormac's own forge, came storming into the room. With the cold exactness of the steel they wore, they bound Roran's hands behind his back with abrasive rope, shoved him onto the table, and then bound his legs too.

"Bind me all you want!" Roran snarled. "Nothing will keep me from—"

Zerebril backhanded the restrained Roran with a gauntleted hand. It didn't hurt as much as Roran thought it should. Maybe Zerebril was just weak, maybe he held back, or maybe Roran's rage kept him from feeling anything.

Zerebril sighed and squatted down to get on eye level with his prisoner. "I don't believe the superstition about treating prisoners poorly. Nevertheless, I don't like doing this to the son of Cormac, even if he was Ardhatazian." The prince sighed, and a hint of pleading crept into his voice. "If you would just make the swords your father did, I would release your brother and treat you better."

Roran bent his head low. "I told you already. A thousand times I told you, I can't! No one can."

"I don't believe Cormac would take his secrets to the grave. He must've known; his forge would flounder without his signature weapons." The prince's eyes meandered over to the torchlight. He blinked twice and then shook his head as if trying to bring himself back into the moment. "Answer, how would that help his family if you couldn't continue his legacy?"

"I *don't know*. He refused to talk about it. I don't . . . I don't think he wanted me to continue his work." Roran fixed his eyes on Zerebril's. There was something almost familiar in how distant they were.

Zerebril twisted up his lips to hide them even further. "But he trained you in the trade, did he not?"

"Well, yes but—"

"Then surely, you can do it." Zerebril's eyes remained locked on Roran, but something about their glaze made it seem like Zerebril really wasn't looking at Roran but at something beyond him. "From my perspective, the view of reason, it would make no sense not to teach you the secret. The only other option is that you are an Ardhatazian traitor and are saving the secret for King Ewen. So, your family is being treated as such."

"We're not traitors! I've lived here most of my life. You are betraying us. Your royal guards are carrying halberds *I made*. And before I die, I'll impale you on one of them!"

The prince breathed in deeply and blinked several times, as if Roran's words jolted the prince awake from a long nap. Zerebril shook his head and then examined his surroundings. The guards shuffled about around the cell. One of them peered into his bucket and cringed at the smell. Henrietta came in and set the tray down on the open end of the table.

"Henrietta, please see to his hands," Zerebril said, tossing the roll of bandages to her. "Use the jar as a salve before wrapping."

Henrietta did as instructed. The poison in the jar, Life Nectar, had unusually powerful and quick medicinal properties when used in small quantities. To Roran, it would only become life-threatening if he drank the whole jar. Life Nectar came from grounding Lake Verdin Borage Flowers, also known as the Verdin Stars. The plants grew in abundance year-round, surrounding the massive Lake Verdin—which technically wasn't a lake—at the center of the continent. It also contributed to Verdin's culturally accepted suicides, something Roran despised. Drinking a jar of Life Nectar would bring a deceptive calm, with only faint internal pain as the body betrayed itself, organs silently shutting down one by one. Within a day, death would claim its victim.

Roran bent further forward, positioning his bound wrists higher up his back and making it easier for Henrietta to do her work. Though he was still visibly shaking with anger, he did not want anyone other than Zerebril to feel it. Maybe the guards, but not Henrietta. Roran felt his rage to be a commodity that could fizzle out or get diluted if forced upon too many targets— needing just one aim, a hot tip in the heated ingot that he could beat furiously against, creating life-giving sparks that would warm the dankness of the cell, replace the mildew smell with ozone.

Prince Zerebril lowered his sword and stood, thinking. Roran noticed that aspects of the prince's speech were slow and deliberate, but too slow. It reminded Roran of how he would try and fail to hide drunkenness from Cormac on the few times he went into the taverns.

"Son of Cormac, you must listen to me. Ewen has won six decisive battles, annihilating our forces as he pushes up the Shatter Rock toward this city. We are scholars, not warriors. If we don't have those weapons . . . all of Wilheim will burn. What you have done to your hands is childish and inexcusable. You have wasted valuable time. I need Cormac's weapons to outfit our soldiers. That's all I'm asking. Prince Gunter . . ." Zerebril closed his eyes and sighed. "He tried to stand alone against an enemy force with Cormac's sword, but they responded with new weapons of their own, strange powers only said to have existed in fables originating from the west or Lichtfangr records. The Ardhatazians mean to kill or enslave us all. You'll die in this castle along with my father and me if nothing is done."

Roran made no response. Henrietta finished applying the Life Nectar and began wrapping his hands. Roran let his head rest on his knees. Though most people would find it difficult to be angry at the prince, who already sounded so defeated, Roran had no trouble finding a way. Most of what the prince said went in one ear and out the other as soon as the sniveling crept into his small voice. Of all people, *Zerebril* was trying to play the victim?

"You want me to feel sorry? For you? You can all rot as far

as I'm concerned. I'd pay to watch screws get turned into your skin!"

Prince Zerebril sighed. "If country cannot motivate you, I am forced to use kin."

Roran jolted up, causing Henrietta to lose her progress on rolling the wraps. "No!" And like that, rage quickly gave way to panic and panic to desperation. "Please! I can't do it; punish me, not Arno!"

"I don't know what it will take, but what you have done today cannot go unanswered," the prince let his head roll back so he could look at the stone ceiling. "If your next sword does not have Cormac's powers, I will use it to . . ." Zerebril shook his head and sighed, "to cut off Arno's leg."

Roran thrashed around as much as he could, knocking Henrietta to the floor. "That will accomplish nothing! The weapons cannot be made! You're just killing Arno bit by bit! Must you take my brother, too?"

The guards on either side of him walked up and, with plated gauntlets, pressed his back down so he was folded against his legs.

"I will come for you in a day's time. If you truly do not know how to make the swords of power, use this healing time to wrack your mind. Surely you saw him do something to the weapons to imbue them with power."

"I don't know! I don't know! *I don't know!*" Roran cried.

"Tantrums do not produce results, only action. Life and limb depend on it." With that, Zerebril turned and exited the cell.

Henrietta finished the wrap and was escorted out by the guards. The torch outside Roran's cell was burning out, and Henrietta replaced it with a new one. Afterward, she looked at Roran again and slowly closed the door. Roran did not move as the door shut, and the darkness once more enveloped him.

CHAPTER 2

WHAT MUST BE DONE

PRINCE ZEREBRIL STOOD at his father's bedside, pressing a damp cloth to the fevered brow of a man who once ruled over the Wilheim Peninsula with dignity and intelligence. Now both of those things were being stripped from the skeletal old man little by little, day after day, as a rough punishment for giving the land peace and prosperity. The massive bed, fit for a king yet far too vast for a frail body, loomed around him like a cage. The veils hanging from the corner posts had been drawn back, exposing the tangled mess of sheets and leather straps binding King Morgen II. His wild eyes darted in panic, muscles straining against the restraints that Zerebril and two guards had strapped in. Still, the king thrashed, a storm of desperation locked within a dying shell.

"One of his bad days . . . leave us," Zerebril said to the two guards. "It's not fitting to see your king in this state."

The guards nodded and left the king's chambers. Low candlelight lit the dark, cavernous room. In the light of day, the rich deep brown wooden armoire and cabinetry were ornately decorated with remarkable craftmanship. Zerebril had an eye for such things, even if they didn't make the furniture any more or less capable of their jobs. However, in the meager candlelight, the wood looked black; the patterns looked like wicked smiles.

Tapestries lined the walls depicting stories from *The Marches*. On one of the tapestries, there was an army standing against the flaming monster Oros. The other tapestry showed a dying man in armor, his sword stuck in the ground, being cradled by a being of blue light as the red sky fell all around them. Zerebril tried not to look at them. They were nothing but foolish stories, superstitions, and banal comforts. They would not save his father, no matter how much the king held to them on his good days.

"I-I can see them!" the king shouted, eyes staring past Zerebril and to the vaulted ceiling.

Zerebril followed his father's gaze and saw the shadows from the candlelight dancing around the corners and arches. He sighed and tried to soothe his father by patting his head. It was hard to treat his father like a scared child on some days and as king of Wilheim Peninsula on others. As Ardhataz pushed further into the Wilheim Peninsula, the bad days were becoming more numerous than the good, especially after Gunter's death.

"It's alright, Father," he said in his gentlest voice. "I'll get you your medicine. It will make them go away."

"The corpse callers will never go away!" King Morgen bellowed. "They'll overtake us all. Rip our souls out and use them for power! Send the Falconer; stop the expedition! If they reach the bottom of the lake—"

"Easy, Father, just a second now." Zerebril winced as his father strained hard against his leather restraints, blood trickling around his wrists. The prince, still in armor from dealing with the prisoner from earlier, felt the metal's weight as he clanked over to the side table where his father's poppy extract had been delivered earlier that day. The scholars said it wouldn't reverse the deterioration, but it would sedate the king so that he couldn't harm himself. It also provided a distracting euphoria.

Zerebril tipped the vial, letting the milky extract flow into the goblet. As the syrupy liquid settled, he hummed—a low, mournful sound that seemed to seep into the dimly lit chamber. At first, the dark of the chamber and the howls of the king resisted the tune. Then, his voice rose, soft but steady, carrying the haunting melody of the Wilheim Lullaby, each note threading through the air like a whispered prayer.

> *Over mountains, over hill,*
> *Over river, lake so still,*
> *We the sun, we shine on all,*
> *Morn to rise and night to fall,*
> *Morn to rise and night to fall.*

King Morgen stilled. His eyes glancing away from the ceiling and toward Zerebril. "Zella. Zella, is that you? It's been so long. You should see our boys. They've grown so much."

Zerebril wrenched his eyes shut. "Yes. I have your favorite wine," Zerebril murmured. If this were under different circumstances, he might have been offended that his unmasculine voice was being confused with his dead mother's. But it worked. "Please drink." Zerebril brought the goblet up to his father's lips, and he drank down the white liquid.

His father's eyes went back to the ceiling, and then he sputtered out the liquid. "Begone! Can't you see I'm talking to my queen!" He yelled at the ceiling.

Zerebril pulled the goblet away before his father could knock it with his shaking head. The door opened behind him. Zerebril turned to see his half-brother leaning against the door frame. Carl, one of Morgen's bastards and given a lowly, ill-fitting name, a title for unnamed slaves given their freedom, was

wearing his green brigandine, armor made from stitching inter-
locking small metal plates into a sturdy over garment. Carl's face
was almost made of stone, his long bow strung on his back.

"You're here? Back from—where were you going again?"
Zerebril asked as the king continued to bellow incoherently at
the ceiling. "And what of the Lichtfangrs?"

Carl moved his mouth from side to side as if he was chewing
on a thought. It never left his mouth, though.

Zerebril sighed and looked back at his father, who had not
noticed Carl's presence. "It will be soon now," Zerebril said to
himself, since Carl rarely engaged in conversation. He looked
down in the goblet, still half full.

Carl sighed.

"I know what you're thinking," Zerebril said, turning to
face Carl. "But I don't think I have the strength to give him
mercy."

Carl folded his arms and frowned in response.

"Could . . . could you? I know what you've been through. I
know most of it is because of your station. Life has made you
hard. Could that hardness be more useful than my intellect?
Could you do it?"

"It's not my place," Carl said.

"Carl—"

"I could do it. But I won't," Carl scowled. "I'm not his real
son."

Zerebril shook his head. He would never get through to
Carl's stubborn skull, no matter how many times they had this
conversation. "I know you were gone for so much of our childhood, but I still—"

"I wasn't *gone*," Carl spat. "I was sent away. By him. Sent to
the Lichtfangrs. He hoped their training would kill me. It didn't.
They broke apart before I did."

"They broke?"

"The organization has been dissolved. Wasn't long before the others started hiring themselves out as mercenaries to the rest of the continent, be it for merchants or to the warring nations in the west."

Though Zerebril was surprised to hear this, that is where the emotion ended. The Lichtfangrs, as far as Zerebril knew, were an ancient, neutral order of odd mystics who protected the nations around Lake Verdin from vague threats that Zerebril had never seen himself. It mattered little if they were gone; if anything, this was more positive news as it meant that Carl was back for good.

"I am glad you're back," Zerebril bowed his head. "Whatever Father's faults, I still respect you. I still think of you as my brother."

Carl scoffed and switched topics. "Your dungeon chambermaid wanted me to tell you she's concerned."

Zerebril cocked his head to the side. "Henrietta? What? Why?"

"Caught me on my way up here. Said to be mindful of how much you torture your prisoners. Said she wouldn't want them to catch Grief Sickness. Careful, 'brother,' you're making more problems for me." Carl glared at the king and then left the room.

Zerebril cursed and then looked down at the goblet. The medicine had begun its deed on his father, calming him to the brink of sleep. The too-large bed had too many pillows as well— large, overstuffed pillows. With the king already restrained, his ailing body, Zerebril's weight in the armor—it would all be so easy in concept.

Even still, looking into his father's softening face, a face that once beamed proudly like the sun he represented, Zerebril could not bring himself to do it. He could not violently smother his father when that same man had created an era of unprecedented peace, at least until recently. He could not harm the man who had proudly displayed the paintings of a six-year-old Zerebril in the throne room. And if Carl refused to be family, this withering man was all Zerebril had left.

Whether for the sake of himself, his father, or the country, Zerebril could not lift a hand against this man. Jealous of the peace that came over his sleeping father, Zerebril closed his eyes and downed the rest of the poppy in the goblet as he had been doing for weeks now.

CHAPTER 3
TO HOLD BACK THE DARK

RORAN PECKED at his food like a chicken, mashed potatoes covering his nose and chin in the attempt to eat with his hands bound behind him. He quickly gave up, rolled off the table, and flopped on the stone floor with a heavy thud. Yes, there was pain, but it was deserved, necessary. Roran welcomed the pain in his aching side, a pain only a fraction of what Arno had been put through twice now. Wormlike, he wriggled until he positioned himself as comfortably as possible on his side.

Unable to use his bucket in this bound state, he let the warm liquid pool around his hips. It didn't matter. Nothing mattered anymore. His father was dead, his sister missing at best, his brother facing cruelty no child ever should. He could tell the skin on his hands had already healed as the itch of scabs that couldn't be scratched nibbled on the corners of his mind. The swelling and damage done to his knuckles had not yet healed, though. Nevertheless, time was running out.

In his desperation, Roran had thought of several reasons for bloodying his hands. The first was to try to prevent further misery from befalling Arno, which had backfired. The second was to release his pent-up energy. The third was a gamble.

Roran had never seen Cormac make his weapons glow. He had always done it at night or early morning before Roran entered the forge. Roran had learned not to ask about the process as Cormac refused to respond to questions about it. Cormac would always turn away and busy himself. It seemed almost painful to talk about the subject, when normally Cormac was eager to show and teach about anything related to weapon smithing. It was his life's work and what made his family prosperous and happy. Why didn't he talk about it? Why leave his son with no ability to continue his legacy?

Prince Zerebril was right: it didn't make sense. Roran snorted at the thought of Zerebril being right, inhaling a strong odor of mildew and his own urine. He had spent the past weeks of solitude recalling everything his father had taught him in the forge that might have hinted at what could imbue the weapons with the glow. Anything Roran could connect, any subtle clues or misplaced oddities, might save Arno's life, maybe even a kingdom.

All he could think of was his father's illness and coughing fits. He seemed to cough—a wet, viscous rattling—almost to the point of collapse for the next couple of days once he finished a glowing weapon. Nothing could cure it, not even the miraculous panacea of the Verdin Star. What Verdin Stars couldn't cure, poppy could be used to numb the pain and provide pleasure. Though Cormac didn't like the idea of numbing anything, he had started taking poppy more and more as the end approached. After each finished weapon, he would cough until the blood vessels in his face burst, then lie down with the poppy, his eyes becoming glassy as he drifted into the ease of a sensationless moment.

Roran's gamble: the pain always came after the weapons were made. It was the only connection Roran could piece together. Somehow, Cormac had been pouring part of his life into the steel, and it had drained him. Though Cormac never knew his exact age—born to a slave mother and sold to pirates—he couldn't have been much older than his mid-forties when he died. For a man whose trade kept his body strong and resilient, he should have lived twice as long. But pain and sacrifice, it seemed, were woven into the craft itself.

Roran was never one for religion—his days were too consumed by the forge to leave much time for reading—but he had caught snippets of Griselda's bedtime stories over the years. Her stories were adapted from books canonical to Wilheim Peninsula's primary religion: *The Marches,* a series of more or less historical expeditions and accounts of drastic change. Though there were no books at the house, Griselda would go into the city's library or listen to sermons when running errands in Wilheim's bustling market district. Like his son, Cormac never put much stock in religion, either, or learning, or reading for that matter. Even when Griselda got her headaches, she seemed determined to stay in the city and learn as much as she could since Cormac couldn't be bothered to do anything other than swing his hammer.

To entertain Arno, she sometimes told stories of men who could "drink" in their surroundings, could pull from the greenery and use it for all kinds of impossible feats, such as throwing a horse or making earthquakes. The stories described them as both heroes as well as parasites that stole life from those around them.

Trace hairs in Roran's patchy beard caught in the rough surface of the stone floor as he tossed and turned. *Was there anything in the stories that could tell me how to make the weapons?* Roran wondered.

Griselda had told him that Verdin was a caldera, with Lake Verdin being at the center of a massive dormant volcano. She said the eruption had created the land of Verdin, since everything else, as far as they knew, was covered in water. The ending of *The March from Pain* stated that the fertile soil from the planet's center came out of the volcano and led to the lush greenery of the continent surrounding the lake and Verdin Stars, while the highlands farther away from the lake were barren. She had also said that mystical power flowed out of the eruption, power that had dwindled to memory over time as the land's power faded away. Though she left this out of the stories she would tell Arno, she said many believe that the miraculous power would again become manifest once God, Imeel-Illin, caused the volcano to become active. Power would flood the land, but everything alive would die in the eruption, and the world would start over.

"Was it the power of some hidden god?" Roran mumbled to himself.

For those following *The Marches*, one of them specifically depicted suffering and death as integral to power and life. Roran, though unsure, suspected this was why it was acceptable to commit suicide, as one sect of the religion believed that suffering and death would create future growth. This was why Griselda insisted on burying Cormac at the base of a tree, untombed, as was Wilheim custom for those of ignoble birth. His life would provide literal fertilizer for the soil and, according to one of *The Marches*, fertilize the life of his kin. This type of burial also avoided some suspected nasty side effects the religion theorized.

But these were just stories to Roran; after all, he did not feel like a blooming flower while his hands were bound, confined to a cell, lying in his own urine, with Zerebril threatening to hack off Arno's leg should Roran fail. For one matter, it was unclear what the followers were marching to or from. It depended on which prophetic scripture was read, notable examples being *The March from Pain*, *The March Through the Mountain Pass*, *The March of Joy*, and numerous others. Each book contained often contradictory tenets and philosophies buried in the miraculous stories of the prophets leading The March. But there was something to what some of the stories professed about suffering that had to be true, for Arno's sake. If suffering did not produce a prosperous life, maybe the sacrifice of body and life could create some kind of power. Maybe bleeding into the sword was what it took to make it glow.

Roran laced and unlaced his fingers—bound together as they were—thinking of his father, who was often awake long into the night, the sparks from his hammer on heated metal illuminating the dark corners of the forge—not eating, not drinking, not sleeping. If it was his "life's work," did it mean he really put his life into it?

There was one other thing Roran recalled about *The Marches* from Griselda's stories: the reason why it was custom to treat criminals and prisoners with respect; the reason why it was law to provide the Way Out; the reason why, until recently, war was incredibly rare in the Wilhelm Peninsula. There was something dangerous about prolonged suffering, too. Though *The March Through the Mountain Pass* claims it was necessary, and power came from it, the power wasn't always positive or controlled, according to *The March from Pain*. He shivered, both from this idea and from his urine-soaked clothes becoming cold. Roran would have to gamble on a religion he didn't believe in and hope that only the positive tenets were the ones that were founded in something resembling fact.

Funerals on Verdin for the long-suffering were done in haste, usually the day of death, another reason for sticking a body in the ground without a tomb. Cormac had died while Roran was in Wilheim getting their shipment of iron. Griselda and Arno had found him collapsed in the forge, blood leaking from his mouth. Roran couldn't imagine what went through their heads finding their father like that and then hurriedly burying him in the yard at the base of a tree. Roran hoped they gave Cormac the Ardhatazian custom as well, dipping their fingers in Cormac's blood and drawing a triangle on their foreheads.

For people who suffered long, suffered from things Life Nectar couldn't cure, Griselda said that their bodies became dangerous. *The March from Pain* said that their suffering could become manifest once it was no longer trapped in their body; one way of preventing this would be burying the body quickly while the suffering still resided there and letting it seep into the ground to find a new host or return to Verdin itself. This superstition was supported by claims that the tree would die a few days after a long-suffering body was buried at its base. In *The Marches,* it was called Grief Sickness, a plague that affected only certain people who had suffered extraordinary amounts of pain for weeks, months, or years. Their bodies would sweat blood and then become dangerous. For those who lived outside the city, it was the subject of mythology. But for those who dealt with corpses—soldiers, undertakes, healers, and wardens—it was a very real threat.

Roran had left on routine and returned to a world shattered beyond recognition. His father was gone—no farewell, no final words. Though Cormac was a man of few words, he never left without saying goodbye, without letting the three know that he loved and appreciated his children.

In the dim light of their home, Griselda and Arno lay curled together in Cormac's bed, their bodies trembling with silent grief. They had messed up his pristinely made sheets, just wanting to be hugged by something that resembled their father. The day's labor of digging and filling the grave had drained them, leaving no strength for the wails their shattered hearts longed to release. Roran climbed in beside them, wrapping his arms around what remained of his family, holding them together as best he could. They nuzzled into him, grief removing any shame or ego or resistance to vulnerability.

Arno was the first to stir, slipping from their embrace only to return moments later, clutching a candle and their father's hammer with a quiet determination. Though night had settled thick and dark around them, he insisted they honor Cormac with a post-burial service—the only tribute they could offer to a man hurried into the earth. Griselda's soft voice filled the room as she stroked Arno's hair, the familiar melody of the Wilheim Lullaby weaving through the air like a fragile thread holding them all together.

Roran rolled over to his other shoulder and out of the puddle. He didn't have time to dwell on that sad scene and the words they shared to commemorate their father, not with his deadline approaching, not with his sister missing. There was also the matter of the sword his father gave him. But that, too, needed to be put on hold. With any luck, it was still hidden where he had stashed it after spotting Prince Zerebril approaching with fifty armed soldiers just days after Cormac's passing.

Roran heard footsteps outside his door and tensed. It couldn't be time already, could it? It was hard to tell when days passed in the cell. Though there was an opening in the ceiling, it didn't open to the outside world but to the floor of another hallway lit by torchlight. This way, guards could easily check on the status of prisoners when they made their rounds by looking down into their cells. Counting rounds was the only sure way he could keep track of time. Roran had counted that a guard's booted feet passed by the opening every 3,000 heartbeats, which he guessed was about every hour, if there weren't any special visitors or reason to pull a prisoner out of the cell. But steps outside his door now seemed far too soon.

He heard the latch and saw the light stream in from the hall-way. Henrietta stood there with a fresh bucket of bread, spit-fired chicken, utensils, and a change of bandages—he could tell from the smell and the way the pewter fork and knife clanked together in the bucket. Weeks of sensory deprivation made him talented at guessing based on limited information, such as counting heart-beats or listening for metal clanking.

Roran looked up at her. He couldn't quite make out her expression since she was silhouetted against the light, but he did hear her sniffle. She stood there for several seconds, thinking about something, or steeling herself for what she needed to do next. Finally, she entered. Roran didn't hear the familiar clank of armor.

Does this mean that she didn't bring guards? Roran thought. *Did she think she didn't need any with me bound at the wrists and ankles?*

Henrietta set the bucket on the table and sighed. "Okay then. Let's get you up."

"Don't touch me," Roran said.

"Roran, please. We have to feed you, and I'm not doing it with you on the floor." Stronger than she looked, the petite Henrietta shot her arms through Roran's armpits, clasped her hands around his chest, and hoisted him bit by bit onto the table until she could prop him against the wall. "Wet?" She held out her soaked hands and pulled at her damp dress. "Why are you . . . oh, silly me. It's probably hard to use the bucket in your state, isn't it?"

"I warned you," Roran said.

She huffed and then forced a small smile. "Can't be helped, can it?" She wiped her hands on her white apron that hung over her grey dress. The dress was loose-fitting and sturdy, clothing for work and practicality, her sleeves rolled up to her elbows.

Now that she was in the room, Roran got to look at more than just her silhouette or eyes. She was older than Roran by about a decade, with small hints of wrinkles starting to appear on her forehead and at the edges of her eyes and mouth. Her hair was mostly concealed in a simple bonnet. Though older than Roran's nineteen years, she was likely only thirty; however, she still had a somewhat matronly air about her. She fussed over his rumpled, wet clothing and brushed his hair out of his face. Unlike Ardhataz, who would turn screws into their prisoners' flesh for each day they had the audacity to continue living, it was important for Wilheim and most of Verdin to treat their prisoners with a degree of respect, even for the most despised criminals. It was fairly common for chambermaids to tend to the prisoner's cell, provide food, and see to injuries. Most of the time, they were accompanied by guards, though.

"I'll see to it you get a change of clothes and someone to clean this up. I'll have a guard come check if you need to do your business when they come by on their rounds, so we don't end up with more puddles. They'll be able to help you more than I can or should."

Roran cringed at the thought of two men holding him over the bucket. Henrietta must have seen his expression.

"For Imeel-Illin's sake, Roran, why did you have to beat up your hands? You're making this much harder on yourself than it needs to be."

"I wanted . . . I wanted to buy Arno more time between brandings."

Henrietta sighed and closed her eyes. "Not that I can do much, but is what you say true? That Cormac didn't pass down his secrets?" She opened her eyes and stepped closer to his face. "Are we really all done for?"

Roran bent his head up and looked at the stone ceiling. "I have not lied. Cormac didn't tell me how to do it. If he ever planned on telling me, he died before he could pass it on, but I don't think he planned on telling me, even if he wanted to."

Henrietta's eyes unfocused and stared at no point in particular on the stone walls. She sat down on the table next to him and they both stared at the torchlight in the hall. Roran was shocked at how close she was willing to get. She probably figured that it wouldn't do him any good hurting the one person who saw to his well-being. Most likely, she had performed duties for years without any incident. How could someone hurt a caretaker? Roran couldn't imagine it. Then again, how could someone permanently maim Arno?

"I have two cups of water in here," she said, motioning to the bucket. "Is it alright if I use one of them to wash my hands before I feed you?"

Roran nodded.

Henrietta forced a smile as she cleaned her hands of Roran's urine in one of the cups. She then dug into the bucket for a fork and stabbed a piece of the chicken. She held it before Roran's lips and gestured for him to open wide by opening and closing her own mouth. Roran accepted the chicken, which actually tasted good, like it was straight from the king's table.

"Where'd you get this?" Roran said while chewing. "This isn't what I normally get." In the darkness, he seldom could tell what he was eating. Most of it was mashed, partially eaten by a guard, or spat on by the time it arrived on the days that Henrietta wasn't working. He was not only a prisoner but an Ardhatazian prisoner. They likely blamed him for the war, for their possible relatives and comrades already slaughtered by King Ewen.

Henrietta smiled and tilted her head to the side. "I am seeing to it that you are tended for. I have my ways. Now open again."

Roran did as instructed.

"Roran, did you ever shave when you were . . . you know, outside?"

Roran shrugged since his mouth was full. Once he swallowed, he said, "I sometimes forgot to. But I usually did. Why?"

Henrietta gestured to her face. "It's kind of full of scraggly tufts. It looks pretty bad."

"What am I supposed to do about it?" Roran frowned. "Oros alive, you sound like my sister." Roran's eyes fell to the table at the accidental reminder as he still could not bring himself to think about what could have befallen Griselda. He looked down and away from the reminder, hoping not acknowledging it would push the potential horrible fates away. But Henrietta's fork still zoomed over and found Roran's mouth, even though he was mostly turned the other way. She had to overextend her reach to feed him as he resisted, drawing closer to him, dangerously close to a prisoner.

"I suppose I can arrange for someone to shave you—"

"No," Roran said. "I don't trust anyone with a razor near my throat as long as I'm in here."

"I see," Henrietta said as she fed him another bite. "What if I did it? Would you still decline, claiming it to be unnecessary? Have you . . . given up?"

Roran scowled at her and fully turned away, now completely facing the wall like a child in timeout, refusing to accept any more food.

Henrietta huffed and set the bucket down on the floor. There was exasperation in the way she slowly bent back up. "I don't want to believe you, Roran. I don't want to believe that you can't do it. I don't want to believe that we should give up," she said. "But something tells me that you wouldn't lie with little Arno on the line. Zerebril is still unsure, but I think he's trying to fight futility with violence as best he can. He's brilliant, but I don't know if he feels what others do, especially since Gunter's death. Both Zerebril and the king are not themselves. Then again, the king hasn't been himself for a long time."

"You're a mother, aren't you?" Roran asked. It was obvious in how she carried herself, the gentle way she moved hair out of his face, the cooing voice attempting to appease him, slow but certain movements, how she justified the terrible things the people she cared for did.

Henrietta didn't respond.

Roran sighed and gestured to the stone walls with his chin. "I don't know how you do this every day. I think a job like yours would be unbearable, and that's coming from the man in the cell. You have to deal with the lowest of the low, make sure they're fed, see to their wounds, clean up their filth. You even got my stinkin' piss on you today. It must be . . . I don't even have a word for that."

"You're right," Henrietta said. "I am a mother." She paused, making a point to deliberately ignore part of what Roran was saying. "His name is Fredrick, and he's no older than your brother. And I take care of him the same way I take care of you. As far as I'm concerned, you're a grown-up Fredrick, only your name's different." She let that sentence hang in the air, like laundry out to dry in the sun. Roran didn't know how much he'd miss sunlight since he spent most of his days aglow in the forge. Henrietta, even when she was somber, still had the makings of the sun in her personality, like one of the Beacons of Wilheim that founded the city.

Roran took his eyes away from the wall and craned his neck to look at Henrietta. She had balled her hands into fists, crumpling parts of her thick dress in her grip.

"So," Roran said. "Will you take Fredrick and flee Wilheim now that you know? Were you still here hoping that I could save you, too?"

Henrietta took her time to respond. It was a question that she had likely been considering for weeks. The war between King Morgen II of Wilheim and King Ewen of Ardhataz had gone on for six months. In that short span of time, due to Ardhataz's proximity to Wilheim, King Ewen had managed to take control of the fringes of the kingdom and win every battle. The amount of fighting and claiming that Ewen had done in just half a year was unheard of. The desperate state of Wilheim and Prince Gunter's loss in battle was what gave Prince Zerebril grounds to come to Cormac's forge and conscript him in service of the king temporarily until the war was won. Only there was no Cormac at the forge when Zerebril showed up.

"Why didn't you fight?" Henrietta asked. "Had you already given up, even then? Before this cell?"

"What do you mean?"

"Surely Cormac had his special weapons at the forge? Why didn't you use one to fight off the prince and his troops? Why did you let him snatch you and your brother? Were you going to take the Way Out like I've heard so many in the countryside already do as Ewen approaches?"

Roran had thought about using the great sword Cormac gave him. Ever since he first started swinging the hammer in Cormac's forge, Roran had dreamed of one day using a blade rather than making one. Practicing with Griselda had only fanned the flames of this dream as they both developed in skill alongside each other. He had once wanted to be part of the royal guard protecting King Morgen or fighting side by side with Prince Gunter as he dealt with minor border skirmishes. Most of his antagonists had been intangible, such as his mother's death or father's sickness. Just once, he wanted to hit something back, something that bled as much as he did.

However, he knew better despite his temper. Roran shook his head and said, "Using weapons made by Pops means certain death for foe and family alike. The weapons make no distinction in who they burn. I could have hurt Arno. Besides, Zerebril didn't exactly announce what his plans were. I think he had to change them when he saw Pops was dead. We thought we were being invited to the castle as an honorable gesture after Pops passed. I knew he was lying since he brought such a large escort, so I took some precautions, but I never imagined this."

"But you did have one? One of the weapons?"

Roran didn't answer.

Henrietta sighed. "Suppose it doesn't matter now. One weapon won't win the war. Prince Gunter is proof of that. We need many to fight Ewen and his strange new . . . beasts."

"What are they? Him using them on Gunter is the first I've heard of them."

"I haven't seen them myself, thank Imeel-Illin. But I've heard stories from the survivors, the soldiers who retreated while Prince Gunter held back the enemy. Prince Gunter only took a rearguard with him to battle; it's as you say, the prince thought that he would burn their whole force and didn't want his troops caught in the blaze. And it would have worked if they only had normal soldiers. But they had something else. Our survivors said they saw something like dogs, but they were made of light. Metal wouldn't cut them. Only Gunter managed to kill a few with Cormac's sword before he went down too. That's why you're so important."

"But I'm not. Not really. I can't do what Zerebril needs, what this kingdom needs, what Arno and Fredrick need. So, I ask again, are you going to run now that you know?"

She put a hand on Roran's shoulder. "I don't know. I don't know what good it would do. I doubt running would save us if it came to that. I can't fight like Prince Gunter. I can't make weapons like Cormac either."

Roran nodded in agreement.

"But what I can do," Henrietta continued, "is care for people. That's how I fight. That's doing my part, even if it means I'm just caring for prisoners. It needs to be done. But there's a special privilege in it that nobody but me sees."

Roran frowned. "And what's that?"

"I get to see the humanity in the people the kingdom has thrown away. I get to see the light in what was thought certain to be absolute darkness. I don't know what kind of evil is tormenting King Ewen, driving him to kill as much as he does, but I'm certain someone like me can drag the light back out of him." She said that with a hint of pride, a small smile emerging from her lips. "I've done it before. It doesn't always work, but even the most hardened criminal can have his world shaken when he's cared for. You do what you can to light the fire in the dark, regardless of reward or punishment. If you don't, nobody can see. They won't know if their pants are on backward or if their shirt is wrinkled—"

"Or if their beard needs trimming," Roran chirped.

Henrietta smiled and then continued. "We're no better than children in that dark, and even men fear that darkness just as much as the young. Imeel-Illin knows my eyesight has suffered, working in the dark of this dungeon for nearly a decade. But I'm the one lighting the torches, and none of you could see without me. Bear the light, Roran, regardless of reward or punishment. I still believe you'll find a way for Arno, for Fredrick, for all of us."

It sounded too easy to say, even if Roran believed that she sincerely believed it and had experience to back it up. It didn't seem like something Roran could ever accept. "What if . . . what if there's no light for me to bear? No torch for me to light? What if I never see anything again because there's no kindling, no spark?"

"I don't have a good answer for that, Roran. I've never had to go through what you are. My hopes and dreams have always been enough of a spark for me. And if not my own dreams, then enabling the dreams of others, like Fredrick."

"I feel like . . . like even my dreams are being taken from me. I can't help Arno in here. Does that mean that there's no hope? How do you keep fighting if you don't have a dream?"

Henrietta shook her head, admitting defeat. Roran had won the argument he didn't know he'd been having. It didn't feel like he had won. He wanted Henrietta to convince him, make him see something that he was missing. It didn't look like she would be able to.

"So, it is hopeless then?" Roran asked.

"I know this won't be satisfying to hear," Henrietta said, a weak half-smile on her face. "But it's the truth, and I don't think you're in the position to accept any more of my hopeful maxims." She paused and sighed. "I don't believe anyone can keep living without dreams."

With that, Henrietta patted Roran on the back, replaced his bucket, and left the cell.

The light was gone again. He repositioned himself against the wall to sit up straighter, since he needed to slouch for Henrietta to feed him.

"How can she still fight?" Roran said to himself. With that

question, Henrietta's remaining warmth was all but snuffed out. Roran thought of what would soon come. Him failing, Arno being dismembered, Wilheim being slaughtered down to every man, woman, and child. Surely it was hopeless?

But for now, his stomach was full of warm food. It was the first thing he could really savor in weeks. It seemed Henrietta had bought him time by caring for him, time to think, time to rest, time to heal as much as he could. He closed his eyes and hoped against hope that bloodying his hands would be enough.

Roran floated over the forge, listening
To the sound of measured hammer strokes
He poked his head in and saw his father
And a younger version of himself
This was the first time
Cormac charged him with the hammering
He handed the hammer to his young son
And Roran, anticipation jumping in his throat
Swung and swung and swung
Lengthening the red ingot
Cormac tutted and shook his head
Too fast, too imprecise, and Roran would know
How heavy a hammer could get after many swings
How much more willpower mattered when muscle slackened
And whether that would be enough
Until his grip slipped
And he hit his gloved hand holding the cool side
Roran nearly broke his hand
On the first day he was given the hammer
And sat in the corner, crying, and pressing his hand to his chest
But there was still work to be done
And blade making could not be interrupted once started

Cormac picked up the dropped hammer
And beat away
Still crying, Roran sat behind his father
The forge grew darker and indistinct as if night
Had crept in through the windows
His pain drew it in and threatened to swallow everything
Tendrils of pitch latching onto the walls
Trying to grab Roran, both versions of him
They turned red as they approached
And stalked, predatory, waiting
But with each blow, sparks flew
Cormac whistled as he worked
And swung the hammer to the Anvil Tune
With each blow, the sword glowed more
The sparks burned the tendrils which screamed
They redirected their attack at Cormac
But Cormac beat those tendrils into the blade
Roran gazed in awe of his father
In his steady swings:
How he fought, how he loved
And how he held back the dark

CHAPTER 4
WHAT A SHORT SWORD IS MADE FOR

FIFTY HEAVILY ARMED guards outlined the perimeter of the king's outdoor forge behind Wilheim Castle. Their plate shone in the fall sun, the last days of true dog-day heat before a blanket of Shatter Rock Mountain snowfall would envelop the city. The turrets and keep of Wilheim's central castle and seat of the king jutted above the yard as it had done so for hundreds of years, no matter what was happening outside the city gates. Panels of stained glass visible from the outside lined the uppermost walls of the keep, where the throne room was located high above. Like all the city's buildings, it was made of polished, white stone, stone that reflected the sun and seemed to saturate the other colors. The green of the grass was more aggressive, the tanned skin of the castle staff seemed to sting those near it, and even the water in the quench tank seemed more insistent to capture the color of the sky. This is the only time Roran could remember vibrancy being painful to look at, his eyes unable to take in the harsh shine of the world from being in the dark for weeks.

Roran could smell the royal guard sweating in their heavy armor. Another curse of being kept in the stone cell for so long was that smells seemed to be more noticeable, especially the terrible ones. Though they must have been scorched in the tight-fitting metal, their armor was impressive. Their plate was painted by Zerebril himself, who had a natural talent for the arts, each one made to match the individual wearing the armor. The Wilheim royal guard stood apart from regular soldiers by wearing sugarloaf helms that had an engraved pattern of inter-locking suns circling the pointed top of the helm.

Though Roran was not an armor smith, he did help make several of the halberds each royal guard had as they stood at attention with the tips pointing sunward. The spearpoint, rear spikes, and ax blade of the halberd were designed to look like sunbeams pouring from the central metal construct.

Roran understood all too well why the royal guard stood watch, encircling the forge like statues as cut from the same stone as the castle itself. Zerebril feared Roran—feared the man in the cage, feared what might happen if Roran's skill proved true, if the weapon he forged would burn to avenge his brother's torment. The prince wasn't taking any chances as Roran had the means, the will, and very few things left to lose.

Prince Zerebril stood at the center of the forge holding Arno's hand. "I have done my best to replicate the exact details you have described about how you and your father made weapons. I have sourced the steel and materials from the same provider in Wilheim, I have transported the tools from Cormac's forge to here, and," Zerebril said, holding up Arno's arm, "I have provided sufficient motivation. If you fail this time, then we will know for certain, and all will be lost."

Arno stepped forward. He looked up at Roran, and Roran resisted the urge to look away. Taking that single step forward seemed a monumental task. Arno's eyes, dark, now had the appearance of being sunk back into his skull. His restless energy once reserved for joy, now channeled into frantic panic—head turning back and forth from the forge to the halberds. Though his hair was combed, and his clothes were clean, probably Henrietta's doing, this was a shadow of Roran's brother.

"Roran? What's going on?" Arno asked, lip quivering.

Roran struggled to breathe and could only manage a curt nod at his brother.

Zerebril continued. "I have provided several master smiths who will serve as your apprentices for this process. You have complete control over them. All I require is a simple short sword that a spearman can use in close quarters. Realistically, we would only need a couple of troops per battalion trained with these swords to counteract those beasts of light. Any more would only endanger our own army. A skilled smithing team like this should be able to make a munitions short sword in a day. Once we know the correct method, we can make several at the same time and increase efficient production. Is this reasonable?"

Roran nodded.

"Good." Zerebril gestured toward Henrietta, who came and took Arno back to the castle.

Arno looked back at Roran the entire slow, unsteady march, his eyes wide enough for Roran to see his own bedraggled reflection.

Zerebril exhaled, noting the looks between the brothers. "Alright then, you're welcome to begin. I'll have official observers taking notes if I'm not out here myself. We need to get every detail to replicate a successful attempt."

Roran began. He gave instructions to each smith, divvying out responsibilities based on skill set, discipline, and experience. One to work the forge, another to sharpen the edge, another to heat treat, another to polish, while others worked on the cross guard and pommel and shaped the wooden handle. Roran would beat the sword into shape himself. With the large team multi-tasking for an individual weapon, though it was inefficient, it could be done in a day for a simple, undecorated military short sword.

Once the forge was hot enough, Roran began the process of heating the ingot, pulling it out, and lengthening the material with his hammer blows. Though his hands felt much better, it was still difficult to fully extend his fingers. His scabs began to open after repeated blows, and soon blood was dripping down his arm. Droplets flew off his hand with each collision of the hammer against the would-be sword. He beat his own blood into the ingot.

Roran put the sword back in the forge and waited. All he could do was stare at it while the heat climbed and singed his face. The other smiths were busy preparing their stations or working on the cross guard and pommel, but eventually, waiting for the heat was all that could be done.

Roran pulled the sword back out and beat it again until his ears were ringing with the thunderous clanging, until the repeated impact vibrations made his hand sore, until his shoulder burned from the exertion of continuously lifting the hammer. Once the sword began to cool, Roran put it back in the forge yet again to wait some more. He wished he could enjoy this familiar burning and pain the way he normally did. Working his hands and body was more healing to Roran than Life Nectar when at home in the forge. He wished he were working alongside his father rather than these strangers.

Roran looked at the other smiths, and they looked at him with apprehension, some with even fear. *Had Zerebril threatened these men as well? Or was the threat of King Ewen's army enough?* Roran thought.

Then Roran noticed that King Morgen II had come out to the forge yard. Rather than purple regal robes made from the pigment of Verdin Stars, the only source for purple or blue pigment on the continent, he was dressed in robes of black. He was not wearing his crown. He seemed to still be in mourning over the loss of his eldest son, Prince Gunter. The king spoke to no one and stood at the edge of the forge. He leaned against a wooden support beam, breathing through his mouth, and watching the process with dim eyes. Zerebril walked over to speak with the king, but the king shooed him away.

When Roran would run into Wilheim for smithing supplies, talk had reached his ears of the king's failing mind. He was once known as King of the Peaceful Dawn, a king who had overseen decades of peace, prosperity, and technological progress to the great city of Wilheim, further solidifying the city as the beacon of civilization to the rest of Verdin. Now, he rarely left the castle, stumbled over his words and body, and spent most of his days reportedly looking at the sky, ceiling, or stained-glass windows. His was a sickness of aging that the Verdin Star could not aid. He lived long and well, mirroring his city, and now he was being punished for it by a very long and drawn-out march to his funeral pyre.

The king seemed to be talking nonsense to himself that Roran couldn't make out. The guards near him shuffled about uncomfortably. One guard dared to approach and the king recoiled, suddenly coming to life as if he was stabbed.

"Burning! Burning . . . uh . . . ohh . . ." the king regained his composure as the soldier moved back. The king shook his head and smiled weakly. "Not a good day."

Only one person accompanied the king as he walked into the yard, someone Roran had not seen before. He had blonde hair, a blonde beard, and was about Roran's age. He was clad in light armor emphasizing mobility rather than total protection and had a bow across his back with a quiver of arrows at his side. He wore a green brigandine with no pauldrons and had smaller vambraces.

Though his expression was just as disturbed as the king's, it was wracked with a different emotion: indiscriminate hate. Whether he was looking at the king, Roran, or the guards, the scorn never left his face.

Zerebril had two guards bring over chairs for the king and his angry escort, but only the king took the offer. Zerebril took the hate-filled man to the side and talked with him out of earshot. Again, his expression did not change when looking at Zerebril and remained a mask of anger throughout the whole conversation, though Roran never saw the man open his mouth.

The sword grew hot enough again, and Roran did the repetitive work until the sword was properly worked into shape. Once completed, he checked on the progress of the other smiths who were shaping the cross guard and pommel. After that, he followed the blade around to each station and supervised the entire process even though these men were clearly skilled and had far more experience than Roran himself.

The royal guests never interrupted; they only observed. They had apparently put aside all responsibilities for the day as none of them ever went back into the castle. Food was brought out to them and was also provided to Roran and the smiths, but even as they ate, they watched Roran and the forge intently with hungry eyes. Despite the stifling heat of the forge being mitigated since it was mostly outdoors, the atmosphere was still heavy with desperation from the moist, hurried breathing of everyone in the yard.

As the sun drifted across the sky, Roran began to sweat more even after the forge went dark when it was no longer needed. The swords Roran had helped make with Cormac would only glow when they were completed. There was no way to know until the very end, which made the waiting nearly crippling. The food had not settled well in his stomach, and it took all his concentration to focus his eyes from smith to smith, station to station. He felt dizzy and would often brace himself against a beam, similar to how the king first appeared. Roran did not believe in anything he could pray to, no verse or song he could chant in ritual, no mantra or poem he could recite to set his mind at ease. Nothing in *The Marches* would distract him from his pain—pain, for Roran, now being the only thing that could resemble religion. He waited, eyes boring into the nearly finished blade hard enough that they could have made a fuller for the sword.

Once all the individual pieces were finished, Roran assembled the sword himself. He tapped the cross guard down over the tang, fitted the wooden handle to cover the rest of the exposed tang, wrapped a leather grip over the wood, and capped it off with the pommel. As it neared completion, Zerebril told a guard to go fetch Arno from Henrietta but instructed the guard to not let Henrietta come out to the yard.

Roran held the finished short sword in both hands, one hand under the blade, the other on the handle. He willed it with all his might to glow. In his desperation, he breathed on it, fogging up the blade, he rubbed the blood from his opened scabs up and down the blade to wash off his breath and wiped that with a clean work rag. Nothing.

Unconsciously, Roran clenched his jaw tight enough that it threatened to fuse his teeth together. Several blood vessels burst around his eyes from the stress. "What more do you want!" Roran yelled at the sword. Roran was no longer holding an inanimate object, but a force of ill will, a sword Roran himself helped make for one terrible purpose.

The king, the angry man, and Zerebril all stood up. Roran turned toward them, frenzy in his eyes. "I don't know what it wants!"

Zerebril grasped the handle of his sheathed rapier with one hand and approached, his expression unreadable. He motioned to several guards with his free hand, who approached Roran from all sides. The smiths quickly vacated the forge.

Exhaustion and hopelessness seizing Roran, he dropped to his knees and let the sword clang to the stone floor in front of him. For good measure, the guards placed gauntleted hands on his shoulders, not enough to restrain but enough pressure to remind him of their presence.

Zerebril picked up the sword and inspected it. He turned to his father and the angry bowman, shaking his head. Just in case, Zerebril walked outside the forge to an opening in the courtyard and swung the blade. It cut through the air as any fine sword would, but no glow, and not a hint of flames followed in its wake. Zerebril bowed his head, his lips completely disappearing in the hard line of his mouth. He closed his eyes and sighed.

Arno was escorted out into the courtyard. The veins bulged in Roran's neck at the sight of his younger brother being ushered along by a guard.

"Sit him on the anvil," Prince Zerebril commanded.

"No!" Roran shouted. "You corpse caller!" Despair turned to rage turned back to grief turned to maddening hate. "I swear I'll turn the screw in every last one of you if you touch another hair on his head!"

Arno jumped at Roran's shouting, terror overwhelming his face as it dawned on him what his brother's frantic cries meant. Though Roran was shouting despicable slurs, Zerebril seemed to not hear him at all.

Arno pulled against his escorts, but a royal guard picked him up, his legs kicking.

"Roran? Roran! What's going on?" he pleaded as he was carried.

Two other guards walked up to the forge. They set Arno on the anvil, two holding his arms and one holding his leg outstretched over the anvil's tip.

"Scoot him forward so that his knee hangs over," Zerebril said, circling the anvil. His brows were furrowed, shadowing his eyes. Despite Roran's howling rage, Zerebril seemed somewhere else, as if he was willing himself to be anywhere but in this place at this moment. His eyes were glazed over, and he looked almost subdued.

By this point, Roran was fully restrained, with several guards pinning him against the floor as he yelled and struggled with his remaining strength. Arno was quietly whimpering, looking from his brother to the prince to the non-glowing short sword the prince held in his hands.

Zerebril picked up a leather strap from one of the work benches and offered it to Arno. "Here, you'll want to bite down on this."

"W-Why?" asked Arno.

"Trust me."

The guards looked away, trying to find anything in the forge they could fix their eyes on to make them forget what was happening. Arno opened his mouth and Zerebril gently put the folded strap in. "Good, now bite down."

Arno did, eyes watering and his hands shaking. His eyes seemed to get larger. The fear and implication in Arno's eyes seemed to draw Zerebril back. He couldn't bear to look into the pleading eyes of an innocent child. Shakily, Zerebril held the sword over Arno's leg, just below the knee to gauge the trajectory before raising it up over his head.

"No . . . no . . . no," Arno mumbled meekly through the leather strip.

"Roran, please; last chance. Tell us the secret. Your father was Ardhatazian, right? If you refuse . . . I have to assume that you are enemies to Wilheim and plan on escaping to tell King Ewen the secret." Zerebril seemed again to be speaking beyond Roran, like the rest of the people there needed to hear the decree rather than the victims.

Roran was hyperventilating, barely able to respond, especially as the guards pinned his flailing body down and pressed the wind out of him. "There's nothing more I can do! Please, cut off my leg instead!"

Arno looked from his brother to his leg on the anvil, breathing faster when he realized what was about to happen, though he kept the leather in his mouth. He squirmed his shoulders only for the guards to tighten their grip.

Zerebril sighed. He then made the mistake of looking into Arno's eyes again, and—to Roran who was nearly suffocating as he subconsciously held his breath—it seemed Zerebril could not do it. He lowered the sword and looked over to his father.

King Morgen II returned Zerebril's gaze but could not offer any sympathy. "If you are to be king of whatever remains at the end of this, you will need to follow through with your promises. And your threats," the king said, his voice croaking as if this was the first time he'd spoken all day. "You must wrangle the shadows in the sky no matter what name they bear."

"I do not believe this will help us win the war, Your Majesty," Zerebril said. "Are you . . . fit to make decisions today?"

Anger spread over the king's face, though he did not answer Zerebril's question. "It means little if it fixes a problem. It's a matter of holding yourself to your word," the king replied. "Do it quickly and be done with this whole sorry attempt."

Zerebril looked back down at Arno's leg and then at his eyes. The prince dropped the short sword and sat down on a work bench, holding his head in his gauntleted hands. "Gunter was meant to be king, not me," he exhaled. "I'm a painter. I don't dismember children."

The king's eyes came to life with the fiery terror of madness. "Children? What children? All I see is rot in my yard! We're all about to be corpses defiled on the ramparts!"

The blood drained from Zerebril's face. "Father, you're not yourself."

One of the royal guards offered a hand to stabilize the king but the king leaped back from it in fright.

The king looked to the angry bowman and swatted at his arm, "Tazzes! Kill the red-haired corpse caller! Kill the screw-turning little one. He's threatening to grow bigger, so we have to take his leg. This is what was said and what must be! We can't break our word, or we'll rot! That's what Tazzes do. They lie, and they rot!"

The angry bowman moved at the mad king's request and entered the forge, furiously stomping toward Zerebril. Zerebril flinched and closed his eyes as if expecting a blow from the angry bowman.

"I . . . I can't," the prince whispered. "I need more . . . poppy . . . mercy."

The bowman rolled his eyes and exhaled. He ignored Zerebril and picked up the short sword instead.

"No!" Roran shouted, his voice barely anything more than a hoarse gasp.

The short sword Roran made was not designed for chopping like an ax but for piercing into weak points or cutting cloth armor. It was thin and had little heft in the blade. As such, it took several swings to make it through.

CHAPTER 5
CAPTAIN

URREM THOUGHT people viewed time all wrong. It was a misconception that the future was theirs to shape. If anything, the only thing they had control over was how people shaped their past. A carpenter can control how the house was built. He cannot control what happens to the house. Urrem thought that every important moment of his past could be captured in the instance a tool struck the ground: a shovel striking the rocky soil, a pick striking the stone, a burial in the snow, a new place and a new home, a glowing blade stabbed in the dirt and the events that would make him captain.

A spear striking a heart. Considered a mercy for someone who would never recover.

Captain Urrem watched the soldier next to him pull a spear out of the chest of a farmer. It looked like the farmer tried to fight back with a shovel. Urrem shook himself out of the daze. Sometimes it was necessary to go into the past to avoid looking too closely at the present.

"Did we happen to come up on da quotas?" Urrem asked the nearby soldier.

"Yes, sir. Captured thirty people, we did. Wrangled thirty

more before we killed the rest who attacked and tried to stop us from taking da prisoners."

"Prisoners? What are dey like? I tink . . . demographics is the word?"

"Dey were varied, sir. We tried to only round up dose who looked cut from sturdier stuff of the younger men and women," said his lieutenant.

"Good, dat should sate King Ewen for now." Urrem turned and examined the smoldering village. Most of the houses were fairly rudimentary, with basic wattle and daub construction. It seems the barns were more cared for than the homes the farmers lived in.

"And da crops?" asked the soldier.

Urrem drew his mouth into a hard line. "Ya know da orders, Lieutenant Malcolm. Burn 'em."

"Da livestock?" asked Lieutenant Malcolm.

Urrem winced, but he knew he had to say it. Despite his rugged features, square chin, and narrow eyes, Urrem was much more capable of feeling than his hardened body suggested. "Same ting," Urrem managed, running his hands through his short, brown, and partially thinning hair. He then put on his helmet, as if it could protect him from the many difficult pangs of war.

Malcolm sighed. Like all soldiers in Urrem's unit, Lieutenant Malcolm wore his standard-issue thick gambeson, a stuffed cloth garment that went down to mid-thigh, with a black tunic. On the chest were the three white mountains symbolic of Ardhataz. They were also given nasal helms, but Malcolm had replaced his issued nasal with a Wilheim barbute helmet he had looted from a corpse. Unlike the nasal helm, which was mostly a metal cap with a narrow metal fixture extending down to only cover the nose, the Wilheim barbute encased the whole head and left a large T-shape in the front to uncover the eyes, nose, and mouth. If the soldiers survived a battle, they were encouraged to loot enemies for their armor if it fit, despite it not matching issued uniform. As long as they wore the black tunic over whatever looted armor they found, they could be identified as part of King Ewen's forces. Despite prioritizing military training, King Ewen's kingdom of Ardhataz was low in iron mineral deposits, with most of it coming from extremely dangerous work Urrem had experienced firsthand high up in the mountain mines. Most arms and armor came from loot or had to be imported from nations they weren't in conflict with, namely the nations to the west. However, wool and animal materials were plentiful, meaning everyone received a gambeson, spear, and wooden tower shield, and the nasal to start. Urrem noticed how many of his men treated looting and getting new equipment as a sign of their battlefield prowess, as if they were advancing in rank shown by how many they had killed and looted.

Lieutenant Malcolm walked away tutting.

"I know, I know. But don't ya say anyting if ya know what's good for ya. I'd rather be building houses dan torchin' 'em too," Urrem said.

What a waste, Urrem thought. He knelt down to pick through one of the burnt husks of a home. He cleared away crisp joists and fragmented wooden shingles. He examined the handiwork, or what was left of it. Though he trusted King Ewen's judgment, he sometimes couldn't quite make out the reasoning for the actions on his own. Urrem admitted to not being very bright, but he was an artist with wood and hammer. Before he was drafted, he would fix the local village's housing issues for free if they provided the materials, while his father built bridges and mine shafts high in the mountains.

Urrem stood up and brushed the soot off his plate. Then his eye caught an old great helm in the wreckage, indicating that this house belonged to a veteran of Wilheim long ago. Being a higher rank, he had first go at the enemy loot. Of the things that fit, he had managed to get a breast plate and greaves. With this great helm, a boxy helmet that completely encased the head only leaving narrow slits for the eyes and round holes near the mouth to help with breathing, Urrem had a chance for a more protective helmet than his nasal helm. He found that visibility and hearing, which bulkier helmets restricted, were more important for higher-rank officers who weren't necessarily on the front lines but still in the field. He needed to see his troops and make adjustments, more so than he needed to worry about an ax to the face.

Instead, he called over one of his men. "Briggs!"

Briggs was the very image of an Ardhatazian warrior—tall, broad, and red as sunbaked clay. His missing front teeth, a glaring gap in his otherwise imposing face, and how he lost them were a treasured memory for Urrem. He had watched it happen —watched Briggs lose a bet with Malcolm and, as punishment, sink his teeth into his own shield. No one had asked him to bite down that hard, but Briggs approached everything with reckless enthusiasm, his own well-being an afterthought to his unwavering determination. And Malcolm kept the teeth.

"Found ya a helmet," Urrem said.

"Did ya now?" Briggs said with his lopsided grin.

Urrem nodded. "Wit' tis great helm," he said holding it up for Briggs to inspect, "da whores won't have to look at yer awful face. Could save ya some money since dey be chargin' ya out the ass on account of ya being so ugly."

Briggs took the helmet and jab in stride, swapping his nasal helm for the great helm. He stuff it over his head and nodded, indicating a good fit. "Don't need to worry about whores chargin' me," Briggs's muffled voice boomed from the helmet. "Yer ma services me for free."

Urrem laughed and clapped Briggs on the shoulder. However, he did feel bad laughing while standing on the burning rubble people once called home. But it was very hard not to laugh at Briggs.

"Me mother's dead," Urrem replied. "Been dead two decades."

"I know," Briggs said turning away. "Why do ya tink she's free?"

Urrem both grimaced and chuckled at the same time. "Don't ya tink dat's a little insensitive?"

"I agree, couldn't feel a ting. No sensation whatsoever, so wide was her cavern. I'm guessing yer pops needed one of dose fancy candle headlamps for more than just da mines."

"Alright, alright! Enough 'bout me parents' corpses."

Briggs clapped Urrem on the back. "Oh, come now, I was just getting started; but probably for da best."

Urrem nodded. "Speaking of corpses, dis place is going to start stinkin' so best be leavin' soon."

"Aye, not to mention da ruckus about to come once dey set the barns a blazing."

Urrem looked Briggs in the eye and leaned in close, "Ya know why we do dat, right?"

"King's orders?"

Urrem smiled. "Yes, official decree. Don't want ya getting distracted from da war effort. Back home, King knows how much ya have relations wit your sheep."

Briggs looked down at his feet and shook his head covered in the great helm. "Ah, ya bastard. Ya finally got me. But . . . at least da sheep are warm, unlike yer ma."

With a quick duck and swift movement of the arm, Briggs punched Urrem in the groin.

Urrem grunted and doubled over.

"Would ya quit doing dat!?" Urrem hollered.

"Never!" Briggs laughed, jogging out of Urrem's reach.

Once Urrem steadied himself after enduring Briggs's verbal and physical onslaught, he turned away from the burning village.

Malcolm, overhearing the conversation, walked back over. "Why do ya let him get away with dat?"

Urrem gestured to the burning landscape around them. "I needed a laugh."

Malcolm nodded and carried on, following the rest of the unit as they finished looting. Urrem then led them back toward camp, their thirty captives in tow.

Urrem was one of several captains whose primary job was not to fight in large-scale open combat against the forces of Wilheim. He was tasked to raid the local area, gather useful tools and weaponry, capture thirty people per week, and burn everything else to the ground. Ardhataz had plenty of food and livestock that traveled with the army, as the nation was well-versed in animal husbandry—especially Briggs—so King Ewen instructed them to burn anything they couldn't carry to demoralize the enemy and prevent any peasant revolts from catching them unawares. Still seemed like a waste to Urrem, though, especially now as he heard the panicking livestock being burned in their stables.

Soon, the sound of screams could be replaced by another sound, which was a great mercy. The sound of mail jostling under their tunics filled the night as Urrem rode on horseback alongside his infantry unit. They all still smelled like a mixture of charcoal and a slaughterhouse, but they had for weeks now, and that smell would not go away no matter how many times they dipped in the river. Just as sawdust was a right bastard to get out from under his fingernails, the smell of weeks and weeks of slaughter clung tightly to his armor, nestled in his pores, and refused to let go.

They walked alongside the Shatter Rock River now, one of the widest and deepest rivers on the continent. Most of the campaign had relied on the river to transport some of the more cumbersome elements of the army. Though they were going upstream, the river would go all the way to Stedtfest and Wilheim to the north back up against the mountains. It made the exhausting journey through the lowlands near Lake Verdin and the massive Stedtfest forest more manageable. What was harder to manage was what came next, after Captain Urrem dropped off the thirty captives.

Much of their livestock and parts to assemble siege weapons for taking Stedtfest and eventually Wilheim were being transported by large flat boats that somehow could travel quickly upstream, a puzzle Urrem couldn't quite figure out yet. However, there was another boat, the largest boat, that Captain Urrem did not like to think about. War prisoners were made into slaves, which Urrem didn't have any qualms with—unlike Wilheim, Ardhataz had an economic boost due to war and slave trade—but the thirty captives he was to bring in every week were not put to work as slaves but rather put inside the boat. Unlike most of the other boats, it had walls and a roof; it was not just flat. Though he couldn't see what went on inside the boat, he could *hear* it.

It was not his place to question the Prophet King Ewen, who could supposedly perform miracles and was vested with holy power. Whatever was going on inside that boat must be by divine mandate. It was said that King Ewen had started manifesting powers, received a divine revelation about holy conquest, and conscripted an army to fulfill the revelation. And it was hard not to believe the stories. Ewen had won every battle, even a battle against Gunter and his Cormac weapon. Ewen had an inescapable magnetism, binding all within reach of his charm and almost divine valiance.

Once Urrem made it back to camp, he dismissed his troops to sleep off any rogue shovel bruises or pitchfork scratches in their tents. They wouldn't need to report for a few days since they hit their quota early.

If only I could end the war early, too, Urrem thought. He loved Ardhataz, believed in the justice they were delivering, but the weight of his devotion paled in comparison to what waited for him at home: Jezerelle. Her eyes—wide, dark, and always carrying a quiet sorrow—haunted him more than the battlefield ever could. Eyes that pleaded for him to hold her, to promise he would never let go. They had only been married three short years before conscription tore them apart. No children yet, no warmth of a family to fill the silence of their home—just Jezerelle, tending the house alone, waiting for a husband she had no guarantee would return.

Urrem bit his lip and made his way over to the river from his campsite. He knew personally how hard it was to weather the mountains alone.

Urrem and King Ewen's royal guard, Shadows of the Mountain, outfitted in full black plate, assisted Urrem in directing the thirty-person chain gang to the boat. The boat was anchored at the moment to the side of the river, tied to several trees to keep it from floating back downstream. They had to walk across a wide plank to get from the shore edge to the boat. Urrem tried not to think about the screams he heard inside the boat, nor did he lock eyes with any of the people he was escorting into whatever lay waiting inside. King Ewen made it clear that this boat and what happens on it was absolutely vital to the success of the campaign.

What Urrem did see were the two figures who stood next to the closed door. One of them was King Ewen, dressed in polished kingly plate with black-patterned detailing. Ewen held his helmet, a great helm with goat horns adorning the sides. Though it added unnecessary weight, the giant man looked the stuff of nightmares when he wore it. He would almost always wear the plate, unless he was fist-fighting.

The other looked to be a scholar by his robes. Not just a scholar, but *the* Scholar. The apparition that had been haunting the trek up the river. Though Urrem did not know much about the scholarly world, he could have sworn that the sun emblazoned on the back of the Scholar's robes was the sigil for the Wilheim Academies.

Ewen towered over the Scholar, and everyone else in the

army for that matter, but his bearing wasn't threatening, at least for now. His bushy red beard and mane bounced as the king laughed at one of his own jokes. The king's cheer made it harder to forget that, according to stories, his hair had once been brown but the hundreds he'd slain personally on the battlefield and in the Highland Pits had dyed it red.

King Ewen was talking, but the robed Scholar was not, except the king still replied as if his comment had been addressed out loud, making it look like King Ewen was talking to himself.

"How many more do ya tink we'll need? Boat's near full," the king asked. His tone was fairly jovial given the boat he was standing on.

No response.

The king nodded. "Hmm, so we'll need a consistent supply den. How many of da monstrous tings are ya plannin' on makin'? What is necessary for da sieges? We do *only* what's necessary."

No response.

The king stroked his bushy red beard and raised an eyebrow. "Very well. Den I'll be keepin' dose five captains busy under Colonel Macblite. We have a fresh batch o' livestock comin' now," the king gestured to the approaching chain gang. The robed figure turned, but with the hood, Urrem could only make out a pale, clean-shaven chin in the night. Urrem saluted the king once his attention turned to the captain.

"At ease, Captain Urrem," King Ewen said. "Tank ya for yer service. Ya be doin' much for me and Ardhataz."

The king opened the door before Urrem could look away. Urrem hurriedly turned around, a cold sweat breaking out on his forehead. Next to him, the people in the chain gang started resisting heavily, trying to jump off the wide plank connecting the boat to the river edge. They were screaming, falling to the floor, refusing to walk any nearer to the open doors of the boat.

The black-plated royal guards, all of which were almost as big as Ewen, grabbed them more fiercely and shoved them inside.

"Don't be so quick to heed him," Ewen muttered to the passing guards. "I'm still in charge."

Urrem, breathing heavily and sweating, his armor feeling much more cumbersome than usual, did all he could to steady himself and not keel over into the river. It didn't work, and he fell to his knees, the sight of what was inside threatening to make him sick. The smell not helping either.

"What's da matter, soldier?" King Ewen walked up to him; his plated legs seemed to clink over all other sounds of the flowing river. It did not drown out the screams.

"I must be dehydrated. Da villagers fought back for a while."

"Well, see to it dat yer well-rested, Captain." King Ewen was close enough to pat him encouragingly on his back.

Urrem did not look up or respond. He was distracted by the king's shadow. Wherever the king walked, no matter where the lamplight shone from, his shadow seemed attached to the river as if he were tethered to it. But this was more than just a shadow. It seemed to have stars caught up in it.

Urrem's eyes followed the king as he walked back toward the Scholar, whose shadow seemed to be doing the same thing. Then the Scholar shivered, as if in a seizure, before going rigid, then softening again. The normally mute Scholar broke out laughing at the faces of the new arrivals in the boat. It was the first time Urrem had heard his voice. The laugh was high, nearly nasally— a squeaky, scratchy noise clearly above his normal speaking registry.

"Can you bear the look on their faces?" the Scholar asked. His lack of the Ardhatazian sing-song dialect a clear marker that he was originally from Wilheim. And an outsider.

Ewen didn't respond.

Why was Ewen dealing wit dis Willy? Urrem thought. *I*

tought da whole point of dis was payback and expansion for our people. Why is he here and treated so well by da king?

"You must tell me more about your upbringing," the Scholar continued. "I am fascinated with certain aspects of your personality. Is it natural? Do you intentionally craft a persona for your troops?"

King Ewen closed the doors as the last of the quota was dragged inside. Ewen turned and eyed the Scholar quizzically. "Ehrm, I don't much like dese kinds of questions. Can ya switch back, please?

"Of course! But I really must insist you tell me more soon if we are going to continue having the scribes compile your March."

Ewen shrugged and waved off the comment.

"As you wish." And with that, the Scholar silenced himself, and Urrem watched, shaken, as Ewen continued his one-sided conversation with a mute Scholar as they walked off the boat and back to the main camp.

CHAPTER 6
GRIEF SICKNESS

RORAN CURLED beneath the splintered table, his breath ragged, his body trembling despite the fevered sweat clinging to his skin. The bowman in green brigandine had flung him to the stone floor like discarded rags, leaving him broken, thoughtless. Even fear had lost its shape—only instinct remained. He clutched the jar to his chest, the only choice that was entirely his, the Life Nectar and what escape it offered. The world beyond his shaking limbs blurred, distant, as if it no longer belonged to him.

He knew he didn't have much time left. There were several ways in which his death was certain: from execution in case he was lying so that Cormac's secrets didn't fall to King Ewen, to just letting him starve as everyone fled Wilheim, to being caught in the battle that was coming. And there was one other way. The way from Griselda's stories. What the jar was meant to end before it could get worse.

Roran could feel *it* consuming him already. It was uncertain how much suffering one could take before *it* came; this mostly depended on the person in case-by-case studies performed by the scholars in the Wilheim Academies. The nameless, inexplicable death that waited for people wracked with extreme and enduring suffering. More than mere physical injury, *it* came for those suffering in the mind, who have died hundreds of deaths day by day yet continued to live.

Though the condition was called Grief Sickness, the *it* which caused the symptoms resisted definition. When someone suffered something traumatic and life-altering, Grief Sickness would sometimes take hold of the person. Not everyone, but some were susceptible to it. Based on what Griselda had said, the victim's blood would get hot, and it was said to explode out of the body—an eruption of red from the pores in the skin. A lethal dose of Life Nectar would diminish the pain but still result in death due to internal organ failure.

Once Grief Sickness started, it could not be stopped, and it was assumed to be always lethal. Most would take the Way Out once it started, as the pain was said to be insurmountable and unending.

Roran's skin burned with fever, sweat slicking his trembling limbs as violent tremors wracked his body. His muscles clenched and spasmed, beyond his control. The more he thought about what had just transpired, the hotter he felt. The muscle spasms would only last for a few seconds but were wretched. He yelled as his hamstrings seized and convulsed. Each convulsion stole his breath, twisting him in agony as if his very bones rebelled against him.

He heard boot steps near the opening in the ceiling. The weight of each step pressed through the wood, a slow, deliberate rhythm that sent a chill crawling down Roran's spine. "Help, please! I don't feel well!"

The hardened heels paused then continued walking. Roran gasped for air. "Please! It hurts so much!" The dull thud of the boots slowly drifted away from his ears.

"You're feeding me to Oros!" he cursed.

But even as Roran cried out, overwhelmed by his own bodily agony, he was emphatically disgusted with himself. *If I'm in this much pain*, he thought, *what did it feel like to be Arno? What did it feel like to have your brother make a sword that chopped off your leg?*

The flickering torchlight scarcely visible from the opening in the ceiling and underneath the cell door seemed to slow, like the flames were being halted.

"No . . ." Roran groaned, before yelping as his calves seized this time. Sweat poured from him in relentless streams, making yet another puddle. Roran felt like time was becoming distorted as the pain made every second feel like an hour. Could he last long enough for Henrietta to come and bring him food and water?

Roran did his best to focus his mind on the present: the cold air he was breathing, the colder stone beneath him, the fire in his chest. *No, not that, something else!* The dark of the room, the quiet, the solitude, Arno's severed leg. "No!" He seized again, this time the muscles in his back. Roran writhed around under the table like an eel cut in half. They didn't bother to bind him again, assuming it no longer mattered what he did to his body. He was going to meet an end one way or another.

Another guard passed by.

"Please . . . please . . . I need water. I need Henrietta."

The boots halted, silence pressing down like a held breath. Then, from above, a voice—low and unseen—slipped through the darkness, curling around Roran and squeezing him tight. "She's not coming back. If I were you, I would take the Way Out and be done with it." His voice was somber, not even the normal leer or disdain, as if he was considering the same approach himself. He walked away, footfalls seeming heavier and heavier.

Roran looked down at the jar in his hands. Why had he not drunk the Life Nectar? He was certain to die by all accounts.

Maybe he hadn't surrendered yet? He was holding the option close, but something kept him from doing it. Though the culture had accepted that this was necessary for those with Grief Sickness, it seemed fundamentally wrong to him. He remembered his father looking down in sorrow at the bodies of an entire family that had taken the Way Out: a husband, wife, toddler, and infant.

After Arno was born, Cormac's weapons became famous. The man moved his family closer to Wilheim to do business more efficiently and with richer clientele who could pay for the weapons, which were quickly growing in popularity. For whatever reason, instead of moving out once the property was purchased, the previous owners of the forge had taken the Way Out as a family; assumedly, the parents made the choice for their children. No one would ever know why.

Roran remembered seeing Cormac's darkened expression, his thick brow shadowing his eyes as he looked down at the corpses. Cormac had paid for a wet nurse to feed Arno, but Griselda was holding baby Arno whenever he wasn't feeding. She walked into the house behind them and screamed, snapping Cormac from his trance.

He pulled his children close, hiding their eyes behind his broad shoulders, shielding them from the grisly sight. "I will never let this happen," Cormac promised to himself just as much to Roran and Griselda. "Ya hear me? My children will always be safe as long as I'm alive to say a ting about it."

Griselda stopped crying and returned her attention to soothing Arno by gently bouncing him in her equally tiny arms.

Roran, eleven at the time, could not imagine what had happened. He could now. But Cormac could not stand the practice. After all, he had lost greatly too and had not succumbed. Roran's mother, Gretchen, had died giving birth to Arno.

Roran seized again, his shoulders cramping. They were getting longer and more painful. Worst of all, Roran had stopped sweating, not because he wasn't hot, but because he was dehydrated. How much longer did he have left? How much more pain would he have to endure before he just died already?

Roran looked down at the jar and started to unscrew the lid. He was not like his father, not strong enough, not skilled enough, not bright enough to hold back the dark and protect the family. He was no sun, unlike Henrietta, his father, or his siblings. What would his dead father say to him if after eight years of beating a prosperous life out of the stubborn iron, Roran had lost it all in less than a month after Cormac's death?

But was it *really* Roran's fault? He seized again, this time large groups of muscles in his legs rather than just in isolation. "Why, Pops? Why didn't you tell me how to make the weapons? You said you would protect us but look what happened because you died! Look what happened because you didn't trust me with the secret!" Roran's abs cramped and forced all the air out of his diaphragm, which resulted in a coughing fit.

Slowly, Roran crawled out from under the table and placed the jar on top. He grabbed the edges of the wood to steady himself, knowing he was likely to seize again at any moment as his fever got worse and worse.

Who would blame him if he took it? Who would know? Who would care? The kingdom was doomed, and Arno was likely going through the same thing he was. Another seizure brought him down to his knees, his face inches away from the jar.

The way Roran saw it, he could die easy, or he could die hard, but death was guaranteed. Why subjugate himself to it? The Life Nectar would numb the pain and allow him to die with far less suffering.

"I'm sorry Arno, Griselda . . . Pops," he whispered and took the lid off the jar. "If the stories are true, I'll see you again, in another life, on the next leg of the March."

He looked down into the honey-like green content in the jar. The Life Nectar moved around slowly, it's lazy sloshing back and forth even more unnerving than if it had moved with the same urgency to expel the pain Roran was consumed by. Roran lifted his arms, brought the jar to his lips, and waited as the green ooze slowly made its way down to his mouth. But it never quite did.

A jolt of pain and cramps ran up all the muscles in Roran's arms as his upper body all seized at once. The jar he had been holding loosely from exhaustion flew from his hands and shattered on the stone floor before he could swallow a drop.

Roran crumpled, his arms locked around his chest. His legs jerked uncontrollably, the violent spasms rattling his bones. A rushing filled his ears, swelling from a distant whisper into a deafening roar—inhuman, endless, like the bellow of some ancient, unseen predator hunting in the dark. Beneath his skin, his veins slithered, writhing with fevered heat, as though something wicked clawed its way through his blood, desperate to escape.

The Way Out was gone, dashed all over the floor, and Roran wasn't even strong enough to crawl over and lick it up.

His suffering was manifesting.

"Fine," he croaked. "If I'm going to die like this, then let my agony kill the lot of you in this castle!"

Would anyone hear him? No. Did it matter? No.

Roran was not strong enough to be like his father, but it seemed like he had no choice but to suffer through it anyway. He opened his mouth to breathe, but a scream forced the air away. His lungs were working against him, vacating air in consistent shouts instead of drawing it in. He began seeing all the faces of those he knew as all nineteen years of his life stretched out before him. Every face he had punched and everyone he had loved unraveled at a blinding speed before his unfocused, listless eyes. Even Henrietta slipped by. What was it Henrietta was saying? Regardless of reward or consequence, bear the light?

No. He was not even given the chance to bear the light.

"Regardless of reward or consequences," Roran mocked, "we're all going to die."

He was wet once again, but not with sweat. Roran looked down at his arms as tiny droplets of blood started to steam out of his pores. His vision faded. The roaring grew louder until the noise seemed to drown out all forms of sensation. He could feel the roar, even smell and taste it.

So, this was the feel of death—the guttural, animalistic roaring that consumed everything and left only darkness. "Good, now I can meet you," Roran wheezed. "Face to face." Roran was fully aware that he had lost control of his senses and mind. If the procession of everyone he had ever known wasn't proof of that, then the thing growing near the wall certainly was. He could faintly see some large predatorial darkness stalking about on all fours at the corner of the cell, waiting for him to finally slip away. It seemed like faint strands of light were slipping off Roran's steaming, bloodied skin and coalescing to form the beast's body. The light tendrils writhed together, as if it was a collective of snakes with one mind taking the shape of a panther.

Roran looked at the light strands being pulled away toward the creature greedily devouring all of his remaining life.

Finally. Something he could punch.

"So be it," he said, pushing himself to his feet. "If you're going to eat me, I'm going to hit you back first!"

The creature was taking on more of a form, outlines shaping, with ridges that seemed to somewhat glow in the dark of the cell. The more it grew, the more it glowed, and the hotter the already stifling hot cell became. It snarled at Roran, a metallic sound like the edge of a sword being dragged across an anvil.

Roran jumped at it, but it wasn't there, not fully. He felt wisps of heat as he passed through the creature's mostly intangible body and went face-first into the stone wall. He saw stars and fell to the ground, but the roaring had stopped. Instead, he heard something else. A voice. Something cruel and cynical. And . . . was that laughter?

"Good show! Good show!"

The room lit up red as all the darkness seemed to be eaten by the redness that appeared in the center of the cell. "I've finally found you," the voice boomed.

CHAPTER 7
FILAMENT OF GOD

Roran hovered in the air
Watching as Arno built a pile of leaves
A dying summer's bounty
In the light of a fading sun
Slowly sinking beneath
The tips of the undressing trees
Roran recognized this place
As Stedtfest, an old home
Before they moved to the Wilheim forge
But when they lived here
Arno was not alive yet
Roran recognized it as a dream
He lowered himself and kneeled
By Arno's tender side
As he stacked his leaves
"You'll remember me,
Won't you? You'll carry me
In your heart?"
Arno asked, his eyes on the leaves
Roran took his brother by the shoulders

"I won't need to
You're not dead
Nothing will steal your life
As long as I steal breath."
Two passing children snickered
They pointed at Arno, his leaves,
And laughed at the futility
"You can't,"
They said,
"Stack something that will blow away."
Roran stood up with balled fists
He didn't care if it was a dream
No one mocked Arno
Not without answering to the angriest . . .
Arno grabbed Roran's shirt hem
He was still wearing the dirty clothes of prison
Arno's voice was quiet but persistent,
"It's more futile to punch a shadow."
Roran bowed his head, smiled,
And knelt back down
"But it would have felt good."
"Roran, your anger
It's not always a bad thing
We are Ardhatazian
We are born angry
You can control it
Focus it on something unjust
Let it give you the strength
To make things right
You can use it
But not if it uses you."
"Arno! Time to come home."
A woman's voice called
Roran looked up and saw her

If he was in Stedtfest
Then his mom
Would still be alive too
And she was
Calling home the child she never met
Her beautiful, kind baby Arno
As much as Roran wanted to run
Run and hug Gretchen, Mother
He knew what this dream meant
And he felt dread
"No! He's not dead yet!"
Roran shouted,
"You can't . . . you can't take him yet!
Without him, the world . . .
I don't know how
To be kind
Without him!"
Roran blinked and
Arno was at his mother's side
"It's okay, Roran.
We'll see you soon."
Roran pulled at his hair and yelled,
"It's not real
It's not real
It's not—"

SCREAMING AND THRASHING, Roran awoke on the floor of his stone cell. His dream was slowly fading from the corner of his memory as dull muscle aches reminded him of his waking life.

Well, that at least meant he was still alive. Hopefully, the same was true for Arno. Though he was exhausted, he was no longer experiencing the terrible pain, the muscle spasms, and the fever. Though his skin was still stained with smears of his own blood, he was no longer actively sweating blood.

"I figured you could do with a night's rest, but it did take all of the patience I had to wait for your fleshy highness to complete your slumber."

Roran jolted alert. Something was in his cell . . . and talking? His last memories came back to him. The stalking darkness. The red thing that ate it.

"Not many people come out on the other end of that. You must feel like the field a swarm of geese shat on. Terrible business, giving birth to these things, your father might know."

Roran sat up against the wall and peered over to the table on the other side of the cell. On top of it sat a glowing red man dressed in aristocratic fashion. He had a wide brimmed hat with a feather, an overcoat atop a buttoned vest and a frilly white undershirt beneath that. He had a red beard that was unusually unkempt and scraggily in comparison to his noble clothing. The beard seemed to float and move in the air as if it was unaffected by the ground's pull and caught in a light wind. Though his clothes made him look wide, he was barely taller than Henrietta.

Roran struggled to speak. "What . . . what . . . ."

"What am I? I suppose it would make sense Cormac never told you. That frumpy seadog-bastard was always so ashamed of me."

Roran used more energy than he had available to growl at the thing for insulting his father.

"Oh, growl all you want if you want to be a seadog too. He is technically a bastard, and colloquially too I might add. He often kicked me out of the forge and sent me to wander the countryside. A good thing too. If he hadn't, I would have never discovered the more refined and superior fashion of the upper class. I would hate to go around wearing a smithing apron and gloves my whole life . . . can I call it life? I'll call it life. Oh right, your question."

Roran had no choice but to listen to the thing ramble. He was too exhausted, hungry, and thirsty to do anything but sit there and occasionally growl.

"In truth," the red man said, his voice gruffer, as if friction was needed to make the noise that resembled human speech. "I don't really know that much about what I am."

Roran frowned. He trained his eyes on the red glow. It seemed like he wasn't one, solid being, but rather millions of tendrils writhing and pulsing in the shape of a man.

"I know, I know, but I really don't. Just because I'm called a 'Filament of God' doesn't mean I'm omniscient."

"A Fil-filame—"

"Yes, yes, Filament of God. Not that it really *means* anything. Definitely not to the likes of you and your thick-skulled bloodline."

Memories started to come back about Griselda's stories. It was a concept that several of the scriptures had mentioned but could only speculate about. It was agreed that Filaments of Imeel-Illin were almost universally bad, being born of suffering made manifest, and great precautions had been taken to prevent them from coming into being such as giving people the Life Nectar, trying to prevent open warfare, or burying corpses of long-sufferers immediately. According to Griselda, they were thought to be associated with the unspeakable "corpse calling" practice west of Lake Verdin. The equally mysterious Lichtfangr organization was created to fight them.

"Did you come from me?" Roran asked.

"Ha!" The red man belted out, speaking and not really laughing. Just mimicking laughter, Roran thought, to mock him. "There's no way a grub like you could make something like me! I earned sentience."

"Then where?"

"From your father. It seems that I can latch onto a host that has similar blood. Otherwise, I feared I might have faded away or turned into a reasonably sized boulder. It took a while for me to find you, though, since you lot buried me in the ground. Thanks, by the way," he scoffed. "If I was a fledgling without conscious thought, like what you just birthed, I would have died already, my energy turning to lifeless mass."

"If you're not from me, then what—"

"Oh, hush! Smoke's practically coming out of your ears. You were about to create something like me, too, but you're not strong enough like Cormac. Despite what the people say, not everyone dies in Grief Sickness. Your father didn't. He gave birth to me more successfully than your mother gave birth to your pipsqueak brother—"

Roran jumped to his feet. "Don't you *dare* talk about them like that!" He stumbled toward the red man but fell to the floor, still too weak to do anything with his anger.

The red man jumped up, walked over to Roran, and slapped him hard across the face knocking Roran into the stone wall.

"And don't you interrupt me."

Roran rubbed his cheek, dumbfounded. It felt like he'd been hit by a flaming hammer. His cheek was warm to the touch while the rest of him felt cold and clammy. The red man started pacing around the cell.

"I don't play games, boy. Now, listen up good. We got things to do after I briefly fill you in. The matter is, your father stuck it out, for his children or some nonsense, but it did let me come into being. When filaments are first born, we're bestial and dumb, kind of like how you are for most of your life. But if the host survives, we latch on and learn from them. We get traits from them. The scholars I played tricks on called us living tapestries, and that more threads get added to our makeup the more we learn and experience. However, most of the time we kill our host in the birth process and then diminish before we can get a footing. That 'Grief Sickness,' as you imbeciles call it, is giving birth to us. More than anything else, intense suffering causes fragmentation and life and God splits, so I hear at least.

The result is me or that panther-looking thing you made. It was going to kill you, too; you're not strong enough like Cormac, but I saved the day. You're welcome."

Roran shook his head and knit his eyebrows together. "But how did—"

"I ate it. We can drink in the suffering of things and other unattached filaments, especially before they develop agency themselves. It makes us stronger and capable of learning more. We grow, and our influence spreads. Again, you're welcome, and I do believe you owe me one. For starters, you're my new host. By all accounts, I'm a great roommate."

Realization dawned on Roran's face. "So, it was you. Pops used you to make the blades?"

"Oh, that, yeah. That was me. I developed a bit of an inner craftsman hanging around Cormac. They were beauties, so many things *burned* with my signature touch. You wretched humans don't deserve to wield them. I tried to convince Cormac that he couldn't sell them, but then the brute started swinging them at me. At ME! I helped him make them, and he has the nerve— anyway, the old frog croaked his last bloody croak and is now molding in the cold, dark ground. Serves him right. There's always a cost. Whether it's ignoring me or using me, there's a cost," the red man laughed.

Roran pushed himself up off the ground and placed his back against the cold stone wall. "Cost?"

The red man sighed. "You really are an idiot. Seriously, watching your brain work is like watching a dog chase its tail. Yes, there was a cost! Cormac made a bit of a deal with me: that his family would be protected. So, as long as he was alive, I held back most of the unsavory things. Your family had legendary weapons, and you lived outside the wall. Have you ever wondered why your home was never ransacked by bandits? Unfortunately, that power doesn't come from nowhere." The red man winked. "Once he died, I couldn't hold things back anymore with my power source gone. So that puny prince came. I would have faded completely before I found you if I wasn't running on so much Cormac juice."

Roran was brimming with fury. "You killed him! You caused this?"

"Now hold on," the red man tutted, holding his glowing threads shaped like hands in the air. "I didn't cause this; I actually protected you for the better part of eight years. I still haven't gotten a 'thank you' by the way. But there was an exchange to it. Cormac didn't always make weapons that needed my particular skills, but each time he did, whenever funds were low, he knew exactly what he was doing. There was no trickery. Even if sacrificing himself to protect his family is the move of a simpleton, he did it on his own. Guess he didn't know what would happen once he died, though, and my power source ran out. We run on suffering; it keeps us tangible, powerful, and conscious."

"There's more of you?"

The red man stroked his floating, wispy beard. "Well, I haven't been around that much, but I have noticed signs of ones that grew past the animalistic fledgling stage. Not many, though, and I haven't had a direct run-in yet. In fact, most of what I know about myself is just learned by lurking around the Wilheim Academies and listening to your sister's stories."

Roran grew almost as red as the glowing thing in front of him. "You were spying on us?"

"Oh, hardly! You get angry so quickly. You really need to work on that. That kind of stuff eventually rubs off on me now that you're my host."

Roran sputtered. "But you're nothing like Pops!"

"Yeah, that's his fault. He didn't like me hanging around. Once each weapon of power was finished, he told me to go as far away as possible until the next one. With each new weapon, and more of his life I siphoned away, my tether to him got a bit longer. I spent a lot of time hanging around the snooty upper crust and academics in Wilheim, trying to learn things and grow further since Cormac is a terrible sport over the whole ordeal. They are quite fun to mess with. One time, I stuck a man to the ceiling. I let him scream for hours before he eventually fell back into his bed."

Roran shook his head. *What in all of Verdin am I dealing with?*

The red man continued. "However, I did leech a few things from Cormac. My nature and powers still rely on his traits. I deal in fire and forge. You give me the raw materials, and I'll fashion a power you can only imagine."

"So . . . you can make more weapons?"

"I mean, yes, but I don't see a forge in this cell, do you? You might need something else to deal with this current predicament."

Roran rubbed his forehead. "I assume you had something in mind? You can kill them, can't you? You can kill everyone in this castle?"

The red man simply smiled.

"And Arno? Can't we get him? Can we do something for him?" Roran brimmed with fury just at the thought of Arno on the floor in his cell, no longer able to stand. He would have to learn how to crawl like an infant; his hands and knees would get calloused and hard from their new purpose. But now Roran could fight back.

"If you're willing to let me feed off you," the red man said. "I can turn your suffering into a way out, and I don't mean that putrid green gunk either. It's all over the floor still. I think it's *hardening*."

Roran took some time to think as the red man continued to pace about, careful to step over the Life Nectar. Apparently, he was pacing impatiently because he interrupted Roran's thoughts.

"I know you can't see what's going on up above you, but it's high-flying chaos. Half of the staff of the castle are rolling up their belongings in their drabby carpets and fleeing, while the other half are begging the king to let them stay here if Ewen comes with a siege force. Each breath wasted in contemplation is another footfall closer Ewen gets."

Roran scratched his head. "I don't know what you can do or what I can offer you. I would wish for my family to be happy, but, if you're to be trusted, that's what my father asked for, and it only worked as long as he was alive."

The red man scoffed. "Start simple, stupid. Get yourself and Arno out of danger and worry about what's next later. I don't know if you realize this, but I have a vested interest in keeping you and your family alive. You're my food source after all."

"So, if I refuse, you fade away?"

The red man hustled over and pointed a meaty red finger at Roran's nose. "Hey, you owe me! I saved you last night, and I'll do it again. I don't have to be a parasite, unless you want me to be. Plus, what other choice do you have?"

"But I don't have anything to offer you right now. There are no weapons here for you to imbue. If I'm following you correctly, I have nothing I could exchange with you for the power to work."

The red man smiled and smiled broadly. "It's not giving up what you have now that hurts but giving up what you could have had in the future. That's what hurts the most and is equivalently powerful. Kill your dreams, and I'll kill your enemies. We don't need a weapon when I can turn *you* into one."

Roran waved the red man away. "I've been down here so long; I've been so . . . broken. I've forgotten that I've had any dreams. What about making weapons like Pops? Is that a sufficient dream to give up?"

"Oh please, that was never your dream. That wasn't even your father's dream. That was just necessary."

Roran put his scabbed hands to his face and tried to think,

but thoughts of saving Arno and torching the castle were the only things he could think of, and he was not giving those up.

"I will gladly remind you of your fleeting fancies. I recall you wanting to become a great warrior. In fact, when you were younger, you considered stealing one of Cormac's, *my*, swords so you could run off and be a soldier, killing and getting fame. You practiced swordplay all the time with your sister in the hopes of one day leaving the forge and cutting a name for yourself out of the corpses of your fallen enemies."

The daydreams did come back, though he wouldn't word it as aggressively as the red man did. Roran pictured his Ardhatazian build and muscle, strong from the forge, easily tossing away smaller soldiers. He even pictured the great sword his father made and how powerful it would make him. Yes, he did want to be a warrior. He wanted to use that fiery rage that never left his hot blood. Once, he imagined it because he wanted to use a sword to win glory, a legacy, one to even outshine his father's. Now, he wanted to wield the sword to kill just about everyone in this castle and the enemy marching toward it. What would happen if he gave away his desire to fight with one of Cormac's swords? What choice did he have?

Roran exhaled miserably, "When was the last time I had a choice I wasn't forced to make?"

"Choice? From where I'm standing, it doesn't look like you've had any say for a while now. Or do they give you menus now in the dungeon? Do you get to choose the color of your bedsheets? Oh, right, you don't have a bed. You have a table."

Roran gritted his teeth. "Alright, I get it." Roran stood. "Fine."

"You have to say it. I need permission."

He turned away from the red man and gritted his teeth. *For Arno*, he thought. *And Griselda. And Mom and Pops.* "I'll give up my dream. I'll give up wielding a sword with my own hands for glory. Just get us out of here. Forge me into a weapon."

"Excellent!" The red man laughed. Roran remembered that cruel laugh from the night before. "Would you care to shake on it?" The red man said, offering his hand.

"Can I at least know your name before I make the deal?"

"Name? I guess I've never really had one. I've been called 'Mongrel Vomit' and 'Dung Wretch' and 'Void Spawn' and 'Da Crusted Drool on Me Mother-in-Law's Jowels.' Your father got pretty creative with his insults—that sailor tongue of his. But I've never really thought of myself as having a name. I'm just me."

"Well, what would you like to be called?"

"I kind of like Void Spawn, now that I bring it up. It has a certain gravitas, doesn't it?"

Roran sighed. "I'm not calling you Void Spawn. If I'm going to have to deal with you, presumably for the rest of my miserable life, I'm going to call you by a proper name."

"Things are named after what they do. For example, you look an ass, smell like an ass, and bray like an ass. It would be fitting for me to call you Ass-face."

Roran rolled his eyes. Why did he deserve to listen to this thing for the rest of his life?

"However, it's harder for me. I do so many things and can change shape, so calling me what I look like doesn't really make sense. I guess it is harder to pinpoint desires now that you've turned the tables on me," the red man said, scratching his beard. "You pick a name then."

"I don't know . . . Camroc?" Roran offered.

"That's just your dad's name spelled backward."

"Fine, no names for now. Let me know when you think of one."

"Deal. Now shake on it." The red man waved his hand, waiting for Roran to take it.

"If you can kill them all . . ." Roran grabbed the thing's hand and firmly shook it.

"Mmmm, yes. That's the good stuff," the red man said, seemingly enjoying the experience. He pulsed and glowed brighter as a strand of light crept out of Roran's skin and wove itself up the red man's arm, assimilating into his fabricated shirt sleeve.

Roran waited. He didn't feel any different. But he did want to let go of the moaning, glowing thing's hand. But the red man wouldn't let go. Roran felt the atmosphere of the small cell get more oppressive, as if the walls were being sucked inward toward the two of them. Up close, Roran saw the nightmare that was the thing's face, thousands of moving strands woven together to give the appearance of human face and expression. Some strands were even dedicated to resembling pores in the skin. *How much had this thing learned—or eaten—to get this many strands?* Roran thought.

"Umm, can you . . . are you . . . my hand, do you mind? Can I have it back?"

"Oh, don't worry, you're not going to need these anymore." And with that, the red man grabbed Roran's other hand, pulled both up to his mouth, unhinged his jaw, and, in a flash of light, bit them clean off at the wrist.

CHAPTER 8
OTHER PEOPLE WILL SUFFER

"HOW ARE WE TO RESPOND?" Prince Zerebril demanded more than asked. He kneeled before his father in the large throne room before the dais. Sunlight twinkled on the stone floor, once a comforting sight to Zerebril, now a reminder that the majority of his conversations with his father were before the twinkling light of stained glass or the fleeting candlelight of his father's quarters as he raged against the encroaching shadows. He forced his eyes away from the lit stone and back to his father, more corpse than man.

King Morgen was seated on the throne, head resting on his hand. Though he no longer wore the clothes of mourning when he sat the throne in an official capacity, Zerebril could see that his face was still heavy as with the black attire reserved for burials. How long was he going to remain in this state? Would he ever recover? *My brother may have brought the kingdom down with him in his death, though he certainly didn't mean to*, Zerebril thought. *The tragedy seems to have advanced father's illness. Hopefully that doesn't lead to Grief Sickness.*

"Lord Father, how shall I respond?" Zerebril asked again, his voice echoing around the vaulted ceilings. Today, Zerebril addressed his father as a king rather than as a child. It was one of his good days, if he could call it that.

The king blinked as if he had just arrived back in the empty throne room. He looked at the sunlight coming through the stained-glass windows and seemed to remember where he was, who he was, and what they were talking about. The poppy mixing with the illness dulled the king's once-quick mind even on days when he was more alert.

"Marshall a portion of the city's garrison to complement the remnants of the standing army. We will try to stop Ewen before he takes the city of Stedtfest in the south."

Zerebril exhaled out slowly and shifted his weight back and forth, his plate armor clinking as he did so. Though his father seemed lucid today, he was still not coming up with sound strategies. "Lord Father, what will we do if Ewen unleashes the new weapons on us? These beasts of light are impervious to our weapons and burn through our soldiers like kindling to the bonfires!"

"What would you have me do?" The king sounded half genuine, half annoyed.

"Should we pull the standing army into the city and prepare for a siege? There's a hope that the walls of Wilheim are enough to keep the beasts out. If we send them out to Stedtfest, I am certain they will all be slaughtered." *Like Gunter*, Zerebril thought but didn't dare utter. "We cannot meet them in open field unless we have a way to counter these new weapons. Doing anything else would seem like a bloody acceptance of our fate."

The king, with difficulty, stood from his throne. "I will not abandon Stedtfest to its death! It will not be said of me that I let our countryside burn while I hid behind the walls."

Prince Zerebril sighed. Weight. More and more weight on Zerebril's shoulders. How was he to stop his father from making poor choices? Though Zerebril never planned on fighting in his armor, he began wearing it around for several reasons. It made him look more official, as Gunter had as the crown prince. More capable and respected, maybe enough to challenge the king.

He looked at his father's once imposing image and felt pity. Though he was better today than most days, that wasn't saying much. Weights of his own seemed to be attached to each wrinkle on his father's face, causing it to droop. His limbs behaved as though they were moving slowly underwater. Though the poppy medicine helped with the pain and somewhat with the lucidity, it did nothing for the years of rule that lingered all over his father's body, evidence of war scars despite never stepping on the field of battle. "I am sorry, Father. My plan to mass-produce Cormac's weaponry failed. But we cannot send out the army just to keep up appearances. They'll all die."

"Appearances? Do you think I do not know what you and everyone else have been saying about me after Gunter was slain? Since before that? It's too late for appearances."

"Then what? Pride? You'll send them to death because of your pride?"

The king paused and sat, more collapsed, back into the throne. His body made an audible thud against the wooden frame even through the cushioning. "On my word, I cannot abandon my people. As king and protector of not just Wilheim the walled city but Wilheim the peninsula, it is my duty to fight and protect them. Even if it is vanity, such is the cost of holding one's word. Even though I am slipping, drifting from here to there . . . I am still the protector of this realm, and I will protect with what I have left."

Zerebril gritted his teeth. *This stubborn man.* It was tremendously hard to react to his father, who could be a babbling simpleton one day and a powerful, though tiring, presence the next depending on if the medicine did its work. *I need some more poppy too*, Zerebril thought, feeling the itch, the need for some relief from all of this.

There was another reason for wearing the heavy armor more

and more after Gunter's death. Carrying nearly half his weight in armor around all day strengthened his scrawnier body, focused his mind. Two things that neither his father nor Gunter could strengthen themselves. He would have to do it instead, even if he was ill-equipped for the roles now expected of him. He would at least look the part.

The king's fingers scratched the bare patch of his scalp, exposed like a wound beneath the hollow of his crown—a crown fashioned from connecting several golden suns in a chain. "Son, we all have talents and sometimes. You are known for your intellect, ability to find solutions, for excelling in the Wilheim Academies, even your art. But your head will only slow you down in the midst of battle. Just so, I am known for being true and firm. It's who I am when I'm permitted to still be me. This was good for Wilheim in times of peace, but I'm afraid I am not equipped to handle times of war. I relied on Gunter for that as I rely on you for counsel and strategy. But with Gunter gone, whose talent is for the battlefield? We pride ourselves on being a nation of progress and scholars, a place of great innovation. But it only attracted others whose talent is for taking. The best I can do is send the army and pray. It is the right thing to do even if it is not one that will end in victory."

Zerebril tried to contemplate his father's response. It wasn't surrender he was proposing. It was useless suicide on a mass scale. Not even to prevent Grief Sickness. Something needed to be done and quickly before his father stoked the flames, before his title allowed him to execute orders without question. Zerebril thought about the pillow on the king's bed, the restraints, asking Carl to kill . . .

"What if we did have someone with the brutality required for war?"

His father suppressed a condescending chuckle. "I know that look. What are you scheming?"

"My-half-brother."

"The bastard?"

"You gave him the name Carl."

The king rolled his eyes. "The concubine named him. Others have named him 'The Falcon,' but why does it matter what his name is?"

"No, she didn't. You named him. You gave him a lowly name, a name of no consequence, a name that means 'free man,' yet I have never seen someone so chained in my life."

The king waved away the lecture. "Point being?"

"Well, judging from his willingness to permanently maim a child at your behest, I would say he could be your sword in Gunter's stead."

The king paused and eyed Zerebril as if he was just insulted. "That was your responsibility. You gave your word; you promised reward or consequences. It was your duty to uphold it."

"The child was eight and did nothing wrong! I thought the blacksmith would break before it came to that. I respect Carl, but that was callous, and you ordered it. You weren't . . . forgive me, you weren't in your right mind to give that order. You're justifying it after the fact."

The king ignored the condemnation and resumed staring back at the stained-glass windows. "The bastard has been doing my dirty work for years now. Though I'm proud to say I haven't had to use him often, your half-brother's ability to discreetly hunt down the unsavory should not be punished."

Zerebril sighed. "Noted. But the real matter is that he could lead an army. He's an excellent archer and a skilled bounty hunter. He has partial Lichtfangr training. How many criminal heads has he brought to you in service of the kingdom?"

The king clamped his eyes shut, as if he had seen something ghastly in the window. He shook his head and looked back at Zerebril. "Yes, skill he has, the fact remains that the man hardly talks. How could he lead an army?"

"He doesn't talk because he doesn't think anyone will listen, given his birth. He does what he's told."

The king nodded. "So, you think making him the general to send to Stedtfest will solve the problem?"

"No. Not at all. That will still end in slaughter at this point, no matter who we send. But I think we can change tactics. Rather than meeting them in open field, we send Carl and a small force equipped with all known Cormac weapons to sabotage the enemy camp. A quick strike force to do reconnaissance and then attack the beasts of light while unaware could take away their advantage."

King Morgen considered the plan, his face getting a little brighter at the suggestion. "This plan assumes Ewen cannot just replace the beasts."

"You're right. But if we take out the beasts and then send in the larger forces once the beasts have been killed, we could take out Ewen's whole army and capture him before he has the chance to do whatever he does to make more. We bait him out with the army to protect Stedtfest, like you suggested. He'll assume they are there to wait for his approach behind Stedtfest's small fortifications. Before he arrives, Carl could strike, send his falcon to confirm the success, and the rest of the army could charge their camp."

"I'm not one for subterfuge."

Zerebril shook his head. "Father, are you concerned about honor? The enemy we face is not. He slaughters civilians and burns crops so that we cannot recover. He doesn't even raid to sustain his army; he just pillages for the fun of it. He has bred his force for destruction only. It is our duty to stop him at any cost."

King Morgen looked back at the window. The sunlight coming through made his golden crown gleam. "Yes . . . you're right. This could work. How many Cormac weapons do we have?"

"We have Gunter's. The light beasts seemed to not want to

touch it. The rearguard was able to recover it once the light beasts were called back. Unfortunately, all others are in private hands of merchants and the like. As we have avoided war for so long, we never used the kingdom's funds to purchase one, as it didn't seem necessary until Ewen invaded." Zerebril paused. "However, Henrietta told me she thought Roran was hiding at least one other weapon on Cormac's property. We'll recover the hidden weapon and find a way to enlist the help of any private merchants and mercenaries with the others. No doubt, they've gone into hiding with the war. I'm also assuming they heard what happened to Cormac's family and will think anyone with those weapons will have a target on their back. That fault is mine, and I will have to undo that damage." Zerebril winced at the thought of Carl hacking at the child's leg. He would need some poppy soon to quiet that memory, too.

Zerebril blinked and resumed his train of thought. "Our scouts report that Ewen's army will reach Stedtfest in two weeks if they maintain their current pace. We'll send our army to meet them and have Carl ride with his small band on horseback once we have several warriors with those weapons. He could reach them before the battle begins. To be certain, if we send our army now, we can create obstacles for Ewen to delay his march. I'll see to that myself."

The king smiled, the first time Zerebril had seen it since Gunter passed. "Talents. I think yours is better than mine. You can apply that intellect to many more scenarios than I can apply verity." The king took a long breath in. "Do you remember Gunter's other talent? The one that was always overshadowed by his battle prowess?"

Zerebril nodded. "He loved singing. He told me he liked to stand in the Wilheim Academy concert hall just to feel the organ vibrate his lungs, even if he didn't understand the lyrics written in the old script."

King Morgen bowed his head. "I wish he never picked up the sword—that he became famous for his singing."

Zerebril winced and longed for the release of poppy.

The king shook his head. "Where is Carl now?"

"He's waiting outside. I believe he is doing . . . crowd control."

The king rubbed the back of his neck. "There is one thing I worry about. This elite vanguard of yours. It's almost certain that they'll all be killed even if it leads to our victory. Do you think Carl will agree to this?"

Zerebril nodded. He hated asking people to do things like this. But it is like his father said, his talents are elsewhere while Carl is almost as good of a warrior as Gunter, though Gunter was more straightforward and Carl sticks to the shadows. "If I am dismissed, I will talk to him straight away."

"You are dismissed. Zerebril, son, the fate of the kingdom is now on your shoulders as well as mine," the king sat up straight and a twinkle returned to his eye. "We can bear it together. Today, I have faith. Tomorrow, I may not. But I trust you'll be able to lead us when my bad days come."

Zerebril bowed, stood up, and strode out of the throne room, his plate clinks sounding in the silence left behind. As he shut the massive wooden door behind him, he thought he saw his father staring into the stained glass, teary eyed.

Zerebril descended the sweeping, curved steps leading from the throne room, his boots pounding against the polished stone. The main hall bustled with urgency—castle staff hurried in all directions, their faces taut with tension as they worked to fortify both the stronghold and the city beyond. Whispers of the inevitable siege threaded through the air like a chilling draft. Few believed Ewen would falter before reaching the city gates.

Stepping into the courtyard, Zerebril found Carl leaning against a pillar, arms crossed, his expression unreadable. The restless press of townsfolk had swelled, their voices a chaotic tide crashing against the line of guards struggling to keep order. A captain of the guard, his face lined with strain, barked commands over the uproar, trying to soothe and command in equal measure. Desperate pleas for sanctuary from those dwelling outside the city's fortified walls mingled with cries of outrage over looters and lawlessness. Fear, raw and unbridled, gripped the air, thick as the coming storm.

Zerebril walked up to Carl, who greeted him with his customary scowl. "We have matters to discuss," Zerebril shouted over the crowd. "Let's go inside to properly talk."

Carl scowled in acknowledgment. He had a repertoire of scowls that had subtle differences to replace the gestures and emotions most normal faces were supposed to make. Zerebril took no offense—he had long since concluded that Carl's face could not feasibly assume any other shape.

Carl followed Zerebril into the entry hall. The room was vast with pillars and vaulted ceilings like the rest of the castle, with many chambers blocked by large wooden doors that led to different wings of the castle. Zerebril grabbed a servant and said, "Please go to my quarters and bring me the glowing sword. Here are the keys. Quickly now."

"Yes, my prince," the servant bowed and scurried away.

Carl scowled at Zerebril as he waited for him to say what this was about. Though he had seen Carl's face so often, it was still unnerving "So, um, how's the bounty hunting work going?" asked Zerebril.

Carl blinked twice as if annoyed and waited for the real question.

"Alright, skip the small talk then," Zerebril said under his breath.

Carl repeated the exact same gesture of annoyed and dramatic blinking. "You are here to scold me for the child's leg."

Zerebril stood stock still. Carl broaching any topic of conversation was unheard of. Eventually, Zerebril shook his head. "No, no .

. . that was my fault. My father . . . our father was right and not right at the same time. If I didn't have intentions to follow through on my threats, then I shouldn't have made them. Now that I am heir to the throne, my father needed to teach me a harsh lesson."

Carl scoffed. "Other people suffer so you can learn." The words should have carried the rise of a question, but Carl delivered them flat, unyielding—a statement, not an inquiry. It settled like a weight between them, heavy with a truth Zerebril had neither the mind, the time, nor the poppy to dull.

"Carl, Ewen is marching on Stedtfest."

"I'm not deaf; I know."

Zerebril sighed. "I think we have a way to stop him."

"You said that with Cormac's sons, too."

"Quiet and listen!" Zerebril shouted. The plate, his voice, his frustration all carried a menace, no, an immediacy that Zerebril scarcely used. And the effect was noticed. The servants paused temporarily to look at the prince before returning to their duties. Carl raised an eyebrow.

Zerebril took Carl toward the wall and out of earshot. He continued in a more hushed tone. "The plan has been modified. We're still using Cormac's weapons; we'll need to get them from other places. I'll track down the merchants and mercenaries and convince them to fight alongside us to save the kingdom."

Carl raised his other eyebrow. Both eyebrows raised, forehead creased, eyelids half lowered conveying some sort of puzzled, shocked scowl of intrigue . . . and maybe disdain? Probably disdain. "And me?" Carl finally managed.

The servant returned with the weapon, Gunter's sword.

Zerebril took it in hand, held it up, and admired its glow. "Thank you," Zerebril said to the servant. "Dismissed."

"My pleasure, your lordship," said the servant, bowing before scrambling off to his other duties.

"Our brother's sword." Zerebril turned back to Carl and

offered the handle of the blade. "I need you to lead them into the enemy camp and take out the beasts so our larger, better-outfitted army can crush what is left, without their advantage. Take this, and our victory is assured."

"Other people will die so you can win."

"Look . . . I . . . I would do it if I were a warrior. But with Gunter gone . . ." Zerebril stammered, partly because of the awkwardness, partly because he was distracted. Did he just feel the ground rumble?

Carl spat on the stone. "I didn't say I wouldn't do it. I just make observations, your *lordship*." Carl took the weapon. "It's not my style. It's kind of big and bulky. I normally prefer my bow or quicker short arms." His tone had changed. Carl wasn't as angry when discussing weaponry or how they're used.

"You only need to learn to wield it enough to kill the beasts. You don't need to wield it permanently."

"If I survive, you're taking it back." Again, that same flat affect, a statement that should be a question, that matter-of-fact certainty that Carl was above asking questions when he thought he knew the answer. Or maybe he knew no one would give him a truthful answer.

Zerebril put his hand on Carl's shoulder. Carl flinched so Zerebril played it off as if he was patting him. "No, Carl. It's yours."

Carl nodded, taking the sword and running his fingers down the glowing flamberge blade.

"It's not really my style, either," Zerebril continued. "I wouldn't wield it for more than a few minutes before getting exhausted."

Carl looked down at Zerebril's rapier and smirked.

"What?" Zerebril asked.

"Nothing," Carl said. "Just an interesting choice of weapon. Especially for someone wearing full plate. Normally, if you wear plate and expect to fight others in plate, you wield a mace or something blunt—"

The ground shook more forcefully; Zerebril was not imagining it. He gathered his balance and noticed that the servants were now shouting and running for the exit.

"What's going on?"

The door beside them shattered in a deafening blast. A wave of debris and stone sent Zerebril hurtling across the main hall, his body in the metal plate skidding and sparking across cold stone as jagged splinters and chunks of wood rained around him. The world swam—his vision blurred and his ears left useless with an unbearable ringing. He shook his head, fighting to steady himself, but the pounding in his skull made it hard to tell which way was up.

He finally managed to climb to his feet and pulled out his rapier. Carl, head bleeding, mumbled unconsciously next to him. The feint telltale glow of the Cormac blade shown but was buried under debris that Zerebril already knew he wasn't strong enough to move.

Zerebril forced his eyes to refocus on where he once stood and noticed a massive hole where the door and frame used to be. Only hints of wooden fragments hung by the hinges that stayed bolted in, though the bricks they were bolted to had been cracked and shifted to complete disarray. Dust swirled in the air, curling around the massive hole in the wall that yawned before him.

In place of the door stood a massive, hulking creature about eight feet tall. He was bear-chested and had red skin. His muscles seemed almost to burst from the skin, pushing his veins to the surface, which were glowing underneath his skin. Streams of light danced up from his veins as if he was growing long strands of hair made of sun fire all over his red, leathery body. Looking down, Zerebril noticed a torrent of blood cascading out from the creature's arms. His arms had somehow been absolutely mangled, wrists and hands gone, only jagged bone sticking out from the stumps of its arms. The blood, superheated, was steaming, puffing into a billowing, ugly, moist red mist that rose up into the air. The creature was holding something in his left arm, carrying it by pressing his elbow to his side. *A small child? Was that the young Cormac boy being carried by this thing?* Zerebril thought.

"Monster!" a servant yelled, and they all sprinted for the door. The two guards posted at the door held their halberds pointed at the creature but did so hesitantly as if they were going to turn and run too.

This attracted the attention of the beast who roared and ran at them, each step more like a leap through the air. Arno was screaming and covering his eyes. The creature trampled the servants and dashed several aside with his free arm.

The beast crashed into one of the guards with his shoulder, not caring that his abdomen had just been impaled by the halberd tip. The guard was flung into the wall and collapsed to the ground, motionless. The halberd, still in the creature, looked like it was going to stay there. The creature tried to pull it out by the haft but didn't have fingers to grip it. In frustration, the creature just coated the wood in its hot blood until the wood *ignited*. Partially burnt away, the haft separated from the metal head of the halberd and fell to the floor. The metal halberd head was pushed out when the beast flexed. Blood flowed from the wound, but it, too, turned to steam and cauterized what should have been a fatal injury.

Seeing the creature impaled yet unphased, the other guard turned to run but slipped as the carpet slid out from underneath him. The creature jumped into the air and smashed the guard under his feet, sending the carpet billowing up around them. A sickly crunch curdled Zerebril's stomach as metal crumpled, bone snapped, and blood poured out from the gaps in the armor, soaking what once decorated the centerline carpet of the hall.

The creature nodded at the pulverized body under its feet in satisfaction before spitting on the mess.

While the beast's back was turned, one servant tried to hit the creature with a tall floor candelabra, using it like a spear. The beast spun around, snarled, and stabbed the servant on the end of his severed arm, the bone where the hand should be coming out the other side of the servant.

Zerebril thought he was going to be sick. It was the same after seeing Arno's leg severed. He couldn't stand the sight of it. Not only that, but the smell of the creature's burning blood was horrendous—unlike anything he had ever smelled. Nevertheless, he approached the beast with his rapier, legs shaking, plate armor clanking, and betraying his brash stand against the monster. Thankfully, he heard the shouts and clinking heavy armor of the royal guard on their way.

The beast turned and saw Zerebril. It roared and dropped Arno, who tumbled to the floor, now coated in the impaled servant's blood. Unable to use one leg, the child struggled to climb out of the pool of blood and viscera, but kept slipping and going face-first into the warm scarlet.

The beast used its now-free forearm to push the servant's corpse off his bone. He struggled, not able to use his forearms alone to unstick the impaled servant. The furious beast used its teeth and yanked the servant's corpse off with a jerk of its head. Then it started to run at Zerebril. Zerebril pointed his rapier out and closed his eyes, not having any time to come up with a sounder plan.

"Roran! Roran! Help me! Please!"

The beast froze and looked back at Arno, who was crying helplessly trying to get all the blood off his face and hands. Unable to stand, all he could do was try to crawl away from the pools of blood from the corpses of the guards and trampled servants.

Did he just call that thing Roran? Zerebril thought.

The beast looked back at Arno and then at Zerebril. Armed guards swarmed the main hall and stood in front of Zerebril. The royal guard of Wilheim, clad head to toe in armor and adorned with their sugarloaf helms, was an intimidating force. They raised their shields, but even they were doing it shakily in the face of such an inexplicably powerful creature. The beast roared in agony, seemingly pained by Arno's cries for help. It ran back and crouched near Arno. Its breathing became slower, and it seemed to treat Arno as tenderly as its hulking body could allow. It held out its left armless stub, and Arno climbed up into the crook of its elbow again. With that, it kicked down the main hall doors and *jumped* over the castle wall, vanishing from sight into the rest of the walled city of Wilheim.

Zerebril stood dazed as his guards attempted to check him for injuries. "I'm . . . I'm fine," he managed. "See to the Falconer; I think he suffered a blow to the head. Retrieve the sword from the debris."

A few of the guards did as instructed, while others went to examine the trampled servants. Only a few of them were still alive, the ones that had been knocked to the side. Eleven bodies lay in a disorganized array around the hall, trampled, crushed, impaled.

Zerebril looked over to Carl, who was starting to come to. Zerebril muttered to himself, "Looks like Roran was hiding something after all."

One of the royal guards brought over Gunter's sword. Zerebril held it to his face, the heat from the glow warming his skin. "Roran couldn't make these weapons, but somehow, he became one." *And what would he do now that he was free?* Zerebril shuttered. *What have I done?*

He needed to steal some of his father's medicine and fast.

CHAPTER 9
HEALERS AND BULLIES

THE SUN SHONE over the hay field, but it was not pleasant. There was brutality in the illumination and heat. Roran came to lying in this field, acutely aware of being itchy as he was shirtless. He raised his hand to shield his eyes from the harsh sun that was directly above him at midday, but he realized he had no hands. He tried to jump up to his feet but just ended up scrambling backward on his back without his hands there to plant in the dirt and support his weight. He looked in horror at the stumps where his hands used to be. They were mangled, cut below the wrist, two chipped bones protruding from each stump.

"Roran!" Arno cried from off to his left. Prone so that Roran couldn't see him, Arno crawled toward him in the tall grass until his face poked into the patch Roran was in.

"Oh, thank Imeel-Illin," Roran said and crawled over to Arno. Neither of them could properly get to their feet. Roran tried to hug Arno while on the ground, but Arno shied away at the bloody stumps. "I'm so glad you're still alive, Arno. Are you alright?"

The jolly look that normally rested on his face was not there. Instead, his face had smears of dried blood and a hollow look. "I

. . . no. No.," Arno said, curling his remaining limbs up around himself as best he could.

"Don't worry, Arno. We'll make them pay for what they did to you."

Arno didn't respond. He just lay there, whimpering to himself.

Roran positioned himself on his knees and then carefully stood up. He looked around and saw nothing but grass. Behind him, he could see a hint of blue, probably Lake Verdin, maybe The Purple Coast to the north. Then the world started spinning and he collapsed back down.

"Roran!" Arno yelled. "You lost a lot of blood! What do we do? I'm scared. So scared. And sad."

Roran jolted back to awareness, his breathing ragged. Blood continued to ooze from his severed limbs, though the wounds had begun an eerie, unnatural healing—some edges cauterized as if seared by an invisible flame. It was not a complete cauterization though; there simply was not enough skin to wrap over either stump.

"What do we do? Roran? Please?"

Roran looked over at his wide and watery eyed brother, so frightened and small in a field where even grass towered over him. "I don't know," he was forced to admit

"But you'll die. And then I'll be alone. Again."

Roran grunted and gritted his teeth. "Being scared isn't helping Arno!"

Arno shied away and looked down at his own bandaged leg.

"Stay here," Arno said. "Lie on your back and hold your arms up."

"What?" Roran asked.

"Keep them in the air. It's what Henrietta told me."

"Harder for the blood to come out?" Roran assumed.

"I have to help you. I have to. Otherwise, I go back to being alone. I don't want to go back."

"Arno, no," Roran pleaded. "You have the same kind of wound as me. I'll carry you on my back. We'll look for help. There must be some farmers responsible for this hay field."

Arno shook his head. "Henrietta took care of my leg. I'll do the same thing she did. Lift your arms."

Roran looked over at Arno's leg. Bandaged heavily, his trousers were cut at the knee so Henrietta had easier access to the wound. Roran knew they would need to change the bandages soon and seek further treatment.

"We need Verdin Stars, Arno," Roran said, head getting lighter. "Both our wounds—they're bad."

"I'll be back," Arno said.

"Where are you going?"

Arno, crawling away, already disappeared into the grasses, but his voice trailed back. "We're near Lake Verdin, right? I can hear the gulls and waves. I'm crawling that way and we'll get you some Verdin Stars to close the wound. That's what Henrietta did for me. I'll be back."

Slowly, his brother's crawling and scuffling faded away, making a path of trampled grass to find his way back. Roran closed his eyes to see if he could hear his brother ripping up grass for a little bit longer. Despite his age, Arno was like Griselda, which Roran suspected was because he always believed he could eventually accomplish any needed task. He didn't pout; more often than not, he acted, even if that action was sometimes silly or ill-conceived. The two of them were never trusted by Griselda to think of plans.

Roran raised his arms, and the threat of muffled sobs shook his body. Even compared to Arno, he was so useless. His brother was crawling through a hay field for him. Roran would have given up and taken the Life Nectar while Arno was crawling through an endless field to save their lives.

The sun beat down on his face, relentless and unyielding. It didn't help that his eyes were closed; the sun bleached the inside of his lids regardless, painting his awareness with a searing red glow. He longed to lift something—anything—over his head to shadow his eyes, but without fingers . . . the thought was useless. Plus, that would mean lowering his arms and potentially getting blood all over himself in the attempt. He would have to bear the prying rays of the sun on his eyelids.

How had they gotten here? Though fuzzy initially, memories from the prior events had started coming back to him like a half-remembered dream. He had broken down his cell door and then every other cell door until he found Arno. He had been surrounded by guards at one point, but he was strong enough to knock down a door. He escaped with Arno in his arms and ran as far away as he could from Wilheim until he passed out in this field. Those were the basics, but details? They were still taking their time to return. He felt shaken awake from a night of heavy drinking: fogged memory, bodily pain, headache, and regret all being present.

Cormac, being a sailor, would sometimes egg Roran into seadog drinking games. Roran never won and the hangovers were fierce. He would still give anything to drink with his father one more time regardless of the following day's pain.

Roran noticed some ants crawling up his arms. The desire to squish them or wipe them away came over him, but he could not do much. *Just bear it*, he thought.

A gust of wind blew through the field alleviating the temporary heat of the sun and enticing the tall grasses to sing their taunting song, a song of peace impossible to achieve. The wind also shook free a large beetle that fell on Roran' stomach.

Roran yelped as the beetle scurried around on his bare chest. Roran rolled to his side and the beetle fell off, returning to the ground. He shivered, partially from the beetle, partially from the blood loss. Roran, who was not very cleanly and would often unknowingly bring home freeloading ticks into his own bed; he never liked bugs. He shivered again—whole body feeling cold, even though the sun was hot. He didn't know how much more of this he could take. He was entirely helpless. And itchy. And why was he shirtless?

"Arno?" Roran called out but no answer came. "Arno? *Arno!*"

What would become of the two of them? Would they even be able to leave this field? Arno couldn't walk and Roran had no hands. He could never smith again, never wield a sword again. He couldn't even properly hug his brother or sister again . . . his sister, who was still missing. Roran tried not to imagine anything that could have happened to her. Was it possible she had it even worse than Arno and himself?

Roran yelled at the sun, the symbol of Wilheim glaring down at him. It was a guttural yell in a universal language, lamentation and hatred and frustration. Wilheim had betrayed Cormac's line and brutalized them until almost nothing was left. But what did it matter? King Ewen's army would burn everything down anyway. "Good riddance," he mumbled. Zerebril's looming face came to him, holding his rapier at his neck in the cell. "And may you suffer at the hands of Ewen for what you did."

Then the memory changed to a more recent one, still Zerebril and his rapier, but his face was terrified, and they were in a large open hall. *That's right*, Roran thought. *I almost killed him, but . . . he remembered Arno's plea, trying desperately to crawl out of the pool of blood. He remembered the mob of heavily armed guards that rushed to defend Zerebril. He was close, very, very close, to making Zerebril suffer at his own hands . . . or at least stabbing him with the bones that remained protruding out.

But obstacles threw themselves up at the last moment—.

He winced from the thought. How dare he label Arno as an obstacle. Arno was out in the field crawling around looking for Verdin Stars. All for him. Roran, if anything, was the obstacle, the burden. He had endangered Arno in order to take life. Yes, they deserved death, but Arno did not need to see that.

He was not as good a caretaker as Griselda, who was gifted at caring for others, especially Arno. Even when she got one of her terrible headaches, she would power through to entertain or help their little brother. He remembered the day their mother died in childbirth, the first time he felt true grief, but also the first time he realized how incredible his sister was.

Eleven-year-old Roran sat in the corner of their wooden home in Stedtfest, watching as Cormac collapsed over Gretchen's lifeless body, wracked with sobs. Wet nurses and servants flurried around him, their efforts to clean and soothe futile against the weight of Cormac's grief. Roran could see it in his eyes—the hollow stare, the tremors—what he now knew as the early grip of Grief Sickness. But only eight-year-old Griselda seemed to know what to do, just eight-years-old like Arno was now. Silent tears streaking her face, she cradled the newborn and settled beside Roran. Forcing a smile, she held out a finger near Arno's tiny hands. His barely open eyes remained unfocused, but his fingers curled instinctively around hers. A choked sound escaped her—a sob, a giggle—both battling for release.

The noise drew Cormac's attention away from his dead wife, and he looked over at the three of them sitting in the corner. By that point, at Griselda's prompting, Roran had put his finger near Arno's other hand. Arno had gripped them both, creating a connected chain among the siblings. Cormac screwed up his face and seemed to push away whatever he had been fighting as he rushed over to the corner and hugged the three of them together.

"I will protect ya as long as I live," he had said. "Dis will not happen again. We will not quietly take the Way Out."

"Roran?"

Roran lifted his head as he heard Arno's voice fighting through the tall grass. "I'm here, Arno!"

"Almost . . . back," Arno shouted, sounding like he was straining with the effort of crawling through the field.

Soon, his head poked through the grasses. His face, in addition to being stained with blood, was now covered in dirt. Hay and grass were stuck in his curly reddish-brown hair. He held a bundle of Verdin Stars in his hands, the purple and blue flowers poking between his fingers. Though it wouldn't be as effective as the more refined Life Nectar, smushing a ground-up mixture of the stem and flower petals into the open wound would still be better and quicker than whatever feeble attempt Roran's exhausted body could muster.

Arno had started grinding them together in his hands, but he found two stones to finish the job properly. He put the flowers and stems on the back of a flat stone. He then rubbed it together with the other until a sticky green substance from the stem had emerged and glued the bits of shredded petals together with the mixture. It would act as both an adhesive to pull the wound shut, a ward against infection, and a stimulant to assist the body's natural healing processes.

"Alright, Roran, can you lower your arms so I can reach them? Just bend your elbows down to the ground so that your . . . stumps are still pointing up."

Roran nodded, drawing his elbows down and close to his chest. Arno crawled over with the ground mixture still on the back of his rock like it were a painter's palette and started to daub the pulpy mash into Roran's open wounds with his finger.

Arno's face paled, his eyes flickering to Roran's mangled arms before darting away. A shallow swallow, a barely contained wince—discomfort radiated off him.

Roran noticed the effects of the Verdin Stars almost immediately as some of the pain started to subside.

"Thank you, Arno," Roran said. "I should be the one taking care of you, not the other way around. I promise you won't have to do this to me again."

Arno didn't say anything, he just kept diligently applying the mixture as if lost in thought. "Roran, do you remember yesterday?"

"It's a bit fuzzy, but I think I have most of it."

"What happened to you?"

Roran paused as he tried to remember before he transformed, before he heard shouts of people calling him a monster. There was his cell, the Grief Sickness, the beast in the darkness, and the red man.

Roran looked frantically. Could the red thing be looming about?

"What is it?" Arno asked.

"I . . . don't know. I don't know what happened to me, not really anyway." This was partially true, true enough for now until he could offer Arno a better explanation once he got his hands on . . . once he confronted the red man again, wherever he was.

"But you remember . . . what you did?" Arno asked hesitantly.

"Yes, I saved you and then ran us into this cursed field."

Arno closed his eyes and furrowed his brow. "I don't mean that . . . thank you . . . but I mean, the other stuff, what you did to everyone else."

Flashes of trampled bodies, tossed-aside servants, crushing a guard in his armor underfoot, and impaling that man on the end of his stump returned to Roran's mind. "Yes, I remember."

Arno finished applying the mixture to one arm and crawled over to the other side and began doing the same to the other. "Did you do that . . . on purpose?"

"I think I was. It's muddled, like being aware of yourself in a dream. Or like the times I'd get really drunk with Pops. But everybody in that castle deserved to die for what they did to you, what they did to us. I only wished I could have killed the prince, the king, that bowman, and all of the guards too. But it won't matter now, Ewen will kill the rest."

Arno stopped applying the mixture and shuffled away.

Roran looked up, bewildered. "What? What is it, Arno?"

"They didn't have to die," he said.

"Arno, look at your leg, look at the reason you have to crawl on your stomach like a snake through this field. Of course they deserved it. There needs to be justice for you."

Arno shook his head, and tears crept in. "No, Roran, they didn't. They didn't! They were just like Henrietta. And you dropped me in their blood! I got it in my mouth and hair!"

Roran tried to inch over toward him on his back, but Arno crawled away indignantly. "Arno, you don't understand, you're too young, but those are bad people—"

"And how old do I need to be to understand Roran? Do I need to be twenty before I know? Does killing become okay at that age? You *murdered* people who were trying to run away, and I had to watch you do it while you carried me through their blood," Arno covered his head in his hands. "It was so much blood."

Roran remembered Arno in the crook of his left arm, covering his eyes and screaming as he tried to kill everyone in sight. "Arno—"

"That's not my big brother! I never want to be like you when I grow up," Arno said bitterly.

"Arno, I'll never leave you alone again. Is that better?"

"Arno looked at his brother through his hands, still partially covering his face. He didn't respond. He just sat there, hands covering his face, trying his best to block out the whole world.

Roran would do anything to get access to his thoughts, to soothe whatever awful thing was replaying in his head, keeping him from speaking.

"I want a different promise," Arno said sheepishly.

Roran nodded, trying to be encouraging. "What is it, Arno?"

"Promise me you won't kill anyone else?"

Roran shook his head. That was too much. "Arno, what if someone is threatening to hurt you? What would you want me to do then?"

Arno thought about it for a second. "I still don't think you need to kill. If you're that much bigger and stronger and faster than everyone else like you were, you could have run away. Otherwise, you're a bully. You had all those muscles, and nobody else did. But you used them badly, and that makes you a bully. I don't want a bully for a brother. I won't forgive you for that." Arno's face was flush with anger, as if he had finally let loose all the pain he had felt over the past month.

Somehow, it hurt worse to be called a bully by his younger brother than it did to be called a murderer. "I promise I won't kill anyone else unless there is absolutely no other way to save us."

Arno crawled back over and finished applying the mixture to the other arm, still frowning, but he did apply the salve with less lethargy. "I'm not forgiving you for what you did to those people."

"Then why help me?"

"Henrietta had to heal prisoners who did the same as you. She didn't have to think they were good people, but she did have to heal them." Arno paused. "I don't know if she or anyone else ever forgave them, but she couldn't let them die either. If she let them die, she said she wouldn't be able to forgive herself. Then there would be two unforgivable monsters in the world instead of just one."

Roran winced. "Do you think I'm a bad person, Arno? Do you think I'm a monster?"

Arno didn't respond.

"I did those things to save you—"

"That doesn't help. If that's true, then all those people died because of me! Their blood is still all over me . . . ."

Oh God, Roran cursed himself. Arno was blaming himself

for other people's deaths. Arno should not have to carry that weight. He was too smart, like his big sister, and he was seeing through Roran's attempts to justify things. Roran could not treat him like a child who could be sated with a half-attempt at explanation. Arno needed the explanation, the reasoning, and the moral, or he would never let a wrong be forgotten.

"It's not your fault, Arno," Roran said. "Don't ever think that. It's their fault for hurting you. They did deserve it and earned their deaths. I was carrying out justice and protecting you."

Arno finished applying the salve and crawled away, refusing to look at Roran. "You don't get it! You've always taken things too far! You broke my only friend's leg over calling me a name!"

"He wasn't *really* your friend, Arno. He was making fun of you for your leaves—"

"If that's your way of protecting me, then I'll have to protect the rest of the world from *you*! You turned into a monster, Roran, you turned into something that's not my brother! And until you promise to never kill again, I . . . I . . . I'll stop speaking to you. I will stop thinking that you're my brother. Because you'll always just be scary."

"I have to kill because not everyone can be as good as you, Arno."

"They won't have the chance to grow if you kill them! They won't have the chance to be better."

Roran sighed and rolled over to look at his brother. Arno was curling up as best he could, but he couldn't balance without his full leg. So, he just laid on his side and brought his knees to his chest.

"Arno, they aren't growing anymore. They're corrupting. They let the world get the better of them, and now they make bad choices because of it. Those choices can hurt innocent people like you."

"People in progress," Arno whispered.

"What?"

"It's something Henrietta said to me when I asked about why Zerebril was doing what he was. She said we think people stop growing in the head as soon as they start growing in the body. But that's wrong. We'll keep messing up like babies do, but as long as we learn from those mistakes, we can keep growing. She said we kind of die as soon as we think we're done growing."

Roran wished he could have overheard that conversation. He wished he could have gotten to know Henrietta more, and under different circumstances. But he cursed her at the same time. It was impossible to be that kind in this world; there was no way to bear the light like she said. That kind of thinking would only get them killed. But was that the point? To do it regardless of reward or consequences? It seemed a foolish thought, especially if he was his brother's ward. He would not let himself or his brother die for a useless ideal. *I'll have to lie to him to keep him safe*, Roran thought. *I can't have him not talking to me, or that might get us killed too.*

"Thank you, Arno, not for just crawling through the field and doing this, but for being a good person. I did those things because I thought they were right at the time. You're helping me see that I was wrong. I need to grow more."

Roran thought he could see Arno's frown dissipate a little despite not entirely facing his brother.

"Do you forgive me?" Roran asked.

"No," Arno said flatly.

Roran's mouth hung open, aghast at the response. He had said all the right things, hadn't he? "But—"

"Pops said things won't change just because you said sorry."

"Then what am I supposed to do?"

Arno paused and turned to look at his brother once again. It took considerable effort. "You can promise you won't kill anymore."

"Arno, I—"

"There were so many. So much blood," Arno said, almost on the verge of tears. "Why did you do that? You scared me so much."

With the faces coming back to him, the weight was starting to loom over Roran too. Arno would not let his brother forget this, no matter what reason he did it for. In his enraged state, Roran hadn't thought about the consequences of his actions. Their faces, their blood, Arno holding justice over his head, all made him feel the weight of killing, something he had never done before and hoped he would never have to do again.

"Then . . . I'll save just as many."

Arno looked up into the sky for a while, unclear if he was pondering what Roran said, or if he was still reliving everything in his mind. "It don't know. Lives aren't coins. There's no trades."

He's talking to me like I took the sun out of the sky. Arno was a dangerous combination of Cormac blood. He was as smart as Griselda but . . . *he's as stubborn as me.*

"Then I'll save hundreds, thousands if I have to."

"That's still the same. Lives aren't like Ellie's math lessons. You can't make the numbers right."

Out of frustration, Roran lost his temper and snapped back. "You're going to get us killed by swearing me to this! You'll see, if I have to show mercy, they'll come back later and kill us."

Arno turned away again and curled into himself, on the verge of shaking, as if Roran had threatened to chop off another limb.

Blood of Oros, this is hard, Roran thought. He needed Griselda. He went and yelled at his brother, his brother who had lost his leg and was still more concerned about Roran's moral compass than his own wounds. "Arno . . . I'm sorry for yelling. But it's true," Roran said pleadingly. "You know it's true. Wilheim will try to kill us. Ardhataz will kill us too. We have no friends. Everyone will try to kill us."

Quietly, Roran could hear Arno whimpering. "If you have to become a monster so that we can live, then I don't want to live."

"Oh, No-No . . ." Roran said, slipping in his brother's affectionate nickname.

"Don't call me that!" Arno snapped.

Roran sighed. "I promise, no matter what, even if it is to save us, I won't kill anyone else." *If I had fingers*, Roran thought, *I would cross them.*

Arno made no reply and turned back.

Roran pulled his arms down and examined the work Arno had done. The mixture was stuck fast and covered all his wounds, except for his bones which still slightly protruded out from the stumps of his arms. He did not like the idea of walking around with exposed bone. Not only did it sound painful when the salve faded, but it also sounded like it could become dangerously infected. He would have to do something about that.

"Arno?"

"Yeah?"

"I have a pretty bad idea, but I think we have to do it."

Arno sighed. "What?"

Roran paused. "There's something we have to get at our forge. If we sell it, we could get ourselves taken care of and set until this war passes. Maybe we can even flee Wilheim. If we get out of Wilheim, get to the land beyond Lake Verdin, we won't be in danger, and I won't have to use violence."

"Not without Ellie."

Roran nodded, remembering the image of him and Griselda letting baby Arno grip their fingers, remembering the three of them huddled in bed after Cormac died. "You're right. We're family, and we'll need to find her. She's probably the one person in this kingdom who doesn't want us dead, aside from Henrietta. Even still, we'll need coin to survive and find leads before we can leave the kingdom."

Roran grimaced as he cautiously positioned his legs under

himself, careful not to touch the ends of his arms against anything, and stood up. With his head a little clearer, he thought he could make out the shape of a farm on the far horizon away from Lake Verdin.

He turned around to face the massive body of water since it was the first time he had seen it in a while. The blue lake stretched over the horizon, impossible to see the western warring nations on the other side. It was hard to imagine something that large was the mouth of a dormant volcano as Griselda had said. How deep was it anyway? How much of the world he knew could be buried under its waters? It would take days to sail across the enormous lake. But on the other side, maybe there was peace.

Ya know, Roran remembered Cormac saying when he had taken the day off to show the three siblings Lake Verdin and what his seadog life used to be like. *It ain't a lake at all. It's more like a gulf or sea. Da ting flows around da Canyon Lands and out and out and out to tings even I've never seen. Forever. I've only seen a glimpse of da vast blue, but I know in my heart dat it is endless.*

Roran was skeptical of finding peace in the so-called "warring nations." But if Cormac was right, then they could go farther. They could keep going out and out until one day, they found a new home of their own, a home where he could tie a wooden sword to his arm and still challenge Griselda to a duel, a home where Arno could find bigger, more colorful leaves to collect, and they could all take turns inventing new games until they all walked together to the next leg of the March where they would see Cormac and Gretchen once again.

He looked down at his brother, who was craning his neck to look up at him. Roran sighed and squatted down. "If I remember correctly," Roran said with a half-smile, "I believe one of your favorite games was riding on my back."

Roran was expecting a giggle or enthusiasm. But Arno was

still quiet. He wouldn't be bought or distracted. Nevertheless, Arno pulled himself up onto Roran's back, latching his arms around Roran's neck and collarbones. Though Roran would be like a dog strangled by his leash for a while, this would have to do.

Roran started walking through the hay field. On Roran's back, Arno whistled the Anvil Tune as Cormac always did when he was hammering in rhythm.

CHAPTER 10
HANDS AND FEET

RORAN'S bare feet memorized the Wilheim countryside, from the gentle tall grass hills that emerged near Lake Verdin to the more gruesome and unforgiving rocky soil and forest underbrush. The familiar landscape became more consistent as they made their way back to the mountains toward Wilheim city. Aside from being barefoot, the walk was grueling for other reasons as well, and Roran was reaching his point of exhaustion even though he had carried Arno for far longer than he'd thought he'd be able to. At his limit, Roran set Arno down on a stone off the road nearing the outskirts of Wilheim near the banks of the Shatter Rock River. His back hurt immensely, the kind of hurt that made him aware of just how many muscle groups were wound together around his spine and shoulders. Though they were different kinds of pain, his back seared with just as much heat as the ends of his arms. Even after setting Arno down, Roran struggled to talk with so much continuous pressure on his throat.

"How are you holding up?" Roran croaked, stretching his arms above his head. He bent forward, pulled himself toward his hamstrings by wrapping his stubs around his legs, and let his spine decompress as his torso hung loosely in front of his knees.

Arno smiled, freckled dimples surfacing over his lightly sweaty face. This was a smile Roran had gone weeks without seeing, where Arno could confidently hold Roran's gaze and not be ashamed to let the world see his radiant glow. With all the pain behind them and ahead, it may not have been an appropriate time for such a smile, but when had Arno ever put restrictions on when he could experience joy?

What Roran had been taking in with his feet, Arno took in with his eyes as the rolling grasslands closer to the lake gave way to forested regions hinting that they were mid-fall. Arno kept looking farther beyond the trees and up to the Shatter Rock Chain, the mountain group that sheltered Wilheim City, growing taller by the hour.

Given the amount of time it took for Arno to answer Roran's initial and rather simple check-in question, it seemed like Arno was deep in thought. Or maybe he wasn't thinking at all. Maybe he was freely experiencing life as it should be outside the sunless, leafless dungeon.

Eventually, Arno answered, "Probably better than you. You sound like a toad."

Roran laughed and then winced as it hurt his throat. "Yeah, well, you've gotten heavier."

"No, I haven't," Arno said, crossing his arms. "I've gotten lighter you dummy. I'm missing a leg."

Startled, Roran shook his head and raised an eyebrow. *Was that okay to say?* Roran thought. *Could he make jokes like that and be fine?*

Arno maintained that grief-erasing smile. Roran let himself smile too. Arno was incredibly resilient, just like Pops.

"If anything," Arno continued, "you've gotten weaker. You turned into a big, red, scary mountain and now you're back to being puny. You think you'll be able to get big again, if we need to run?"

Roran went to scratch his scraggily beard but then lowered

his arm when he saw there was nothing with which to scratch. He still hadn't seen any sign of the nameless red man that bit off his arms and turned him into a monster. The thing had left him with blood on his hands—rather, his bones—without a word.

The pain in his arms was starting to win the wrestling match for Roran's attention over the pain in his back, and he winced. The salve was wearing off and his exposed bones at the end of his arms were starting to burn and sting and throb and be every other agony word his language had a name for. Thankfully, they had gathered more Verdin Stars and Arno had kept applying the salve to his arms every couple of hours. In turn, Roran had helped as best he could to steady Arno while he checked his leg bandages. Arno's wound at the severed knee had fully closed thanks to the Life Nectar Henrietta applied. Little surprise there, she was a much better healer and likely had a more refined version of the Life Nectar than the bootleg mash Arno was forced to make.

But if he kept smiling like Arno did, would he be able to dull the pain? It was worth a shot. "Oh, Great Healer," Roran said dramatically, "Lord Arno, can you work your wonders on my arms again?"

"Sure, but you didn't answer my question. Can you get big again?"

Roran sighed. "That's because I don't have an answer. There's still so much I don't know about what happened to me."

Arno shrugged, pulled some more flowers out of his pocket, and began grounding them on the stone he was sitting on. However, before he could apply it, Roran started to hear the familiar sounds of his trade, only now there was inherent danger in the noise. Thin, articulated metal plates moving over another metal surface. Riveted chains in heavy sheets bouncing on moving muscles. Shod hooves clambering on broken roads. He lifted his head and looked toward the direction of Wilheim.

He picked up Arno in his arms by shooting his stumps underneath Arno's armpits, the way Henrietta had done to him. He lifted Arno farther away from the road until they were more concealed in some bushes.

"Hey, what are you doing!"

"Shhh!" Roran whispered and pointed up the road with his stump.

Arno followed the tip of Roran's protruding bone and saw gleaming plate reflecting in the sunlight. Zerebril on horseback was at the front of a large army leaving Wilheim.

"He's taking the garrison?"

"Garri-what?" Arno asked.

"It's the forces stationed inside a walled city to defend against sieges. But that would leave Wilheim defenseless. Where's he going with them?"

"You ask these questions like I would know," Arno replied.

"Hush."

Behind Zerebril were hundreds of soldiers. All were armed with un-visored barbute helmets, mail hauberks, gambeson, vambraces, greaves, pauldrons, and a green tunic with the Wilheim sun emblazoned on the front and back. Though Roran and Cormac did not specialize in making armor, the war demanded they make rudimentary greaves and pauldrons that were fairly simple and could be done in bulk. Only the cavalry unit and Zerebril were on horseback and covered in metal plate from head to toe due to its expense and cumbersome weight. Horses could carry full plate better than infantry could march with it at a distance.

Wilheim's forces seemed more armored than any regular soldier. Despite this, they somehow had still lost every battle to Ewen and helped arm the enemy with their fallen troops. Though Wilheim was richer, they did not have a sufficiently trained force, which cost them dearly in each battle. For arms, they carried long spears resting on their shoulders, a short sword at their waists, and a kite shield on their backs. Roran had made his fair share of spearheads and was positive that many of those soldiers were walking around with weapons he had personally made.

Even despite their weaponry, armor, and numbers, they march to suicide if they leave the walls, Roran thought. *Good.*

Roran fed his hatred as he stared Zerebril down through the bushes as the prince passed on horseback.

As if sensing his brother's thoughts, Arno looked over at him and frowned. "Don't even think about it, Roran."

"I'm not, I'm not. Plus, I'm in no shape to take on a whole army."

"Good, maybe you're not that big of a dummy after all."

Roran smiled. "Thanks." Still, this desperate move by Wilheim bothered him. What were they planning without a sure means to win?

Once the garrison passed, Arno finished applying the salve, and they headed home. It took another hour of walking before they reached the forge, cottage, and small clearing in the forest that was trusted to house their memories.

"Griselda!" Arno yelled.

"Shhh!" Roran whispered. "We don't know if Zerebril is still looking for us. I'm guessing they would kill us on sight even if they aren't actively searching."

The forge stood dark next to their small cottage, and the yard seemed barren. Dead grass and leafless trees dotted the property. Though the seasons were beginning to change, everything should not look so lifeless since it was still warm outside. Perhaps there was something to burying the corpse of a long-suffering individual that killed the life around it, or more likely the red man ate the life around it to sustain himself until he could get out of the host and find an heir to Cormac.

Roran walked Arno back to the tree where they had buried their father; tongs and a hammer were crossed over each other on the dirt mound to indicate the spot. "Hey Pops," Roran said. Though he couldn't see Arno, he could hear him sniffle.

The tree itself looked much worse for wear. Dead for sure. The bark was unnaturally cracked open all over. Roran looked up at the tree. It had been one of the largest trees nearby, a tree Arno liked to climb all the time, but now it looked too fragile. Its leaves had fallen, and its bark had taken a sickly grey color. Is this what Filaments of God did? Did they eat life to sustain themselves?

"Walk over to that branch," Arno said, shaking Roran out of his thoughts.

Roran first checked the size and thickness of the branch to determine it would hold before he did as he was told. Arno reached up and grabbed the branch. Once he had both arms secure, Roran let Arno hang.

"I can still climb trees!" Arno said.

"Correction, you can still dangle from trees," Roran said, clinging to the always-bright mood Arno possessed. "And I bet you can't dangle for long if I tickle you!"

Roran reached up to tickle Arno's armpits only to realize that he no longer had fingers. He sadly looked at his stubs and lowered his arms.

"Come on," Roran said, gesturing to his back, "There's a couple of things we need to do here." Arno climbed onto Roran's back, and they walked into the forge.

It had likely been over a month since Roran had returned, though he wasn't exactly sure as he lost count of days somewhere around the third week in the cell. The forge had mostly been raided by Zerebril when he brought the tools to the castle forge, but it still had enough to properly function. It was disorganized and dusty, as it hadn't been properly cleaned since Cormac was still breathing. Weathered tools hung on the walls, soot-covered ingots were stacked in the corner, and barrels of hafts pointed accusingly at the ceiling.

"Alright, Arno, this is going to be tricky," Roran said as he walked around the centered furnace. "So, we need to work together to get this up and running for a little bit. I once promised to teach you how to work hard so you can steam like me and Griselda."

Arno nodded vigorously from Roran's back so that Roran could tell he agreed.

"Well, today's the day."

Roran could hear Arno giggle with excitement at the prospect.

"First things first, we need a better way of getting you around or I'm going to suffocate." Roran walked over to a rack of ordinary hafts that had not yet been tipped with the metal spearheads. "We're going to cut one of these up and make you a crutch."

With effort, Arno pulled himself up over Roran's shoulder so he could nod and smile at his brother.

"Good, in the meantime, you'll need to be my hands and I'll be your feet. If we work together, we can cover for each other's missing limbs."

"You got it, boss," Arno said enthusiastically. While he was farther up on one shoulder, Arno reached over Roran and grabbed one of the hafts.

"Though Zerebril took a lot of the tools to the king's forge, Pops always had spares. He wouldn't let a broken tool interrupt him from making a blade. There's bound to be a saw here somewhere . . . there!" Roran walked over to his old workbench. It was mostly preserved, as if Zerebril had mainly focused on taking Cormac's tools. He probably did this because Roran's tools were in rougher shape since tool upkeep was much less fun for Roran. He examined the saw on the table. It was nearly dull, but it could still cut.

Roran set Arno down on his workbench chair. Arno grabbed

the tool and made sawing motions in the air rapidly while mimicking the sound.

"Hey, don't play with that. We need to keep all our remaining limbs," Roran said while giving Arno a semi-stern look. Arno slowly set it back down on the table. *Was that a joke I am allowed to make? Did that make Arno sad?* "Arno?" Roran asked. "Can I make those jokes? We don't have to laugh at stuff like that if it hurts."

"Henrietta said it would hurt worse to not talk about it," he responded with a smile.

"Right." Roran nodded thankfully. "This might be a bit tough, but can you stand on one leg and use your hand to support yourself against my shoulder?"

Arno nodded and pulled himself into position.

"Good, now grab the haft. We need to see where to make the cut; hold it with your other arm near your armpit."

Roran eyeballed the measurement and planned to cut it a bit shorter if necessary. He could always add padding, which would be essential anyway to make up for it being short. Roran held down the haft with his forearms while Arno made the cut.

"Slow and steady, use the full length of the saw rather than using one part of it quickly," Roran instructed when he saw Arno's mirrored eagerness, like the first time Roran had swung the hammer.

Soon they had fashioned together a T-shaped crutch from pieces of the haft and leather wrapped around some cotton at the top for padding. Arno tested it out after Roran positioned him correctly. Arno's face lit up as he was more mobile again.

"This is great!" He laughed. But after a couple laps around the forge, he was breathing heavily. "But it sure is tiring. I feel like I'm jumping around from place to place."

"You kind of are. This is meant to help out in a pinch. It's something you can't really travel with by yourself, but I needed you to be able to at least stand on your own for the next step."

Arno stopped moving about and looked at his brother. "What else?"

"I'm making you a harness so you don't have to put me in a chokehold whenever we're walking long distances."

Arno laughed. "Like a saddle? Do I get to ride you like a horse? Are we making reins too?"

Roran shook his head and smiled. "I'm *not* your horse. If anything, you're *my* backpack."

"So, no reins? I won't get to steer you?"

"No reins."

"Aww. That would have been a lot of fun," Arno said with a frown.

"Only for you," Roran said.

"Well, sometimes, I think you need to be steered."

"Anyways," Roran said, waving off Arno's comment. "We have many leather straps meant to wrap around weapon handles or belt armor shut. We'll tie these to make shoulder straps and attach them to one of our wooden boxes that hold scrap. We'll cut some holes in the back of the box for your leg and stump, add some padding, and you'll have a little wooden carriage."

Now that Arno could move about on his own, albeit with considerable effort, the next project went more quickly. Roran held the box in place, while Arno sawed down to make slots where he could situate his legs. Roran had Arno add a belt to the straps in the front. This way he could run with Arno on his back and not worry about the harness slipping off since he had no hands to readjust straps that threatened to slide off his shoulders.

Once the straps were fashioned, Roran slung it over his shoulders, squatted down, and Arno sat down into it.

"Hey," Arno said, concerned. "I'm looking backward! I won't be able to see what's in front of us like this."

Roran chuckled. "That's what you got me for, remember? We're working together. If Wilheim gives chase, you can be my eyes to watch my back, and I'll take you forward to where you need to go."

Arno sighed, "I guess that makes sense. So, we'll be like a double person when I'm on your back, right? We'll have more eyes and limbs than anyone else, even though we're missing a few."

"You're exactly right," Roran said. "There's just one more thing we need to make for now." Roran walked over to a box of pauldrons that hadn't been shipped out before Cormac died. "We're going to make covers for my arms. To do this, we'll need to heat up the forge, get two of these nice and hot, and then bang them into a narrower shape. We're going to make them fit to my arms instead of wide to fit over the shoulders."

Arno nodded, and they set to work. They lit the forge, heated up the shoulder plates, and then used the horn of the anvil to hammer them into rounded, narrower shapes. This took a while, as Arno couldn't hit the metal very hard with one hand holding a crutch and the other swinging a hammer much too big for him. But they eventually got them shaped to where Roran was satisfied. They added belts to each arm cover so that Roran could strap them on and lock them in place. Unfortunately, he couldn't put them on yet. He had been putting off the thought of what he had to do next.

Arno sat back down on the workbench and sighed. He wiped sweat from his forehead.

"Am I steaming yet?"

Roran looked him over. Arno was exhausted, still in dirty prison clothes. And Roran was still shirtless.

"No, not yet. You need to work a little harder. But for now, catch your breath. We should put on our clothes while we're here. We can fetch supplies and put them in the box-harness thing with you." Though this was necessary, Roran was savoring every second before the final phase of the arm caps, when he had to get the saw back out.

Arno pulled at his mud-covered shirt and nodded. His long crawl near Lake Verdin had permanently stained the front of his clothes brown.

Taking a break, Roran carried Arno in the new harness and left the forge to walk into the house next to it. Like the forge, it was evident that someone had been rummaging about, looking for something. All their food had been taken to Arno's dismay.

"Roran! I haven't eaten in two days!" Arno complained. "And someone had to go and take our grain? Our vegetables for stew?"

Though Roran hurt for Arno, he strangely wasn't that hungry. He should be starving from carrying Arno all this way. He pushed the thought away, left the kitchen, and wandered into their rooms to get clothes. Though everything was dusty, their clothes were still there. Arno changed and helped Roran get a fresh tunic over his head. It was a much longer process, needing to set Arno down on Roran's bed, have Arno unstrap the harness, have Arno pull the green tunic over Roran's head, strap the harness back on, and get Arno back in. Everything had to be done in a painful, slow, multi-step process.

As they walked back to the forge, Roran took one last opportunity to stall by poking his head into Cormac's room. His bed was still disheveled from when the three of them huddled there after Cormac's death. It was hard not to imagine Cormac getting ready in the morning by making his bed, pulling on his neatly folded clothes, eating his morning oatmeal, donning his apron, and entering the forge. Cormac was a tidy man of simple routine. He would be horrified to see his bed unmade and forge ransacked.

"Arno?" Roran asked.

Apparently also deep in thought, it took a second before Arno answered, "Yes?"

"Can you make his bed for me?"

Arno didn't answer.

Trying to lighten the mood, Roran mimicked their father's heavy Ardhatazian accent and said, "Ya can't be leaving an unmade bed, No-No. It's a ting undone that could distract yer hammer blows."

Arno chuckled. "That was terrible. But I'll do it Woe-Woe."

It was worth the peace of mind to make his bed for him, even if it did take a tedious amount of time to get Arno out of the harness. Roran found relief in finishing something his father couldn't. But he couldn't put off the saw for much longer, and they reentered the forge.

"I know you're tired, Arno," Roran said while he helped his brother out of the harness. "But now comes the hard part. And to be honest, I'm not going to like this very much either. Could you do me a big favor and tell me jokes, stories, sing songs, anything to keep my mind off what we have to do next?"

"What? What's next?"

Roran grimaced. "You have to saw off the parts of bone jutting out from my arms—"

"What! I'm not doing that!"

"Arno—"

"No, I'm scared. I don't want to do that."

"You have to. Otherwise, these covers won't fit. They'll get infected too if I don't cover these wounds with skin growth helped by the Verdin Stars."

Arno cringed at the thought of it and rubbed his own arms.

"Like I said, I need you to do something to distract me. I'm sorry for making you do this, but there's no other way. I'll get sick if these bones are constantly exposed. I need to shear them off and apply Life Nectar until the skin heals over the ends of my arms."

Arno shook his head, the joy having vacated his face.

"Arno, look at me. You're my hands, remember?

"I won't hurt you!"

"You will be saving me," Roran smiled. "Even if it hurts."

Arno looked down at the floor and closed his eyes.

"Arno," Roran said, kneeling down to address him. "You're the only one who can save me. If this isn't done, then I'll die. But if we rub the Life Nectar on before we start, I'll feel the hurt less. I'll be fine," Roran forced a smile. "Promise."

Arno nodded and swallowed. They washed the saw and Roran knelt in front of the anvil. They strapped Roran's arms to both ends so he couldn't move away. Arno rubbed on fresh Life Nectar over the wounds and bones. It was still going to hurt; this was for Arno's peace of mind.

Once ready, Arno hobbled over with the saw and one final piece of leather. "Here," he said, gesturing with the leather to Roran's mouth. "You'll want to bite down on this . . . trust me."

Roran closed his eyes and nodded, exhaling out all the air he had trapped in his diaphragm. *Arno should not know that*, he thought bitterly. Nevertheless, Roran accepted the piece of leather and bit down. He looked down at his arms and pictured the saw about to cut open Zerebril's face instead.

Roran's little brother, eight years old, held a dull saw in his hand, looked Roran in the eye, and scrunched up his face. Arm shaking, he held the saw hovering in the air above the bone. Forced now to look at it, the sight of his bones was ghastly, dun and beige and stained red with some cut fibers and muscles still partially attached. Would he be sick?

Four protruding bones. Two for each arm. Maybe twenty-five back-and-forths per bone? One hundred total cuts, Roran counted, sweat starting to form on his forehead. *You can do this. Encourage Arno, don't scream, don't show the pain. You'll be fine.*

However, this was a wood saw, not a bone saw a butcher might have. This saw was not designed to cut through bones, and it took more than Roran had anticipated. Arno did his best to whistle Cormac's Anvil Tune to distract Roran, while Roran bit down on the leather and did his best not to distract Arno with any indication that he was in terrible, unspeakable pain. They both protected and complemented each other in their own way: the hands and feet of one body.

Roran focused all his rage at Zerebril and it kept him conscious. His face reddened as he threatened to bite through the leather with every slow, grinding saw motion. As soon as Arno had made the final pull of the saw and sheared off the last of the bone, Roran allowed himself to pass out on the anvil.

CHAPTER II
ARM FOR LEG

RORAN WOKE a little later still strapped down to the anvil. Though his wounds had been covered by Arno while he was out, that was the worst kind of physical pain he had ever felt, worse than being on fire in a forge mishap, worse than Grief Sickness, worse than getting his hands bit off. And it was all Zerebril's fault.

Roran recovered his wits and tried to move, but he was still strapped to the anvil.

A light flickered on in the forge. "Hey! Ass-face! Enemies are approaching. You better beat it, or you and the pipsqueak will look worse than those arms of yours."

Roran shook his head and looked closer. In the mouth of the forge, he could see the telltale signs of a red glow. "You!" Roran shouted.

"Shut it! Do you want them to hear you? They're carrying *my* weapons, evil thieves. Meaning they could kill *me*, not to mention you."

Roran bit at the straps but could not get his arms loose. They tied him down tight to keep him from squirming. "Where's Arno!?"

"Oh, him. They already caught him. The angry blonde bastard has a knife to his throat to make sure you don't transform. I probably should have led with that. Oh well."

"What?!" Roran tried to look behind him toward the door but could not crane his neck far enough with his arms strapped down. "I'll kill you myself if you don't do something!"

"Whoa! Remember, vested interest! Are you angry about the whole biting-your-hands-off thing? Nothing personal, but we needed a lot of juice for that stunt at the castle."

"Can I transform again?"

"Well, you could, but . . . you know, I'm guessing you don't want pipsqueak's throat cut," The forge sparked as the red man's essence talked from the forge. Did he laugh at that last part?

Roran continued to struggle against the straps when he heard a voice from outside yelling in toward the forge.

"Son of Cormac!" the voice yelled. "I have your brother hostage. Do anything like you did at the castle, and I will cut his throat like I cut his leg."

Rage lit up in the pit of Roran's stomach. *The angry bowman is here*, Roran thought. *Good, now I can kill him myself.*

The bowman continued, "If you drink the Life Nectar we toss into the forge, I will let Arno go free. You can then at least die on your own terms and save your brother. That's worth something, trust me. Do not come out. I want you nice and far away."

If I could get free, Roran thought, *then I could get my great sword I buried under the anvil.* He looked down at his arms. *Nevermind.*

Roran heard a glass jar roll behind him. It came to a rest near his knee. He could feel its coldness against his leg . . . again.

"Umm . . . a little help?" Roran asked the forge.

The red man stuck his wicked, grinning face out of the mouth. "What would you trade for my help?"

"What will give you enough juice?"

"Hmm," he considered. "I quite like this forge. It's very

homey. I'm sure you have a lot of fond memories here, too. What if you could never return here again?"

Roran's heart sank. He could never come back home? Could never light up the fires? Could never visit his father's grave?

"I'm waiting for your answer, son of Cormac," the bowman yelled. "The longer you draw this out, the more likely it is for my knife to slip. Save your brother. A life for a life. Down the jar and you'll pass away easy. It's a far nicer death than a monster like you deserves. You wield power held by corpse callers, and we all know what kind of monstrous things they did to get that strength. How many people did you defile to get that kind of power, huh? Son of Cormac?"

Roran cursed. He looked into the forge as that dastardly red face poked out. "Fine!" Roran spat.

"You have to say it," the red man said.

"You can take my home in exchange for your help."

"Good, I'll assume your word is as good as a handshake, you know, considering—"

"Shut it! Get this over with!"

"I've killed your kind before," the bowman continued. "Judging by your lack of response, I'm guessing you want to find a way out. There isn't. I was a Lichtfangr. I was trained to fight things like you, things that emerge from the dark places of humanity. Death waits for you, whatever you do, as I know it waits for me. Don't give it to the child, too."

The red man crawled all the way out of the forge and rolled his eyes. "Is he bragging?"

"Hurry up!" Roran hissed.

"Has anyone ever told you that you have a nasty temper, and it makes you less fun to be around?"

Roran gave the red man the meanest look he could muster.

"Fine, fine," he muttered. "Can't go getting you killed and whatnot." The red man held up an index finger. A strand of light emerged from Roran's arm and wound itself around the red finger. His nail grew to a sharp point, and he cut the straps, freeing Roran.

"Is that it?" Roran spat. "That's all you're going to do?"

"Hush, I am preparing to make an entrance," the red man said, sucking in air and glowing more intensely.

"Hey! What's going on in there? I see red!" That was a different voice than the bowman's.

How many people did he bring with him? Roran thought, sliding over to the wall and risking a peek out the window. Roran counted three men, but they all had Cormac weapons. The bowman was holding Gunter's great sword with one hand, letting the ricasso sit on his shoulder. The other two had glowing, ornate short swords that Cormac and Roran had made for Rodrick the merchant last year.

The two men were twins, also in similarly light armor as the bowman. One didn't necessarily need heavy armor with a Cormac weapon, as most enemies would never get close enough to land a blow. Stray arrows were the biggest concern. All heavy armor would do was slow down the wielder and potentially allow them to cook in their own flames.

"There's only one way out of this that guarantees Arno's life," the bowman said.

"Yeesh," the red man said, appearing next to Roran. "That guy's even uglier than you, and he's twice as angry! I would stay away from him if I were you. He's pregnant."

"What in Imeel-Illin's name are you talking about? *He* can't be pregnant."

"Oh yes, he can, and he is. He's ready to pop; blade's been in the forge for a long time by the looks of it. He may not be able to give birth to one of your kind, but he can to *my* kind. He's been wearing that scowl for years, something's been eating him up from the inside for a while and he's probably strong enough to let it out given how long he's been pregnant. And since he's a Lichtfangr—a pregnant Licthfangr—nasty sort."

"Please, stop calling him pregnant."

"But he is . . . whatever," the red man said, waving his hand to dismiss the thought.

"What are we going to do?" asked Roran.

The red man made the gesture of cracking his knuckles, even though there was no joints to pop. "I'll cause a distraction."

"That's it?! That's all you can do for me losing my home?" Roran nearly shouted.

"Shhh!" the red man whispered. "They have my weapons, they can kill me, and then everyone's dead. You gave me enough for quite the theatrical display, just you wait. I'll work best from afar and then you can kill them when you transform."

"I don't know how to do that again," Roran said.

"You get more stupid by the day, don't you? Don't you feel it? You've begun to change.. It's in there already. You exchanged your dreams of sword-wielding and your hands. That physical offering of your body ensures a lasting effect, just like how Cormac's offering of years off his life permanently infused the swords," the red man said. "Here," he tossed over the metal arm covers Roran and Arno had made. "You might want to put these on. Punching things with those wounds will not be fun; it'll still hurt with the covers, but it'll hurt less."

The red man fit the covers to Roran's arms and locked them in place.

"If you don't give us an answer, we're going to . . ." the bowman paused, seemingly distracted. "What in Oros's shit is that?"

Roran looked out the window and was surprised to see that the red man had already vanished and appeared outside.

One of the twins eyed it up and down. "Who are *you*?"

The red man tutted, "You know, I still don't really have a good answer for that. But I can do you one better, I'll answer as if you asked, '*What* are you? '"

"And what is that?" the other twin asked.

The red man roared, "I'm part god!" Everything that was once alive on Cormac's property burst into flames. The grass they were standing on sizzled instantly and blackened. The blaze on the woods doubled the height of each tree, creating looming pillars of flame. Flame exploded from the red man himself as well, creating a red mouth that threatened to consume them.

The three men jumped back and fell down as the mouth of flames flew over, singeing their fabrics and hair. The bowman had let go of Arno in the chaos. Arno was trying to hobble away on his crutch, but there were flames encircling the whole property, and he was doing all he could to not accidentally place his crutch in a burning pocket of grass.

"Oh no! Arno!" Roran yelled. He sat back down, closed his eyes, and tried to find that foul power inside of him. With his heightened emotions, he was able to find it much easier than expected. A smoldering darkness sat in the pit of his stomach, like a coal sizzling and waiting to be ignited.

You called? It seemed to ask.

How do I transform? Roran asked it.

Stoke the flames, it responded.

Roran felt a kind of fire in his stomach, unnoticed until now, something that he had been subconsciously drawing from, making it so he didn't need to eat. He had to stoke it by drawing in air to reignite the flames. Roran breathed as deep as he could and held his breath, pushing all the air deep into his diaphragm. He could feel himself getting hotter and hotter, the longer he held his breath and the harder he pushed the air down.

Arno scrambled around looking for any opening to the flames and lost his balance, falling to the blackened grass. The three hunters got back up on their feet and drew their glowing weapons, bearing down to face the man on fire.

One of the twins leaned over and asked, "What do we do, Carl?"

"Wait!" The red man bellowed. "Your name is Carl? Ha!

How bland!" The red man held his palm to the sky and drew in some of the surrounding flames to his hand, creating a massive ball of fire.

The red man looked over to the forge, "Time's running out, Ass-face," he muttered and chucked the fireball. The twins jumped back as far as they could until their backs were up to the walls of flame. However, Carl stood his ground, raised the great sword, and the sword absorbed the incoming fire.

"Braver than I thought," the red man said. "Really hoped you didn't know it could do that."

"I didn't," Carl said. "But I saw you do it and thought it might work."

Carl charged at the red man, flashing his glowing hot sword.

The red man tipped his wide-brimmed hat at Carl and flew up into the sky, arms outstretched and laughing as he twisted like writhing smoke. "And that's where I draw the line, up to you now, Ass-face."

Roran, now eight feet tall, veins glowing white under his red skin, fire strands trailing from his veins, and eyes demanding blood, walked out of the forge. His shirt burned off his skin as the white-hot filaments bristled and elongated to float around him.

The twins stepped in front of Roran while Carl ran and grabbed Arno, who was curled up in a ball. The twins started flourishing their swords from left to right, faster and faster, until the swords' glows brightened and burst into flames of their own. The three invaders had regained their composure after the red man's assault and were now ready to bear down.

Roran never thought he would have to fight against weapons he and his father created. The twin on Roran's right struck first by bringing his blade out of the flourish, above his head, and cracking it down. Like a cattle whip, a stream of fire cracked from the sword toward Roran. Roran barely dodged it by turning his shoulder, and the fire lashed into and destroyed the Cormac family house behind him. Roran watched in rage as the roof collapsed on his home.

"You'll pay for that! I'll turn every screw I find into your pathetic bodies!" He roared, his voice taking on the same grinding noise the red man had. He rushed forward and closed the distance much faster than the twins were expecting for the bulky monster. The twin on his left whipped his own flame tendril, which blasted Roran right in the chest.

His red bulk was launched back in an explosion that smashed him into the remnants of the family cottage. Roran's chest was a mess of blistered and blackened skin, but his blood steamed from the wound and began to heal it. Grabbing the nearby wooden debris, Roran jumped to his feet and threw two massive planks at the twins.

The twins jumped out of the way, but Roran was upon them in a single bound from the house. Roran brought his arms up and both metal covers connected with either twin in uppercuts to their chests. Roran heard the individual plates in their brigandine fracture with the force. Both of them gasped as all the air was forced out of their chest. The blows launched the twins into the air, over the flames, and out of sight.

Roran turned and fixed his gaze on Carl. He held Gunter's great sword in one hand and Arno's arm in the other. In the perilous environment of raging flames, Arno was a liability, an obstacle. Carl raised the great sword over his head to kill Arno. But when Carl tried to bring the sword back down, he found that it wouldn't budge. Roran had caught it between his metal covers and was pressing them together hard enough that it trapped the blade in the air. Roran kicked Carl while his arm caps vice-gripped the blade, forcing Carl to let go as he flew. Carl tumbled backward doing several somersaults before hitting the wall of the forge with the back of his head.

Roran walked over to finish him off, but Arno yelled, "No, Roran! He can't hurt us now! Don't be a bully!"

"He cut off your leg!" Roran roared back.

Unafraid of his brother, Arno hobbled up to him on his crutch while the flames grew higher all around them. Arno reached up and poked Roran's chest, which had nearly fully healed. "And you created a new one for me. You don't take, Roran. That's not you. You are a creator!"

Though frustrated, Roran nodded at his brother. The flames were getting higher and closer and there was no point in arguing. He disappeared into the forge and knocked the anvil over. By now the flames had reached the walls of the forge too, having leaped over from their burning house. Roran smashed the stone tile that he buried Cormac's sword under and knocked away the stone fragments as best he could. But it wasn't there. Panicking, Roran pounded the dirt, seeing if he would be able to feel it under a layer of sediment. It definitely wasn't there.

The fire had reached the ceiling of the forge, and wood started to splinter and crack. Roran shook his head, grabbed the straps of Arno's harness with his teeth, and rushed back out of the forge.

"You knocked my new weapon away," Carl said. He was up again, one arm around Arno's neck, the other with his dagger pointing toward Roran.

"You're not going to knock me out twice," Carl continued. "So why don't you just—"

Roran didn't let him finish. He rammed his shoulder into Carl and Arno, sending them to the ground. Roran climbed over the top of them, his arm covers pressed into the blackened grass to support his weight.

Carl tried desperately to stab at Roran's neck, but could only reach up high enough with Arno on top of him to stab Roran's shoulder. Roran flexed his shoulder and snapped the blade off at the hilt. The blade pushed out followed by bloody steam that cauterized the wound.

"Let him go!" Roran yelled.

Carl did not loosen his grip.

"Let go or I'll kill you!"

Though Arno was too scared to speak, he shook his head as much as he could in Carl's grip.

Roran looked from the resolute, determined death mask of Carl, to the cowering face of Arno. And though Arno didn't want Roran to kill, what choice did he have?

"We're all doomed to become weapons for higher powers," Carl spat. "My life has always been forfeit."

"Fine," Roran growled. "You took his leg, so I'll take your arm!" Roran bent his head down and bit through the arm holding Arno. He yanked his head to the side and ripped Carl's arm off at the shoulder. Carl yelled in a frenzy, but Arno latched his arms around Roran's neck now that he was free.

Carl writhed on the ground while he was bleeding out. Seeing him writhe like that took all the rage out of Roran. Roran thought he would be thrilled to inflict the pain, but there was nothing there. Hearing the man's cries, feeling the heat of the flames creep as they devoured his last place of refuge, smelling his own burning blood, tasting the chips of bone and muscle from Carl's arm . . . he *was* a monster, and he was dwelling in a hellscape that used to be his home. Nothing about this gratified him. He was hollow, a fire burning on fumes.

Roran let the fire inside him die and he shrank back to his normal form, feeling dizzy, cold, and shirtless.

As the flames threatened to engulf them, Roran told Arno to strap up the harness and climb on. Arno did.

"Hey!" Roran said looking up into the smoke-filled sky. "Mind helping us out of this fiery death trap?"

"Oh, I suppose," the red man responded, though Roran could not see him. The fires didn't dissipate, they seemed to get *bigger* as they rose higher and higher into the sky. Roran understood as soon as the red man appeared. Somehow, the red man was sucking the flames and smoke back into his hand, creating a massive ball of fire the size of a house.

"Get going!" he said, "I've got to do something with all of this power; it can't go back in me."

With Arno holding onto his crutch, seated in the harness, Roran started running for the first gap he saw in the flames.

Behind him, Arno trembled and watched as everything played out. Carl, getting his bearings, ran out of the flames too toward where the twins had been launched. Once Roran had put enough distance between themselves and their old home, the red man condensed the fire in his hand and launched himself back down, punching the center of the forge and creating a massive explosion. The shock wave shook the earth and nearly knocked Roran off his feet.

He looked behind himself to see what Arno had. Where their home used to be was a large crater four times the size of the original property. The flames were gone, and it was eerily quiet other than their ringing ears. But it was quiet enough that they could hear small chunks of dirt and building debris falling from the sky all around them.

"Bye Pops," Roran muttered.

"Bye," Arno said with a slow, sad wave.

True to his word, the red man had destroyed his home, the only tangible thing left that had any connection to his father and Griselda. Now the only home he had was strapped to his back— just Arno—but Roran would protect him whatever may come. As long as Roran could fight, nothing in all of Verdin would be able to hurt another curly, auburn hair on little Arno's head.

Roran turned around and started jogging south through the wilderness. Arno kept staring at the newly made hole until it was out of sight.

Though Roran had many pressing questions about what had just happened, one of them overshadowed all the rest. Who took the sword Cormac had given to him?

PART TWO
NEW PROTECTORS MUST BE MADE

CHAPTER 12
LEGACY

THOUGH GRISELDA WAS WELL aware that the glowing great sword was not designed to cut firewood, she didn't have much of a choice. There was no ax. Yes, this kind of labor was far beneath what the sword was made to do, but she would freeze if she didn't hack some of the low-hanging limbs off the trees. Besides, the sword would never chip or get dull from hacking at things it wasn't designed to hack at. That's the beauty of her father's legendary weapons. Even if a great sword wasn't designed to cut wood, a Cormac-made great sword could be used to do so much more.

The blade sang as she swung it through the air, chopping halfway into a branch. Then, using the undulations like a serrated saw blade, Griselda pulled the sword back and forth, heating it up and severing the rest of the limb. She had to be careful not to get the blade too hot or it would set the branch, and the rest of the tree, and the rest of the forest, ablaze. So, she had learned during her stay in the wilderness to only hack off limbs no thicker than her well-muscled arms.

Griselda collected the fallen limb in her left arm, hair falling into her eyes as she bent over. She had started making the preparations for camping as the sun sank behind the trees, casting the forest into a noisy gloom. By this point, Griselda had gotten used to all the noises: frogs croaking, crickets chirping, rodents rustling, broken branches falling when a breeze knocked them loose. The first night in the woods she had spent almost entirely awake. But now she could get a few hours of light sleep, occasionally jumping awake at some miscellaneous sound nearby. Though the forest surrounding Wilheim was not as vast and dense as the forest south of Stedtfest and contained relatively no predators, it was still unnerving to sleep in the dark alone. Normally a heavy sleeper, Griselda could only manage a few hours of broken sleep in the deep, mountainous woods, every rogue sound snapping her upright and sending her heart pounding in her chest.

She was wearing men's trousers, which she had looted when her dress became impractical. The low cloth of her dress would catch on fallen branches and thorny bushes. Though she needed to choke her waistline with a belt just to keep the pants from falling, they were lighter and made woodland navigation much easier. Griselda never liked dresses all that much anyway, the loose fabric often tripping her in practice duels with Roran. In ditching her dress, she also looted a beige men's tunic and brown leather vest. She was focused on survival, and excess cloth that would either catch on things or weigh her down when it rained was not a good way to survive in the forests outside Wilheim.

Griselda propped the great sword up against a tree. She dropped the branch limb in the center of the clearing on some sticks she had already gathered and arranged some hefty stones around them in the shape of a circle. She propped up a simple tent, a rope stretched from one tree to another with a bundle of water-resistant cloth hung over it. To make the triangle shape, she held the corners of the cloth in place with more rocks.

Griselda unrolled a padded sleeping mat underneath the makeshift tent. She had scavenged the camping equipment and new clothing from a ransacked caravan. All the valuables, jewelry, fine silk, tools, weapons, and coins had been taken. What was left were scraps of food and the camping gear used by the merchants. Ever since she found the aftermath of the raid, she stayed off the road. However, she had gotten lost.

Now that camp was set up, she could start cooking her dinner. From underneath her backpack, she grabbed the great sword and held it up in the dying light of day. Three or four weeks ago, her brothers were taken from her while she hid in the woods out of sight. She had been a coward, but what realistically could she have done? There were fifty armed guards, and she had no means of fighting them. She didn't have the sword yet. It was not the smart thing to do to come out of hiding.

Though she knew it was irrational, she couldn't help but let the memories of her cowardice turn to anger. She flourished the sword from side to side until the glow intensified, and then she stabbed it into the pile of sticks. They burst into flame. Other than cutting branches and starting fires, she had managed to find a few more possible uses for the glowing sword, save the one that it was designed to do: protect her family.

Roran had shown her where he kept it in case of an emergency. A weapon worth so much could not be left in the open. However, Roran had not considered how heavy an anvil was for anyone other than himself.

Griselda had to move a workbench, prop its backside with as many stones as she could find, place her back against the braced workbench, and then push the anvil with everything her legs could muster. The bench still moved more than the anvil, and she had to reposition it several times to fully get the anvil off the stone it was covering. She almost considered leaving the anvil in its new place off-center from the room, but it didn't feel right. Cormac had always kept his tools and forge immaculately clean and tidy. She wouldn't watch her brothers become prisoners *and* leave Cormac's shop out of sorts.

Once the sticks were properly lit, she pulled the sword from the pile, set it inside the tent, and then dropped a larger log on top of the small fire. The sword's soft glow also provided a source of light on par with a torch, but it looked less conspicuous since it was more akin to moon and starlight.

Griselda rummaged through her backpack. From a book she had looted off the traders, *Wilheim's Woodland Wonders: A Catalog of the Area's Flora and Fauna*, she had identified and collected edible nuts, berries, and mushrooms on the forest floor. Without a ranged weapon or knowledge of traps, she couldn't get any meat. Well, she could use the sword as a ranged weapon, but it would also mean burning the forest down to hunt rabbits.

She nibbled on the berries as she arranged the mushrooms on a small pan that she held over the fire. According to her book, these mushrooms could cause diarrhea if not thoroughly cooked.

When her house became unsafe to stay at, Zerebril's men coming by to pillage tools and materials from the forge every few days, Griselda tried to stay in a nearby inn, which was also outside the walls of Wilheim. Though she thought it was a bad idea, she couldn't think of any better options. Immediately, she drew eyes from everyone inside. The sword, which was too big to conceal or even have its glow stifled in a scabbard, stopped all conversation. Griselda didn't make it ten steps into the inn before deciding that the sudden silence was a bad sign and fled back out into the night. From there, she had slept in barns on piles of hay after the farmers had finished working, and she made sure to leave before the workday started the next morning. Then she found the raided caravan and went into the woods.

Griselda had taken the idea of being lost remarkably well, as far as she was concerned. If she couldn't find her bearings, it also meant that any cronies Zerebril sent after her would also have a difficult time.

After eating a few berries, she ate the nuts while the mushrooms finished cooking. According to the book, she could live almost entirely off these hearty nuts, but they did not taste very good, and so she ate them a bit begrudgingly.

While lost in the woods, Griselda had hardly moved other than to scavenge. She spent most of her time reading the few books she could carry with her. Books were considered precious, depending on who wrote it and what subject, but the raiders had apparently not considered them. The three that she had been able to carry with her were all written by scholars from the Wilheim Academies, making them incredibly valuable. They were mostly practical for wandering merchants but very insightful given Griselda's current predicament. She had *Wilheim's Woodland Wonders: A Catalog of the Areas Flora and Fauna*, which she consulted regularly. Apparently, the scholar, Adadain Flussel, had written it for his degree in botany over the course of several years as he did field work in the forest, surviving on his own and seeing how long he could live without any other human aid. Griselda found the chapter on camping very useful.

With the mushrooms fully cooked, Griselda picked them out of the pan with her fingers after they had cooled. Despite being singed on the outside, they were still spongy, a texture Griselda thought a bit unpleasant. Berries were really the only scavenge-able food that she didn't find distasteful. She had to restrain herself from eating them all at once and instead opted to save a couple for a snack throughout the day. Plus, according to Flussel, eating too many berries at once could also cause diarrhea. If Flussel was to be believed, nearly everything caused diarrhea. Griselda had wondered if truly so many things had this kind of negative impact on the human digestive system or if Flussel just had a weak constitution. However, she was not willing to put Flussel to the test with her own stomach.

The second book Griselda had was *Trading Trades: Craft, Commodities, and Crooks* by Wilfred Fortinbras, a retired trader and now professor teaching at Wilheim's College of the Collo-quial. Griselda found that the scholars had some unnatural and slightly annoying draw toward alliteration. The book was divided into three sections, one which outlined the value of the work of certain skilled craftsmen and what proper going rates were for their work, another section which detailed tradeable commodities other than Wilheim's coined currency for when a trader was in a different kingdom, and lastly, Griselda's favorite section, details on how to deal with tradesmen specifically. Professor Fortinbras said to assume everyone was a crook trying to swindle her out of her valuables with the least possible effort, as it was the safest mindset to have. He then went into specific types of people he had dealt with on his adventures, complemented with outlandish stories in places like Ardhataz, port cities around Lake Verdin, and faraway places Griselda had never heard of on the opposite of the massive lake, which, Professor Fortinbras pointed out, wasn't technically a lake. Like her father, Fortinbras had also seen the mouth near the canyon lands connecting it to some massive body of water farther beyond. She had finished reading this book yesterday and had taken care to memorize Professor Fortinbras's categorization of people, as it could be useful for interactions outside of trading.

Once finished with the mushrooms, Griselda set the pan aside and sat down on a stump near the fire. She finished the second book yesterday and spent most of the day scavenging. She would soon need to move to a new place with more resources. Since the sun was almost completely set, Griselda propped the glowing sword behind her for some additional light as she began to read the third book, *The Collected Marches of Verdin*. Unlike the other two, this one had little practical value for a merchant that Griselda could see initially. It was a large tome that contained several of the March hagiographies gathered over the years. If the merchant wasn't religious himself, Griselda assumed he probably knew about various religious traditions as a way of building rapport with clients based on what she read from *Trading Trades*.

Griselda had only skimmed *The Marches* in the Wilheim library, as Cormac didn't have much of a need for books, but she had gone to Wilheim proper to fetch household needs and listened to sermons on certain stories from *The Marches*, stories she would then paraphrase, half-remember, butcher, or outright change to entertain Arno as bedtime stories. Griselda had also spent an hour or two in Wilheim's comprehensive library before and after each errand, much to Cormac's annoyance.

Griselda smiled wanly. Cormac was always sending her and Roran into the city in his stead. When she asked him why, he had said, "When dey hear my accent, dey don't hear da tune. Dey hear dirt. Dey mistake da fire in my beard for blood. Ya both at least have some of yer ma's blood in ya. Da red's not as prominent in yer auburn hair. Ya grew up here and didn't catch da accent. Better ya both do it. Need to learn da city yerselves anyways."

Griselda rubbed the dirt off *The Collected Marches of Verdin* and thanked her father for sending her into the city, to inadvertently learn how to read.

She had put off reading this for practicality, as the other two books seemed to offer more pertinent advice. However, this collection of the most notable Marches contained much more abstract knowledge and editor commentary. It also contained painful memories of better times.

The scholar Rufus Redaway had organized *The Marches* in a theoretical chronological order and made commentaries on the parables, stories, and sayings from each individual March and added speculative insight from the interactions, intersections, and differences between *The Marches* as a collective.

Wilheim prided itself on being one of the most learned cities on the continent and had mandatory public schooling within the walls for children up to the age of twelve. Being on the outskirts and responsible for Arno's care while Cormac and Roran were busy in the forge, Griselda didn't get a chance for this education.

However, she tried to teach herself as much as possible at the library and by asking girls her age in the city what they were covering in classes.

Griselda propped open the tome and began reading Redaway's introduction until she heard a small noise close by. Footsteps, by the sound of the rustling. She closed the book and grabbed the sword behind her. She held it up to shine a light a little farther than the small fire could send. Tracing the perimeter of the camp, she listened and scoured the growing darkness until she found two gleaming eyes reflecting the light back at her.

The eyes were close to the ground, not a threat unless it was a man crawling through the woods. She lowered the sword to cast the light closer toward the target and saw a small fox. By the looks of its size, it was young, somewhere between a pup and a full-grown adult, a time for testing boundaries and discovering the world.

Though she had caught it approaching, the curious little thing had not scampered off. "You're a tad brave, aren't you, little fox?"

It walked up in a zigzag, exploring the surroundings while avoiding direct confrontation with Griselda, sticking its head in the air to sniff.

"You probably smell the mushrooms," Griselda said as she watched the young fox sniff the pan. "I'm not quite sure what you eat, little fox, but I have some berries you could try if you'd like?" Though the fox would look over at her when she spoke, it mainly ignored her as it nosed its way around the campsite.

Griselda pulled the remaining berries from her pack, set the sword down, and crouched near the fox. She offered a couple out to the fox's nose by fully extending her hand. The fox caught the scent and hesitantly approached Griselda's outstretched fingers.

"It's okay," she said. "I won't hurt you. Keep being brave and you'll get what you want, little fox."

The fox drew close, sniffed her palm, looked at her, and then ate a few berries. "That tickles," Griselda giggled. The fox plucked a few more away from her hand with its mouth, dropped them on the ground where it was easier to eat, and made tiny, wet chewing noises.

"You are a darling," Griselda smiled. "As sweet as Arno but as brave as Roran. The two of them together make for the traits of a noble prince. You wouldn't happen to be the Valiant Prince Gunter, would you? On his next leg of the March in the body of a fox?"

The fox's red and brown ears twitched. It nosed its way back into Griselda's hands for the remaining berries. It licked her palm to get any remaining berry juice and then backed away.

"All done? Hope that was enough, seeing as that was the last of them."

The fox made no indication of response and instead continued to sniff its way around the camp. It eventually poked its head into Griselda's tent. "Hey now, that's my private quarters; a prince like you cannot intrude on a lady without permission!"

The fox went fully inside, and the flap swished shut. Griselda huffed and stuck her head inside the tent, too. The fox had curled up on her bedroll, eyes still watching her. "Gunter, this is most unbecoming of a prince," Griselda chuckled.

The fox started to close its eyes.

"I'll have you know that this is not your den."

The fox fully closed its eyes and yawned.

"No fair, you're too darling to disturb now," Griselda sighed.

She left the fox alone and pulled her head back out. She propped herself up against a tree trunk with the sword beside her to provide more light. As the fire gently crackled less and less, Griselda continued to read the introduction to Redaway's tome, but found her mind drifting to topics that she had been trying to avoid.

What was she going to do? Surely she couldn't wander the

wilderness forever making friends with the local wildlife. Were her brothers still in captivity? What was happening inside that castle?

She looked over at the sword. She had considered walking up to the castle demanding a trade, the sword for her brothers, but she thought better of it; Griselda demanding a prisoner trade with Wilheim's nobility probably wouldn't end well.

She remembered the first time Roran had brought the sword out of the forge and shown it to her and Arno, claiming it was a sword Cormac made for all three of them. Griselda was suspicious of this, as it was obvious Roran was the only one large enough to wield the sword in any efficient capacity. At least, at that moment. Despite mentioning this, Roran, stubborn as ever, insisted that Cormac made it for all three of them.

"What should we name it?" Arno had asked. "All special swords have names!"

Roran hadn't considered it and had a blank look of puzzlement on his face. He scratched his chin, a thin beard growing in that he had neglected to shave that morning. "How about you two name it?" He had offered.

That night Griselda and Arno, rather than the normal bedtime story, began brainstorming the best names for the great sword. Griselda had written down a list of candidates Arno had come up with using some charcoal and cheap paper Cormac had used for filling orders or making lists of needed materials.

Arno was filled to the brim with whimsy and enthusiasm having been given the chance to name what may become a legendary weapon. Unfortunately, that did not make him very good at coming up with suitable names for the great sword. They were, however, very original, with the notable ones being "Fart Flame," "Bastard Blaster," and "The Sad Feeling After Waking Up to a Wet Bed" that he shortened to just "The Nightmare That Caused the Bed Wetting." Griselda was sure to note wasn't that much shorter. Eventually, Arno devolved into nonsense words with various intimidating adjectives.

To Arno's credit, he did focus mainly on flame-centric names. Roran said that the sword technically had a flamberge blade, a blade that undulated back and forth, writhing like a serpent or tall flame. Though difficult to make, the undulations had several benefits according to Roran, such as cutting better and distributing shock. Roran couldn't help but gush about the sword's design. He said the blade design would also be great at parrying and trapping spear shafts to deal with opponents at range if they managed to dodge the emitted sword flames. The sword made the wielder a one-man army, capable of dealing with most threats close up with half-swording, mid-distance with its length and undulations, and at range with the flame projectiles. He even boasted that, due to it being a Cormac weapon that would never lose its edge, he wouldn't have to worry about sharpening it, which would be much more tedious than a sword with a simple straight blade.

Griselda rolled her eyes remembering her brother. Roran could be so hard-working in some capacities, but could not be bothered to do basic upkeep, such as regularly shaving, bathing, eating, or even maintaining his tools or tidying his space. He directed all his efforts toward creation with little thought to anything else. On more than one occasion, she heard Cormac grumbling to himself while alone in the forge, cleaning up after Roran. It's things like this that tended to make him impulsive or careless, which Griselda capitalized on when they sparred.

Eventually, her and Arno had come up with a proper name to match Roran's description of what the blade could do. They had named it . . .

What was that? Griselda thought as she heard a sound in the night. More footsteps. Perhaps Gunter had left or brought his friends? She poked her head in the tent and saw the fox was still in there, sleeping soundly.

The fire was dying down and night had fully enveloped the woods. Griselda's heart quickened and she stood up as the footsteps continued to approach. She grabbed the sword and held it up in the direction of the sound. They were coming in too fast but not heavy. Meaning there were multiple sets of feet rather than one set running.

"Who's there?" Griselda called out, doing her feeble best to sound intimidating and not like she was shaking.

She heard whispers in response, men talking to each other, then a laugh.

"I said *who's there*? Answer if you don't want to be run through with my Cormac weapon." *Surely that would frighten them off, right?*

"I thought I saw the signs of its telltale glow," one of them responded. They approached into the sword's light. There were four of them, rugged bandits by the looks of it, with mismatched light armor looted from bodies. They had beards and dark eyes that did not reflect the sword light back at her. The speaker had a thin sword and shield. The other three had axes.

"What are you doing all the way out here?" asked the one with the sword and shield, apparently the leader of the pack.

"Trying to avoid trouble, and you?" Griselda barked back.

"We heard a young lady with a glowing sword had been spotted in the area. Some high-up royal brat is paying quite a bit for mercs with those kinds of weapons. If you don't mind, we can take that heavy thing off your hands and use it properly." He didn't sound unkind, but there was something off about his unreflective dark eyes that made Griselda shiver.

"This is my father's last blade. It belongs to my family, and I am going to keep it that way."

Strong words for someone with a shaky voice, Griselda thought, chastising herself.

"What's your name?" one of the ax wielders asked.

"Griselda, daughter of Cormac. My father made these weapons, and I know how to use them."

They whispered to each other, but the one with the shield kept a neutral expression. "I don't doubt you know how to use it . . . but would you use its power in the forest you're camping in? You'd burn everything down around you. No one needs to get hurt. We just want the weapon so we can get Zerebril's heavy purse."

So Zerebril is after the weapons after all.

"Just let us take it, we'll let you go."

I don't trust them, those eyes will get everything they want, more than just the sword, Griselda thought. *I'm not letting someone walk up and take something that doesn't belong to them, not again.*

"So does your silence mean you're considering it? Well, let me put it in no uncertain terms. You will give us the blade, or we will take it from you with force. There is nothing to consider." The bandit eyed the book that Griselda had been reading. "You can read, so you must be smart. Do the *smart* thing. Or I'll have to be much less friendly."

Griselda stood up as straight as she could and held the sword out in front of her. "I don't care if you call it the smart thing. I'm doing the right thing. This is *your* last warning. Come any closer and you will all be dead over coin that Zerebril will never give you." Griselda started slowly spinning the sword, heating it up but not causing it to ignite. The glow increased, lighting up the men's scarred faces and tattered armor.

All four of them looked at each other and stepped forward.

"Circle her!" The shield bearer snarled, his demeanor becoming more animalistic. "Lop off her hands if she wants it that way."

Griselda steadied herself and sank into her stance. With this big of a sword, one heavier than she was used to, she would need to make each strike efficient, letting the momentum of the sword carry her from position to position. She analyzed her surroundings as they began to circle her. She would need to stay in the center of the campsite, otherwise the length of the sword, from pommel to tip being about as tall as she was, would get caught in a tree trunk.

"Last chance girl," the shield bearer said. "It's four on one and we are stronger than you."

Roran's boasts came back to Griselda. "Even without the power," Roran had said, "great swords like this were designed to ward off multiple opponents. It turns the wielder into a one-man army."

For you and Arno, Griselda thought. *I won't let them take this from us. I will get this back to you.*

The sword brightened in response as Griselda began to flow. She made a chain of sweeps from side to side and overhead, letting the weight of the sword pull her from stance to stance, as she danced in the middle of the clearing. The wide, controlled swings were able to protect her from all directions as long as she kept the sword in motion. The sheer intimidation of the large glowing blade would make them hesitant to draw near . . . hopefully.

One axman approached when her back was turned, but the sword was swinging behind her as well and he jumped back. The sword was glowing brighter and brighter; she was running out of time before this got bad.

The shield bearer stepped forward and tried to slow the blade down by sticking his short sword in its path. Griselda hardly noticed as the momentum of the great sword slapped the short sword away and almost knocked it out of the shield bearer's hand. He jumped back, startled.

Griselda got used to the sword's feel and what it was capable of. It was designed for destruction, designed to burn and send an untold number of souls to the hereafter—the next leg of the journey. And so, she and Arno had named it End March.

She engaged. While the sword was swinging lower, she let it smash into the campfire and send the flaming chunks of wood at one of the axmen. Having no shield, he tried to protect his face by holding up his ax and hand. The embers broke on impact and scattered into his face, mouth, and eyes. He dropped to the ground writhing in pain.

"Idiots, she'll kill us all we if don't stop that sword from swinging!" The shield bearer said. The two remaining axmen lunged at her, bearded ax hooks trying to catch and slow down the sword to create an opening.

Griselda felt the handle of the sword heating up as the friction-sensitive weapon increased in temperature. The tip of the sword, being what was traveling the most distance with each swing, would heat up the most while parts like the handle and ricasso could still be held by gloved hands. Griselda was not wearing gloves and so she would get burned if it properly ignited. One axman did catch it in the hook of the bearded ax and trapped it, but the heated sword created a shower of sparks on impact. The axman jumped back in shock, allowing Griselda to sweep the sword clear through the neck of the other axman who thought the sword was trapped. More sparks as End March's undulated blade ripped through the man's clothes, flesh, bone, then flesh and clothes on its way out, the friction setting parts of the shirt collar on fire.

The man's torso fell to the ground while his head fell the other way. Griselda flinched at what she had just done. She had decapitated the man more because that was where the sword was heading, not intentionally; she couldn't stop the momentum. His eyes . . . they were still open and staring up into the darkness. She had to force down the urge to vomit at the head of the man rolling around the campsite. Blood, more blood than she thought could possibly fit in the human body, drained from both the head and the torso. She grimaced. *Don't think about it. If you think, you're dead*, she told herself.

"Oros's shit!" said the remaining upright axmen, who tried to back away.

Don't think about it, or you're dead.

"Idiot!" the shield bearer said. "I'll deal with her."

Don't think about it, or you're dead.

Taking a life had never been something she imagined she would do, could do. She knew it was irrational to bear the guilt, but all the things that decapitated man had lived, from his infancy to his beheading, were now dropped onto her increasingly sore shoulders as End March did its brutal work.

By this point, the man hit by the embers had gotten back to his feet and joined the fight again. That still put her at three to one, better than four to one at least.

"Stop the sword from moving, and we win," said the shield bearer, almost trying to reassure himself. "Then we get the blade and the girl. We'll make sure you pay for our friend here."

As he approached, he let his shield down. Griselda lunged at the opening, bringing her sword down from over her head. But he was goading her to commit to the swing. He raised his shield at the last moment. Wood and metal cracked and splintered as the great sword cut halfway into his iron-rimmed kite shield and into the arm holding it, shattering the bone.

The shield bearer shouted in pain but then forced a smile. "Got you!"

Griselda tried to rip the sword free, but it was stuck in the shield, and the man kept maneuvering it so that she couldn't get leverage to yank the sword up.

The man pulled her in at the cost of tremendous pain in his arm and held his thin sword up, pointed at her neck. The other two bandits whooped and hollered at her sides.

"Looks like . . . we get an additional prize," he said. Despite his bravado about his plan working, his face was pale in the glowing sword light.

Griselda grunted. "You must not know how these weapons

work," she said. "They are sensitive to friction. Meaning the more they rub against material, the faster the fire comes."

Griselda kicked the man in the groin and gave one final yank on End March as it ignited against the wood and his arm. His whole left side caught on fire, bright and hot enough as if night and winter did not exist, but the sword was still stuck fast, and Griselda had to let go lest she get caught in the flames too. Her knuckles were red from the heat pouring down from the blade already.

The shield bearer waved about, which only made End March hotter, causing the fires to spread more quickly. As he flailed, licks of flame snaked through the air, crisping the reddened fall leaves on the ground. One flaming tongue snapped at Griselda, lashed her left arm, charred her tunic, and burned her skin, the toll for certainly taking another life. Her skin continued to glow as it burned before she patted it out. She would pay. She knew it. She would pay for every life, every set of shoulders missing their head, down to every hair now cursing the air with the smell of burning death. She knew it irrational with her mind, but the feelings that came from watching a man's flesh char outside in, organs heating, eyes melting, teeth popping, were feelings that could not be guided by reason. Her left arm now bore a blackened brand, skin that would never heal, the cost of legacy and its uses, a brand that she knew already was bound to burn her mind as well. This—this she would never unsee.

Barely alive, the man dropped his sword as he tried to remove the shield from his arm. Griselda grabbed it instead, End March's light now harsh and sinister and repelling.

Don't think about it, or you're dead!

One axman, the unburned one, stood open-mouthed as their leader failed to get the shield off his arm due to it being pinned in place by End March. Griselda lunged and stabbed him right in his gawking mouth, sword end protruding out the back of his neck. She removed it quickly to deal with parrying a blow from the last man standing. The sword had the reach advantage over the shorter ax, and Griselda used continuous thrusts to drive him back. With this blade being easier to handle and quicker, he wouldn't dare try to catch it this time. Like Roran, the man tried to defensively bat her away, but she flowed with the momentum —body moving with memory if her mind could not do anything but smell a man roasting—and kept up the offensive until he backed into a tree trunk. With nowhere to run, Griselda pierced him through his leather jerkin, and out the back, sticking him to the tree. The man coughed up blood and then his head drooped forward on his limp neck. Griselda let go of the sword handle as if it too could burn her.

The shield bearer had finally stopped screaming as the shock, blood loss, and intensity of the flames did their work, cooking his brain inside his skull. Griselda ran over and, with trembling hands, dumped her water skin to put out the fire before it spread to the trees. She choked back tears at the grizzly sight and threatened to vomit once again, the smell now being the only thing she could perceive, something so foul, it seemed to brutally dull her other senses.

They were dead. Now she would think about it, even if she didn't want to. Could she live with that, continue to do it, even for her brothers? Mutilate others and herself in the process? How many would she kill?

Shaking, she put her hands on her knees, and she let herself feel the weight of everything that had happened. And when that was not enough, she collapsed and lay on her back, feeling the warmth of the men's spilled blood seep into her stolen clothes.

Hyperventilating, her arms shaking at the lives they ended, her chest heaving up and down, her rasping breaths becoming the only audible sound in the once noisy forest, her mind raced in every possible direction with no inherent purpose. Her whole body was trembling. She clasped one of her hands over her mouth to silence her noisy breathing, in case anyone else heard her, but then pulled it off. It was drenched in blood, and she had wiped it on her face and mouth, tasted it. Rolling over to her side, she spat the blood off her lips.

End March turned Griselda into something other than herself. The fear she saw in their eyes as they stared at the rapidly moving glowing blade. The momentum of the blade carried it through a man's neck as if it had a mind of its own, a mind bent on dismemberment. Allowing herself to flow, allowing the weapons to do their work without her direct intention had resulted in the grisliest of deaths, deaths that she couldn't get out of her head, no matter how many times she blinked the starless night sky away.

Even these hardened highwaymen, with all the terrible things they had seen and done, even they had looked at her like she was a monster. And she was. She killed four men and was now lying in their blood and viscera. What would Arno say if he saw her do that?

But she had to. There was no other way. She closed her eyes, tried her best to slow her breathing, and thought, *May you find better lives on the next leg of the March.*

And then she heard footsteps.

"No . . ." Griselda groaned. "No more. No more death."

The footsteps, stealthy this time, did not slow in response to her pleas. She was too tired to react quickly, and before she knew it the footsteps were next to her ear.

This is it, Griselda thought. *I'm sorry, Roran and Arno. Father, Mother, I will see you soon.*

She braced for the slice of a blade but instead felt something cold and wet on her skin. A fox tongue licked the sweat off her steaming forehead.

CHAPTER 13
DRASTIC TIMES

ZEREBRIL'S MOUTH WAS DRY. He stood on the wooden battlements overlooking the dense forest outside Stedtfest as the night grew deeper and deeper, the clouds above obscuring the stars and fast-moving moons. Somewhere in those trees, a blood-thirsty army was on its way. There would be no terms, no mercy, no survivors left in Ewen's wake. To the rest of Wilheim, it had appeared the king of Ardhataz had gone completely mad and slaughtered without remorse or clear purpose.

Zerebril shivered. It was getting colder; snow might make its first appearance in a couple of weeks. Eleventh of Fourth Fall's March—that was the day, only twenty days before true, calen-drical winter came, though that hardly seemed to matter. Storms would blow down from the enormous mountain ranges that encircled the entire continent and bring blizzards. It was a bleak time of the year, made bleaker still by the approaching army.

Zerebril turned to look over Stedtfest. Since it was located on the Shatter Rock River and surrounded by thick, tall trees, the town had mostly used wood in its construction. Though Zerebril had initially feared that this would make the town incredibly prone to fire, their engineers and architects were smarter than he had originally thought. When Zerebril arrived, he found that the log wall surrounding the city was treated, thick, covered in moss, and the area near the river was generally moister. The townspeople, in preparation of the oncoming army, had also soaked animal hides and layered them around the outer wall. Somehow, they had not given up, or, at the very least, they were too ready to fight to the death. The people of Stedtfest were gritty woodsmen, strong of back from long bows and ax blows.

There was no way Ewen would be able to use trebuchets or ballista in this dense forest either. That meant if he couldn't knock down the wall or light it on fire, then he would have to climb over it. In anticipation of this, Zerebril had set up posts for his army immediately when he arrived in the city. There were dozens of watchmen on shifts on the perimeter watching for ladders, fire, or movement through the day and night.

A large portion of his army had also cut down the trees nearest to Stedtfest for a couple more strategic advantages. This allowed for greater visibility around the city for at least one hundred yards. It would also prevent Ewen's forces from climbing the trees and hopping over that way. Though he wished he had time to make a larger killing field in front of the walls, he couldn't make it too big, or it would allow Ewen to move his siege weapons into effective range and out of lethal reach of the Stedtfest long bows.

The extra wood was used to heighten the walls. Zerebril also had his men cut the wood, sharpen it into points, harden the tips with fire, and place them around the walls like pikes to discourage anyone trying to quickly approach on horseback. As an additional safety measure, Zerebril had his soldiers dig pit traps and trenches in the hundred-yard expanse between Stedtfest and the new tree line. The traps were small but deep. Anyone who stepped on the covering would fall six feet onto sharpened wood covered in livestock dung. If Ewen could use terror tactics, so would Zerebril. He had set all of this up in a matter of days.

And it was thirsty work; Zerebril wet his lips with his tongue, pieces of skin peeling off as his lips started to chap. It's not that there wasn't water, there was, but Zerebril was thirsting for something else, something that lingered at the corners of his mind, promising a fog, a relief, an oblivion from all of this struggle and pressure to save something that already was surely doomed.

Zerebril gripped the edge of the wooden wall with his heavy gauntlet. He peered into the darkness, constantly aware of his tongue in his dry mouth, his teeth clattering together as he occasionally shivered, and the restless craving of mercy that twitched his eyelids.

Did he really believe that this was all for nothing? Was that why he craved the mercy, the poppy, so much? Was he just biding his time and doing his duty until his time ran out? Or was he still hopeful, but having hope in such bleak times was so painful that it justified numbing his pain?

Whatever the case, sedated or not, Zerebril had done everything he could think of to stave off Ewen for as long as he could. However, he knew that this would all be for nothing if the light creatures were not dealt with, creatures they still knew little about other than the reports from when they killed Gunter. Any scouts sent ahead to find out more about the creatures never returned. All the information they had was that the light beasts could be killed with Cormac weapons.

And his half-brother Carl, whose team had the Cormac weapons, had not arrived yet, which was beginning to make Zerebril's jaw perpetually clenched. He knew that he had gotten Rodrick the Merchant's twin guards in exchange for tax exemptions on all activities in the city, but was Carl having trouble procuring others? What could be holding him up, given the gravity of this situation?

A watchman with a torch passed behind Zerebril, the light barely making the mud below him visible, let alone the tree line a hundred yards away. By his count, a watchman would pass by any given span of the wall every twenty seconds. Was that enough, with such oppressive darkness?

Zerebril turned and climbed down from the wooden battlements. He had one more way to delay King Ewen if he needed to for Carl, though it would cause irreversible damage to the surrounding area. If Carl did not arrive by morning, Zerebril would take drastic measures to ensure Ewen slowed long enough until their only hope at stopping the light beasts arrived.

If the light beasts were slain by Carl's vanguard and their Cormac weapons, Zerebril could destroy the enemy camp, their means of production, their food—since the idiot Tazzes were burning everything—and leave them crippled. From there, even if Ewen still tried to siege the city, Zerebril's defensive precautions would be more than enough to break King Ewen's remaining forces.

Zerebril arrived at his quarters, which the officials of Stedtfest had arranged for him. Every night he would survey things to reassure himself that everything that could be done had been. But almost every night now, the shadow would creep up, and his overthinking would plague him. For times like these, with his brother gone, it was time for the mercy. It was hard to sleep without the poppy, so he had stolen as much as he could from his father's doctors without arousing suspicion. He almost took more, hardly caring if he got caught as long as he had the relief.

The glass vials rolled around as he frantically pulled the drawer on his bedside table. The shadow was getting closer, and he needed it fast. Half of the vials were already empty. He shivered again despite being in a warmer environment.

Though he understood what was happening, becoming addicted to the strong opiate, Zerebril was helpless to stop it. He had tried to ride from Wilheim to Stedtfest without taking any. He had failed. The shivers became hard to hide after that much time without the only thing that could slake his thirst. His whole body ached and longed for it, as if each muscle group could slowly override his normally impressive intellect for the sole purpose of getting more mercy.

He held a vial up before his eyes, both hatred and desire mixed in equal measure. He wanted to squeeze the vial with one hand until it shattered, while the other hand urged him to dump it down his throat. Eventually, one side of him had to win. And which would it be? Had he forsaken hope, or did he cling to the whisper that Wilheim could be saved? Which was more painful? Either way, both were painful enough to demand a respite, a relief, a brief mercy. Zerebril uncorked the vial and downed its contents. He sighed with shuddering breath, waiting for a medicinal miracle to take its divine effect. He lay on his bed, and the shadow crept away at last. In the embrace of mercy, Zerebril could drift into something resembling sleep.

Zerebril walked outside the walls
Of Wilheim
He was younger and holding
The hands of his big brother
Gunter, in armor Zerebril had painted
With the lyrics of Gunter's favorite verses
Was leading him
Through the forest
Away from Wilheim
Zerebril laughed and ran ahead
Deeper into the dense woods
Until he saw sunlight
And emerged at a wide clearing
At the top was a hill
Zerebril knew this hill
The sky darkened with smoke
Zerebril turned to scan for Gunter
But he wasn't there

How could he be
Zerebril knew
And knowing in dreams
Was as good as seeing from afar
As Gunter fought and died on that hill
Zerebril tried to sprint back to Wilheim
But he was slowed, suddenly wearing
His plate armor, so heavy
He called for his brother
The sky darkened more
And when he finally emerged
Back where he started
Wilheim was burning
He heard a roar
And a massive red creature
Handless arms bleeding steaming blood
Burst through the outer wall
And knocked him awake

Zerebril nearly jumped out of his bed as a knock came from the other side of his door. He slowed his breathing. "What is it?"

From the other side, a messenger said, "Just thought you should know . . . the Falcon didn't arrive."

Apparently, it was morning. Though Zerebril had slept, he had been plagued by nightmares yet again.

Zerebril tried not to let the sorrow bleed into his tone. "Very well. I'll arrange for a delay. Tell the town officials I'll have to execute the final defense. We've spoken about it and agreed to use it as a last resort."

"I will, sir."

Zerebril heard the wood creak as the soldier walked away from the door.

According to the troops that survived where Gunter fell, King Ewen was largely transporting his troops, equipment, and food along the river to increase their pace and keep his troops fresh. However, Zerebril still had some leftover logs from the tree removal around Stedtfest and had a terrible idea for how to put them to use.

Fine, Zerebril thought, *if you want to travel by river, I'll give you a sea.*

CHAPTER 14
DRASTIC MEASURES

"CAPTAIN URREM!" bellowed King Ewen.

Urrem was looking over the side of the boat in disbelief when he heard the king come stomping up next to him.

"Captain Urrem," the king said again. Ewen clapped a heavy hand on Urrem's shoulder and forcefully spun Urrem around. "What exactly am I looking at?"

Urrem looked into the beady bright eyes of the red-faced, red-bearded king. King Ewen stood about a foot taller than Urrem and was wide in his exquisite polished plate with black engravings. Looking up at him was like facing down a red avalanche.

"I don't really know what could a' caused dis . . . yer lord-ship," Urrem uttered.

"Course ya don't," Ewen sighed. "Yer a soldier, and a carpenter before dat, if I'm not mistaken? I need da Scholar." With that, Ewen stomped away. Urrem could have sworn that there were indents in the wood where Ewen's broad feet thudded.

Urrem exhaled. Though King Ewen was mostly pleasant to his troops, he could still be frightening. Urrem turned around and looked back at the wilderness. Instead of there being a river that the boats could travel up with soldiers on the shore, there was a new swamp that did not exist yesterday.

The river had gotten shallower, grounding some of the boats, while the water expanded in all directions, jumping the river banks, and flooding the forest. Soldiers were muttering, carrying their belongings above their heads while wading forward in knee-deep, sometimes waist-deep, water. The horses were skittish and resisted being pulled through the water while carts became virtually unmovable, their wheels sinking into the mud.

"Clever Willies must have clogged da river," Urrem muttered.

Not only was the water an inconvenience to quick travel; it was cold. This was mountain run-off water while winter approached. Soldiers were shivering as they trudged along. Urrem heard a soldier sneeze. *Oh no*, he thought. Stagnant water forming over what was once a forest floor had unsettled the landscape tremendously. Bugs were flying all around their helmets, looking for safe places to land. *Bugs, cold water*, Urrem thought, *dis could not only mean slowed travel but also disease.*

King Ewen's crew had stocked up on Life Nectar when they passed around the southern edge of Lake Verdin, but that was meant for wounds and wouldn't be enough if everyone came down with fever. How could this have happened? Did this mean that King Ewen's revelations weren't accurate? Had something finally stood up against the king, who was divinely mandated to win?

Urrem shook his head—dangerous thoughts. Like King Ewen had said, Urrem was a soldier now and was not expected to think. That was for his betters, for Ewen and the Scholar.

Urrem caught sight of his unit traveling upriver, trying to push a horse-drawn wagon out of the mud. The captain jumped off the boat and waded over to his men.

"Captain!" Lieutenant Malcolm saluted.

"Stuck in da mud?" asked Urrem.

"Oros take ya ass-wagon!" exclaimed Briggs as he repeatedly kicked at the wagon with his boot. However, to perform the kicks, Briggs had to lift his leg high out of the water. Eventually, he lost his balance and fell in.

Malcolm rolled his eyes at his troop's display. "Y.yes, sir. Dis river has been screw-turned by Imeel-Illin himself. Flooded river's been getting our wagon stuck more often dan Briggs fornicates wit his sheep—"

"Dat only happened once!" Briggs said, poking his head out of the muddy water. "And she forced herself on me!"

Malcolm shook his head. "Da horses can't bear dis drudgery."

Urrem nodded and looked into the back of the wagon. Most of it was unworn armor and food for his specific unit; then he noticed that the wagon had two wooden planks running along the sides for seating.

"Lieutenant Malcolm," Urrem said. "Have da men break da wagon seat planks off da sides. Get some rope and tie it to da front of da wagon . . . wait, hey!" Urrem shouted as Briggs, soaking wet but quickly drying off from the internal heat produced by his fury, scrambled up to climb into the wagon. "Don't climb up dere; ya'll only sink it further. Remove da planks witout climbing into da wagon."

Briggs glowered but nodded.

Malcolm fished a rope out of the side of the wagon and began fastening it to the front of the wagon. Once the planks were free, Urrem angled them under the wheel of the wagon so that the wheels would roll up onto the wood instead of deeper into the mud.

From there, Urrem grabbed the long rope and pulled it around the tree as an anchor. "Alright, men," he said. "I want ten of ya pulling on this rope wit me, five of ya pushing the rear, and six of ya lifting the wagon up on the sides. If we have any luck, we'll get da wagon unstuck witout having to unload it to make it lighter."

On the count of three, everyone did their duty, and the wagon rolled free onto the planks. Lieutenant Malcolm clapped Captain Urrem on the back. "When did ya get so smart?"

Urrem shrugged. "I've had to get lumber wagons unstuck before. Anyway, I'm needed back on da boat. The officers are going to meet wit Ewen to decide what is to be done about dis. Have men walk in front of da wagon and test da ground for any soft or deep spots. If dey find someting ya can't just skirt around, sink da planks down in da water over da soft spot before da wheels get dere."

Malcolm saluted, and Urrem returned to the boat. As he climbed up the boat, he saw disturbances in the water coming from behind the boat. Waves were being made as if a serpent was swimming in the water, but nothing was there to create the waves. Something was lifting the grounded boats and pushing them upstream. He double-checked, but whatever had made the waves was gone. He looked around at the trees in the Stedtfest forest. They all seemed to groan as they drowned in the water, or maybe it was the wind. Behind him, where the army had been, where he saw the disturbances in the water, branches and leaves started falling from the dying trees.

Urrem sat himself down around the king's massive, circular table on the boat dedicated to war meetings. Around this table sat the entire command structure of the army. King Ewen did not sit; rather, he walked *on* the table, placing himself above everyone else. He could also address each of his staff more personally by walking over to them whenever they were speaking. The man was charismatic if brutal.

The table itself had various necessary items: a map of the

land, charts on food stock, reports on casualties, schedules for weapons and armor maintenance, catalogs of available horses, bills of health on each boat and wagon, instructions for assembling siege weapons, and some things that Urrem had never seen before. Each item was in front of a specific person who could pass it around the table if necessary. At the table's center was a large, padded mat.

The Ardhatazian high officers of war sat stiffly around the table, the spontaneously created swamp having a visible impact on the rigid postures of every commanding officer in the room.

Three generals responsible for land assaults, sea assaults, and siege craft, plus defensive fortifications, were seated in higher chairs equally spaced around the massive table, creating a triangle of command. Under the three generals, there were three colonels responsible for different specializations in accordance with their generals' designated area, and under each colonel, there were five captains responsible for field command of troops. There was a scribe who took notes during meetings, and the king's eight-year-old son. In total, there were sixty seats at the table, each with a name card and a specially decorated chair patterned to their specific area and rank, though not all of them were filled.

There were eighteen open seats, as one colonel and their five captains had stayed behind in Ardhataz to oversee the defense of the country according to their areas of expertise.

Everyone was meant to be seated; however, there were two people walking around. The king, who was pacing on the table, and the Scholar, who had no seat and paced around the entire table rather than on top of it.

As Ewen paced on the table, he made eye contact with each officer and provided a reassuring half-smile as he appeared to mull over his thoughts. As far as Urrem could tell, the king tried to make each officer feel valued and known personally. Ewen had known details of Urrem's life that he didn't remember disclosing to anyone.

Urrem peeked over his shoulder as the hooded Scholar skulked behind him. Urrem shivered. Though he didn't really want to know the answer, he couldn't help but look down at the Scholar's shadow. In the brightly lit room, his shadow behaved as normal. Urrem couldn't make up his mind as to whether that was a good thing or whether he was seeing things when the shadow bent toward the water the other day.

Ewen's nearby footfalls reverberated around the room and snapped Urrem's focus back to the center of the table.

The king kept the war room incredibly organized. No one was allowed to talk over each other; no one was allowed to talk at all unless they raised their flag. The scribe would note the order of flag raises and let the king know who was next in line to speak.

Right now, nobody spoke. The king just paced back and forth in contemplation. Urrem, having only recently been promoted to captain for his actions at the Battle of the Highest Hill where Prince Gunter fell, had not yet spoken in one of these war meetings.

It was not unusual for the war room to be quiet, given how it was organized and how King Ewen always responded with much consideration to each point raised by his officers. But under the silence, Urrem thought he could hear many, many questions. King Ewen always seemed like he had a well-planned reason for each of his unorthodox or even irrational actions, though some things he would not explicitly share.

However, the looks on the officers' faces said it all. They had been burning the land on their way to Stedtfest, which seemed ludicrous, especially if they needed to retreat. Then there was the entire wing under Colonel Macblite, whose sole mission was to gather a quota of hostages for . . . something . . . something unspeakable in that boat. On top of that, Ewen had been trusting portions of their military strategy to this Scholar who appeared out of nowhere several months back. Urrem could practically hear teeth grinding down to nubs around the room.

"So," King Ewen finally said, "da enemy has decided to dig their own grave for us."

Around the table, many eyebrows raised.

"What could I possibly mean? Well, according to our scouts posted around Stedtfest, dis little act of damming da river and flooding da area has had a significant impact on dem as well." He stroked his beard and walked in a circle, his eyes moving from his shoes to his officers, to the ceiling, to the Scholar, but never allowed to linger on any specific place. "Dis act of slowing us down reeks of desperation. We have won every single battle on our conquest through da countryside."

Officers around the table nodded, seeming to forget their questions and concerns.

Ewen continued, though Urrem noticed that he was intentionally making his Ardhatazian accent more pronounced. "So, dey be trying new maneuvers to slow da inevitable, but in doing dis, the Willies mutilated deir crops and land. And what be da meaning of dat, Siege Master?"

The Siege Master, General Macintosh, raised his hand-held flag depicting a trebuchet on a background of stone wall. Even though Ewen directly asked him a question, the flag-raising was still customary. Ewen nodded, prompting him to speak.

General Macintosh was a balding man with black eyes that seemed far too small for his large head. Despite his large, prominent forehead, he was thin, and his voice was a bit nasally. "It means dat dey won't be able to last a prolonged siege witout starving first," he said as he folded his hands on the table and shifted in his seat. Macintosh peered around at the other branches before continuing. "A lengthy siege of Stedtfest won't be necessary, but in da long run, killing da food source in dis area means dat da walled city of Wilheim will be dat much easier

204 • ANTON JONES

to take when da time comes. Dere will be lasting consequences to dis such as food shortages, delayed travel and communication, and economic strife."

King Ewen clapped and smiled. "Exactly! Dey be mere weeks away from total collapse. Foolhardy is what it is. By da end of dis, dem Willies will all be begging to be subsumed into Ardhataz."

Captain Trayhaz raised his flag. Trayhaz was seated next to Urrem and in the same wing under Colonel Macblite. Like Urrem, his sole mission for the foreseeable future was to raid and gather hostages.

"Ah, Captain Trayhaz. How's the wife doing?"

Muirza was her name. Though Urrem didn't know Trayhaz, yet, as they married on the customary pillar recently, Muirza was one of Jezerelle's longest-lasting friends.

"Well, your lordship," Trayhaz said. "I just received word that she gave birth to twins."

"Twins? Excellent! Two strong lads no doubt." King Ewen smiled broadly and clapped again, which was louder than whatever Trayhaz was going to say next.

Trayhaz seemed to have thought better and held his tongue.

"So, what's on your mind, Captain?"

"Your lordship, forgive me if I don't hold all da pieces of information, but . . . ." he hesitated and swallowed before speaking. "If our victory is assured such as ya claim, then why burn da land we will be inhabiting? Why continue to gather hostages? Surely we no longer need dese fear tactics since da enemy is already desperate?"

King Ewen nodded in understanding but held firm in his stance. "Captain Trayhaz, as someone tasked wit dat business, I do respect your opinion on da matter. However," King Ewen looked over at the Scholar, "we must keep it up, even when da enemy no longer fights back."

Murmurs went around the table, and King Ewen stamped his

plated boot on the ground, demanding silence. Nobody was to speak unless the flag was raised.

"Officers of war, dis is indeed bloody, but it has a long-term purpose. Da Wilheim Peninsula is only da first stop on dis leg of the March." Ewen let it sink in for a bit, hinting at future implications. As he spoke, he rotated around the table to look each officer in the eye. "Soon, da other countries on da continent will make war wit us as well. I need not remind ya dat we are situated between da Wilheim Peninsula and all da smaller warring countries in da west. Once word gets to dem of our victory, dey'll finally unite and form a coalition against our might. If da Willies are not screw-turned so deeply in da ground by dat point, den we'll fight battles on both sides of our mountains. What we burn now we'll rebuild but rebuild it da Tazzian way. Dis be justice for what was done to us."

All around the table there were more nods of agreement and a few fists beating chests. Though no one was allowed to speak without the flags being raised, it was not unusual for officers to beat their chest in acknowledgment.

"We be changing our legacy, one grueling slog through da mud at a time. I've seen it." He paused and scratched at his beard. "As ya may have guessed, da captured are being used to make weapons, yes. I dare not divulge da details 'bout dese weapons as dey must not leave da boats but know dat it is for ya own good and da good of Ardhataz and da continent as a whole."

The Scholar nodded as well but otherwise didn't speak. Urrem noticed that Ewen kept making nervous glances at the Scholar, waiting for his nods in the pauses of his speech.

"But women and children? We can hear dem," Trayhaz blurted out without raising his flag. "Do we need to torture da women and children as well?"

King Ewen's face grew stern, a tight line replacing his jovial smile. He looked back at the Scholar again before standing taller and readdressing Trayhaz. "Like I said, Captain, we cannot divulge da details about da procedures. I invite ya up to da table if ya be wishing to stand your ground."

Urrem froze. Captain Trayhaz wasn't necessarily his friend, but he could tell the man's character from his concerns, and now he was a father of twins. Urrem's stomach knotted up and it seemed like every other officer's did as well. What would Jezerelle do if Muirza became a widow?

Captain Trayhaz stood up. Urrem's hand shot out instinctively to Trayhaz's arm to hold him in his seat, but Trayhaz shrugged it off. Trayhaz fiddled with his necklace, a chain through a hole in a small silver horseshoe.

King Ewen nodded solemnly and stepped onto the padded mat at the center of the table. He called up two captains to help with undoing his plate. He removed his breast plate and greaves, until he was shirtless and in trousers, his broad, hairy chest exposed.

"I am not as naïve to tink my authority absolute. I respect yer right to challenge me on anyting ya tink might lead Ardhataz astray," Ewen said as Trayhaz also removed his armor and stepped up onto the table.

The other officers cleared away the reports, maps, and other miscellaneous war room items in case the conflict left the mat.

"I am grateful for such policies," Trayhaz responded. "Even if I do dis as a matter of conscience, I will not deny being a bit excited to fight a warrior such as ya."

The king clapped, and the smile returned. "Very good!" King Ewen looked over at his son, who had been doodling on his own version of Wilheim's map. "Pay attention, young bull, soon you'll be doing this in my stead."

Urrem noticed the king's son smile and nod, but it did not stop him from doodling.

Trayhaz and King Ewen shook hands to acknowledge each other and then assumed combat stances, fists raised up to protect the chin, elbows held in tight to protect the body. Any officer had the right to challenge the king according to Ardhataz ancient custom. If he could best the king's champion, then the officer's say would win over the king's for that particular matter. Most Ardhatazian kings enjoyed the fight and would elect to be their own champion until age got the better of them. Since this happened often enough, Ewen was well-known in hand-to-hand combat. He had never lost a fight.

They both traced the line of a triangle, the Ardhataz symbolic mountain, on their chest, signaling the start of the fight.

Though Trayhaz was not weak, being promoted for his combat experience, King Ewen still towered over him. Trayhaz moved from side to side on the mat while King Ewen occupied the center, meaning he had to move one step to follow Trayhaz every time the captain took three. Trayhaz shot out a couple of quick jabs to test King Ewen's guard and to gauge his reach. Ewen didn't flinch and let the blows slide off his elbows. Trayhaz risked a kick to Ewen's thigh, and still the king did not budge.

Urrem hadn't seen the Right to Challenge enforced before, though he had heard about it. The two seemed as friendly as could be before the fight, but it did not cure the sinking feeling in Urrem's stomach. These fights could be dangerous, no matter how chummy the two were before getting on the mat.

Trayhaz threw a left hook to try and get around Ewen's guard. It connected, but Ewen's head didn't move even a little despite the punch landing on his cheek.

The stories were proving true. Urrem had heard that King Ewen did not fight back for a while during challenges. Just as he demoralized his enemy with scorched-earth tactics on the field, he demoralized challengers by showing them how ineffective their strength was compared to his own. This led to one of two things: weakening the resolve of the challenger or riling them up until they made risky moves.

Trayhaz was the latter. He jumped in close and risked

several shots to King Ewen's dense, muscled body before jumping back out. Though Urrem could see the red marks where Trayhaz's fists made contact, Ewen didn't seem like he noticed.

Satisfied with gauging Trayhaz's strength, Ewen left the center of the mat and walked Trayhaz down. Trayhaz evaded him while keeping himself away from the corners of the mat, where a challenger would be disqualified if they stepped out.

Trayhaz threw some more jabs, but they were even less effective as he threw them while backpedaling, taking away their force.

Slow and steady, Ewen kept pursuing Trayhaz around the mat until he managed to corner him. Trayhaz threw one last fury of desperate punches, which only left him winded and didn't slow Ewen down at all. Ewen, still breathing through his nose, loaded his hips and delivered a momentous left hook targeting Trayhaz's body.

Ewen was slower than Trayhaz, and so Trayhaz saw it coming. He lowered his elbow to his side to block the blow. Urrem closed his eyes and cringed, knowing what was coming next.

Though Trayhaz blocked it on his elbow, the size difference between the two made blocking an ineffective strategy. Trayhaz's only hope was to evade, which Ewen had taken away.

The blow cracked Trayhaz's arm and then the ribs the arm was protecting. Trayhaz's body collapsed around the punch as Ewen followed through, rotating his hips and shoulders through his target. The force of the punch knocked Trayhaz off the mat and to the ground.

Several of the officers winced as they heard the bones crack on impact. Urrem felt sick.

King Ewen nodded in acknowledgment to the challenger and walked over to his son. "Willem, up ya go," Ewen said, gesturing with a nod over to the crumpled Trayhaz.

Prince Willem nodded and walked over to Trayhaz, who was clenching his ribs on the ground.

"It's alright, ya did well," Prince Willem said. Willem knelt and patted Trayhaz's head. Though only eight years old, Willem was already a sturdy child and helped Trayhaz to his feet. Ewen walked over and offered his hand. Trayhaz, wincing, tried to raise his broken right arm, but couldn't. He was forced to take the king's hand and shake it with his left arm.

Ewen smiled broadly and clapped Trayhaz on the back, causing another wince.

King Ewen turned away from Trayhaz and addressed the other officers. "I am chosen to lead dis next March by Imeel-Illin. But I still treasure ya all as I would my kin. Even as I am chosen by God, I am still human and in need of ya counsel. All of ya act as my eyes and ears, able to see and hear tings when I'm tending to other business," Ewen looked back at the Scholar, but this look was different. Instead of looking for affirmation, it was one of defiance. He turned away from the Scholar. "Stand ya ground if ya must, and I will respect it."

Many of the officers nodded in response. Prince Willem helped Trayhaz back to his seat before walking back across the table to his own. Trayhaz breathed heavily as he sat next to Urrem.

Though Urrem was appalled by some of the things he was forced to do, it was hard to go against King Ewen's force of character.

As the meeting adjourned, Urrem stayed back to help Trayhaz to the medical tents.

"Well, I guess congratulations are in order," Urrem said through a half-smile. "Jezerelle and I am happy for ya and Muirza. I'm sure Jzerelle will insist we bring da lot of ya food on a regular basis."

"Dey're not lads."

"What's dat now?" Urrem asked.

"Ewen hoped dey were strong lads," Trayhaz winced as he spoke, his breathing heavier as Urrem helped him out of the chair and toward the boat's exit. "Dey're lasses. Identical."

Urrem steadied Trayhaz's gait with a hand on his back. "Does that change anyting?"

Trayhaz smiled through the pain as Urrem pushed open the door. "No," he said, looking down at his horseshoe necklace. "I reckon it don't change a damn ting."

Urrem returned the smile as the wash of noise that the doors barred back returned to his ears. The sloshing mud and water, the horses' exhausted whinnies, the grumbling soldiers, all were present and fighting to be heard. But the quiet smile exchanged between the two captains, the celebration of new life, seemed to put the war far away, at least for now.

Urrem often caught himself dreaming of home too. His wife tending the land by herself. Trayhaz's wife raising twins by herself. That, more than the noise outside, returned the grim looks to their faces. After all, Ewen had implied that the Wilheim Peninsula was the first of many stops on this new March.

CHAPTER 15
CHANGES

RORAN BREATHED in through his nose and out through his mouth as he kept up the slow jog, the scent of fallen leaves and decaying branches catching in his nostrils. He was trotting along south, with Arno in tow in the backpack carrier they had built together. Running had taken up large chunks of their days—days of dwindling daylight as winter approached—attempting to evade all signs of Wilheim as they searched for any signs of Griselda. And it was for Griselda, the hope of reuniting his family, the fear of what was happening to her without his protection, that spurred Roran to keep running.

They had stayed off the major roads and trade routes, instead following game trails that ran parallel to the Shatter Rock River. They questioned every hunter populating the forests, and there were very few this far away from the city with the threat of Ewen approaching. No one had seen or heard of Griselda. They would head as far as to Stedtfest to find her. The only bit of good that had come from the other hunters is that Roran was able to get a new shirt.

Despite not hearing any good news, Arno couldn't help but

marvel at the height of the trees as Roran jogged with him in the harness. The forest surrounding Stedtfest had some of the tallest, sturdiest trees on the continent. They would tower over even Wilheim's outer wall if positioned side-by-side. In truth, the trees sprouted above the understory, proudly standing resolute, aloof from the conflicts happening at their base. They were sentinels who couldn't interfere, the hardiest organism on the planet, but also completely vulnerable to bipedal mammals and their petty problems.

"How long do you think it took to grow that tall?" asked Arno.

"Probably longer than Ardhataz has been a kingdom," Roran replied. Since Arno pointed it out, Roran also let himself crane his neck back as far as he could to look up at the titan tree. Arno stuck his finger in Roran's ear.

"Hey!" Roran laughed. "None of that!"

Though Roran laughed, the reminder that Arno was on his back made him aware of how much the skin on his shoulders was getting rubbed raw by the wooden box. His skin had been tougher since he left the castle, but Arno still needed to apply Life Nectar to his back each time they stopped to rest. He'd either develop a calloused back or he'd find some cloth padding to get the wood off his skin. He didn't know which would happen first.

At least his stumps were now completely covered in new skin. Though there were still some problems with having his arms in the metal caps while he jogged, such as Arno needing to clean out the sweat and dead skin crusted inside the metal, it was much better than getting an infection from open skin or exposed bone.

Arno interrupted Roran's thinking with a voiced thought of his own. "How long *has* Ardhataz been around?"

Roran grunted. He was not the historian of the family. "Well,

Griselda might have a better idea of that than I. But it hasn't been around as long as Wilheim."

"And how long has Wilheim been around?"

"No idea."

"Oh," Arno said, displeased that his curiosity wasn't being sated.

Looking to keep his brother entertained, Roran did the best he could to remember any of the histories he had heard in passing. "Wilheim's been around for practically forever. In fact, Ardhataz only came into existence because of Wilheim."

"Really?"

"Oh yeah," Roran said, glad to have a captive audience. "Wilheim never had a good idea about what to do with their prisoners. Grief Sickness made them scared of keeping jails, but they couldn't execute everyone either."

"Well, yeah," Arno agreed. "So, what did they do?"

"They made it someone else's problem," Roran said, jumping over a fallen branch. "They sent off their prisoners to the harsh mountains of the Ardhataz plateau, the highlands where nothing really grows, and there are few natural resources."

"That's mean too!" Arno said indignantly.

"I don't think they were concerned about the meanness of the punishment. They just didn't want to risk people suffering Grief Sickness on their own land. Not everyone who suffers develops it, and I don't know why some do and some don't, but Wilheim didn't want to take any risks, I'm guessing."

Arno sighed, and Roran could feel him adjusting in the harness. Each time Arno moved, Roran felt it as the harness rubbed more skin off his shoulders. Of course, Roran would never let Arno know.

"They probably hoped their prisoners would all die in the harsh lands," Roran continued, sucking in air and communicating each sentence on his breaths out. "Unfortunately for us, it made them much stronger. They're all originally from Wilheim, which is why they mostly speak our language."

"But you went through it, right?" Arno said, circling back. His interest was now more focused on his brother rather than the abstract history of centuries past. "The Grief Sickness? You had it, and they didn't send you away."

"I think they stopped exiling people there once we recognized Ardhataz as an official country."

"What was it like?"

"Huh?"

"The Grief Sickness?"

"Oh, umm . . . right, yeah. They stopped sending people to the highlands a while ago, once everyone united around . . ."

"Roran," Arno interrupted. "What was it like?"

"I . . . umm . . . well, not fun, I guess."

Other than Roran's footfalls at his gentle jog, silence lingered between the two. Then Roran's shoulders burned as Arno turned around in the harness. He leaned on Roran's shoulder as much as he could, staring at him with knitted eyebrows.

"I can guess that it was 'not fun,' Roran," Arno said flatly. "You know, with its name and all, that much is pretty clear. So, what happened?"

"I don't know; I don't really want to talk about it. You sure you don't want to know more about—"

"It's okay, Woe-Woe, you can tell me. I promise not to tell anyone else."

Roran slowed his pace to a walk. He had tried as much as he could to forget the whole thing. Like his father before him, he wanted very little to do with the whole business unless it was absolutely necessary. He didn't want to talk about him giving in, lying on the floor of a prison cell in a pool of his own blood as it oozed its way out of his pores like lava. Something he and Arno now had in common, lying in a pool of blood. He was going to end it all, and Arno could never know that. Roran would never let Arno think that the Way Out was an option.

"It's hard to describe, Arno," Roran said finally, "I don't really remember much about it."

Arno huffed. "You're lying, I can usually tell. You took too long to answer me."

"I don't know, Arno!" Roran burst. "It's hard to talk about. Just get off my back about it, okay?"

"I am strapped to your back," Arno said, a bit bemused. "I don't want to make you hurt again by talking about it. But Henrietta said that not talking about hard stuff could sometimes hurt someone just as much."

Roran sighed. "She talked to you a lot, didn't she?"

"Yeah, I think she was sad and wanted someone to talk to. Or maybe she talked to me because I was sad—or both. But whatever the reason, it helped. And if I'm going to be riding on your back, I need to know what to do if it happens again. Just like putting the Life Nectar on your arms and back, or cleaning out your metal caps, I need to be your healer while you get to be my horse."

"I'm not your horse . . . anyway . . . you do raise a good point."

Arno patted Roran on the top of his head. "Good horsey, you're starting to listen. You want a carrot?"

Roran rolled his eyes. "Alright, alright," Roran said. *But I only need to give him the aftermath. Not what caused it*, Roran thought. He picked back up to his steady jog. "I was sad, but you know, *really* sad, after seeing what they did to you. It caused my body to stop working and for me to sweat blood. I almost died, but the red man saved me somehow."

"Oh, that's good . . . I think," Arno said, scratching his head. "Speaking of that red man, who is he? What's his name?"

Roran paused to address Arno's question. What was that thing's name? "Umm, he doesn't have one."

"What do you mean he doesn't have a name?" asked Arno. "Everything has a name. Even your sword has a name."

"I mean just that. He doesn't have a name. He never thought of naming himself, and he won't accept any of the names I thought of," Roran said.

"Hmmm . . . seems rather odd. Maybe he'd like one of the names I could give him?"

"Well, Arno," Roran huffed as he lightly jogged along the path. "I don't want him around. We shouldn't name him like he's our friend. He's a monster, and he feeds off our lives."

Arno cracked his knuckles loud enough for Roran to hear it. Roran never thought he would miss the simple feeling of cracking his knuckles.

"Maybe you could *try* to be friends with him?" Arno said. "Seems like he could come in handy."

Roran cringed at the expression and then shivered at the thought of the thing's wicked, cynical laughter. "Arno, he ate my hands."

"Yeah, but . . . hmm," Arno wandered off into thought, but then his stomach growled. Food had been an issue as they traveled. Neither of them could really hunt, and they didn't know what was edible. The only positive was Roran's increased durability since he first transformed. He didn't seem as hungry as he thought he should be, somehow getting nutrients from another source.

"Arno," Roran said. "Put one of the berries in my mouth. I'll test them for you."

"Horses don't order their rider," Arno laughed. "But I guess I can feed you since you're being good."

Roran rolled his eyes again, but Arno couldn't see them from back in the harness. Roran rolled his eyes in the opposite direction to try it out. It didn't feel right.

Arno's hand appeared in front of Roran's mouth.

"Open wide!" Arno said and popped the berry in. "Good

horsey. I'll be sure to comb your mane," he said, yanking at Roran's tangled, messy hair.

"Would you cut that out!" Roran grumbled. He swallowed the berry and now would have to wait. He had been less incapacitated by poisonous berries, and so he had been tasting one or two for Arno, seeing how they impacted his digestion after a day or two, and then determining whether or not they were safe for Arno to eat. However, they were down to their last group of berries, not having found any trees bearing fruit in two days. But Roran didn't seem to notice the fatigue, despite carrying Arno and running through the woods. It troubled Roran to know where he was getting his energy from. If he had learned anything about the power and the red man, there was always a cost. *Come to think of it . . . Pops never had much of an appetite, either, for how much he worked.*

"How about Beans?"

Roran snapped back to focus on his conversation with Arno. "To eat?"

"No, his name," Arno suggested. "Beans make me fart. He seems to be full of hot, stinky air, too."

Roran chuckled. "I like your reasoning, but I don't think he'll go for it. He's too full of himself to settle with a name like Beans."

"Hmmm. Where is he, anyway? We haven't seen him since our home."

"I honestly don't know," Roran replied. "He mentioned something about having a longer tether from being around longer and getting stronger. Said that he could go as far as the Wilheim Academies while Pops was in the forge. He could be anywhere doing anything. I think he can sense when his food source is in danger and then come find us."

"You mean us? We're his food?"

" . . . yeah," Roran exhaled, uncomfortable with the thought.

"How about Rump Roast?"

"I seriously doubt he'll let you name him after a food. He thinks of us as food. He won't let us do it the other way around."

Arno pondered. "Well, why not? It's not like he can do anything to us. He wants to keep us alive, right? So that he can live too? If he's going to be rude to us, then I'm going to do the same to him. See how he likes it." Arno punctuated his thought by folding his arms and smiling resolutely.

"Arno, are you just thinking of food names because you're hungry?"

"No . . ." he said sheepishly.

"I don't think we're going to find anything more on this side of the river, so I think we'll cross and go to the proper trade routes. We should be far enough away from Wilheim by now." *I hope.*

"So, you'll look for a bridge or ferry?"

"Yeah, it's too big and deep for me to swim across. I don't think I could really swim anymore, even if I wanted to. Especially not with you on my back. But there's bound to be a way soon since we're getting close to Stedtfest."

"Uh-huh . . . hmmm . . . Roran?"

"Yeah, Arno?"

"How long have you been running?"

Roran breathed out, noticing he hadn't really been breathing as much as he should. "Umm . . . I guess all morning."

"And . . . you're not tired?"

Roran did a mental check of his body. His feet were fine, his muscles felt energized and alert rather than tired, he didn't feel like he was sucking down air. It felt like he could do this all day. "I guess not."

"Don't you hate running?"

"Well, no . . . I like sprinting, I hate running long distances . . . oh. Huh." Roran stopped his jog. "Now that you mention it, we should rest."

He sat down on a rock, and Arno undid the harness.

"Could you tend to my back?" Roran asked.

"Sure," Arno said.

Once out of the harness, Roran laid himself on the ground. Arno crawled over with Life Nectar in hand and lifted Roran's shirt.

"Well, that's funny," Arno said.

"What?"

"There's nothing wrong with the skin on your back. It's not like it has been the past few days. There's just two scars where the skin was rubbed off." Arno lowered Roran's shirt and climbed up to sit on the rock. "But that's okay. I have two scars on my back, too!"

Roran tried to block out the memory of his failed swords being used to brand Arno. That wasn't his fault. That was Zerebril's. Plus, something more concerning was bothering him.

Puzzled, Roran lay on the ground a little while. What was happening to his body? His body felt fine, but there was something else that felt off. Something deeper. He didn't fully feel like himself. Running long distances, not eating, not needing sleep or rest, seemingly forgetting that he needed to breathe sometimes, it seemed like the humanness of Roran was being sucked away and replaced with something else.

"Oooh," Arno giggled. "That's a funny-looking leaf! I think I'll hold on to this one."

Roran grinned. It was good to see that Arno, at least the most important part of him, was unchanged despite the harrowing experience of being imprisoned, getting branded for his brother's failures, then having his leg cut off.

"You eating dirt and grass down there?" Arno asked since Roran was still lying face down.

"I mean, I probably could, and nothing bad would happen."

Arno laughed. "What?"

"I seem to be . . . never mind."

"What? What!" Arno said, jostling Roran's shoulder with his one good leg.

With effort, Roran rolled onto his side in the leaves so that he could face Arno. Arno had a hungry smile on his face, ready for new information to digest. With Arno on his back for so much of the time, it did Roran good to see his beaming, overeager smile.

Roran sighed and pushed the fear of the changes away for now. "Well, Arno," he said. "If I can eat grass . . . maybe I really am becoming a horse."

Arno awkwardly lunged off the rock and fell on top of his brother in his signature dogpile. "Woe-Woe's becoming a Horse-Horse!" Arno laughed.

"Careful! Knock it off!" Roran said, trying to hold in the laughter while concerned that his brother could hurt himself on one of Roran's metal caps.

"Woe-Woe's becoming a Horse-Horse," Arno continued to tease and now tried to tickle Roran, who couldn't do much to grab and throw Arno off of him.

"Arno . . ." Roran struggled. Though Roran was being tickled, this was no longer funny. He was trapped, pinned down . . . "Arno!"

Arno continued, seeming not to notice Roran's change in tone, his deepening voice. Trapped, pinned down, watching Arno, helpless, as a sword was raised over his brother's leg. Hack. Roran was sweating. Hack. His pulse was pounding in his head. Hack. He shut his eyes.

"That's enough!" Roran bellowed and shoved Arno off. Roran's voice echoed throughout the woods, and when it came back to Roran's ears, it didn't sound like his normal voice. It sounded ominous, like metal grinding on metal.

He shook his head and quickly got on his knees, realizing he had just shoved his little brother. Hard. Arno had landed several feet away and banged his little head on a thick tree trunk.

Roran jumped to his feet and rushed over to Arno, who was rubbing his hand against the back of his head and grimacing.

Seeing Roran lumbering toward him, Arno yelped and scooted back away from Roran around the tree trunk until his back hit the large rock where the harness still sat. The terror in Arno's face crushed Roran's heart.

"Arno, I'm sorry! I didn't mean to . . ."

"You're not a horse, Roran," Arno said in a small, quiet voice. "Horses don't push their brothers away. Horses are nice. They eat carrots out of my hands."

Roran's pulse returned to normal as he let out the breath he had been holding. Arno was okay, even if Roran was becoming less and less of himself. "I'm sorry . . . I am really, really sorry, Arno."

"Saying 'really' *really* doesn't make it mean more. You remember what dad used to call you, right? Do you *really* want to be that?"

Da angriest man in da world, Roran heard Cormac say. But looking at Arno's lack of leg, he had one more legitimate reason to be angry, even if he didn't want to be.

"I . . . I know," Roran said, walking over to sit next to Arno, both of their backs leaning against the rock.

He breathed in deeply and let himself look up at the blue sky just barely visible through the branches of the monstrously tall trees.

"Arno?"

"What?"

"If I keep . . . changing . . . can you promise me something?"

Arno was quiet for a second but eventually nodded.

"I'm carrying something inside me. I don't think it's always a good thing. I think it eats away at things, at me, at my surroundings. I don't know what it is going to do to me. But as long as you don't change, I hope I won't change either. I know it's a lot to ask you, and I keep having to do it, ask things of you, but can you promise me you won't change?"

Arno chuckled. "You're silly sometimes, Woe-Woe. Of course we're both going to change. I have to grow and stuff. You grow too, just much faster, and redder, and you shrink back down afterward."

Roran smiled. "See, that's what I'm talking about. You stay who you are, and I'll do my best to stay me. Deal?"

"Deal!"

CHAPTER 16
RODRICK THE MERCHANT

WITH HER GREEN hood up over her head, Griselda became hyper-aware of the thick rain drops thudding against the cloth. Her wet clothes clung to her skin as she climbed aboard the back of the wagon. Three other passengers were in the wagon bound for Wilheim.

Griselda had decided it was time she come out of hiding. She wasn't sure how, but she needed to do something to free her brothers from the dungeon. And she didn't want to be anywhere where she could be hunted again.

She was wearing her last good pair of clothes scavenged from the raided caravan. She had to dispose of the others she was wearing once she realized they were soaked in blood. Her left arm itched as her skin scabbed over the burn scars.

End March was being concealed in the water-resistant tarp that made her tent. It was tightly bound several times to stifle the glow the sword emitted. Though the sword was no longer lighting up her surroundings, it's massive handle, ornate pommel, and long quillons with the ring guards all poked out the top of the wrap. Many people would be able to tell by the size of the weapon and the craft of the exposed parts that it was expensive, just not how expensive it was.

Griselda unslung her backpack and set it down next to her on the wooden bench, the pan hooked on its outside rattling as she did. She rested the long bundle of sword across her lap and looked at the other three passengers. It was harder to trust strangers, now that a few of them had tried to kill her. And she had to kill them.

Griselda could see her breath in the cold rain. She wrapped her arms around herself and permitted a shiver.

Though she had practiced swordplay with Roran, she never imagined she would have to use a sword on another human being.

The faces of the other three passengers were concealed as well, visible cold breath escaping their hoods at varying intervals. As far as she could tell, the two seated across from her, a man and a woman, were a couple. They were both snoring, which could be heard over the rain, presumably having been on the wagon for quite some time. There was another man seated next to her opposite her backpack. He was rounder with a pointed beard that attempted to cover his double chin. He had a heavy red cloak wrapped around himself, covering any kind of clothing that might indicate his occupation to Griselda. He eyed the sword handle but said nothing, quickly glancing at Griselda when he thought she wasn't looking and then switching back to looking down at his own pudge.

His glances made Griselda sweat despite the cold rain. *Based on his rotund stature, I would easily win if he tried anything,* Griselda thought, gripping the handle of End March. *If it came down to it, I could kill him. But why am I thinking like that? Judging whether or not I could and would have to kill people?*

She screwed her eyes shut. Their bloody faces appeared again. Only for a fraction of a moment, like the bright afterimage of the sun if she carelessly looked up at the sky after emerging from the family cottage. But they were still there, and Griselda feared they would never be banished, never quite leave her alone ever again. She would never be able to close her eyes and not see them briefly, never lie down to sleep and wonder if anyone was outside in the dark with clothes from corpses and sharpened blades.

As the wagon rolled down the well-worn path through the woods, Griselda attempted to quiet her mind. She failed. She didn't like that her back was exposed to a wide expanse of dark forest, a forest capable of hiding grizzled men with hollow eyes. Her heartbeat hadn't slowed down since she lit that man on fire, heard his threats then his screams. Cooked food hadn't smelled the same since and, against her better judgment and the book's advice, she had been eating more and more of the berries.

She needed a distraction, so she pulled out Rufus Redaway's commentary on *The Marches*. The rain was beginning to subside, making it somewhere between a gentle drizzle and a fine mist depending on the tree cover, so Griselda needed only to hold a sliver of her cloak in the air over the book to keep it from getting wet.

She had finished the introduction which then put her at the oldest March, *The March from Pain*. However, from the little she remembered of this March, she recalled it was not a fun read. The language was archaic, even after attempts at translation; the author was sparse in describing things and assumed the reader would know other things impossible to decipher countless years later. The book often depicted events happening and then not giving any sort of reflection as to what they meant. And the content of the story was downright miserable. A king had tried to save his people, failed, watched his world end, was kidnapped, tried to rebuild his old civilization in a new place, and then saw his new world end again with a volcanic cataclysm. It was *not* the story she needed to quiet her mind.

She skipped ahead to the chronological next March, *The*

March of Joy. Rather than following the story of a singular miserable individual like *The March from Pain* does, *The March of Joy* was a collection of parables and stories by different authors about different historical events and figures all attempting to communicate how to live a fulfilling life in the face of the pain so odiously detailed in the first March.

The first story, by an unknown author with an unknown context and motive, cataloged a story of people living in a cave complex from the third-person point of view. Rufus Redaway's footnotes had little to offer regarding the rhetorical situation surrounding the story other than that it was hypothesized that the survivors of the Lake Verdin volcanic cataclysm would have had to be underground if there was anyone in the area at all. Redaway noted that a heavy layer of ash pervaded the soil surrounding Verdin at certain levels when building projects required deeper foundations. He suspected that when the ash was in the air, it would have made living above ground nearly impossible.

Griselda turned the page. The fat man in red glanced over, assumedly trying to see what she was reading. Griselda clenched her teeth at his unsubtle gaze.

But she pressed on with the opening of the first story. Originally, it was unnamed, but Redaway had named it "The Parable of the Cave Dwellers: An Ancient Etymology for Verdin Burial Rites and the Founding of Wilheim."

Redaway had translated the story from an archaic form of the language that would evolve into the modern tongue spoken across the Wilheim Peninsula and Ardhataz. On one side of the book, Redaway had translated the text as literally as possible, retaining the old idioms and idiosyncrasies. On the other page, Redaway had updated the text line by line for a modern reader.

They hit a large bump, and the woman's head lilted onto her husband's shoulder.

"Do you want to know what happens in the story?"

Griselda's eyes snapped up to the large man swaddled in his red cloak. She tensed and said nothing.

The chubby man knitted his eyebrows, seemingly not expecting Griselda's hostile posture and silence. "Well, it's actually quite pleasant. It was a favorite of my father's. He used to tell it to me as a bedtime story." He paused, searching Griselda's expression, and then smiled, seeing if he could put her at ease. He wouldn't, but he seemed determined to try. "But that was many years ago . . . and many, many more pounds ago. Ha!" He said, slapping his stomach.

Griselda opened her mouth to respond but then thought better of it and looked back down at her book.

"Did I almost get a chuckle? Self-deprecation usually breaks the ice . . . at least, that's what Fortinbras said."

Griselda's mouth hung open as it dawned on her why this large man was trying to talk to her.

"Recognize the name? He wrote *Trading Trades: Craft, Commodities, and Crooks*, which I suspect you are also carrying."

Her hand moved back to the handle of End March.

"Woah, woah, woah!" he said with his hands in the air. "You can keep them! I left the books for a reason. I had already memorized the best parts, you see. Didn't think they were worth carrying over some of the other items in the caravan."

Griselda took her hand off the blade and put it back on the page of the book. "I'm . . . I'm sorry for your loss. It looked brutal, the wreckage of your caravan."

He shrugged his shoulders. "It happens. I grew up in the warring nations of the west before my father and mother sent me to the Wilheim Academies. I got used to bloodshed at a young age."

Used to bloodshed? Griselda thought. *How? Did that mean that this unassuming, fat man had killed people? Or watched people die frequently? And got used to that sight?*

"Part of the reason my father told me that story was to comfort me after a raid when people we knew died. It provides a rather optimistic take on death, or at least," he huffed, "gives our corpses a purpose in the aftermath. That's all we can truly know anyway."

She looked back up at him after being jostled by another bump. "Fine," Griselda said. "The ride is too bumpy for me to do any serious reading. What happens?"

He smiled, recognizing the permission to keep flapping his fleshy lips. "The descendants of the Red King were hiding underground after the sky turned black and everything got cold. It was far colder for far longer than it should have been. The air was poisonous, and they hadn't seen the sun in months. The young died of starvation, the old died of asphyxiation, or at least that's Redaway's guess. The new leader, Ilir, the grandson of the Red King, led his people into these strange caves that had glowing stones embedded into the walls. Though they could breathe, and see in the dark thanks to the glowing rocks, and build new homes in the cave without the ash collapsing their roofs, they were all still starving."

Griselda's stomach rumbled and she really hoped this man didn't hear it. She didn't want him to offer her any of his food, of which she expected he had plenty stashed away in the inner pockets of his cloak. The berries had not been enough lately. She spoke up hoping to distract from the rumbling noises. "So, how did they solve that problem?"

"You assume they solved it?" He responded with a wry smile.

"Well, of course, someone had to live to pass on the story."

"That," he said raising his index finger into the air, "is only a valid argument if you believe that this story is historical and not merely some fireside chronicler's fancy."

Griselda rolled her eyes, "Well?"

"They didn't solve the problem. They kept dying."

"And?" Griselda mockingly asked, knowing there was something more to the story. "This is in *The March of Joy* after all; it can't end with everyone dying." *Could it?*

"You do realize that everybody dies eventually, right?" he chuckled.

Griselda huffed, irritation showing in the red cheeks beneath her freckles. "Yes. I would appreciate it if you didn't treat me like some child," she said. "Like you, I . . . I already am well-acquainted with death. But that's not the point of stories. If they are happy stories, they stop telling what happened before the heroes die. If they are sad, they tell the stories up to the hero's death."

"And what about the stories that tell what happens after the hero dies?"

Griselda frowned. "Well, then he must not have been the real hero of the story. Just some sad sod who died before the happy end another character got to experience."

The fat man smiled deviously. "That's where you're wrong . . . Ilir was definitely meant to be the hero of this story."

"Just get on with it then!" Griselda shouted, a little louder than she meant to. She looked over to the couple across the wagon and was relieved to find that they had not been disturbed.

The man shrugged. "Fine, fine. Ilir and his family started to take the dead bodies of the starved and place them in a more remote part of the cave system. They were starting to smell, and the people feared the disease their bodies could bring. Fever can hit much harder when you've been hungry for weeks."

Griselda nodded, trying to ignore the large vacancy in her stomach.

"Ilir and his family took the bodies to a section of the cave they found that glowed the brightest, hoping it would guide whatever remained of his friends and family on the next leg of the March. The cavern was so bright from all the glowing walls it might as well have been daylight, like the sun never left them and decided to instead set into the cave and stay there until the sky cleared up.

"After that, Ilir tried to find alternative food sources, but nothing seemed to live or grow in the cave network. They were able to get by for a while off of newts and small rodents that found their way into the caves, but they ran out of even the small critters eventually. They started eating their shoe leather, their pet dogs, anything they could. They were safe from the volcanic aftermath, but they would all still starve in the soft glow of the caves. Ilir decided he would venture back out of the caves to see if the sun had returned but found that the exit had collapsed by the weight of ashfall. Only a small gap was large enough that children could fit through. They were far too weak by this point to open it farther and they couldn't risk it collapsing more by trying to widen the opening. So, Ilir sent his daughter, Amalie, who was only eight, along with the other children of the survivors, out back into the sunless sky of the overworld."

Griselda imagined Arno trying to lead a pack of children through a land of ash. She doubted he would have the presence of mind to figure out how to survive and lead. At least, not as she currently knew him. Maybe when he was older.

"The children were forced to abandon their parents to certain death in the caves. Not that their fate seemed much better. But, as you suspected, this is *The March of Joy* after all. Amalie eventually found a village that had been protected somewhat by the ashfall, as it was in the crook of a mountain range. They were still surviving off their livestock. Amalie told the villagers about their parents. After they were fed and rested, Amalie, the children, and a few kind villagers took their tools back to the cave entrance and tried to widen the hole.

"Eventually, they did. Amalie ran back into the glowing caves, but to her dismay, nobody was there. Their cave homes still stood, but everyone had vanished. There were no bodies or any signs of life. Amalie took the group to the edge of the complex, where her father Ilir would take the bodies just to make sure they had checked every corridor for their parents. And that's when they found their salvation: mushrooms. Glowing, edible mushrooms. It was a miracle! So many mushrooms that it could feed the children and the remnants of the villagers above the caves for months. Their parents must have found a way to grow them and then escaped the caves once they got their strength back. Amalie brought the mushrooms to the village in the crook of the mountains and would make weekly trips back to the caves to collect more of the mushrooms as they seemed to keep growing. Amalie continued to hold the room sacred and bring the dead there, hoping her father Ilir would one day return to the caves to bury his dead and find her there. And so, Amalie, the children, and the villagers continued to live nearby in the crook of the mountains which would later become Wilheim. They outlived the constant dark clouds and the sun once again shone down on the land. For her bravery, Amalie is known as one of the beacons of Wilheim, and one of the bonfire pits in the city squares is named after her as well as her father."

Griselda sighed. "They didn't know, did they?"

"What, that the children's parents didn't escape the caves?" the man laughed. "That Amalie was likely eating the fungus growing from her parent's bodies? No. It doesn't seem the author made that connection, or if he did, he never directly stated it. According to Redaway, who also noticed the implications of what they were eating, the author chose to focus on the fact that Amalie survived what her parents could not by escaping to a new home, a message that seemed to stay important to our people and carried over from *The March Through Pain* and later into *The March Through the Mountain Pass*. That's what 'Wilheim' means, after all, in the old script. The want for a new home."

Griselda regarded the man for a second, who seemed to grow a little more somber. "Your parents didn't escape to Wilheim either, did they?"

He shrugged. "Who knows? I have trade deals in my hometown, but I've never run into them again. I've built a trade empire spanning the Peninsula and across the lake," the man said, raising his chin higher in bravado. "But . . . none of my sources said they ever found them. One day, maybe, if I expand my network to Ardhataz and beyond, then I'll find them again."

Griselda felt her eyes getting misty. She would never see her parents again, either. And now all she had left was a fool's hope of saving her brothers if they were still in Wilheim. She looked back down to her lap at the book sitting on top of End March and closed it.

"In these times," he said, "with the Tazzes coming, I think it's important we stick together."

Griselda looked over at the chubby, bearded man. He was still staring at her sword, but with an unreadable expression. His hand up in the air as if he was going to place his hand on her shoulder.

"Excuse you," she huffed. "I don't need to be comforted." Griselda wiped her eyes.

The man made a show of haughtily exhaling. "Fortinbras was wrong again. Vulnerability would not win any maidens."

Griselda screwed up her face in disgust. *Was that all an act?* "Not if you're using vulnerability like it's some sort of tool, you piglet."

The fat man blew raspberries, seeming more horselike than piglike. "Fine. I guess the game is up. What are you doing with a sword like that then?"

"It's not for sale," Griselda said. She tried to be very firm to discourage whatever the man was thinking.

"Everything can be bought, but I'm not so much as interested in the weapon as I am the one who wields it."

Griselda pulled a knife out of her pack and pointed it at the man.

"Woah! I didn't mean I was interested in you for *that* reason .
. . although—"

Griselda stretched out her arm until the knife was at the
man's double chin.

"Point taken! Now if you please, take your point away from
my neck. I won't make any further advances or comments about
your attractiveness."

Griselda drew her arm back from him but still held the knife.
The nerve of this man, she thought. *He's a merchant after all; I
should have expected him to manipulate me from the start.*

"Oros's wings, girl, you're trying to make my heart explode
or something . . . huw-wee," said the chubby man, trying to
regain his breath. "What I was trying to imply, is that I'm interested in hiring more guards. My two best guards were
conscripted into Prince Zerebril's service. But . . . I suppose I
can't run my business if Ardhataz sets everything on fire, so fair
trade. I have back-up mercs, but they are otherwise occupied at
the Academies for the meantime."

Griselda raised an eyebrow. *This man thinks that I'm a
mercenary?*

"Anyway, with the twins gone, more of my caravans have
been raided. Which is, of course, why I'm riding this humble
wagon with you now. I'd pay well for your protection," he said,
nodding at the covered End March.

Griselda tried to hide her fear. *What does he know about this
weapon?*

"My name is Rodrick. As you can guess, I'm a merchant," he
said, trying to ease Griselda back into the conversation. He cast a
quick, shifty look over at the sleeping couple. "I run caravans
between Wilheim, Stedtfest, The Purple Coast, Port Maw, and all
the small port towns running along the west side of Lake Verdin.
You might have heard of me. I'm very famous round these
parts."

Another bump in the road. Griselda said nothing. Instead, she indicated she wanted him to keep talking by raising both eyebrows and looking expectantly at him.

"Stone wall, huh? No matter, I'm usually the one running my mouth anyway. That's my business. Yours is the swinging . . . with the sword, I mean. Curse me for my innuendos," he said slapping himself in the forehead. "To be clear, you would be hired to protect my caravans from bandits on their routes. The job is not easy, and the pay matches its difficulty. For someone wielding a blade like that, the going rate is 200 silver Wilheim coins per week."

Griselda failed to keep her eyes from bulging out of her head. Cormac's family was not without means; she had taken a purse of ten gold coins, which equaled 1,000 silver, from Cormac's stash at home. However, she suspected they should be significantly richer given the price of the blades. Cormac must have it squirreled away in something. But making 200 silver per week on her own was incredibly lucrative, especially for someone with no official tradesman skills.

"I'm guessing that bought your attention," Rodrick said, smiling.

He must know about the sword. Had Griselda met this man before? Did he say twin guards? Her memory was fuzzy, but she did remember Cormac and Roran making another set of twin swords for a customer last year. Nevertheless, no matter how tempting the offer . . .

"I—" Griselda hesitated. "I can't."

Rodrick didn't even flinch. Griselda guessed this was a man accustomed to getting turned down but finding a way to weasel into a deal anyway.

"Can't because . . . ?"

"For a number of reasons . . . the first being I'm not a trained fighter."

"Ha, good one. You don't need to be a trained fighter with one of those," he said nodding at End March.

"What do you mean 'one of those'?"

Rodrick scoffed. "Girl, you're not fooling me. A blade that big isn't put in a scabbard. There's only one reason why you would laboriously cover it like that: the glow. You bundled it up so much it would take you ages to get it out and actually use it. My twin guards also had the weapons. Your secret's safe with me. I'm not going to give any more to Zerebril; he's got enough of my things. Taxes and such. Taking my twins and such. Spiteful, artsy little dung hill of a prince, and such," he muttered to himself.

Though this was intended to relax Griselda, it did not. She grabbed the handle of the blade reflexively and started to scan the woods surrounding the wagon. She had been practicing flourishing the blade every day since she was attacked by bandits, getting a feel for what the sword was capable of and how fast she would need to swing it before it created those dreadful flames. Even with lengthy practice sessions, reading no longer being a priority, she was not comfortable enough with the sword. All her muscles tensed as she thought she saw movement in the forest nearby.

"Easy girl, it's alright. Honestly, what can anyone do to you while you're holding that? So, what's the other reason why you *think* you can't accept the offer?"

Griselda swallowed and refocused her gaze on Rodrick. "My family is in danger. I'm heading to Wilheim to buy their freedom."

A glimmer of recognition passed over Rodrick's face. "Oh . . . oh no," he said with a chuckle and wobble of his chins. "It's you, isn't it? The missing daughter of Cormac."

"Shhh!" Griselda said, thrusting the knife back out toward his neck. Griselda looked at the couple who still seemed sound asleep. She then checked the man steering the horse at the front of the wagon. He didn't seem to pay any attention to what was going on behind him, probably a learned skill. The less he knew about the travelers, the safer he'd be.

Rodrick held up his hands. "Like I said, you could easily kill me and everyone here, and everyone in the forest seven times over before anyone was able to draw a blade. I'm on your side. I think it's terrible what they did to your family."

"What do you know?"

He sighed, hands still raised. "Listen, girl, you don't want to hear it from me. I'm not the most . . . skilled with bad news. But I'm sheltering someone on the inside who can give you the details. Assuming you, one, don't send me to the next leg of the March; and two, take a tour of my estate in Wilheim. My source is there and is paying very well to locate a boat across Lake Verdin."

Griselda pulled the knife back.

"And three, stop trying to shave my beard with your knife whenever I say something you don't like, girl. I tend to make some unfiltered remarks, and I'd hate to have a dagger at my throat anytime I open my mouth."

Griselda stared at the man in deliberation. Though he was repulsive and a stranger, he seemed relatively harmless, just another person in danger of losing his way of life as Ardhataz approached. She still didn't trust him, but he was unlikely to hurt her. He was also a lead, a lead that could get her brothers free.

Griselda shrugged. "Might as well. I'm on my way there anyway and should see all options. My name is Griselda, so please stop calling me 'girl.'"

"Fair enough," Rodrick said.

"But," Griselda said, closing her eyes as if bracing for a blow, "could you at least tell me if they are alive?"

Rodrick shrugged. "That's the thing. Nobody knows—" Rodrick was cut off as a blur of movement approached the wagon from behind.

Griselda tensed but then slowly, with great effort, relaxed as a red puff of fur jumped into the wagon.

Rodrick almost fell back out of the wagon. "What in the blazing belly of Oros—"

"Oh, hush," Griselda said, smiling.

The fox jumped up into her lap and laid down on top of End March. He looked up at her expectantly.

"This is Gunter, who apparently thinks he's my pet fox now. Or at least thinks that I'm his food dispenser. Trouble is . . ." Griselda sighed and looked over at Rodrick. She would ask if it was for Gunter. She could live with that. "I've run out of food. You don't happen to have any jerky tucked in that cloak, do you?"

"What? Pet? Gunter? No! No food at all," Rodrick said crossing his arms.

"Please . . ." Griselda said. She put her head behind the fox who was now also looking over at Rodrick. Together, Griselda was convinced that their sad pairs of eyes could pull at the heartstrings of any human alive. But that relied on Rodrick being human.

"Do you think your pouts could buy me? Do you think me some sap that would bend over for any cute pairs of eyes that looked at me and begged?"

Griselda sighed. That's right, Rodrick wasn't human. He was a merchant. And he already admitted to being desensitized long before he became a trader on the open road. "Fine, a trade then," Griselda grumbled.

"Good, you're a quick learner," Rodrick smiled. "I will feed you if you promise to protect me on our way to Wilheim. Don't want you running off and leaving me to the screw-turning scourges robbing my caravans in these hills if we see any trouble."

"Both of us. You'll feed both of us," Griselda nodded at the fox.

Rodrick blew another horse-ish raspberry between his meaty lips. He pulled out a chunk of deer jerky from his cloak, tore it in half, and handed the chunks over to Griselda.

Griselda let a giggle slip as Gunter ate one of the pieces out of her hand. She quickly stuffed the remaining chunk in her own mouth. "Deal," she said as she chewed the tough meat. "I'll protect you on our way to Wilheim, but that's it."

"We'll see," Rodrick scoffed. "You might grow to like what I have to offer."

CHAPTER 17
VANGUARD

ZEREBRIL WAITED in the war room, fists clenched in his gauntlets. He had been informed that scouts had spotted Carl and four others on their way to Stedtfest.

About time, he thought. *But only four?*

He had not wanted to dam the river, as it had just as many consequences as it did benefits. Once the normal pathway was blocked, the river had fanned out in a ninety-degree spread, flooding the forest, the fields, and parts of Stedtfest itself. It also partially flooded the hundred-yard gap of traps between the tree stands and Stedtfest, making the whole place a muddy pit. In response, Zerebril set down a number of planks from the town entrance to the trees that could be pulled in quickly or lit with oil and set on fire in case the enemy slipped past their scouts. This wooden pathway would make sure that Zerebril could lead a cavalry charge as soon as Carl sent his falcon, without being slowed down nearly as much as the enemy was.

Zerebril tapped his fingers on the table. Only four bearers of Cormac's weapons were available from the description the scouts gave, other than Carl himself. He knew that Rodrick's twin guards were two of the four, which meant two more had joined as well. That would have to be enough. However, there were hardly any warriors who proved a capable match to Gunter; he had held off an entire battalion until Ewen's beasts came. Zerebril was told by the retreating rearguard that his brother lit everything on fire, slew five of the beasts, then was killed by another five. Math was unreliable for battlefield outcomes, but, theoretically, five bearers could bring down twenty-five beasts, maybe more since they would be prepared for them and not exhausted from fending off a battalion.

A knock came at the door.

"Enter," said Zerebril.

One of the twins pushed open the door. They both wore green brigandine matching the colors of Wilheim's troops, had shoulder-length brown hair, and wore the same unreadable expression. If Zerebril remembered correctly, they were named Arthur and Dale. They were sons of one of Wilheim's professors, but they were attacked while the professor was visiting Ardhataz. Their father was killed, and the twins were sold into slavery, fighting in the Highland Pits until they bought their freedom and returned to Wilheim. They were enlisted by one of the richest merchants, that slime-ball Rodrick, who had heard of their reputation as fighters and outfitted them with Cormac weapons.

They came in without a word and sat at the table. They are almost as stoic and silent as Carl, preferring to only communicate with each other through stern looks. *Great*, Zerebril thought, *more Carls*.

They were followed by a girl a little older than Zerebril himself, maybe early twenties. She had short blonde hair, cut boyishly like Zerebril's. She was laughing at some joke Zerebril had not heard. However, unlike Zerebril, she was outfitted more like the twins, with a green brigandine and not full plate. He had no idea how she could be laughing with such a sour crowd. Still giggling, she sat down at the table without addressing Zerebril in any way. It seemed like all three of them were pretending that Zerebril didn't exist.

Oh, Zerebril thought, *that's why she's laughing. Connor is here.*

Unlike the previous three, Connor did wear full plate. He had a broad smile, short brown hair, and was taller than the other three. He had a green tunic over his plate with the Wilheim sun emblazoned on it. Despite the Wilheim colors, the reddish-brown short beard indicated he had Ardhatazian heritage. Zerebril was unsure how the other members of the group would feel about his ethnicity, given who they were fighting, but if Zerebril knew anything about Connor, and unfortunately, he did, Connor wouldn't let a matter like that hinder him from charming the trousers and dresses off everyone in a mile vicinity.

Though there was another complication: Connor's father was a renowned slaver. Though slavery was outlawed in Wilheim, Connor's father, Machaze, had made quite a business in Ardhataz before sending his son to the Wilheim Academies, which is how, regretfully, Zerebril knew him.

Zerebril mostly kept to himself during his stay at the academies; however, Connor had gotten drunk almost every night. He was lively, intoxicating, and jolly despite his father's wretched business practices. These were all qualities Zerebril did not have, but he also didn't see much use for talents involving being good at parties. When Zerebril took the poppy's mercy, he did it alone so he could stifle the world; he did not do it to socialize.

Eventually, Connor was kicked out of the Wilheim Academies and showed his other talents instead, namely his fighting prowess. He had bought a Cormac mace with his father's slaving money. But he wasn't wearing it on his belt.

Zerebril's face reddened as he saw Gunter's sword slung over Connor's back. Zerebril jumped up from his seat and slammed his gauntleted hands on the table. "Why? Why do *you* have my brother's sword!" Zerebril yelled.

Connor kept laughing at whatever joke he had made before they entered. "Oh, Z, please stop calling it Gunter's sword. He's dead. You might want to learn to live with it. Plus, I've named it."

"You what?!"

"Oh, that's the funny part," the girl said. "He named it . . . he named it Professor Mathilda!" She slipped into another round of laughing.

"That's right," said Connor, looking at the girl and enjoying his ability to make her laugh. "The rugged, beautiful woman was the only one to have stabbed me in my heart. Now I will use this sword to stab many more."

"Yes, yes . . ." The girl continued through her laughing. "He asked her out and she called it off after one date."

"I got a kiss," Connor said defensively. "It was just not meant to be, being that I was her student at the time. She still wasn't interested after I was kicked out, either."

Carl, hanging back in the doorway, shoulders and torso obscured fully by a heavy cloak, and muttering to himself, said, "I heard that was a fabricated story. There wasn't a kiss."

Zerebril was visibly shaking with anger. He leaned forward on the table to steady his trembling arms. Though this stopped the shaking, it did not drown out the sound of his heartbeat or the veins pulsing in his forehead.

"Yeesh, Zerebril," Connor said, finally looking at Zerebril intently. "You look like you could use a drink. Maybe something a bit stronger, if you like."

"You tried to date our professor?! Never mind, why do you have . . . *Professor Mathilda*?"

Even the twins were shaking their heads in disapproval.

"Carl traded it to me, seeing that he can't use it anymore. I traded him my mace, Dean Macbrick, the only man to have broken my heart."

The girl stopped laughing and raised an eyebrow.

"He expelled me; I didn't try to date him," Connor said, shrugging.

"I'm not calling it that," said Carl, who kicked the door shut. Sure enough, the glowing mace, Dean Macbrick, was hung in Carl's belt.

"What is this?" Zerebril said, walking over to Carl. "You have a band of maniacs and vagabonds with you." Internally, Zerebril winced as he said that. If Carl was the preferred person out of this batch, they were treading deep in Oros's dung.

"I heard that!" said Connor. He seated himself next to the girl, and they whispered about Zerebril conspiratorially.

The heavy dark green cloak over Carl's shoulders shifted and slid around unnaturally. Maybe it was too big and needed more brooches?. He had the hood down so that all the world could plainly see his scowl. "If you want the job done," Carl growled, "then these are the people you want. Mercs with a reputation and needing the gold coins you promised."

"Speaking of which, where is this fabled gold treasure trove of yours?" asked Connor, stretching and placing his arm around the girl's shoulder.

Carl answered before Zerebril could. "It's not *his*," Carl leered. "We got the fortune from Cormac after raiding his house."

Zerebril sighed as Carl tossed a large purse onto the table. Its thud echoed around the room and the coins spilled out. "There's forty Wilheim gold coins in it for each of you," Carl said.

The girl's face paled. "That's a year's worth of caravan duty!"

Connor scoffed, "Sophia, please, you're being swindled if that's all you make in a year in your line of work. You're worth more than that. Who's your employer?"

Zerebril ignored Connor. "For one battle, this is more than enough. You're being paid four times more than a general. But the risk is also great."

"From what I hear, it's suicide minus the Life Nectar. That's not even mentioning having to worry about the rest of these idiots lighting me on fire in the process. Except for you, Sophia," Connor corrected after receiving a hurt look from Sophia. She shook his arm off her shoulder, and Connor rolled his eyes.

Carl walked behind Connor and made a point to kick his chair leg very hard as he passed. Carl sat down on the opposite side of Sophia, who was visibly uncomfortable as soon as the cloaked, scowling man sat down.

Zerebril took his seat at the head of the table, the twins on his right and Carl, Sophia, and Connor on his left.

Two servants carrying a tray of food entered once Carl had unclogged the doorway. They set the pig roast down on the table with carrots and onions surrounding the pig.

"Oh, it's about time!" Connor said. "I've eaten nothing but potatoes for three days on our way here!" Connor hopped up and immediately set to carving the roast.

"So, Carl has already told you the plan?" Zerebril asked.

"Shhh . . . not now, Z," Connor said as he continued to cut and then serve the food to everyone at the table. "Food first. Food always comes first. Schemes later. I don't think straight on an empty stomach."

"Affirmative," Arthur said.

"He gets angry without food," said Dale.

"He stops making jokes and just starts trying to fight people," Arthur said, shaking his head.

"Tried to fight me already," said Dale in agreement.

"You probably deserved it," said Connor, plating onions and carrots alongside the cut meat. "What were we fighting about again?"

Dale rolled his eyes and held his tongue. Having Connor forget an argument was usually the best one could hope for. The trademark Ardhatazian stubbornness and temper ran hot in his blood.

Zerebril sighed and accepted the plate that Connor offered him. Once Connor had served everyone a plate, he pushed the whole hog over to his spot on the table and started eating from it while it was still on the platter.

The entire room paused, mouths open to stare as Connor downed the rest of the meat at double the speed.

The nerve of this man, Zerebril scowled. He looked around to see Carl scowling, too. *Oh great, Connor's antics are turning ME into Carl.*

"Do you chew your food?" asked Sophia, who was still staring as Connor made a spectacle of the amount and speed at which he ate.

"Oh, sure," Connor said between bites. "For the big chunks, I do. But chewing isn't always necessary for the smaller chunks."

Sophia scooted away from Connor and looked like she was going to be sick.

"You should see Professor Mathilda eat. There was a woman after my own heart . . ." he shoved in another hunk of pig. "She wouldn't even talk until her plate was clean. Made the date a little odd for the first bit, but she was done in under a minute—"

"Alright, enough," Zerebril growled. "No more talk about our professor. We're here for Stedtfest now. So, Carl, you told them, right?"

Carl scowled. "I wouldn't ask them to do it without telling them what it would cost."

Zerebril nodded. "Then you'll do it?"

The twins nodded. Apparently finished with his food, Connor pushed the pig back to the center of the table so he could put his feet up on it instead. He leaned back in his chair but also nodded when Zerebril looked over at him.

"That's why they're here," said Carl.

"Good. According to my reports, King Ewen should be approaching within two days. The dammed river slowed him down, but it has not stopped him. The success of this entire operation lays in your . . . capable hands." Zerebril shuddered at the thought of leaving the fate of Wilheim and Stedtfest to the likes of Connor, who couldn't be relied upon to wake up before noon.

"As soon as they make camp," Zerebril continued, "you'll launch your assault. Worry only about killing the beasts and then send the falcon once they're all dead. One of you and myself will come with the cavalry once their advantage has been taken, and you can safely retreat. I don't want you swinging those weapons of yours with my cavalry nearby."

"Whoa, Z. You're riding into battle too?" asked Connor. "Almost brings a tear to my eye. I never thought I'd see the day."

Zerebril ignored Connor. He still wasn't sure if he should ride into battle. He'd be almost entirely useless, but could he make these people sacrifice themselves if he wasn't putting his own life on the line? Could he trust them if he wasn't personally out there? Zerebril shook his head and asked, "Does this plan seem reasonable?"

Sophia shrugged. "Makes sense to me."

The twins exchanged a look and then nodded.

"Is that all then?" Connor asked. "I've never been to Stedt-fest, and I want to check out the local flavor in case the town's a scorch mark in a couple of days." Connor looked around at the wooden logs framing the square room. "Frankly, I'm not impressed with their woodwork on the building designs. Sturdy for sure, but there's no flair at all. It's not like we're going to lose a cultural hub even if Ewen flattens the place."

Carl leaned forward so he could scowl at Connor around Sophia. Sophia leaned back and looked down at her lap, trying to avoid becoming a casualty of the Carl glare.

"What next?" Arthur said.

"Routing the enemy here means that we get time before they can build up their forces again, if not outright victory. Ewen has confidently led his entire army to one place if the reports are to be trusted. And why shouldn't he be confident? He's proclaiming himself a prophet and leader of the next March. He's won every battle with hardly any casualties and taken down our best fighter."

"Second-best fighter," Connor said.

Zerebril slammed his hand on the table again, louder.

"Alright, alright, I get it. Z has decreed this table to be a no-fun zone," Connor said, throwing up his hands.

If he comes back alive, Zerebril thought, *I will have definitive proof that a just god does not exist.*

Apparently not finished eating, Connor took his boots off the table, pulled the pig back in front of him, and continued stuffing his face.

I need to ignore him, Zerebril thought. He breathed in deeply and held his tongue. *Just a little longer. I only have to put up with him for a few days.* It seemed like everyone else was doing their best to pretend he wasn't noisily scarfing down food as well. *Could this man be trusted? Did he have a choice?*

Zerebril sighed. "Don't go too far from the barracks. You'll need to be ready at a moment's notice once they are spotted. Connor, that means no getting drunk for two days. Can you manage that?"

"I don't know, Zerebril, might be hard. But I reckon it probably isn't as hard for me to avoid drink as it is for you to take the stick out of your ass."

Zerebril shook his head. *I guess I deserved that for stooping to his level.* This time even Sophia elbowed Connor.

"Oh, what are you elbowing me for? Z's got no teeth. We have a mutual arrangement here. Honestly, Sophia, I sometimes question your intellect. I mean, you insist on carrying a shield with your Cormac sword. What's the point of that?"

"It's for arrows, you moron," she huffed.

"Sure, but you can knock those out of the sky long before

they get to you with the flame lashes. Shield will just weigh you down."

Sophia blushed. "I'm not skilled enough to do that yet. I only just got the sword when the last guard retired a few weeks ago."

Connor scratched his chin thoughtfully. "Then it seems everyone could do with a bit of practice, other than the twins. There, Z, you have a way to keep me out of the taverns. Sophia will have the twins teach her flame lashes. I'll show *the Falconer* here how to use Dean Macbrick, since the explosions it creates can be . . . slightly harmful to the user."

Carl raised an eyebrow. "In what way?"

"Well, unlike the sword variants of Cormac's weaponry, the flanged mace behaves differently. The swords ignite with friction and can create those famous flame whips. Dean Macbrick, however, ignites on impact to devasting effect. The harder the impact, the nastier the explosion. If you don't want your arm blown off," Connor smirked as he said that. "I'd suggest pulling your blows a bit. Thrusting works well as it's a smaller impact that puts the explosion farther away from you. Even that will shred through the best plate armor. If you want the most out of the weapon, you might as well treat it like a damn trebuchet and just heave the thing. Though finding it after the explosion can be a bit of a pain. My employer, a debt collector, would have me blast down doors and walls of the debtors who thought they could hide—"

"I get it," said Carl.

"Yes, well, I need a tune-up, too. I'll need to see what Professor Mathilda is capable of before going into battle." Connor inched closer to Sophia. "Perhaps we could spar for a bit afterward?"

Zerebril sighed and said, "You're dismissed." Connor was painful enough as it is, but watching him flirt was nauseating. That probably meant Sophia would be the pick for leading the cavalry charge in order to minimize Connor's tendency to be distracted.

Zerebril walked up and grabbed Carl by the cloak while everyone else left.

"Brother, it is good to see you," Zerebril said. "I was worried you wouldn't make it."

"You call me brother more now since Gunter is dead."

Zerebril frowned. "Yes, well, did you have to give his sword to *Connor* of all people? I know you said it wasn't really your style, but I think a sword of that importance should stay in the family."

"I'm family now."

"You've always been to me."

"As you say."

Zerebril sighed. "But the sword—"

Before Zerebril could finish, Carl pulled his left hand out from the cloak and untied the string that fastened it around his neck and unpinned the brooch. The cloak fell, revealing that his right arm was completely gone.

Zerebril's breath caught in his throat as he looked from Carl's shoulder to his scowl and back to his absent arm. "Oros's blood! What happened?"

"Our big red friend."

"What?!"

"He was at Cormac's forge when we went to search the place for any remaining weapons and coin based on Henrietta's tip. The little kid found us making off with Cormac's stash. We tried to use him as a hostage against his brother. Didn't work."

Zerebril sat back down and placed his hand over his head. "So, it really is Roran then, isn't it? He was the monster at the castle?"

"Seems like it. Looks like he had another friend too that could also use otherworldly power. The types of things old

Lichtfangrs would fight. Bastard hucked a fireball at my head without even having a Cormac weapon."

Zerebril shook his head. "I don't know how they did it. Short of eating one of Cormac's weapons, it should be impossible. Unless they were corpse calling, but where would Roran have gotten the corpse? He was in the dungeon! Did your Lichtfangr training teach you how to deal with that kind of a threat?"

"Does it look like it?" Carl said, nodding to his missing arm. "Whatever the case, I can't wield a great sword with one hand. So, I traded it for the mace."

Zerebril nodded. "But your bow?"

Carl didn't provide a verbal answer, only another scowl.

Zerebril banged his gauntleted fist on the table. This turn of events could kill the whole plan. "How will you lead the vanguard now? You can't string your bow! You're fighting with your nondominant hand!"

"I suffered for your victory."

"W-What?"

"I *suffered* . . . suffered *long* in the name of a family I have never been welcomed in. For certain people, that comes with some perks. Or so I've been told." Carl walked up and knelt in front of the seated Zerebril.

Zerebril, looking at his face more intently, could see something was off. Carl's skin, or at least the veins, seemed to be partially glowing in his face.

For the first time in Zerebril's memory, Carl smiled. It looked unnatural and sinister. "I no longer need to wield a weapon, even one made by Cormac," Carl said. "*I* am the weapon now."

Zerebril stared at him, eyebrows bunched together. Carl refastened his cloak, still smiling, and exited out the door. The two servants came back in and started clearing the plates and food as Zerebril continued to sit and think. Zerebril blinked rapidly as if to recollect his thoughts, shifting in his chair to the tune of his metal plate clinking. *What in all of Verdin did he mean by that?* Zerebril thought.

He stood up and went to the doorframe. He saw Carl descending the stairs from their banquet room in the tavern down to the cobbled streets below. He had an uncharacteristic pep in his step for someone who had just lost his dominant arm to the shoulder. Yes, Verdin Stars, while they would not regenerate the limb, could rapidly heal even a wound like that, but Carl seemed unburdened mentally as well. Was he also taking poppy?

Zerebril shook his head. Carl's eyes would have shown the glaze if he had taken it. He shivered as he remembered Carl's parting smile. His eyes were focused and unflinching, piercing with pinhole pupils situated above that unnatural smile. Zerebril continued to watch Carl as he caught up to the twins and they walked toward the barracks situated near the main gate and partially built into Stedtfest's tall, layered palisade. At the very least, Zerebril wouldn't have to worry about those three being unfit for battle, whatever their moods or unusual dispositions.

From the top of the stairs on the side of the tavern, Zerebril looked down to his right and saw Connor and Sophia making their way around to the proper entrance to the tavern. Now those, too, Zerebril might need to keep an eye on.

Zerebril let his weight pull him in his heavy plate down the stairs. If those two were going to walk into a tavern in their full gear, Zerebril would too. He followed them up to the bar in the tavern and sat right next to Connor. Connor, too focused on Sophia, didn't seem to notice at first until Sophia pointedly looked at Zerebril.

Connor turned to address Zerebril. "Can I help you?"

"If I can't trust you two to stay out of the taverns, then I will follow you around and kill your fun. After all, I bring with me the 'no-fun zone.'"

Connor rolled his eyes. "Fine, suit yourself. Barman! Get this lost child your strongest drink. The kind that will make him shit the stick all the way out of his ass."

"The Gumption?" the barman asked.

"Perfect. Stuff will either kill you or make your chest hair grow its own chest hair."

The barman did his best to keep his laughter to himself, nodded, and began pouring Zerebril a drink.

"I'm surprised the tavern's still open, considering," Zerebril said as the barman passed him the tankard.

"Ya'd be surprised," the red-haired barman said, wiping the spilled alcohol on his leather apron. "What better time to drink dan da end of da world?"

Zerebril leaned in toward the barman and whispered low so that Connor, who had resumed his conversation with Sophia, couldn't hear. "Well, if you don't want the world to end, make sure you give these two the weak brew. This is your vanguard responsible for saving the town. Don't get them too drunk or Stedtfest will . . . it won't be here in the next few days."

"Noted," the barman said and then turned away to address his other customers. The barman was right. The tavern was crowded with woodsmen, hunters, and seemingly some of the Wilheim garrison—everyone bent on having one last good night before their homes were set ablaze. At least, these are the people who decided not to flee to Wilheim's walls or across Lake Verdin. For one reason or another, be it age, duty, mobility, responsibility, or otherwise, these few had chosen to stay and were now living up what time they had left.

Zerebril took a sip of the tankard and cringed. He hated the taste of alcohol, no matter what its reported effects were. Sure, it could make you forget, make you numb, but did it have to taste like horse piss? The Ardhatazian Gumption especially was not suited for human consumption; it should only be used as a paint remover or sterilizer.

Connor chuckled, noticing Zerebril's disdain for the drink

clearly written on his face. "Still can't stomach the stuff, can you, Z?"

"No, I don't drink. But I will if it means it stays out of your gullet."

"Don't drink, you say . . . that's not what your palace maids tell me. They say you've been in a right drunken stupor lately." Connor looked over his shoulder at Sophia and then whispered to Zerebril, "I've been paying them some conjugal visits, you see."

"You have to be married to use that term—but stop trying to sleep with my staff. Stop trying to sleep with our professors. And stop trying to sleep with—"

Connor lifted Zerebril's tankard back up to his face before he could blurt out Sophia's name. "Shhh, hush now, Z. It's going to be okay."

Zerebril choked down the Gumption before yanking the tankard out of Connor's hands and staring daggers at him.

"Just drink and forget. Relax a little. We'll be fine. I know I make jokes about this place being turned into a graveyard, but I'm sure *we'll* at least be fine. Do you know how good I am with one of these?" he nodded down to Professor Mathil—Gunter's great sword resting against the bar.

Zerebril's gaze lingered over the sword, glowing unashamedly in the bar in full view of everyone remaining in Stedtfest. But they all seemed much more concerned with their own problems than to investigate what Connor and the glowing sword were doing here.

"You'd be better if you got yourself a shield too," Sophia chimed in from her seat on the other side of Connor, now refocusing back in on their conversation.

Connor smirked over his shoulder back at her. "You can hush, too. It's a two-handed weapon."

"And it will always be inferior to my one-handed sword because of that," she smiled, comically over exaggerating the smile to show all of her pristine white teeth.

Flustered, Connor turned fully around away from Zerebril on his stool to confront her. "Shields aren't everything when you've got proper armor, the kind your cheap-ass employer should be outfitting you with. You know, Professor Mathilda swore by great swords—"

"Professor Mathilda this, Professor Mathilda that," Sophia said, downing the rest of her tankard. "You bring her up an awful lot while still trying to schmooze other girls," she winked at him. "Not really a sound strategy."

"I only do it because I don't know enough about *you* yet," Connor said, trying to recover. "But I plan to fix that. Barman, another for the lady here! Purple Coast ale if you got it. I appreciate a woman who can keep up with me."

Zerebril rolled his eyes as the barman obeyed. Zerebril tried to catch the barman's eyes and gesture to cut them off early, but the barman purposely ignored Zerebril's attempts to get his attention.

"Speaking of not knowing enough about people," Connor said, drinking and returning his gaze back to Zerebril. "What's the deal with Carl?"

Zerebril sighed. "I thought you might know. You were traveling with him after all."

"Sophia and I met up with them only three days ago. By dat point, he'd already had his whoopsies with his arm. He's been force-feeding us potatoes and cackling to himself when he tinks we aren't looking ever since."

"Cackling? As in laughing? Carl doesn't laugh."

"He does now," Sophia said. "And not just that. He's been talking to himself too."

"Yeah," Zerebril said. "He talks to his falcon."

"No, not to his falcon," Sophia said after another sip from her tankard. "Whatever red thing he and the twins faced a week ago, it seems like it really did them in."

"Do you think he's—" Zerebril paused, trying to figure out

how to word his thoughts. "Do you think he's fit for battle, at least as fit as the two of you?"

Connor shrugged. "Dat depends. Barman, another for me. Bring yer ass over here and hit me wit the stiff drink!"

Zerebril leaned his head back and stared hopelessly at the dark wooden ceiling. Connor's Ardhatazian accent, which he normally tried to play down, was coming out and would get more pronounced the more he drank. It was getting later, and the crowd was getting rowdier to match the dip in sun.

"And one more for da lady here, for da road. Too noisy in here now. She can't properly hear all da complaints—compliments I'm paying her," Connor said, raising his eyebrows at Sophia.

Sophia scoffed.

Zerebril groaned.

The barman laughed.

"Why are the Tazzes here?" bellowed a gruff voiced from behind them.

Oh no, Zerebril thought, groaning. He looked over and saw the barman rolling his eyes and turning away to busy himself with another customer. Connor looked positively giddy, a spark in his eyes and a smile pulling at the corners of his mouth that he was trying unsuccessfully to hide.

"Oh boy," Connor said. "Here we go." He stood up and turned to address the man who called him out. "How can dis Tazz help ya?"

The man swaggered and swayed, already deep in The Gumption. Looking like a carpenter by trade, tool belt and hammer still around his waist. He had muscles, but there was no possible way this man would stand any chance against Connor in armor. Was he some kind of idiot, or was this just one of the many reasons Zerebril avoided drinking in bars? Zerebril saw Sophia put her gauntlets back on, though she kept drinking.

"Um . . . friend," Zerebril stood, placing himself between

Connor and the carpenter. "Yes, he's from Ardhataz initially, but he fights for us now."

"Ah Z, it's cute ya tink ya need to stand up for me," Connor said, placing his hand on Zerebril's pauldron and forcing him to sit back down. Though it was simple motion executed with almost casual deference, both Zerebril and the stool were nearly squashed under Connor's force. Whatever problems he had with Connor, Zerebril had to acknowledge that he was incredibly strong.

"Let da man speak. He has da right ain't he?" Connor laughed. "He's just defending his town from da big bad Tazzes."

"Connor," Zerebril said through his teeth. "If they already don't like, don't make it worse."

"Someone's got to defend the town," the carpenter said, spitting on the wooden floor and ignoring Zerebril. "Nearly everyone's fled. The town's now full of the city snobs in their polished armor. Probably don't know a spear from their ass. And these are the fighters that are going to save us? The pampered academy boys who have never seen real combat behind their big stone wall?"

"What? Da garrison?" Connor snickered. "Dey won't save ya, dat's my job." Connor pointed his thumb at his enthusiastic smile.

The carpenter scrunched up his face and then looked at Zerebril. "Prince? You hire him? His going to betray us to his kind."

Zerebril was so caught off guard that the man recognized who he was that he couldn't recruit his faculties to respond.

The man then looked over at Sophia. "And what? Is the Tazz shagging our women, too? It's not enough that you're killing and enslaving us? You have to replace us with your ugly red babies too?"

Sophia smiled, set down her tankard, and in one swift motion, stood, turned, and launched a gauntleted right hook into the man's chin, sending him to the floor.

Zerebril tilted his head back and groaned loudly.

Connor's face reacted in slow motion as it went from smug condescension to pure open-mouthed elation. His eyes went wider as Sophia planted a sloppy kiss on his still open mouth. Connor raised both fists over his head in triumphant victory as Sophia continued to slobber up his face like a hungry dog.

Zerebril's frustrated groan turned to a look of sheer disgust as his nose wrinkled up and eyes tried to hide what they were seeing behind a squint. The carpenter remained motionless on the floor, unconscious. If Sophia didn't knock him out already, the Gumption would have with one more swig.

"Alright!" the barman yelled. "Da three of ya are done. Out of here!"

Well, Zerebril thought, *at least he'd be out of the tavern for the night. Guess he and Sophia have some sparring they must see to.*

Connor walked toward the exit like he was ten feet tall, Sophia and Zerebril following.

"At least you're having the time of your life," Zerebril said under his breath.

Connor turned and snorted as he watched Zerebril trail him. He put an arm around Sophia. "In case ya didn't read da book about social cues, yer not welcome to follow us, Z."

"I didn't think you could read at all, Connor," Sophia smirked.

"I don't need to read when I'm already an expert. Also, nice hook."

Sophia shrugged. "It was hardly fair. I had a gauntlet on."

"Still," Connor said. "Form was great. Ya even rotated at da hips and feet. Ya sure yer not being underpaid by yer boss? How long have ya been merc-ing anyway?"

Zerebril ignored them and shook his head. "Why in all of Verdin would I want to follow you two? If the horse piss won't make me sick, hanging around you any longer certainly will."

"Hush, Z. It's past yer bedtime. Run along now," Connor cooed.

They parted without even giving Zerebril a second glance. Zerebril scowled his most Carl-esque scowl.

"I really am becoming Carl," Zerebril said to himself as he walked back to his quarters in the barracks. "Or, at least, what Carl was. I don't know what Carl has become now."

I am the weapon now, Carl's voice repeated.

As long as Zerebril could direct that weapon toward Ewen, Zerebril could deal with Carl's odd—well, odder—behavior. He could deal with all of them as long as they saved Stedtfest.

CHAPTER 18
CITY OF LIGHTS

GRISELDA WALKED through the walled city of Wilheim following the huffing and puffing Rodrick. Thankfully, it seemed Rodrick didn't have the stamina to walk and talk at the same time. Not hearing him talk was a mercy she would gladly accept. Both still had their respective red and green cloaks up, even though the rain had stopped. Griselda didn't know who Rodrick was hiding from, but she was glad he kept the hood up—his renown alone might attract unwanted attention.

She stared at all the familiar and lavish buildings, all made of polished white stone, neatly organized, and several stories tall. Compared to any other city Griselda knew of, Wilheim was a beacon of architectural advancement, partially due to the students from the College of Building and Design who were well paid to construct buildings and provide the city's layout. Wilheim embraced its status as a beacon of enlightenment, hence the sun emblazoned on every public office and the bonfires in each city square. Each of which was named with a memorial plaque after an important historical figure central to the sprawling utopia's legacy. The city, whether day or night, would never know true darkness because of the blazing fires, and they had created a public servant office of fire tenders who stood guard and kept the fires at a manageable height. Griselda thought it seemed like an unnecessary hazard for a primarily symbolic tradition.

Though the architecture was immaculate and impressive, the people running in and out of the buildings looked anything but. Everyone was in a state of panic as they walled up their windows with planks, bought the remaining food supplies, and ushered their crying children through the throng of frazzled people. Many people were buying tickets on wagons or on boats out of Wilheim to cross Lake Verdin. This was a people who had lost faith in their city and rulers' ability to stop the looming threat, the threat of Ardhataz, Griselda's kin—barbarians who all resembled her in skin, hair, and eye color, even if she didn't have the accent.

Griselda didn't blame the people for panicking, didn't blame them for the dirty looks given to Wilheim citizens with Ardhatazian ancestry. With the rumors about what King Ewen was doing to the countryside and what he was about to do to Stedtfest, Griselda thought these people were reasonable for trying to flee, even if it meant the uncertainty of starting over in a new land with a new language, tradition, and religion. After all, her parents had done it too. And given the rumored state of the fading King Morgen, there seemed to be little in the way to even slow down Ewen's March, stories of which were already being compiled at Ewen's insistence to solidify his status as a divine prophet and liberator. Though the propaganda may work in Ardhataz, everyone in Wilheim had a very different opinion and was calling him the Blood-Red King as a parody of Wilheim's pseudo-historic Red King. But their opinions wouldn't matter as they were being erased from memory, one twinkle at a time, until all of the lights of Wilheim were snuffed out.

Griselda was shaken from her thoughts when she felt something tug at the bottom of her pant leg. She spun around and found that Gunter the fox had followed from the cart and snuck into the city. He nipped at her expectantly. Rodrick didn't seem to notice and stormed ahead, blustering to himself about the rabble in the streets.

Someone almost stepped on the fox and yelped when they saw it. Griselda picked Gunter up and pulled out some berries from her pocket. "Is this what you wanted?"

It barked and let its tongue roll out. Griselda held up her hand to the fox and hurried up to catch Rodrick.

So much for being inconspicuous, she thought. She was carrying a fox like she used to carry Arno while the handle of a massive sword poked way up above the back of her head. Even if everyone was losing their minds in the chaos, someone would be bound to at least remember the sight of her.

Wilheim was massive, and they had to walk several blocks before they left the market district and got to the upper-class estates. Beyond those estates were the Wilheim Academies with individual colleges clustered together. The castle keep was far to the east, backed up closest to the Shatter Rock Range that hugged the northern sections of the city. The Shatter Rock River was divided by a human-built dam so that one side of the river ran through the castle keep and the other ran through the center of the city proper, thus providing water to the whole city and to the castle in case of breach to the exterior wall. Still blustering to himself, Rodrick approached a large wooden gate painted with a host of geometric patterns. Griselda hoped she wasn't meant to be paying attention to anything he was saying, because she definitely wasn't.

He finally turned around after unlocking the gate, and his eyes bulged out of his head at the sight of the fox being cradled in Griselda's arms.

"How did—that's not coming in my place! I will not have it soiling my rugs."

Griselda smirked and pushed beside him onto the grounds.

"Tough, Rodrick. We had a deal. He's still your charge as long as I am."

The mansion was at the center of the yard with stone pathways making a square around it. There was a garden, a shed, a fountain, and a statue in the four corners of the property.

Griselda passed the statue, eyed it, then spun around. "You had a statue commissioned of yourself?"

Rodrick blushed. "Well, I don't see why not. I built a trading network spanning Wilheim—the Peninsula, not just the city—with plans to expand farther to the other side of the lake and Ardhataz."

"Your statue, when was it commissioned?"

"Last year," Rodrick said.

Griselda tried to hold in a laugh. The statue version of Rodrick was generous, drawing in his gut, broadening his shoulders, erasing his double chin with a fuller and more prominent pointed beard, dressing him in full plate armor with sword outstretched and pointing to where the sun would rise.

"What's so funny? Look, I didn't pay that much for it if that's your concern. I have some friends in the College of Arts who needed to make a statue for their final project to graduate."

Griselda laughed harder since he missed the point. "It's just . . . it's just that your statue is very . . . optimistic."

"I don't know what you mean," he sputtered. "And seriously, get rid of the varmint."

Griselda rolled her eyes, turned around, and continued to walk toward the front of the house. She could feel she was getting closer to Roran and Arno, and she didn't want to waste any time arguing with the egotistic merchant.

She fed Gunter another berry from her pocket and knocked on the massive wooden doors. "Hello! Anybody home?"

"I'm out here," Rodrick said indignantly.

"Right, I know, but I'm guessing you have servants. If you have a statue of yourself, then surely you have servants, right?"

"Well, about that," Rodrick said, passing Griselda and unlocking the doors. With effort and heavy breathing, he pushed the doors open to reveal a completely empty house, minus the floor rugs. Any wall furnishings, candlelight fixtures, and furniture were absent from the entire building. The floor tiles were marble polished to mirror reflection. Columns, likely unnecessary in actually supporting the weight of the house, were of the same white, cut stone modeled after the rest of the city's architecture.

"You see," Rodrick said, "I'm moving across the lake too. I had my staff go ahead of me to secure a modest location in the canyon lands to the north. This city and country are doomed, and I'm not about to sit here with my thumb up my ass while Ewen kicks down the front gate and prepares his bag of screws."

Griselda walked around looking at the rugs that were all intricately designed with patterns. They had lettering surrounding the patterns in a language she had not seen before.

"Like I said, while I was escorting my second to last caravan of my belongings to the docks, we were attacked. It's why I was in the wagon. All that's left to take now is my rugs . . . and my stowaways."

Griselda's ears perked up as she heard a young boy's voice echoing through the house.

"Rodrick's back!" the boy said.

Arno? Griselda hoped.

The boy ran down the stairs. He was wearing a simple yellow tunic and brown trousers that didn't fit his bright green eyes. A women of similar eye color walked down the stairs after him.

Griselda sighed. This was not Arno.

"Ahh, Fredrick," the merchant said. "How have you been? Keeping busy in my empty house?"

"Well, it was *really* boring. But my mom does tell good stories, so we managed," Fredrick paused and stared at Griselda. "Why do you have a fox? Can I pet him?"

"He's wild. I think he only likes me because I feed him berries."

"Ooooh! Can I try feeding him?"

"Sure," Griselda smiled. She knelt down and handed Fredrick a berry, who then handed it to the fox. Though initially suspicious, the fox did eat it out of the young boy's overeager hand.

"That tickles!" he laughed.

Griselda smiled. "I know, right?"

Fredrick's mother walked up behind him and laid her hands on Fredrick's shoulders. "And who is this? Our escort?" she asked, eyeing the sword handle.

"To be determined. I'm Griselda," she said, offering her hand and shifting Gunter to her shoulder.

Her green eyes lit up as she smiled in what looked like recognition. "Henrietta, pleased to meet you!"

"Yes, well," Rodrick muttered, "I may have promised that you, Henrietta, would give Griselda a bit of information in exchange for my safe trip back to Wilheim. I may still be able to persuade her to stick around for longer, but—"

"He says you know what happened to my brothers," Griselda blurted out.

Henrietta sighed. "Oh dear." She turned Fredrick around. "Why don't you go jump in the fountain?"

Fredrick giggled and dashed out the front door.

Rodrick stared at her open-mouthed. "Have you been allowing him to jump in *my* fountain?"

Henrietta shrugged. "I don't see the problem, you're not bringing it or that ridiculous statue with you, right?"

Rodrick huffed and walked over to the window, face turning red as Fredrick whooped and jumped into the fountain. "The thanks I get," he said.

Griselda realized she instantly liked Henrietta. Really,

anyone who gave Rodrick a hard time was bound to get on Griselda's good side.

"Well, I suppose you're eager to hear news," Henrietta said, though her shoulders were hunched.

"Yes, please. How do you know?"

"It's a bit of a long story."

"Then just the shortened version is fine."

Henrietta exhaled. "I worked in the castle. When I was young, I was the king's chambermaid. I didn't know any better, and Fredrick was born when the king made an advance. I saw how the king treated his other bastard, and so I kept Fredrick a secret from the crown. But I was still a problem for the king, even if he didn't know about Fredrick. To hide me as his mistress, he had me working in the castle dungeon as the chambermaid to the prisoners."

Griselda perked up. "Then you must have seen them if you worked there!" Griselda immediately regretted her excited reaction, the part that caught what happened to her brothers, but not what happened to Henrietta and Fredrick. "But," Griselda began again, "excuse me—I'm sorry for what the king did to you. It's just . . . I need to make sure nothing bad happens to my brothers, too."

"History," Henrietta waved the comment away. "Ancient history. But, as for your brothers, I have to warn you dear, what happened to them wasn't good."

Griselda felt one of her sudden headaches coming on like thunder rumbling in the distance, a warning of relentless pounding and strife. She brushed the strands of her hair out of the way so she could rub her temples. After blinking hard, she nodded, prompting Henrietta to continue.

"Zerebril was desperate and tried to get Roran to mass-produce Cormac weapons to stop Ewen. When that didn't work, they . . . . tortured Arno."

Griselda sucked in air, but it felt like it went nowhere. It didn't go into her lungs but got caught in her throat as she felt like she was choking on her own breath. Her dirty clothes, loose from travel and wear, suddenly seemed to tighten and constrict around her torso. She balled and un-balled her hands to give her something else to focus on. It didn't work.

Henrietta winced, "They believed it could . . . motivate Roran to produce better results."

"H-how could anyone—" Griselda gasped, as a chill ran up her spine.

"Hurt a child?" Henrietta asked, finishing Griselda's thought. "I'm sorry to say, but it happens more often than you think."

"What did they—no. I don't want to know," Griselda muttered. "Not now."

The headache grew in intensity, and Griselda walked over to the stairs and sat on a step. She let Gunter down, who sat next to her, and looked up. She also unslung End March and set it on the floor. Henrietta followed and sat next to her, very close, rubbing Griselda's back with her hand.

"Are you alright?"

"Fine, just a headache. I sometimes get them."

Henrietta moved one step above Griselda and sat behind her. "I might not be able to offer the best of news, but I think I might be able to help with this, at the very least."

Henrietta gently placed her hands on Griselda's temples and massaged them.

"Sometimes, these things come from pressure or tension in the shoulders and neck. I'm no healer, but carrying that heavy sword around if you're not used to it might do something funny. Now, try to relax your neck."

Griselda did as she was told, and Henrietta moved her head from side to side, gently stretching the muscles in the shoulders and neck. Rodrick stayed at the window and continued to watch as Fredrick played in the fountain. Gunter trotted up next to

Rodrick, placed his paws on the low sill, and also watched Fredrick play.

"Does that feel better?" asked Henrietta.

"A little, but I've had these before I grabbed the sword."

Henrietta kept moving Griselda's head back and forth, side to side, and tilting it up and down. "I guess that's the weapon Roran hinted at then."

Griselda stiffened and turned around, "What?"

"I was his chambermaid. I personally saw to feeding him, cleaning his quarters, and bandaging his hands."

"His hands?"

Henrietta nodded. "He tried to break his hands so that they couldn't force him to make another sword and torture Arno when it didn't work."

"Oh, Roran," Griselda choked. She lay down on the lengthy stair step and put her throbbing head in her hands. "I think I'm ready to hear the last bit."

"What do you mean?" Henrietta asked, switching again to rubbing Griselda's back.

"They're dead, aren't they? I don't think Rodrick wanted to tell me for fear that I might not escort him back. I've . . . I've been bracing myself for it. I'm ready now."

Henrietta sighed. "I don't know, dear."

Griselda blinked. "What?"

"I don't know what happened to them."

That was not the response Griselda was expecting. A little light flashed behind her brown eyes. Not quite hope, but a need to know, similar to when she was speeding through a book to get to the end. "Why not?" Griselda asked.

"Zerebril told me to stop taking care of Roran but to treat Arno's injuries. I did as commanded. Once I finished dressing Arno's . . . wound, I left the cell and heard some bestial roar. I stumbled back to the wall as this massive red beast was coming down the hall and one by one, punching the cell doors down with his . . . mangled arms. I swear it's the truth. He released each prisoner intentionally until he found Arno. While the beast ignored the other prisoners, it grabbed Arno and ran off with him."

Griselda blinked in disbelief. "What? But why take Arno?" She had been clinging onto Gunter for dear life the whole wagon ride, knowing in the back of her head that she was going to get the news and then decide to work for Rodrick since there were few good options. But this confusion and subversion shook up her headache even more.

"I can only guess, but Griselda, I think that thing was Roran. He had similar facial features, and he looked at me . . . with—I don't know how to explain it. But Zerebril thought it was Roran, too. Zerebril had the Wilheim scholars investigate the aftermath, and they determined that Roran's cell was broken from the inside while the others were broken from the outside. Something happened to him, likely Grief Sickness, though even that would have looked different."

"Grief Sickness," Griselda mumbled, remembering *The Marches*. "The books said it could turn certain kinds of people into monsters before it killed them. Not everyone, according to the book, but Roran had brooding in his blood," she sighed. *Oh, Roran, what did you do?*

"Some of the scholars said that as well, but they also suggested that I slipped him some kind of western . . . corpse-caller potion," she said, struggling to say the filthy words. "Zerebril kicked me out of the castle when he heard that theory. Since Morgen is . . . well, he's not himself all the time anymore, Zerebril was able to dismiss me."

Rodrick turned away from the window, looked down at the fox, shook his head, and began pacing around his empty house. Gunter wandered out into the yard to join Fredrick in the fountain.

"So, they escaped?"

"They did. Roran apparently *jumped over* the wall. But no one has heard anything about them since. That's all I heard before I was dismissed and lost my access to information."

Rodrick huffed and turned to Griselda. "And what will you do with that information?"

"What choice do I have? I need to look for them or at least find out what happened. If Roran was jumping over walls while holding Arno, then someone would have had to have seen something."

"Shame," Rodrick said. "You do what you got to do, but my offer is still on the table if you change your mind. Either way." Rodrick turned back to face the window, "me and my passengers have got to get out of here."

Henrietta moved and positioned herself in front of Griselda. "I know there's not much to go off, but your brothers are strong. Nothing seemed to kill them, even the worst of days. I think they're still out there."

Griselda nodded and stood up slowly, the headache getting worse again. "Thank you for taking care of them as best you could."

Henrietta nodded and then left out the door to check on Fredrick, who was still splashing in the fountain.

Griselda walked over to Rodrick, her head pulsing with each step, making it harder to think. But she still needed some answers. What Rodrick was doing for this mother and child didn't seem to line up with his egotistic personality. Henrietta clearly wasn't *with* Rodrick, the thought of which almost made Griselda chuckle. "So," she said. "Why are you helping them?"

"You can probably guess," he said.

Griselda thought. They didn't look like they had much coin, and certainly a chambermaid job didn't provide wealth or connections. Unless . . .

"The story about you coming over from the western nations. Was it true?"

"Yes, yes, but I'm not doing this because of some shared sympathy or solidarity in not wanting to break up families with children or any meek thing like that."

Griselda thought as much as her headache would allow. "Then . . . you're interested in what Fredrick will turn into, aren't you?"

Rodrick nodded. "I'll be taking care of them until he comes of age. If there is still a country here when Ewen is done with it, Fredrick has some claim to the throne. He's an investment of an uncertain return. The king won't be around for much longer, and word has it that Zerebril just rode to Stedtfest to challenge certain death. There may be a vacancy soon. If nothing comes of it and Ewen just drops a puppet on the throne, at the very least, Fredrick and Henrietta will be pleasant company. But if I'm right, I could put a new king on the throne and have him in my debt."

Griselda walked over to the window and watched as Henrietta jumped into the fountain, too. Apparently, Fredrick had convinced both her and Gunter to take a swim.

"Do they know your intentions?"

"Of course, they had to pay for safe passage somehow."

Griselda nodded. "Take care of them; they seem like good people." She watched as Fredrick created joy in others just by being curious and energetic. Much like Arno, who had pulled her and Roran into the yard, Fredrick had pulled his mother and a wild fox into some rich merchant's palatial water fountain.

"I intend to," Rodrick huffed. "All of my investments are well looked after."

Griselda grabbed her sword and slung it back over her shoulder. She walked outside into the yard. Though she had a headache, it was impossible not to appreciate the beauty of the garden and the other buildings of Wilheim poking over Rodrick's fence. It was supposed to be getting colder, and Griselda thought this might be the last warm afternoon before the coming winter.

So, despite her headache, she got a running start and jumped into the fountain too.

The fox yelped and jumped up and down. Fredrick whooped and splashed Griselda and his mother.

Griselda drew Fredrick in by the shoulders and knelt beside him, submerging herself up to her waist in the water. She dug the rest of the berries out of her pocket.

"I have a favor to ask of you," she said.

"What's that? How can I help?" Fredrick replied.

"I want you to take care of my fox friend here," she said, handing him the berries.

Fredrick's face lit up. "Really?!"

"Yes," she laughed, glancing over at Henrietta, who smiled and nodded.

"This fox annoys Rodrick, and it would make me happy if you kept annoying him for me."

"You got it!"

Griselda smiled, a full-toothed, wide smile, the first one since her father's passing. "His name is Gunter."

"Like the prince?"

"Yes," Griselda nodded. "You'll be his new big brother now. Look after each other." She turned to Henrietta. "Is it alright if I hug him?"

"Go ahead. He might as well be Arno, only his name's different," she said.

Griselda hugged him and planted a kiss on the boy's forehead. Fredrick was startled by the kiss. He took a step back, blinked, and then rubbed the kiss off his forehead.

Griselda laughed at his reaction. "Take care now, both of you." And with that, she stood up and left out the front gates.

She would need to make a stop at whatever stores were open for the journey. With the money she had, there was plenty for supplies and then some for the foreseeable future. First things first, she would need proper gauntlets that would allow her to wield the sword without burning her hands.

Griselda looked down at her palms, calluses forming from the recent training with End March. If she wanted to be prepared, maybe she should stop by the Wilheim Academies that housed the College of Combat to see if she could learn proper technique or at least watch a public duel. There's a possibility other higher-up people in Wilheim knew more about her brothers' where-abouts, information that may have only become available after Henrietta's dismissal.

She turned back to look at Rodrick's estate one final time to mentally wish them good fortune on their journey to the canyon lands across Lake Verdin. At the very least, she wished that Henrietta and Fredrick would never be separated.

CHAPTER 19
TO BE A WEAPON

King Ewen had guided his troops up a nearby, partially wooded hill and out of the water. There, they made camp in preparation for the assault on Stedtfest. They had spent the day assembling the siege ladders, scouting the terrain from their higher vantage point, and sharpening their weapons. Thankfully, Urrem would not be needed to help construct the trebuchet, as the Master of Siege didn't think it would be necessary once he heard of Stedtfest's wooden defenses. Urrem was not under General Macintosh, but his carpentry expertise made him useful in assisting with the assemblage of siege craft, and he had volunteered to be useful if he was not on another assignment. He liked building things; he just tried not to think about his creations leading to the destruction of other creations.

Though they were on the hill, the flooded area was only a hundred yards from their encampment, where the boats were anchored. Urrem, flat on his back, in a tent canvas over stiff dirt, was incredibly on edge for someone who was meant to be sleeping. Two major things were keeping him awake.

When they ate as a unit a few hours before, about half of his men talked as if tomorrow would be just another day; the other half knew and kept their mouths shut. This was not going to be like any of the skirmishes running up the Shatter Rock. This was a numbers game, the kind of numbers game only very strong or very weak men can play. The first thing keeping him awake: concern for his men, knowing that they were all to be loosed as flimsy arrows at a wall with the hope that enough loosed arrows would eventually create some sort of opening.

Urrem rolled over onto his side and stared at the traces of firelight still visible from the remnants of the campfire, quietly insisting that there was still light in the dark.

That's how a normal assault would play out. However, Ewen had the boat, and it was anyone's guess how those things would fare in a siege. And what they would do to the people behind the palisade—the second thing keeping him awake.

Urrem rolled over again, returning to his back and exhaling. In his tent, he had nearly bored holes into the fabric above him with his eyes alone. Urrem could not shake away the thought that his men were not ready, and neither was he. Few had done more than raid farmers, and their gear reflected that, most of them still in standard issue supply. With only a gambeson and nasal helm for most of them, they might as well be as protected as scare-crows. So much death was coming at dawn, inevitably for his men as well as for everyone inside the wooden walls.

Urrem's unit was one of many responsible for approaching in shield wall formation while carrying a siege ladder. The shields would help with the approach as that would deal with most of the arrows, but once his men had scaled the walls they would get torn to pieces by the more heavily armed Wilheim troops inside the defenses.

Was there anything he could do to prevent it? Could leading like Ewen ensure the success of his unit? Taking example from King Ewen, he knew everyone in his unit by name, their history, and their hobbies. Urrem's favorite question around dinner campfire was to ask what his troops would be doing if they didn't have to swing a sword. His favorite answer so far involved descriptive relations with Urrem's mother, Briggs, of course.

Urrem smiled slightly and rolled his wide-open eyes. Reminiscing was at least better than worrying. Deciding he was just going to be annoyed from lying awake, he put on his boots to go for a midnight stroll. He put on his black Ardhatazian tunic over his torso. The white symbol of three mountains overlapping themselves now on his chest and close to his heart. Past, present, future, forever in the mountain's shadow—its protection—even when the Ardhataz highlands weren't in sight.

Poking his head out of the tent, he saw that Malcolm was still sitting at the campfire, poking at the dying embers with a stick. Trayhaz, coming from his own unit's encampment when he saw Malcolm was awake, had ventured over and joined him as well, though both seemed content to sit in quiet contemplation.

"Trouble sleeping, too, Captain?" Malcolm asked.

"Someting like dat," Urrem responded. He pulled up a stump and sat next to Malcolm. "Ya too, Captain Trayhaz?"

"Well," Trayhaz sighed, "I've been having difficulty sleeping as of late on account of me broken rips and arm." He managed a pained chuckle. "Why did it have to be my right side? I prefer to sleep on my right side."

"Have dey at least been treating you well in da tents?" Urrem asked.

"Aye," Trayhaz nodded and drank some from his skin. Trayhaz was shirtless, but he had bandages wrapped around his ribs. His silver horseshoe necklace rested against his bare chest.

"What are da bandages for?" Urrem asked.

"Oh, you won't believe dis," said Trayhaz. "Life Nectar only works on open wounds. It doesn't seep into yer skin well. So, for it to work, da docs had to lacerate me bruised areas and den rub da goo into da wounds. Da bandages are for da wounds dat da docs made, not Ewen," he concluded by throwing his hands up into the air, then winced. "Least I get to drink. Heavily."

Malcolm couldn't help but laugh at Trayhaz's display of malcontent. Trayhaz smiled too, obviously trying to make his woes into some form of easy entertainment as a brief distraction from what's to come.

"But," Malcolm said, "ya do get a pass from dis next scuffle."

"Aye, dat's fair," Trayhaz said, nodding.

"It's only a wee scuffle though," Malcolm said, making gesture to its small size by looking through his thumb and index finger. "So, I tink we'll manage witout ya."

"What is yer unit tasked with if yer out of commission?" Urrem asked.

"Guarding camp and . . . tending da boats," Trayhaz said, his face going pale.

Both Malcolm and Urrem didn't know how to respond to that. They waited to see if Trayhaz would offer more, but he didn't seem like he would.

Urrem gritted his teeth. Though he knew he shouldn't ask, he had to know what was going on and why. "So, ya've been in dere?"

Malcolm looked at Urrem with eyebrows raised, surprised Urrem had the nerve to ask the question to Trayhaz so openly.

"Aye," Trayhaz said. "Ewen broke me ribs for speaking out on da boats, den he makes me work 'em personally. Believe ya me, I'd rather be marching toward Stedtfest at sunup den spend another minute on dat boat."

"And?" Urrem prodded.

Trayhaz took another drink from his skin. "We're screw-turning, but I'm guessing ya already knew that. I've never seen it done before now, let alone do it meself. People tied to cross beams, limbs strapped down so we can turn screws, countless screws, into der flesh. Da worst part is da noise of it. Not just da screams, dough dere are plenty of dose. Me and my men at least started giving da poor bastards towels to bite down on. Dere's another noise. The screw pulls the muscle fibers as it twists, causing dem to tear or rip from the bones. Dat, dat ya can *hear*."

Malcolm had a look of pure disgust on his face, which he didn't seem to be conscious of. "But why in Imeel-Illin's name would anyone do such a bloody act? Dese are civilians! It's not like dey're traitors being punished. Are we corpse-calling?"

Trayhaz shook his head. "No, corpse-calling's different. We haven't stooped dat low yet. What we're doing is forcibly inducing Grief Sickness. Da screws are covered in Life Nectar, so da wounds heal around da screw and don't get infected. Dis means dey stay alive and are able to have more screws turned into dem. Because we don't let dem die, some of dem succumb to Grief Sickness as dey start sweating blood. But der are some stronger ones who don't die from Grief Sickness. Deir pain eventually manifests enough, and we can use da beasties. Da Scholar seems to be able to control dem once dey manifest so dey don't burn da whole boat down and ransack da camp."

The fire crackled. Trayhaz shook his head and spat, as if bringing it up had left a bad taste in his mouth. He took a long drink, as if there was a poison inside of him and the alcohol could kill it.

"I did suspect someting," Urrem said. "I just didn't realize how—what's the word . . . meticulous—how meticulous da whole process was. It's planned to da point where it is all calculated . . . and I don't know if dat's better or worse."

Malcolm put his head in his hands.

"What we're doing," Trayhaz continued, "we're telling ourselves it's justice for Ardhataz's centuries of neglect and use as a penal colony. We're now using da monsters dat Wilheim was afraid to create demselves in deir prisons when dey sent our forefathers up to da mountains."

Urrem did see the irony. He wondered if Ewen did that intentionally or if that was accidental poetic justice.

Trayhaz repositioned himself, wincing as he did so, so that he could lean in closer to both Malcolm and Urrem. "There's one man in der . . . he's da one dat frightens me the most," Trayhaz said, lowering his voice almost to a whisper.

"Who, da Scholar?" Malcolm asked.

"No, not him, dough he's a fright too. Dere's another."

"Someone who enjoys turning da screws?"

"No, here's da ting. He's one of da prisoners."

Urrem frowned and looked at Malcolm who looked just as miffed.

"He's . . . covered," Trayhaz continued. "From foot to neck. Screws so close together and clustered around his body dat we might as well have fashioned him a suit of armor made entirely from da heads of screws. And he's still breathing. Ya can't tell from his head because it's encased in an iron mask, but his chest rises and falls. Dere's a few holes punctured into da ball of iron on his head for air, but he never screams. He just endures, day after day, screw after screw. We're running out of skin for da screws. Most of da prisoners can only take getting one of deir limbs covered in screws before dey succumb to Grief Sickness or just refuse water and let demselves die. Not him; he refuses to die. Da Scholar's particularly interested in dis screw-turned man."

"I'm guessing," Urrem said, "he tinks he will make a beast with more umph den da rest if he finally gives in."

"Yer right," Trayhaz said. "It seems to be da case dat da Willies dat survive longer have a better chance of making da beasties. But dat's why we need da numbers. Not everyone gets Grief Sickness. Some people just die. It's about one in six dat gets Grief Sickness and den about one in five of dose are strong enough to make a beastie."

"Thirty," Malcolm said, doing the math. "One in every thirty. Dat's da reason for da quota."

"Aye," Trayhaz nodded. "It's da reason why we take dem

from all ages. The children . . . they're just as likely to create them too."

The noise of the fire crackling filled the silence. A bird screeched in the distance. Urrem guessed that morning was drawing near.

"I don't understand why," Malcolm finally said. "Why do someting so monstrous? To civilians of all folk."

Urrem rubbed his hands together and sighed. "I know why, even if I don't much like da answer," Urrem said. "We have to fight monsters with monsters."

"What do ya mean?" Malcolm asked.

"I saw one. Not the beasties. One of Wilheim's monsters.

Malcolm nodded. "It's how you got promoted to captain, right?"

Urrem nodded.

The bird screeched again.

Trayhaz breathed in deeply, fiddled with his silver horseshoe, and mustered the strength to stand. "Well, I'm going to see to my unit. Dawn's coming soon and I'll get untold ribbing from yer troops if I'm still here when dey wake up."

"Briggs," Urrem sighed.

"Briggs," Trayhaz nodded.

"Fair enough," Urrem said. "Try sleeping on yer left side."

"Ya suggesting I didn't tink of dat? It don't work," Trayhaz said over his shoulder as he left the light of the fire.

Once again, the fire crackle filled the silence, smoke drifting up to the dark branches overhead. The fire was running low, but the sun was likely around the corner, and it would be pointless to stoke the fire with another log.

"Captain, can I ask ya someting?" asked Malcolm.

"Yes, Lieutenant?"

"We've only dealt with scared peasants with tiny pitchforks. What's proper battle like?"

Urrem sighed. "Well, I'd hardly call da Battle at Highest Hill a proper battle."

"What happened dere? We were on a raid when it went down."

Urrem hesitated. "I don't know if talking about it will do anyting to help ease ya mind."

"Dat bad huh?"

Damn it, he thought. Urrem always found a way to stick his foot in his mouth. It's a miracle an idiot like him was promoted at all. He was frightening his soldier more by leaving the details up to his imagination.

"It's just, we only really fought one man. Well, one monster. Da reason why we're making our beasties."

"I heard. Prince Gunter, right?"

"Right," Urrem said. "He had taken position at the Highest Hill, a cliff dat overlooked da Shatter Rock River just on da inside of da Wilheim border. From dere, he was raining fire down on our boats as if he was Oros himself. Not seen anyting like it before. We needed to stop him from sinking da boats, so Colonel Macblite had three of his captains who were not raiding take their units up da hill to engage Gunter."

"And?"

"We did."

"Well, what happened?"

Urrem picked up his own stick to absently poke the fire. Remembering the details of that fight was difficult given the speed at which it happened, but not impossible. The harder task was putting it into words that were accurate but would not startle his lieutenant on the eve of a battle.

"What do ya know of Cormac weapons?"

"I heard Gunter had one, dat dey're imbued wit da power to summon fire or someting. Dat dey can do impossible tings."

Urrem nodded. "I saw a lot of impossible tings that night. I prefer to have smarter people tell me what's possible and what's impossible nowadays."

"Like what?"

"Yer going to make me tell ya, aren't ya?"

Malcolm had set down his fire poker and now only had his attention on Urrem. "I can't force ya to, sir. But I don't see any other point to sitting around a campfire if we're not going to share some war stories."

Urrem let out the air he'd been holding in. "Fine den. Our three captains, all dead now, had tried to flank Gunter. We positioned ourselves so dat Gunter's back was to da cliff and da three of our units could attack him left, right, and center. Given what his weapon was capable of, we were told to drop our shields, which would just be heavy firewood at dat point, and make a mad dash to overwhelm him. Dere was no cover on the hill leading up to the cliffside. Just 300 yards of grassy incline."

Urrem shivered. The seasons were getting colder, despite the fire. Dawn would be coming soon, and he heard another bird screech announcing the coming sun.

"We could see the glow even from dat far away," Urrem continued. "Gunter was a big man, and in full plate he looked towering. With a massive great sword dat was glowing and reflecting light off his plate. Like some harbinger of death ready to guide hundreds of people to da next March. He was standing at da top of da cliff, waiting for us, just patiently waiting as if he didn't have a care in da world while 300 men were getting ready to charge. Great sword tip on the ground, both hands on the pommel, daring us to come at him."

Malcolm shrugged. "I guess I don't know what's scarier. Having to fight three hundred men by yerself or needing three hundred men to fight one man."

Urrem nodded. "Once we started da charge, I swear on my ma's grave, I saw him kick his sword into motion and start flourishing from side to side like this." Urrem paused to spin his stick, which was now on fire, around his head and sides. "I swear, dat sword, it's like having a hammer dat builds every part of da house for you. Once da sword was glowing, it started creating dese tails of fire in its wake. He swung da sword above his head in wider and wider arcs, turning da air around him into a whirlpool of fire, spewing hot death into the air in all directions which then rained down on us as we ran at him."

Urrem paused, dropped his stick, and looked at Malcolm. Urrem grabbed Malcom's gambeson by the sleeve. "Ya see dese? Fabric, cotton, wool—it's flammable. Not like wood, but under dose temperatures, everyting might as well be tinder."

Malcolm swallowed but nodded.

"Three hundred men, in an instant—just roasting sausages. I felt like I was standing on da surface of da sun. Our numbers meant not a ting; we could have sent everyone we had and it wouldn't have mattered. His back to a cliff, aiming da fire down-hill where he could arc it much farther, he could have beat Ewen's entire force dere. And I tink he meant to, he seemed to knowingly trap himself in da fire, like he was going to bring us all down with him. I realized very quickly dat fighting was no longer a priority. I started rescuing any survivors who were not too badly charred and bringing dem back to da edge of his effective range."

Malcolm offered Urrem a wineskin, which he took a swig of. Even talking about the flames made his throat dry.

"Tanks," Urrem said. "I was promoted for da number of lives saved on paper. But da fact is we had three dead captains. I wasn't promoted for doing anyting combat related. It's why I don't tink I have much ta offer ya for tomorrow."

Malcolm frowned. "I wouldn't make light of what ya did, Captain. Rushing into dose flames to save as many as ya can? Dat's a leader. I'd follow dat man more dan one who could swing a sword better dan me. So, how'd we beat him?"

"King Ewen's beasties. Monsters for monsters. What

Trayhaz said is going on down boatside, it's how we beat bearers of those Cormac weapons. By my last run into da flames, Gunter was done swinging da sword since no one was charging him anymore. He stabbed da sword into da ground, I tink to cool da blade. Dat's when dey attacked. Dese bear-looking animals, glowing as bright as his sword was, pounced on him while his back was to da cliff. It seemed like dey climbed up da cliff side while Gunter had his attention focused on us."

"Ya were . . . a diversion," Malcolm said, realizing why the raiding crews were sent instead of the more heavily armed soldiers.

Urrem nodded. "Anyway, one of da tings jumped on Gunter's back and tried to get through his plate. Didn't work very well, and Gunter was able to pull da sword out of da ground and defend himself. He killed five, but dey kept jumping at him, not letting him heat da blade back up. Da remaining five got him to the ground and mauled him, beating him into the ground so dat his plate no longer mattered.

"When dey were done wit him, some of dem carried off his body. Feedin' I guess? But da others started running toward me! I couldn't move. Dey were fast, and my head couldn't grip what was happening. Tankfully, dey ran past me. Apparently, Gunter did have back up stationed in da woods nearby and da beasts charged after dem. Dey couldn't go too far dough."

"Why?" Malcolm asked.

"When dey ran past me, dey had dis glowing trail. It looked like a string of stars dat reached way back off da cliff and down to da river. It's like a leash or tether or someting. I tink it's why we've been using da river so much. Da tings are leashed to it."

Malcolm took a swig from the wineskin too. Urrem knew his story didn't help, but it was best that his troops knew what they were dealing with.

"Lieutenant. If we run into a bearer tomorrow, someone wit one of dose weapons like Gunter's . . . ya don't fight, ya run. Ya hear me?" Urrem said with force. "Dat's an order. If ya see one, ya run. Let Ewen's monsters do da dirty work. Dat's what dey're for."

Malcolm nodded.

The horizon was starting to glow, a glow not too dissimilar to Gunter's sword. With the light of day, the heat of battle would soon be upon them. Urrem frowned as it seemed like he kept hearing unusual bird screeches.

"What's dat?" Asked Malcolm.

"What do ya see?" responded Urrem, rising to his feet.

Malcolm pointed to a tent pole. "Is dat a hawk?"

"Oh," Urrem relaxed. "Hawk, eagle, I don't know da difference. Whatever it is, it's been squawking all night."

Malcolm shivered. "It's a bad omen."

"Nonsense," Urrem said "It's breakfast. I'll get my spear."

Urrem jogged back over to his tent and poked his head inside to grab his spear.

Then everything was upside down. A thunderclap threatened to burst Urrem's eardrums. The blast where Urrem had been sitting was so violent it threw him through his tent and down the side of the hill. He rolled, tangled in the fabric, until his ribs collided with what he guessed was the trunk of a tree. His spear had been knocked from his hands, likely still on the top of the hill somewhere. He untangled himself as he heard other explosions in different areas of the camp.

Urrem scrambled back up to see what had happened, though his ribs ached. Once he crested the hill, he became nauseous. Malcolm, his friend and lieutenant, was in pieces. Urrem tried to rip his eyes away, but he couldn't. They stayed trained on the gore and fragments that were just having a conversation with him. He had lost Malcolm before the siege assault even began. Where the campfire had been was a glowing mace embedded in the ground. The bird flew over and perched on the handle of the weapon.

Air refused to come into Urrem's lungs. Malcolm's head rolled down the hill behind Urrem. He watched it tumble down, a startled expression still on Malcolm's face. It was happening all over again.

Urrem heard clanking as a blond man clad in a green cloak appeared from the other side of the hill. He walked over and wrenched his mace from the ground, and, as he did so, let the cloak slip off his shoulders. He only had one arm. His bird hopped off the mace and onto his shoulder. The Wilheim sun blazed on his green brigandine.

"I wish you were strong enough to pick it up and drop this thing from high above," he said to his bird. "I can't toss this very far with my left hand. I'll have to figure something out."

Urrem ducked behind a tree. Had he been seen yet? It was still mostly dark, even though the sun was beginning to rise. He heard more explosions and cries as attackers seemed to be coming at their camps from multiple sides.

Urrem looked around for his spear. But what was he thinking? Shouldn't he just take his own advice and run? That man was clearly a bearer of a Cormac weapon.

"Oi! Who are ya?"

Urrem groaned. That sounded like Briggs. Urrem risked peeking around the tree to see what was happening. It was indeed Briggs and two others who had gotten out their swords and were circling the bearer.

Oros's shit! They were dead if he didn't intervene. But what could he do if he gave away his hiding place? Nevertheless, he crouched down and continued to look for his spear.

"Whose body is dis? What have ya done?" Briggs shouted.

The bearer approached them. "If you don't want the same fate, splattered over the hillside, then you'll tell me where Ewen keeps his beasts."

"Oh, I'll tell ya where he keeps 'em," said Briggs.

Oh no, Urrem thought. He could tell by Briggs's tone that this was not going to end well.

Briggs lunged with his sword. "He keeps 'em in yer ma's—"

The bird flew off the bearer's shoulder as the bearer side-stepped the lunge and kicked Briggs into the fire.

The other two men, men Urrem didn't know but who were likely responsible for the night watch, both lunged at the bearer from different angles. In a fluid motion, the bearer ducked one sword swipe, pivoted, and used the momentum of his arm carrying his mace to spin into the second Ardhatazian watchman. The bearer then thrust the mace's rounded tip on top of the flanges into the second watchman. The branches rattled all around Urrem with the force of the concussive blast. The watchman's torso became a red mist. The explosion sent the bearer into the air as well, but since he seemed to expect it, he landed on his feet.

"Ya bastard!" the other soldier shouted.

The bearer scowled and rolled his eyes. "Where are the beasts?"

Urrem finally found his spear. He poked his head about the hill and cocked his arm back, ready to heave the spear at the bearer's back. He steadied himself and breathed out. *One shot. Don't miss.* He launched the spear through the air. Perfect throw. The tip would bury itself in the bastard's back—

The spear froze in midair. From the bearer's right shoulder, where a human arm should be, sprouted something else entirely that caught the spear. It was twisted strands of steaming blue light that formed some kind of an arm, like long glowing thick hairs with a will of their own.

The bearer turned and looked Urrem dead in the eyes. "Is this yours?"

Urrem froze to the spot.

The bearer smiled unnaturally. "I guess I'll return it!"

Urrem snapped himself out of it in time to duck as the blue

limb launched the spear so fast that it whistled through the air. The spear impaled the trunk of the tree behind Urrem and went all the way through it and out to the other side.

"Imeel-Illin above," Urrem whispered. "M-monster . . . Run!" He yelled at Briggs and the remaining watchman. "Let the beast handle him!"

"Yes, yes, listen to your Tazz friend," the bearer said as Briggs rolled out of the fire and resituated himself. For once, he did not have any witty retort.

To Urrem's dismay, Briggs just roared and charged instead. The second soldier followed in too. The bearer jumped up into the air and threw his mace into the ground, creating another explosion that propelled him upward and over the two dazed soldiers. The bearer flew through the air, his bird flying beside him as he used his blue limb to extend, grab onto a tree branch, and propel himself through the air, sustaining flight as he swung himself behind the soldiers and kicked Briggs in the back. Urrem had seen squid before in the lake, and a rapidly expanding and shrinking tentacle was the closest thing he could compare it to. The bearer stood on top of Briggs's back, used his blue limb to stretch and writhe out to retrieve his mace, which then retracted back to collide with the remaining standing soldier. His upper body was annihilated, chunks of it scattering into the air.

The bearer knelt next to the head of the shaking, grounded Briggs. "Now, where are the beasts? And if you say anything else about my mother, I'll drop this mace on your head. All it takes is just a little force and . . ."

Run. It was all Urrem could do. He turned to sprint away but he heard the familiar animalistic, metallic roaring of the things he saw on the hill.

"Ah," the bearer said. "It looks like they'll come to me after all. As for you," he said to Briggs on the ground. "I would listen to your friend in the bushes and run. I'm not here for you. I'm here to test my strength against those."

Briggs, a man twice as large as the bearer, scrambled to his feet and took off fleeing into the woods.

Three beasts jumped out of the tree line. They looked much like the sinewy strands of light that made up the bearer's right arm. No flesh or muscle, just bodies composed of pulsing strands of light. They moved like a four-legged predator, stalking around the bearer as he waited. They had no eyes or discernable facial features, just the outline of a body made entirely of glowing veins. Somehow, despite having no vocal cords, they emitted a terrible, vibrating, alien roar, the noise of an anvil being dragged over rocks. Behind them, their floating tethers stretched all the way back to the bottom of the hill and into the water.

"So, you're the living weapons I've heard so much about," the bearer said. "But I trained as a Lichtfangr, so you're not new to me."

The beasts responded with a pulsating, metallic rasping noise.

"Know this. You were made by Ewen as weapons capable of killing bearers. I made myself into a weapon capable of killing *you*."

CHAPTER 20
DESPITE COWARDICE

THE SUN PEEKED over the tree line, a red mourning lighting up Zerebril's face as he stood on the wooden ramparts above Stedt-fest's gate. He heard Carl's falcon screech as it dove out of the sky and landed on a wooden post adjacent to him.

Thank you, brother, he thought. *If you didn't scowl so much, I'd say you were the spitting image of Gunter. You match his courage at the very least.* The falcon chirped at him, opening its beak and eyeing Zerebril with one eye while its head cocked to one side.

"No time to lose then. Sophia!" Zerebril turned to address the cavalry lined up at the gate. "Time to sally out and crush their remaining forces."

Mounted on her armored horse, she called up to him. "Aren't you supposed to lead the charge with me?"

Zerebril nodded. "I thought better of it. I may wear plate, but I'd be useless on the battlefield. It's best I observe and order from up here."

Sophia rolled her eyes. "Fine, this is where I want to be anyway."

Zerebril thought he heard her mutter, "Coward."

He shook off the insult and ordered the gates opened. Sophia's role was to lead the charge and that was invaluable for finishing Ewen off. Zerebril could hear the damage done even from where he stood by the other four. Arthur, Dale, Connor, and Carl had created quite a racket, and the smoke was visible from the ramparts.

In a column, Sophia led the cavalry out across the wooden planks and to the tree line. Though Zerebril did not follow any tenets from the Marches, thinking them as man's best guess at discerning the will of Imeel-Illin with half of the necessary information, he did squeeze his eyes tight and hoped God was watching and wanted Wilheim to stop the brutal invaders.

Despite allowing himself to hope, he still had Wilheim's garrison line along the walls of Stedtfest with buckets of arrows. Men were also at the gate ready to light the oil-covered planks across the killing field on fire.

Coward. No, he was not a coward. He was smart. He was prepared. He knew his strengths and weaknesses. Still, something about Sophia calling him a coward bugged him, even more than any of the insults Connor would hurl at him. It was like she wanted him out on the battlefield knowing that he would certainly die. It made him itch for the poppy mercy as he felt the shadow creep over him.

It was Gunter's long shadow, a shadow that stretched and stayed in Verdin long after his death. Was it fair for people to compare the two princes? Not at all, but Zerebril knew it was unavoidable. Being in Stedtfest while a siege was imminent proved he was already doing far more than he normally would. He was not a trained fighter and would lose to a couple of peasants if he wasn't wearing plate.

What would his shadow be like had Gunter lived and he died? What would Gunter be doing right now? Would Gunter be compared to Zerebril? Would Gunter be raiding his father's medicine to cope with the loss of his brother?

Zerebril shook his head and swatted away a mosquito. *Not today*, he thought. *You're needed here, now, not in the past. Father said that the kingdom is on both of our shoulders.* God help him, that pressure didn't help either. He needed more of Gunter's traits, a man who could put the weight of the kingdom on his back, face down an army, and smile.

Though Gunter was gallant and kind, he was also a bit thick-headed and stubborn. If Gunter were still alive, he'd probably get himself killed by insisting he take on their entire camp by himself. He had every right to be confident in his abilities. His last stand had nearly worked and delayed King Ewen considerably.

The falcon flew off back toward the war camp, likely trying to locate its master, Carl. Zerebril shuffled from plated foot to plated foot. Though the cavalry had to navigate through the trees, they should be fine in the column. Ewen would have cleared the area for camp, too, making it possible for horses to run around. It was not an ideal tactic, but it was far quicker than sending infantry. Any minute now. But time to wait was time to think. And thinking might not be best for him at a moment like this. Gunter's shadow crept back up.

When Zerebril's father had finished his kingly duties, he would sometimes take Zerebril and Gunter down to the hill country at the southern end of Wilheim's border with Ardhataz. They had a hunting ground that Gunter and the king would frequent, but Zerebril would stay back and draw the landscape. He was decent at capturing the scenery, not so good at drawing people. When Gunter and the king came back from their hunts, Gunter singing in triumph, Zerebril had glued his drawings to the trees around the camp. Gunter said it was like having someone record his memories of things he was too narrow-minded to focus on. Gunter was staring at the ground for boar tracks and dung while Zerebril was painting the sky.

Zerebril had stopped drawing and painting when his studies

304 • ANTON JONES

at the Wilheim Academies intensified. Despite this, Gunter would still leave him gifts in his room of the latest paints, brushes, and other art utensils. Gunter left no letter, no card, and never acknowledged that he'd even given Zerebril a gift.

In return, Zerebril gave two gifts to his brother. Zerebril had commissioned the Cormac sword for Gunter, with design specifications similar to the weapon Gunter was already familiar with. They both supported each other's craft, Zerebril, who creates, and Gunter, who protects those creations.

The second gift was Zerebril creating a modern translation of an old script hymn, one of Gunter's favorites in melody, but he didn't know what it meant in the old script. Zerebril had painted his translation of the lyrics on Gunter's armor before he went to the Highest Hill.

In a way, Gunter had given Zerebril one last unacknowledged gift, too. Gunter disobeyed their father and set out to confront Ewen with the Cormac blade after hearing about the burning countryside. Gunter would not be able to sleep while people in his care were having screws turned into them. He had set out to ambush Ewen at the Highest Hill, the region Zerebril and Gunter used to travel to for hunting and painting. According to the rearguard who survived that battle, Gunter had destroyed half of the enemy boats and killed an entire battalion that stormed the cliff to stop him, temporarily halting all mountain-brute forward progress. Gunter's last gift to his brother was time. Time to strategize and prepare to fight back against a foe who outmatches them in every regard other than resources. Zerebril had used some of that time unsuccessfully with the Roran incident, but he was still given enough to arrive in the woods of Stedtfest and turn the forest into his canvas. He was using his skills not just to create, but to protect, like Gunter did. Unless he spent that time cradled in the mercy of poppy.

Either way, that time was up. He could only hope that Gunter's last gift had not been in vain. Zerebril spotted a lone horseman at the edge of the clearing. But they did not wear Wilheim colors. The armored horseman was massive and wore an intricate, polished plate with black engravings. Infantry soon appeared behind him, lining the whole southern and eastern sides of the forest opposite the Shatter Rock River.

Zerebril shouted to the troops below. "Arm yourselves! The enemy is here to siege! They have rallied from the assault and mean to take advantage of our less defended position. Light the walkway, then close the gates!"

How had this happened? Carl sent the falcon. Sophia's cavalry would have run right into Ewen's troops. Where did they all go?

Ewen roamed back and forth on his equally massive armored horse, surveying the expanse between the tree line and Stedtfest. He looked at the burning wooden walkway, the path of flame having traveled quickly due to it being pretreated with oil. The lines of archers on either side of Zerebril knocked their bows but did not draw yet. The men of Stedtfest were renowned foresters, solid archers, and good at crafting long bows. The infantry was in their effective range, but Zerebril would wait to give the order to fire until they had fully left the cover of the forest. Chaos was his best strategy. They would have to worry about arrows from above and traps from below.

What was Ewen waiting for? Zerebril knew he would not send a messenger with terms. His slaughter was unconditional, meant to demoralize the spirits of Wilheim, and likely to send a message to Ardhataz's neighbors. With the infantry in place, Zerebril counted fifteen square units, each spaced out by about fifty feet. They were in shield wall formation, and he could see the top of a siege ladder poking out the front of each formation. *So that's your game,* Zerebril thought. *Overwhelm the ramparts from several sides with ladders to climb the low walls.* Zerebril had predicted that most other siege tactics short of waiting out the population to starve would be useless. But

306 • ANTON JONES

damming the river had probably made Ewen anxious to get into a proper city and give his soldiers a rest from the newly created wetlands. If he stayed out there for too long, winter would be here, and his soldiers would freeze or succumb to disease.

It made sense for him to attack as soon as he arrived. And in those moments of waiting, it was remarkably quiet. The birds stopped chirping. No insects droned. Even the roosters in Stedt-fest didn't announce the dawn. All he could hear was the sound of the nearby river running through the city, spitting out on the southwestern side and then hitting his dam. Even the archers near him seemed to be holding their breath.

Ewen trotted along at the tree line, personally inspecting each unit, saying things that could not be heard across the muddy expanse. Zerebril held a spyglass up to watch him. His men did look haggard. They were already coated in blood and mud, presumably from engaging and cleaning up after whatever happened to the vanguard and the cavalry unit. What he wouldn't give to have one of those weapons right now.

"Idiot!" Zerebril muttered to himself.

He should have kept one bearer back with him to fire from the walls. *No time for the past,* he reminded himself. *Don't think, just be here.*

King Ewen lifted his visor on his helm and bellowed across the expanse. "Ya know who I am! Ya know why I'm here! Dere is nothing ya can do! Dere will be no surrender! So, try to make dis fun! Put up a good fight, would ya?"

Fun? Did he think this was a game? Zerebril wondered. He looked back into his spyglass. *Was the king smiling?*

Ewen turned to his troops and Zerebril could still audibly hear his declarations to them. "Dis city is already yers. Go claim yer warm beds. Kill all bearing arms. Dey will do da same to you. Take captive da nobility or da unarmed. We'll need dem for later. Three mountains to climb! For da past wrongs Wilheim has done to us, for da present will to be greater, and for da future glory of a united Verdin under Ardhataz!"

Ewen raised his fist, horns echoed through the trees, and his soldiers charged out of the cover of the forest and into the killing field. Though much slower in shield wall formation, they could still trot at a decent pace. The fifteen square formations of mountain brutes, clad in miscellaneous armor, black tunics with three white mountains, and curved wooden tower shields advanced to their destiny and Zerebril's demise.

"Archers, loose!" Zerebril shouted. Though they had already begun independently, Zerebril felt the need to give the command in case anyone didn't get the idea. In total, around 500 archers had lined the walls and were shooting down arrows. Not as much as he would have liked, but it was enough to keep the shields up and honest. At this range and since many of Ewen's troops were in simple gambesons, arrows would be fatal if they found a gap in the shields. The large shields did make up for the light armor as arrows embedded themselves in the wood.

As for Ewen's forces, Zerebril found it hard to estimate given the tight formations. From his scouts, Ewen had an estimated 20,000–25,000 troops currently with him after Gunter had killed many on the boats and on land. This was nowhere near that many. He'd guessed that each square had about 300–500 soldiers. The unified squares made it easier to estimate how many troops were in each line and then multiply it roughly by the depth of the formation. Times fifteen squares, that's anywhere between 4,500–7,500 troops for the assault. *Where were the others? Were they sneaking around? Staying back? Had the vanguard taken out that many men? Or was this first round just a test to see how Stedtfest's defenses would hold up?* Zerebril shook his head. Too much thinking. Now was a time for action.

Ewen's troops, distracted by the arrows pelting their shields, wouldn't be looking down to see the slightly out of place muddy leaves and sticks they were walking over. The first line of men in one of the formations fell into the spike pits, exposing the men carrying the ladders with no shields.

"Archers, focus on the formations who fall in the traps, they'll have gaps in the shield wall!" The archers obeyed and sent a volley targeting the disarrayed formation. Many of the arrows found their marks and pierced through the gambeson the soldiers were wearing. This only made more men in that formation fall over each other, slipping in the mud, and trying not to trip over corpses or fall in the pit. The archers sent another volley and decimated the group. They broke, abandoning their ladders and sprinting across the muddied expanse to shelter themselves as parts of other formations that had not broken yet. Zerebril exhaled the breath he was holding. *One down*, he thought, *fourteen to go.* With each destroyed formation, the archers could focus their fire a little better.

Ewen's troops slowed down and started looking down at their feet, making some adjustments rather than running straight to the wall. But looking down loosened the shield wall, and some arrows found gaps. Soon enough, gaps were created in the formation closest to the one that first fell in a trap due to paranoia about their footing. They too slipped in the mud over the corpses and collapsed. The archers concentrated their fire on that one, and it broke in the same manner as the first. With the collapse of two formations right next to each other, there was now a large gap in Ewen's siege crews.

"Infantry! Prepare to fend off the ladders!" Zerebril shouted and gestured to pass the orders down the wall. "Group yourselves around their two centers of mass. Ready the water, the logs, and yourselves!"

Another formation fell into a pit and broke. *This is working,* Zerebril dared to hope. He had concentrated the traps in the center of the predicted assault path, which would create a wedge and split the bulk of Ewen's forces into two, forcing one half deeper into no-man's land and pinning the other against the flooding river. The squares were growing with men from the broken formations, narrowing the gaps between each unit and squeezing them into tighter quarters. Their pace slowed further as the left mass of troops were crowded into the more flooded portions of the muddy expanse. The tighter the units, the less they could maneuver around the traps, even when they spotted them. Soldiers, close enough to hear now, were screaming as they were bunched into the spike pits. The archers jumped on each opening, loosing volley after volley at vulnerable formations.

"This is for Gunter," Zerebril growled. He raised his spyglass back to his eye to see what Ewen was up to. He stayed stationary, just outside the tree line. Though it was hard to tell as they remained in the woods, he had several other people with him, including numerous well-armored soldiers in black plate, not nearly enough for a whole unit, but he had something else he was concealing back there.

Whatever it is, Zerebril thought. *I'll be ready for it.* Zerebril figured Ewen would have sent the beasts by now if he had any left. There was no reason to suffer this much loss when he had that big of a trump card. Or was there? *Stop that! Just focus on what's in front of you. Act on one thing at a time,* Zerebril scolded himself.

The soldiers crossed the flooded trench just outside the wall, which forced them to swim to the other side, a difficult task while carrying a shield and being pelted with arrows. The archers focused on the swimmers and many of them did not make it to the other side. Soon enough bodies piled up in the trench so that the soldiers could cross over, boots on their fallen countrymen, while still raising their shields.

They had made it to the wall, but Zerebril could see what it had cost them to do so. Their eyes were hollow, teeth perpetually clenched, arms and legs visibly shaking under the gambeson. He almost felt sorry for them, until he remembered Gunter and the burning countryside.

Archers in the gap region continued to fire on the flanks of the troops while the ones near the ladders pulled out two-handed axes.

The rear of the shield formations suddenly dropped their shield, and Tazzian archers of their own poked their bows out, loosing arrows at Zerebril's troops waiting for the ladders. Though a few men fell, they quickly ducked behind the wooden crenulations affixed to the top of the ramparts days before.

"Switch to water!" Zerebril shouted. Instead of taking the time to poke their heads around the crenulations, draw their bows, and aim only to get picked off by Ewen's more ready archers below, Zerebril ordered his men to start hurling prepared boiling water over the walls at the soldiers pressed up against the fortifications. Sizzling and screams reached Zerebril's ears from below, and the boiling water made the muddy terrain even more hazardous.

Ewen's archers provided decent cover as the soldiers revealed the ladders and pushed them up the wooden walls. Stedtfest's walls were not nearly as tall as Wilheim's, and this allowed Ewen's troops to have shorter ladders that could be positioned at a less steep angle, making it difficult for the defenders to get leverage and push the ladders off. They effectively turned their ladders into bridges that could not be repelled. The tops of each ladder were covered in metal to prevent the axes from severing them from the landing points on the walls. But Zerebril had planned for this, too.

"Logs!" He shouted.

The Stedtfest infantry climbed the steps up to the ramparts. With all the trees they felled, some were kept uncut and ready for this exact scenario. Zerebril had ordered that the men drill handles into the logs for efficient transportation. Ten soldiers lining the sides of the logs grabbed the handles and marched them up the stairs at each point where a unit had landed their ladders.

"Roll!" Zerebril shouted.

The infantry, together with the archers, heaved the logs over the crenulations and dropped them on the ladders. The sounds were sickening. The logs rolled down the ladders and crushed hands and heads of climbing soldiers. If the soldiers bailed over the side of the ladder, then the logs would continue rolling until they crossed the center of the ladder. All that weight in the center caused multiple ladders to snap in half and fall to the ground. The logs then came tumbling down on the soldiers pressed up against the walls below.

Nearly every ladder broke under the weight. Some of the logs had rolled off the side before reaching the centers of the ladders or were redirected by some brave soldier who didn't bail over the side. Some of the Tazzian troops started to break and run back to the tree line.

"Regroup around the remaining ladders!" Zerebril commanded. His men moved swiftly on the ramparts to various concentration points where the ladders had held. By Zerebril's count, only three were still stationed, one on the far side and two near the river.

Then something happened Zerebril had not seen coming. Not all of the soldiers moved over to the standing ladders. Instead, they stayed in their positions, and some of them grabbed the logs Zerebril had just cast over the side and leaned them up against the wall. Using the handles on the sides as rungs and footholds, Zerebril had effectively given these troop much sturdier ladders.

That backfired, he thought. "Focus arrows and boiling water on troops lifting the logs!"

It took a lot of men and time to lift and position the logs standing vertically against each wall, time that archers took advantage of by picking off men carrying them. When enough men were filled with arrows, the log would fall and sometimes crush more of their troops. Even with the new tactic, only two logs were positioned in place. In total, there were still only five points of entry. Though Zerebril had fewer numbers, that was manageable.

However, the troops that Zerebril thought had lost morale and fled to the trees came running back out with more ladders. Though they weren't in formation, they didn't have to worry about the arrows since the archers were now preoccupied with the much closer threat of the ladders and logs that were already in position.

Close-quarters fighting began as Ewen's troops finally made it to the tops of each ladder or log. The archers went below the ramparts and continued loosing arrows through slits in the log walls. As the archers went down, Zerebril's Wilheim garrison—heavily armored infantry clad in mail, barbutes, pauldrons, and the Wilheim sun emblazoned on their green tunics—defended the choke points. Around each ladder were two layers of Wilheim infantry. The circle closest to the ladders used short swords, maces, and axes to hack at the Tazzian nasal helms as they appeared. Behind the first layer stood men with spears and poleaxes who could also stab or chop at the enemies from over the shoulders of the first layer. There were plenty of men to replace the layers if the choppers got tired.

Though a few more ladders did arrive, there was enough of the Wilheim garrison to go around and defend each choke point. After seeing that going up the ladder would lead to a halberd to the face, Zerebril hoped that would dissuade the men from climbing. It was certain death with no hope to overwhelm the choke points with the number of ladders that had landed.

Zerebril puffed up his chest. He had won. Any sane commander would pull back his troops to avoid too many casualties. He had created the ultimate death trap with over half of the Tazzian troops from the fifteen formations lying dead in the mud. *So why hadn't Ewen ordered a retreat?* This time, Zerebril allowed himself to think. *Ewen wouldn't send his men to a sense-less slaughter. There must be something else he's up to.*

He pulled out his spyglass again and scoured the expanse. No other units had appeared. Just Ewen with the ones in black plate by the trees at the edge of the clearing. But he was *still* smiling. Zerebril shivered. This had to be some kind of diversion. Zerebril frantically ran around the ramparts looking for anything that might be off. Then he heard the screams coming from the other side of Stedtfest where the river entered the city.

Zerebril grabbed as many troops as possible who weren't busy at the ladders and ran into the town. He went alongside the river until he saw the corpses. Civilians had been torn to pieces. The elderly who could not flee had stayed but could not pull a bow string either. They had congregated in the center of the town only to be ripped apart. Cloth, not plate, tunics, not mail, all covered in blood. Ludicrous amounts of the dark red, an even more grisly sight than what was happening in the killing field. Zerebril was going to be sick.

These are not normal wounds, Zerebril thought, forcing down his revulsion.. *They looked like they were killed by claws and teeth.*

The soldiers Zerebril had brought from the wall whispered prayers and muttered curses at the terrible sight of the bodies strewn over the stone streets.

Zerebril looked at the thick, densely packed bars of iron that the river filtered through. *No,* he thought, *there's no way anything made it through that.*

Suddenly he saw something glowing in the water. On the other side of the gate, what looked like glowing yarn was funneling its way through the gaps in the bars. The heat coming off the tendrils made the water bubble as it contorted the strands of its body.

Zerebril had heard of these things, but seeing one of them move was beyond his comprehension. Zerebril breathed in

rapidly as his senses took in less and less of the world he thought
he knew. Confronted with this thing, the world was now much
larger as it was darker, the multitude of things he didn't and
could never know squeezing in on his throat.

The light beast finished snaking through the bars and
returned to its original houndlike shape. Not including the beast
that just entered, there were two other tethers of stars that
stretched from the river and into the city. Three of them, three
unkillable beasts, were loose in the city and prowling to corner
his troops at the ladders. The vanguard hadn't gotten all of
them.

The light beast climbed onto the shore and bore down on
Zerebril and his troops. He stood there stammering, shaking,
unable to make his mouth work.

Coward, Sophia's voice echoed in his head.

Zerebril gritted his teeth to keep them from chattering,
snapped his visor down, and drew his rapier. His troops from the
wall stared down at the dismembered corpses and then charged
in with rage.

The beast pulsed with light, and with that light came an
unsettling, vibrating roar. The soldiers tried to stab at it with
spears, but the light veins shifted themselves around the points.
One soldier tried to hack at its limb with a sword, but the sword
didn't cut through the light strands, it just stretched them away
and then tangled themselves around the sword. The sword was
yanked from the man's hands and hurled into the river. It looked
like a bunch of men trying to fight an oversized, animated
spiderweb.

The beast responded by slapping the now unarmed man
away, knocking him to the ground. His mail had protected him
from being cut or burned, but he hit the ground hard, helmeted
head bouncing off the cobbled stone, and did not get back up.
The spearman continued to prod at the beast. The beast's arteries
nearest the spear hafts began to steam and then swiftly moved

through the haft, chopping off the spearhead and leaving the men with pointy sticks.

"Our weapons are useless against it," Zerebril mumbled. His troops looked back at him and then fled away from the beast.

There was no point in running or fighting. This was where Zerebril would fall. His planning wasn't enough. The time given to him by Gunter had been wasted on poppy, and he was about to be torn apart by the same monsters that killed his brother.

The beast stalked up to Zerebril slowly, sizing up its prey. Scorch marks littered the ground where its veins stepped. It had no eyes for Zerebril to meet, just a mass of glowing, pulsing tangles that moved like a panther.

Zerebril had lost. It didn't matter how many of his soldiers remained if their weapons couldn't hurt the things. Stedtfest had fallen. His breath hitched in his throat as though someone had clumsily sewn his windpipe shut. Wilheim would fall. He heard his plate shaking, layered over a body that could not discern if it should fight or flee. And his father would fall too. As sweat dripped down from his eyebrows and into the corners of his eyes, he lost his grasp on the last glimmer of hope he once had. He collapsed to his knees.

The beast inched up to Zerebril, now right in front of his visor. He could feel the heat coming off the creature, slowly cooking him in his armor. It growled, a sound almost too low for Zerebril to hear, a sound that seemed to reverberate through his useless metal skin.

But it didn't attack.

As his sweat started to turn to vapor from proximity of the heat, Zerebril closed his eyes and gritted his teeth. "What are you waiting for?" He shouted, banging his armored hand against the stone street. "Just kill me!"

The beast didn't respond. Instead, it looked away as someone else in plate approached from behind. Bearing a shield and a glowing sword, Sophia ran up to the beast and stopped. Her sword lowered at the beast. It moved its head in her direction but didn't otherwise seem to stir, almost like it didn't completely acknowledge her. Its head moved back to Zerebril.

"So, he *can* control them," Sophia said.

"Sophia? Is that you?"

"Oh, is that Zerebril under that helmet?"

He dared to lift his visor. He did so slowly, not understanding why the beast seemed to be staying in place and not attacking. "Yes! Now kill it," he whispered. He didn't know if the things could understand his language.

Sophia lifted up her visor. "Hmmm. No."

"What? Why?!"

"Because," she taunted, "King Ewen paid me triple what you did. My orders are to bring you to him."

Zerebril's helmeted head fell forward. He let out a final breath of surrender. The money he had taken from Cormac was not enough. Zerebril could almost hear Roran laughing at him, and his shoulders slumped.

"Nothing to say?" Sophia rolled her eyes and kicked him in the chest plate. Awkward in his armor, Zerebril waved his arms and fell backward on the ground. "I liked it better when you were kneeling, but on your back will do," she said, lowering her glowing longsword to Zerebril's exposed face.

"This . . . what we do here today, it will kill tens of thousands of people," Zerebril said from the ground, his voice barely a whisper.

"You know, Zerebril," Sophia replied. "Holding one of these weapons, you kind of get used to death. It doesn't matter who dies, as long as it's not me."

CHAPTER 21
CAPTIVE

IN ARDHATAZ, there are no tombstones. Instead, there are stone pillars set into the ground marking the places of marriage. Carved into the pillars are the names of all the friends and family who were able to attend the ceremony. It's another thing that's necessary to strike the ground. Handles are carved out of the stone so the couple can climb up the pillar and get married standing on top. For the briefest of moments, for the longest of moments, an Ardhatazian couple is above everyone else, can see farther than everyone else, can hope more than everyone else. During the speaking of the vows, the newly married couple is above its king.

Urrem had memorized both his own vows and the vows said to him by Jezerelle. Even if it was harder to remember every detail on her face, the vows remained fresh in his memory.

He stood on that pillar above the sparse trees three years ago, holding Jezerelle's hands and looking into her eyes.

I vow, Urrem had said, *to be bound to ya, as steadfast as da stone we stand upon.*

And I vow, she had said, *to make this binding a pleasure, not a duty.*

I vow to hold ya above da mountains, above da clouds, so dat ya never feel da storms of winter.

And I vow to hold to you even in the depths of Lake Verdin, in waters so deep we can scarcely see.

I vow to find da strength to always return home. He smiled. *Even after a night of heavy drinking with me mates.*

From below the pillar, his new friends gave a hearty whoop and holler.

She smiled back. *And I vow to be the new home you always return to.*

Sometimes it was necessary to go into the past to avoid looking too closely at the present.

Urrem made another pillar the day they took Stedtfest, just as tall and wide, but made of wood. The Willies had even put handles on it. The log he held up so that the troops could storm the walls of Stedtfest was gone from his mind in the moment. All he thought of was setting the pillar before his wedding day, where he would stand above it all with the one he loved most.

The men climbing this pillar of wood did not get to stand above it all. They were forced up for their country and were not met with a bride at the top. Only death.

Urrem was not specifically tasked to do this, "washing da field," but he knew it had to be done. For the sake of his men, the countless still laying in the mud, possibly still alive.

With his spear, Urrem navigated the corpses, poking them with the butt and then stabbing them through the heart if they didn't move.

Each time he made a thrust through a corpse, he heard a sickening gurgle as water rushed out of the muddy, bloated bodies. He moved to the next corpse, poked it with the spear, checked the pulse if the eyes were closed, and then stabbed again. There were thousands of corpses. It would take Urrem days to do this by himself. Why had no one been ordered to do it?

Time was of the essence, after all, the whole point being to finish off a comrade who could not be saved by Life Nectar but wasn't dead yet. He took it upon himself to spare them from Grief Sickness. If they could catch it, then chances are they would be lying in a field of corpses, barely alive, full of despair, and certain that nothing could save them. He had heard from his own father long ago that Grief Sickness was the most painful way to die, even more painful than burning. He would not let his comrades go out that way.

And then he saw them. Black armor on the horizon, checking the corpses just as he was, except not with a spear. Four Shadows of the Mountain, the elite forces, were prowling around the corpses. Head to toe, they were clad in the blackened armor, except for their gauntlets. Each of them had removed their gauntlets.

Urrem approached their position hesitantly. With their limited visibility, their visors always down, it was possible they hadn't seen him yet. It was possible for him to turn and head back to camp, to not stick his nose in whatever they were doing.

"For Malcolm," Urrem whispered, and he continued his approach.

Each one would kneel down next to a corpse, hold their ungauntleted, outstretched hand over the corpse, grunt, and then move on. But their hands—

Urrem's breath caught in his throat.

Their hands were glowing! It seemed they had some ability to sense something about the corpse by the glow of their hands.

"What are you doing out here, soldier?"

Urrem almost jumped out of his skin. He turned around and

was face-to-face with the Scholar, a nasty smile shining eerily out of the man's hood.

The Scholar cocked his head playfully, seeming almost to relish in his ability to make Urrem's skin crawl. "Rank?" the Scholar asked with his unnaturally scratchy, high-pitched voice when Urrem failed to answer.

Urrem was paralyzed. Everywhere the Scholar went, unnatural things trailed in his wake. Urrem looked down at the train of the Scholar's robes. Before Ewen marshalled the remaining troops from the ambush, Urrem had seen the Scholar—

"Name? Rank?" the Scholar repeated.

Urrem swallowed. "Captain...Captain Urrem."

The smile disappeared from the Scholar's visible lips, the only thing visible. "Captain, you say? Orders?"

"N-none. I'm out here on my own accord. Honoring da dead by not letting dem catch Grief Sickness if dey can't be saved."

"Hmmmm. How noble of you," the Scholar said. "As you can see, we can handle that just fine. I admire your initiative, but from here on out, I would be careful where you go poking your nose around."

"What are dey doing wit dem?"

"Hmmmm?"

Urrem blinked and pointed at the Shadows. "Dey're not making sure da corpses are dead by stabbing dem. Dey're just waving their hands over dem."

"Curiosity is another virtue I hold in high regard; however, that will also not suit you here. Rest assured, anyone still alive will be tended to. Anyone with Grief Sickness will be looked after."

Urrem felt himself sinking in the mud, or what he hoped was mud for he dare not look down.

"Dismissed, Captain." The Scholar smiled and shooed Urrem away by flicking his fingers back toward the outer gate.

. . .

The gates to Stedtfest opened before Urrem's bloodied form. It was not his enemy's blood that he was covered in. It was not his own either. Some of it was dried from Malcolm's violent end. The rest of it was from the blood that rained down on him as he held the log in place to act as a ladder when his own unit's broke.

He walked on the cobblestone streets, looking at the sturdy but modest wooden structures. Homes, taverns, trade shops, and vendor stalls lined the road, all made of wood. All of it was good workmanship, people who had carved a living out of the wild forest and made peace living alongside it. The town would burn quickly if that were Ewen's wish. How long had it been since Urrem worked as a carpenter? How long had it been since he had built his home with Jezerelle?

Unlike the natural wooden structure of Stedtfest, there were three unnatural horrors that morning. The first was the mace bearer, and the second was senseless slaughter as yet another diversion. He had let it happen to him again.

He was surprised by how quickly Ewen recovered and marshalled his forces once the bearers were dealt with.

But that third horror.

Urrem followed the line of exhausted troops into the town square where he could hear dull thumps, gasps of breath, and . . . cheers. It sounded like Ewen was taking his right to beat the leaders of the enemy force. And, knowing Ewen, he would be making a show of it. Though many of the soldiers went in the direction of the cheers to see the spectacle of Ewen mashing some poor sap's face into the ground, Urrem had seen enough for the day.

He took off his nasal helm and sat on a low stone wall, looking up at the sky and just breathing in as much as he could. He had to make up for all the times he held his breath as an arrow whizzed by him on the assault across the killing field.

As he breathed in through his blood-crusted nostrils, Urrem saw Sophia making her way toward the direction of cheering.

The officers had known about the insider, though no one had ever met her. But that long sword made her unmistakable. She had done as much as she could for Ardhataz, trickling information to Ewen until she arrived in Stedtfest. She couldn't get information to Ewen about the planned ambush since Zerebril seemed like he wouldn't let her out of his sight. And apparently she had another very annoying bearer who kept trying to woo her at night.

But she made up for it by leading the cavalry unit into the waiting mouths of the beasties and then showing the beasties where they could sneak in while still remaining close to the river.

From where he sat, Urrem could see dozens of bodies strewn around the streets. Some of them were looted bodies from the Wilheim forces. Others were civilians.

But even that wasn't the third horror he had seen that day. As he fled from the mace bearer, he saw some of the boats being attacked by another Cormac weapon bearer whom he recognized. One of the twins who fought his way to freedom by making a name for himself in the Highland Pits. He had set fire to *that* boat. Whether he had known it or not, all the civilian prisoners who were already being tortured finally met their cruel end by burning alive.

All but one. The Screw-Turned Man had washed ashore on the side of the river. His movements were jerky, muscles not able to contract properly with the screws in them. His breathing was audible through the holes in the iron that encased his head. The twin, horrified, ran in the other direction.

Urrem thought it odd that the twin had run at the sight of the Screw-Turned Man, but then realized he was running from something else. The Scholar had shown up—and that was the true horror, the reason Urrem was now paralyzed whenever he saw the man, if the Scholar could even be called a man. He had never seen anything like it. Even after the light beasts. Even after watching a bearer massacre his friends. What the Scholar could do . . . well, it would be hard to sleep after seeing that.

The Scholar quickly restrained the Screw-Turned Man with dark tendrils that shot out of his shadow, tendrils that looked exactly like the things that lashed the beasts to the river. The tendrils whipped about the Scholar, smashing into tents and their own troops as if they were hard to control. Eventually, the Scholar focused them on the Screw-Turned Man and pinned him down. He was determined to not let the wretch escape.

More cheers erupted from the town square. Someone was really getting the piss taken out of them if the troops were cheering like that.

Urrem sighed. He wondered what would happen to the quota now that the boat was gone. Would they build another to create more beasts? Was three enough to storm Wilheim now that their bearers had been dealt with? Did they have more bearers waiting behind the stone walls? And what in all of Verdin was the Scholar doing with any Ardhatazian he found with Grief Sickness? Surely, they weren't getting the same fate as the tortured prisoners, right?

Urrem let himself fall on his side. He pulled up his legs as if treating the wall as a necessary bed. Wherever he went, it didn't matter which side of the war he was on, there were monsters waiting, ready to tear people limb from limb. Whether it was the bearers, the light beasts made to counter the bearers, the hybrid beast mace bearer who claimed to counter the beasts, or the Scholar who seemed to be a monster in his own tier, there was no escape from the bloodshed. He was just as trapped as the Screw-Turned Man.

He thought of Jezerelle's face with effort. After months on campaign, it was a struggle to remember what she looked like, the exact color of her eyes. The color of her hair. The color of her cheeks when she smiled.

The only color he had seen recently was red, and he was covered in it.

CHAPTER 22
DREAM PROPHECIES

All he can do is watch helplessly
In a half-remembered dream

Griselda and her metal hands
Practice ending lives
In the Wilheim Academies training grounds
A breastplate to conceal
That her heart is now an alloy
That it cares
Yet it has killed
And may make
A habit of doing so

Urrem is rewarded
Quick thinking
Logs for ladders
With a promotion
Title of colonel
In branch of siege
Since the old one

Died in the bearer raid

King Morgen stares at glass
Color swirling in rays
Depicting a history of triumph
Incongruous with
The dark throne room
Praying he is not down
Another son

Henrietta travels toward a port town
Preparing to board Rodrick's ship
Fredrick holding her hand
A great expanse of blue
Sea and sky await
What is ahead
What is behind

In her last moments
Gretchen births Arno
And many will die
In a vain attempt
To keep him safe
In his last moments
Cormac fights a monster
Knowing he could never win
But fight he does
Light the fires one last time
Hold back the dark
Just a little while longer
In his last moments
Gunter stabs the blade into the ground
The brightness fades
Heat dissipates

How many must he kill
How many must he save
The protectors
Are dead
They lasted a moment
And what remains
What is behind
What is ahead

CHAPTER 23
STAND UNWAVERING

IN THE TOWN CENTER, Zerebril, still in his armor, was dropped to his knees. Sophia and Ewen's troops had taken his rapier but didn't bind him. They must have thought he was not a threat. Next to him knelt Connor, out of his armor, hands bound behind his back, with a cut lip and swollen-shut eye.

"You!" Connor shouted at Sophia. "You betrayed us?"

"No," she shrugged. "I just took another job."

"But—but we sparred together! Does that mean nothing?"

Sophia scoffed and shook her head.

"You bitch!"

Sophia walked over and kicked him in the stomach. Connor doubled over. "That's it," Connor coughed. "I'm naming my next weapon after you."

Sophia smirked, seemingly satisfied by the implications of that.

Zerebril looked around. Troops clad in black tunics outlined the square. Many of them had looted the mail, pauldrons, and barbutes off the fallen Wilheim garrison. *If Connor's here,* Zerebril thought, *does that mean the twins and Carl escaped? Or were they bought too?* He continued to look around, searching for any way out of this.

The Tazzes started beating on their shields slowly, in rhythm. *What was going on?* The black-plated soldiers from the tree line soon entered the square and formed a wall in front of the regular infantry. The beating got faster, and Zerebril heard the jovial, booming laughter of Ewen as he entered the space. He raised his hands in acknowledgment of his soldiers drumming, like he was welcoming applause. He had removed his armor and was only wearing trousers, his big red beard barely discernible from the rest of his dense, red chest hair. He lumbered toward Zerebril like a rust-colored bear.

The Blood-Red King, Zerebril thought.

The king stood before Zerebril, looking down and smiling. He clapped Zerebril on the shoulder. "Dat *was* fun. Ya nearly had me dere. So, ya are as clever as yer reputation suggests."

"I-I have a reputation?"

"Hmmm . . . well, no. But Sophia did give me da goods on yer character. Maybe dat counts."

It was getting hard to hear over the beating and roar of his troops. Ewen raised his hands to silence them.

Turning back to Zerebril, Ewen said, "How do ya like da black plate?" He gestured to the massive soldiers covered in the pitch-like metal. "Sophia says yer a man who appreciates da arts; ya even put some design into yer own armor, I see. Dese snazzy fellows are da Shadows of da Mountain. As a special treat for being me elite, I gave dem front row seats . . . well, standing room."

"To what?" Zerebril asked, scared of the answer.

Ewen smiled, "To me personally beating yer ass."

Zerebril was so caught off guard by his tonally off, cheerful attitude. He couldn't formulate any response.

"Alright, Prince, to yer feet," he said, lifting Zerebril off his knees. "One more ting to do, and it's even more fun."

A boy appeared behind the king and looked at Zerebril.

"Ah, Willem, care to watch dis un' too? Was watching me beat da piss out of the jester dere not enough for ya?" the king asked the child.

"I have more to learn," the child replied simply.

"Good lad!" said the king and clapped Willem on the back. He urged the boy over to join the wall of troops.

The child's gaze haunted Zerebril. Not because the child was anything out of the ordinary, but for who it reminded him of and what he had done—the ever-present shadow that changed form. Gunter dying alone. His father, helpless without his stolen medicine. Arno, screaming as his leg was severed. The poppy had allowed his mind to grow dull, left unable to respond to Roran or Arno's pleas for help. The mercy took the pain at the cost of Zerebril's mind drifting like wind. Now he would pay for that.

"If you're just going to kill me," Zerebril muttered, "get it over with." He wasn't sure if he was talking to Ewen or the shadow. "I've been asking all day. Just end it."

"Nah," Ewen said. "I don't kill unarmed royalty. Plus, ya won my respect, like yer ugly friend over here," he said, gesturing to Connor. "Now, he stood up to a good clobbering!"

Connor spat out some blood in response.

"Deal is," Ewen continued, "yer going to fight me; it's the Ardhatazian way. If ya can beat me, I'll let ya go. If not, ya'll be joining ugly here."

"Joining him for what?"

Ewen paced about and scratched the top of his head. "Ya see, Prince, Wilheim so graciously spat us out in da most horrid place in all of Verdin. As such, dere's only three ways of making a living in da Ardhatazian highlands. Ya can raise livestock, ya can pirate merchant vessels in Lake Verdin, or ya can fight in da Pits. And da Pits always need fighters, willingly or not. Ya'll be sent to Ardhataz as prisoners just as yer ancestors did to us."

"You-you're selling us into slavery to fight in the Pits?" Connor stammered. "Don't you know who my father is?"

"I do," Ewen chuckled. "Dat's why it's so funny. Plus, a fighter like ya? Ya'll have a grand ol' time. Ya've got Tazzian blood. As for da high-born Willy here," Ewen motioned to Zerebril. "Yer fate's yet to be decided."

Ewen raised his hands to his face and balled his fists. "Now, I don't expect ya to be familiar with dis custom, so let me give ya a few pointers. Da Shadows of da Mountain are da boundaries. Dey won't interfere," he said, looking around the circle, "unless dey want me to clobber dem too."

Zerebril looked down at his gauntlets. Was this man really expecting Zerebril to fight him?

"Normally, ya would be fighting bare-chested too. But yer a bit of a whelp. Weight disadvantage is no joke." He held out his hand, measuring his own height and then lowering it all the way down to Zerebril's height. "So, I'll let ya keep da armor. I like challenges. Ya know how to fight, right?"

Zerebril was trying to get his thoughts together and couldn't make any sort of response.

"Hmmm. Well, dat won't be too fun den. Ya Willie royalty not teaching proper etiquette of the fist, eh? How about ya make another rule in yer favor to even da odds den? Make it reasonable."

Zerebril racked his brain for any way that he could turn the tides in his favor. None of Ewen's troops would fight at his side if he made it two on one. Connor looked like Ewen had already beat him bloody and couldn't fight anymore. It would have to be some sort of limitation on Ewen himself. Or a weapon.

"I'm guessing giving me my rapier wouldn't be reasonable," Zerebril said.

"Aye, I won't allow dat."

Right then, Zerebril thought. *What could I possibly use? I don't know what would help me to win a fistfight. But if this man is all about respect and warrior spirit or something, maybe . . .*

"Is grappling allowed?" Zerebril asked.

Ewen nodded.

"Then I choose to not have an additional rule. In fact, I will remove my armor as well." It would only slow him down and make him tired much faster anyway, especially since he wasn't used to fighting in it. He wouldn't be able to get up quickly if Ewen knocked him over, either.

Ewen cocked his head and raised an eyebrow. "Ya sure about dat?"

"I am."

Ewen shrugged and snapped his fingers. His troops jogged over and helped Zerebril out of his armor. "Ya have me respect," Ewen said. "But dis will make da fight much less fun for me. I might have to get another round with da ugly one."

Connor groaned.

"What, no more witticisms?" Ewen chuckled.

Connor slowly shook his head.

"Fine," Ewen turned to address Zerebril. "Now, no biting, hair pulling, or groin shots."

Zerebril nodded as the soldier lifted his coif off his head. There was a black-clad soldier on each of his limbs, unfastening the armor. Zerebril was out of his element. He had no idea how to think his way out of this. But there was a gamble on the edge of his thoughts.

"Instead of a rule against you," Zerebril said. "I want a condition if I win."

Ewen grinned and waved a big, meaty finger at Zerebril. "Now dat's more like it!"

"If I somehow manage to win, you'll release us as promised, but you will also take your troops out of Wilheim. You'll end the war."

Ewen's smile broadened to show all his teeth. His soldiers murmured to themselves. Ewen walked up to Zerebril and offered his hand. "Ya have me word as king of Ardhataz," said Ewen. "If ya make me surrender, den I'll end da war and withdraw my troops. I'll even throw in an extra boon. I have yer brother's sword; took it off ugly here when da Scholar wasn't looking. I'll return it to ya if ya beat me too."

"You have Professor Mathilda?!" Connor shouted.

King Ewen kept his hand out but looked over at Connor. "He's an odd one, isn't he?"

Zerebril nodded, reached up, and shook Ewen's hand. *That actually worked? Good, now the only problem left is this over-muscled hairball.* But that was proper motivation. Like his father had said, the weight of the kingdom was back on his shoulders. He could be the sole reason this war ends. He sighed. *If only it had been Gunter who was fighting him.*

The troops finished getting the rest of the armor off the prince. The prince removed his undershirt. He was toned but scrawny compared to Ewen.

"Are ya ready, Prince?"

Zerebril nodded and raised his fists to his chin.

"Good, begin!" Ewen shouted as he traced a triangle over his heart.

The soldiers erupted in cheers. Zerebril realized this must be a practice many of them look forward to.

Ewen settled into his fighting stance: elbows to the side, left fist outstretched, right fist on his chin, and knees slightly bent. Given Zerebril had no hand-to-hand combat experience, he mirrored Ewen.

Ewen inched closer, and Zerebril inched back. He rotated around the town square, getting a feel for how far away he could scramble if he needed to. Ewen maintained his back to the center of the makeshift arena as he pressed Zerebril. Zerebril found himself tempted to drift away farther, but thought better of it. Ewen was going to press him into the corner of the square into a wall of troops, which would not end well.

Instead, Zerebril gingerly leaped forward and jabbed at Ewen's stomach before ducking out and around him.

Zerebril's hand hurt. Why did his hand hurt? Did he punch a man or Wilheim's stone wall?

Ewen nodded in acknowledgment of the clean hit but held a smile on his face.

Oros's blood, Zerebril thought. *That did nothing.*

Ewen inched closer and closer, again trying to put Zerebril in the corner. And again, Zerebril resisted, leaped to the left, and punched Ewen in the side. Nothing. No response. Ewen didn't even look like he felt it.

"Slick little Willy, aren't ya?" Ewen said.

Ewen still hadn't thrown a punch. All he did was slowly move forward. Was he saving his energy? Was he tired after the battle and fight with Connor? Or was this intentional?

Zerebril decided to press the offensive. He reached up and tried to jab at Ewen's chin. Ewen didn't block it; in fact, he lowered his hands at the last minute so Zerebril's punch made it through his guard. He *let* the punch hit him. The soldiers started laughing, but none of them taunted. They hushed back up when Ewen glanced their way.

Zerebril jumped back out of reach. Obviously, Zerebril was not strong enough to do any sort of damage to Ewen. He'd have to win by getting him in a chokehold. But how would he manage that? He was quicker on his feet, but Ewen always stayed in the center, making it less distance for him to rotate to catch threats, if they were even threats at all. The only time he wasn't in the center was when he tried to corner Zerebril.

Zerebril drifted over to a corner, and Ewen followed. It looked like Ewen was expecting Zerebril to try and slip past him again while landing a shot, so Ewen had widened his stance to make himself more difficult to get around. Perfect.

Zerebril dove between Ewen's legs.

"Ya wee weasel!" Ewen blustered, shocked at the tactic.

Zerebril quickly got to his feet behind Ewen and jumped up on his back. He locked his arm under Ewen's jaw and squeezed with all of his might.

The soldiers fell silent. Ewen tried to pull at Zerebril's arms, but Zerebril had the better vantage point. Ewen's face turned as red as his hair.

This will work! Zerebril thought. *It's not in vain!*

Then Ewen squatted down and jumped. He launched himself, Zerebril in tow, up into the air and positioned himself to land on his back, which meant Zerebril would hit the ground first with a bear-sized man landing on top of him.

Zerebril braced himself for impact. *Whatever happens, don't you dare let go—*

Everything went black. The deafening ringing in his ears called him back to consciousness. Zerebril had smacked his head against the ground, and Ewen's weight had knocked the wind out of him. He flashed in and out of consciousness, relaxing his grip and letting Ewen break free.

Ewen stood and held his hand to his throat, gasping. "I got to give it to ya Willies," he said. "Ya fight hard to survive."

Zerebril shook his aching head. The ringing wouldn't stop, but he found his wind and slowly got back to his feet. Ewen stood by in the center of the ring and gave Zerebril time to get up.

Zerebril regathered his bearings. "I'm not fighting for my own survival. I'm fighting to protect the lives of my people."

"I say," Ewen smiled and nodded down at Zerebril's legs. "Ya *are* making dis fun."

Ewen raised his fists and started his approach again. Zerebril tried to spring out of the corner but found he had significantly less strength than before the fall. He looked down at his leg, which had nothing to push with.

My leg's broken, I just haven't felt it yet.

Instead of jumping out of the way like he did before, he only hobbled right into Ewen's first thrown punch, an uppercut to the stomach. As soon as Zerebril had gotten his wind back, Ewen knocked it out again. It felt like he got kicked by a horse. Ewen stepped back to see how Zerebril would respond to the blow.

Ewen smiled as he saw that Zerebril, despite having a broken leg, had not crumpled from the punch to the stomach. Zerebril had bent over but righted himself and attempted to raise his fists again, gasping and coughing, his leg violently shaking.

The soldiers were even quieter than before.

Connor spat out more blood but was otherwise staring at Zerebril as wide as he could manage with his swollen eye.

Zerebril, more falling than anything, lurched toward Ewen's legs to take him down. But Ewen didn't budge. Instead, Ewen raised his hands over his head and slammed them down on Zerebril's back, smashing him to the ground.

Ewen walked back to the center of the ring and waited to see what Zerebril would do. Zerebril was drifting in and out. The pain from breaking his leg had caught up to him and it burned fiercely, making it agony to even wiggle his toes. He couldn't put any weight on it, but still, the weight of the kingdom loomed over him. With that in mind, Zerebril got to his feet, putting the majority of his weight on the other leg and tenderly moving toward Ewen.

Ewen raised an eyebrow. "Ya do know yer leg's broken, right? I heard it snap myself. I imagine ya might have cracked a few ribs by now, too."

Zerebril could barely hear what Ewen was saying over the ringing in his ears and the pain in his leg and sides. His vision was getting fuzzy, making it hard to gauge the distance between

342 • ANTON JONES

them. It didn't matter. Deep in his heart, a fire was awakened.
Dull thumps and suffering rang around his head. Zerebril was
beaten bloody and broken against this wall of a man. Not that he
cared. All he cared about was making sure his people didn't hurt
like he was. He would fight through anything now. That was his
responsibility, and so Zerebril stumbled toward his foe.

Ewen sighed and raised his guard. "So be it." He cocked
back his fist and launched it at Zerebril's head.

Zerebril raised his hand to block it, but the blow was not
being stopped. It smashed his arm into his head and sent him
careening to the side, hopelessly attempting to keep his balance
on his one good leg. It didn't work, and Zerebril toppled to the
ground. The ringing intensified. Shapes were becoming less
distinct. Black stars lingered in the corner of his vision, threatening to grow and eat everything. Shadows he could now actually see, not just a metaphor.

Ewen waited for Zerebril to get back up and approach again.
Zerebril shook his head, pushed himself up, and then continued
his hobbled march toward the Blood-Red King. Ewen nodded
and threw another punch, this time to the other side of the head.
Zerebril had learned that Ewen's punches could not be blocked,
so he leaned back on his good leg, evading it.

Ewen's mass carried him forward as he overswung. Zerebril
punched him as hard as he could as fast as he could several times
to the body while Ewen regained his balance.

Nothing.

Ewen's side was red, but he did not seem to visibly feel any
of the blows. Ewen swung again from the other side at Zerebril's
body, which he could not dodge in time on his broken leg. More
cracks, ribs breaking, black stars and shadows growing and
growing.

Zerebril gasped and fell to his knees. He was losing, and
because of it Wilheim was going to burn. There was no way he
could do anything to Ewen in this state. Might as well let the

blackness creep in and take over. He breathed heavily, each breath created sharp pains in his ribs, but he needed to breathe more than he needed to avoid pain.

Why was he still breathing anyway? Why was he still fighting? He looked up at Ewen and started seeing double. Except Ewen's double looked suspiciously like Gunter.

I was always looking at the ground, he heard Gunter's voice say, *while you were painting the sky.* Zerebril looked up. It was a beautiful day. His head, his heart, his cracked ribs, his broken leg —they all pounded. But that patch of sky sure was something. Through his ringing ears, he heard the noises of the Highest Hill hunting grounds: the birds, bugs, scurrying rabbits, the Shatter Rock River below. And Gunter singing, dragging back a boar through the woods.

Gunter had given him a little more time to enjoy a beautiful day. And the only thing left to do was to fight to make sure he kept it that way.

Zerebril picked himself up one more time and forced his legs to stop shaking. He forced the black stars from his field of vision; despite his cowardice, he would force himself to be unwavering. An odd smile played at his lips as a blurry Ewen and Gunter walked up to him. They eventually focused into one.

Zerebril wanted to remember the lyrics to Gunter's favorite hymn, but his head throbbed. All that came to mind was the lullaby, the release, the end, the final sleep.

Normally chatty, Ewen was quiet as he raised his arms at the broken prince's approach. He cocked back his fist one last time, and Zerebril lost all tangible sensation. Only a small but growing sound, a rising rush in his ears. His mother and now his brother and soon his father all singing.

Over mountains, over hill.
Over river, lake so still.

We the sun, we shine on all.
Morn to rise and night to fall.
Morn to rise and night to fall.

His last glimmer, before everything went black, was looking up at the sky as he fell toward the ground.

PART THREE
EVEN IF THERE'S NOTHING LEFT TO PROTECT

CHAPTER 24
NEW DREAM

"I WIN . . . AGAIN," Arno said suspiciously. He picked up the berry from the stump and plopped it into his mouth.

They were playing Sundial, an old Wilheim staple game. Twelve rocks were arranged on the stump. Underneath one of the rocks was a coin. The dealer would slip it under one of the rocks and then the player had three chances to guess which rock was concealing the coin. Once a guess was made, the dealer had to give a hint: right or left, indicating the closer proximity to the rock concealing the coin.

The two brothers usually preferred more advanced board games, but this worked when they didn't have the games with them. Roran decided that any spare food they scavenged could be won in a game of Sundial. Though there wasn't much—a spare mushroom, an extra nut—it did create a fair way for them to divide food that couldn't easily be divided.

At least, Arno thought it was fair. Roran had been making bad guesses intentionally to make sure Arno would get all the food. And Roran was afraid Arno was starting to catch on.

Arno eyed his brother from the other end of the stump. Roran shrugged.

"I'm not good at games relying on chance," Roran said. "But if we do a race, or an arm wrestle—well, maybe not that one anymore. I'd win if it were a game relying on physical skill."

"Sure Woe-Woe, brag about being able to beat me in a race."

Roran winced. With all that had happened to them, for better or worse, he no longer had the luxury to worry about slips of the tongue. They had bigger problems, and Arno would have to see that eventually. Arno would need to mature and let go of ideals he clung on to. But then again, Roran didn't want Arno to change either. Like most things lately, it was a lose-lose scenario. Arno either would need to change at the cost of what makes him Arno or stand tall, hold fast and suffer when the world could not meet his expectations. There was nothing to be done, so instead of sermonizing Arno on one side or the other, Roran doubled down and did his job as a proper older brother by not holding back on the good-natured ribbing. "To be fair," Roran said, "you never would have beaten me in a race, whether you had both legs or not."

"Well, you—you smell!"

Roran chuckled. If anyone had an idea how he smelled, it would be Arno, who had been strapped to Roran's back for days at a time while he did hard labor.

"But really, Roran. Maybe we should play a different game for the food."

"It's alright, No-No," Roran said, nodding his head to the harness resting nearby on the forest floor. It was about time they saddled up and got back on the run. Arno did the straps and sat in the harness. Roran stood, and the run began again.

Roran secretly hadn't eaten anything for a week. He wanted to see how far he could go, but he still hadn't found a limit yet. He felt fine, not even a stomach growl. He pretended to eat some berries and nuts but hid them behind his back when Arno wasn't looking.

He wasn't eating, but Roran hadn't noticed any other changes happening to him, other than a small tickle in bottom of his throat, possibly the first signs of a cold. Though it was troubling, he felt great, and how good he felt physically distracted from how concerning it was that he was surpassing basic human needs. Oddly enough, it was Arno who seemed a little low on energy. That seemed impossible to Roran. Roran was jogging and carrying Arno through the game trails along the Shatter Rock River, and Arno was tired?

"So, feeling any better today?" asked Roran between breaths.

Arno let out a long exhale, as if he was waking up from a nap. But Roran doubted he could get any sleep in the harness while Roran was jogging.

"Still tired then? How's your stomach?"

"You know," Arno finally said. "I had a dream last night."

"Well, was it a good dream?"

Arno sighed. "Hard to tell."

"Was I there?"

"Yeah," Arno paused. "But not really, at least, not like the *real* you."

Roran gritted his teeth. Had his big, red transformation given Arno nightmares? Did he want to know? No, he didn't, and so he decided to not inquire any further unless Arno willingly offered more.

He didn't.

After some more time and silence, enough silence that Arno could have drifted into his half-sleep again, they noticed the river was starting to behave oddly. Animal tracks had started to disappear from the surrounding area, as if things no longer drank from it. It was getting shallower and shallower, to the point where Roran could walk across it.

"Roran, can I ask you something?"

"What is it, Arno?"

Arno paused, taking time to formulate his question. "What is your new dream?"

"I can't really remember last night's. A lot of things were jumbled together."

Arno let out a weak chuckle. "No, silly. Not that kind of dream."

"What do you mean?"

"You said that Beans took your dream in exchange for the power. So, what's your new one?"

Roran furrowed his brow. He looked over his shoulder to get a glimpse of Arno staring up into the sky and branches. "Huh, I haven't thought about it."

"You should."

"Well, why is that?"

"You said it yourself," Arno replied. "It's important to have dreams, even if they are as simple as steaming from working hard."

"I guess," Roran said. "Right now, it would be to get you and Griselda somewhere safe."

Arno scoffed. "No, Roran, that's what you *have* to do. That's not a dream, silly. A dream is something you *want* to do for *you* without any other things making it messy. You know, like having a dream to have a really big treehouse. That would be just for me. Yeah, I'll still do stuff for you too, like cleaning your gross metal caps, but I got to have something for me too."

"I don't know," Roran said, looking over to check at the status of the river. "Does it have to be realistic?"

"I guess not. Because one of my new dreams is to put a sword where my leg used to be!"

"Um, that sounds dangerous. And impractical."

Arno laughed. "It doesn't matter. It's a dream. It's fun to think about."

Roran thought for a moment. "Now that you mention it, if we had some help and a working forge, we might be able to build you something a little more feasible."

"See? That's why they're important. Also, that's why I keep you around."

Roran laughed. "Let me see," he continued, the steady thumps of his feet against the dirt trail mixing with bird song. "When this is all over, I think I want to open up my own forge. Only, instead of making weapons, I'll make tools to help people like you, Arno."

"How will you forge without hands?"

"I'll hire apprentices. I can still supervise and design things. Plus, I can probably fashion a metal cover that I can attach a hammer to."

"I knew you couldn't resist finding a way to still beat things up with a hammer," Arno chuckled again.

Roran looked over his shoulder to see Arno with a very self-satisfied smile, still looking up at the sky.

Roran turned back and looked at the river, which was getting shallower still, and the width was increasing too.

At one point, where it was shallow enough to see rocks and sticks consistently poking out, Roran decided it was time to cross the river to get to Stedtfest.

"I wouldn't do that."

Roran turned around and found the red man leaning against the side of a tree.

"Beans!" Arno shouted. "Can you just appear and disappear? Can you poof to any place on the continent?"

The red man looked puzzled. "Beans? Poof? Whatever. Don't touch the water."

"Why not?" asked Roran.

The red man held out two fingers. "One: Stedtfest is on fire. No point in going that way. Ewen's murdering everyone there. Two: there's something in the water."

"What?!" Arno shouted. "But . . . but Griselda could be there!"

352 • ANTON JONES

"Like poison?" Roran asked. "The water is poisoned? Or is it disease?"

"No," Beans said, stroking his floating, fraying beard. "I'm not entirely sure what's wrong with it, but the whole river is like that. I just know that it would be a bad idea for a host to interact with the main body of water. I can smell danger of some sort.

"You can smell?" asked Arno. "Does Roran smell bad too, or is it just me?"

Roran rolled his eyes.

"Well, not really smell, but sense," Beans continued. "Plus, nothing's on the other side of the river that isn't on fire."

"Ewen destroyed Stedtfest? It's already gone?" Arno asked.

"Currently in the process of it," said the red man.

"So, there's still time to save it," Arno said.

The red man and Roran sighed at the same time, then exchanged confused looks. Roran didn't think he would ever share the same emotion as the glowing red thing, but apparently, Arno could have that effect on people.

"Listen, pipsqueak," it said, floating over and sticking his face in Arno's, the heat from his presence becoming more and more noticeable. "The only thing over there is death. I've been keeping tabs on the goings-on, and it's a bloodbath."

Arno crossed his arms again. "Well, Beans, that means a lot of people need our help."

Roran wiped sweat from his brow with his forearm. "Arno, if we go over there, I might have to fight. You know what that means, right?"

"But people need our help!" Arno pleaded.

The red man stayed silent as he leaned against the tree, possibly sensing that the brothers should resolve this one without his interference.

Roran exhaled. "There's just no pleasing you, is there?"

"Doing nothing while people die is bad too."

"But how will we cross the river? You heard what Beans said."

"I'm not responding to that name," Beans mumbled.

Arno thought for a moment. "Do you think you could push over a tree, and then we could cross?"

Roran looked up at the massive tree Beans was leaning against. Could he seriously push over something that big? Something that had been a guardian of the forest for hundreds, possibly thousands, of years? "I guess I could try."

"You're not seriously considering going to a battlefield, are you?" Beans blustered.

Roran ignored him. "Arno, could you undo the belt?"

Arno reached over Roran's shoulders and unfastened the belt that kept the straps from slipping off Roran's shoulders. He then squatted down and shimmied the straps off.

"It'll be good to know how strong I can be," Roran said.

Roran closed his eyes, drew in all the breath he could to his lower diaphragm, and stoked the fire.

"Oh, right!" Roran said, taking off his shirt before he ruined it. He couldn't afford to keep lighting his clothes on fire or ripping them as he grew.

Once situated, he continued to stoke the fire. His veins started to glow beneath his skin. He grew several feet taller and wider. Arno gasped, watching his brother transform. Twigs under his feet snapped at the increase in weight. Roran's head hit a low branch as he grew. He seemed even larger than the last time.

Transformation complete, he walked up to a large tree nearest to the river and pushed with his metal caps on the trunk. His feet dug into the ground as the base creaked but held firm. He repositioned himself and pushed again, but nothing happened. Roran backed up for a running start. He sprinted at the tree and threw his shoulder into it, which smashed the bark and created a circular indent. He did it again. Needles and cones fell from the top of the tree as the whole thing shook. His shoulder bled from the points of the bark, but the wounds steamed and healed.

But it didn't seem like he would be strong enough to knock over this healthy, massive tree. He leaned against it and breathed in heavily.

"Can this be done?" Roran asked Beans in his deeper voice.

"Now why would I tell you something that would get you killed?" Beans asked flatly. "Like I said, you need to stay alive for me to stay alive. Keep it up, and I'll arrange a way for you to lose the rest of your limbs. I'll leave your meddlesome torso in a room, chained to a wall so you don't get yourself killed."

"Don't listen to him, Roran!" Arno shouted from his seated position on the ground. "You find a way. You always do!"

Beans groaned. "It's like this family has no self-preservation instincts. Even blasted worms have that! You two are dumber than worms!"

Ignoring Beans, Roran focused on his breathing, seeing if he could stoke the inner flame more. As he focused, he noticed something was off. He could feel strength streaming into him, not just from his breath from the fire, but from outside of him. From the tree. It seemed like he was drawing in life and strength that the tree possessed and reallocating it inside of him. He could feel the tree almost as if it had a wish to grow to touch the sky, to remain as a sentry until the end of time. He felt that wish . . . its dream . . . and Roran took it out of the tree.

The tree started to groan, and the parts that Roran was touching started to turn black with rot and age. Roran shook his large head and continued to stare at the indent in the tree, a tree so large it would take four Rorans in his large form to fully wrap himself around it. The indent started to shoot cracks up along the base of the trunk. Incredibly loud snapping echoed around the forest as the wood, under enormous strain but now too weak to support the mass at the top, began to buckle. Using his new strength reserves, Roran gave one final push with everything he had, and the tree came toppling down toward the river, chips of bark shooting out from the trunk and bouncing off Roran. The tree, first slowly then quickly, came crashing down through the surrounding branches and collided with the ground, bridging the river.

Roran exhaled and shrank back down.

Beans looked livid as he watched Roran put his shirt back on. "You idiots! You complete buffoons! You witless apes!" Beans fumed. "Oros take you, you dense imbeciles!" Beans continued to hurl a stream of insults at them as Roran let Arno refasten the straps. "Ass grease! Puppet cheese! You don't know what you're doing or the powers you're messing with!"

Roran smiled at the insults as he hoisted Arno up. At the very least, it was fun to make that thing angry. "I made a promise to my brother to be better. I intend to keep it," Roran said to the spitting red man.

"Fine. Put yourself in another situation where you'll have to make a sacrifice. See if I care." Beans vanished.

"Stuff it, Beans. Nobody likes you," Arno reached up and patted his brother on the top of his head. "Thank you, Roran."

Roran huffed, climbing up onto the tree trunk. He did feel bad for ending the tree's legacy—especially after having felt its intuition, its desire to grow—but he would topple anything for his brother.

"We got to be careful though. We'll sneak around and see what we can find, if there's anyone we can help."

And maybe, Roran thought, *we'll see our old friends there.* He remembered Zerebril was riding down this way, possibly to confront Ewen's army at Stedtfest. If he was lucky, maybe he'd have a chance to set things straight the only way Roran knew how.

CHAPTER 25
THE COLLEGE OF COMBAT

THOUGH GRISELDA'S coin purse was significantly lighter, she felt the investments were worth it. She had an armor smith take a couple days to fit her with a cuirass, gauntlets, and cowters. Though the blacksmith had recommended full plate, Griselda was not trying to spend all her money. She decided to go with more mobile attire. She didn't think she would need full plate on her arms, as the length of the sword would protect her forearms from being targeted. She compensated with splint vambraces and splint rerebraces. The gauntlets were heavily padded for insulation, allowing her to grip the handle even when the sword started to heat up and would even let her grip the ricasso. She dared not touch the blade itself, but this would make her much more versatile and able to use End March without fear of her getting her hands burned. She opted out of pauldrons as she needed more shoulder mobility for the wide or overhead swings the sword needed to keep momentum for ignition or to fend off multiple attackers. Again, the length of the sword made her pretty comfortable without greaves as anyone targeting her legs would have to dive past nearly six feet of quickly moving death. She did, however, invest in a gambeson, padded chausses, and more mobile and traditionally male clothing to wear when she was out of the armor.

She also purchased a belt and scabbard for a shorter swept-hilt side sword if enemies got too close. The smith made it to her specifications, shorter and broader than traditional side swords so that it could take and deal more damage to armored opponents. She could throw down a gauntlet for more precise maneuvering of the side sword and to more effectively find gaps in heavily armored opponents. Though she didn't think many opponents would get that close, this was more so to counter quick attacks when End March was still on her back. The blacksmith fixed two hooks to the back of her cuirass so she could hang the great sword by the hilt.

All of this, though it took time and money, was necessary now that she had a sword-shaped target on her back, making her one of the most lucrative people to kill in all of Verdin. She wasn't expecting to jump into any fights, but fights might come to her anyway.

She walked through Wilheim in her armor, with End March on her back. Though the glow of the blade was still covered in tent tarp, she drew many, many stares. The panicked people hopping on wagons or carrying their belongings froze to watch her walk by before resuming their hurried frenzy. The infrastructure of the city was starting to collapse with everyone finding ferries across Lake Verdin. The blacksmith said that she was his last order before he packed up shop.

King Morgen was initially reluctant to let people flee the city, but he realized it was futile to use the remaining garrison to stop people from trying to escape. As a result, Wilheim was becoming more hollow by the day, with only the quick scampering of soon-to-be refugees to break the increasing silence of the city.

I can't flee until I find my brothers, she thought. As she was waiting for her armor to be made, she had ventured over to the College of Combat to watch the daily duels featured there. While

Ardhataz's Highland Pits were much more brutal, with many of their matches being to the death or dismemberment, Wilheim's arena in the center of the College of Combat was more of a display of tactics, respect, talent, and sport for officers to observe. There was generally less interest from commoners, and the majority of the audience were people in the college who would go on to become unit commanders. However, with the war and most of Wilheim's forces sent to Stedtfest, the stands were as equally empty as the rest of the city. There were still duels, but they were mostly retired soldiers or professors from the college itself. And they all fought with blunted training weapons.

As she stood before the Wilheim Academies front gate, she could tell the numerous colleges that made up the whole were similarly quiet. Only one or two professors strolled about with papers clasped in their arms. Like the rest of the city, each college had an ornate building of white, polished stone. Many of the buildings had various designs that accentuated their purposes. The College of the Colloquial had an open agora, the College of Observation had an observatory, the College of Arts had a rotating display of sculptures students had worked on, and the College of Combat had a large wooden list at its center with classrooms dedicated to various types of warfare or weaponry underneath the stands.

Griselda entered the stands surrounding the list and found no one else there to observe the upcoming bout. Standing in the middle of the arena was a lone combatant. He was in full plate, visor down to conceal his face. He stood there waiting, with a great sword similar to End March, minus the glow, resting point down in the sand of the list. The plated warrior nodded at Griselda as she sat, and Griselda waved back. Several minutes passed, and Griselda began to fidget. It seemed like the other combatant wasn't showing up.

The combatant made a point to sigh in an exaggerated way, loud enough that Griselda could hear it through the armor and in the stands. He waved for Griselda to come down to the list. She had hoped this might happen eventually.

Griselda jumped to her feet and hopped down into the list.

"Name?" the combatant said, voice heavily muffled behind the visor.

"Griselda."

"Program?"

"Umm . . . what—"

"You're not a student here, are you? Figures, they've either been sent to Stedtfest or fled. I'm guessing my scheduled opponent did likewise. So then, you're an opportunist looking to learn?"

"Yes, sir."

"Actually," said the combatant, lifting the visor, "It's 'ma'am.'"

"Oh . . ." Griselda said, taking in the combatant's facial features. She was a middle-aged woman with freckles around her nose and upper cheeks. Though most of her hair was concealed, Griselda did note some longer, grey blonde strands on her sweaty forehead. Despite her age, she appeared very fit and comfortable in the armor and with the larger sword.

"Apologies," Griselda said, bowing.

"Don't worry about it, happens a lot. Most of the time I have my visor down intentionally so my male opponents don't treat me any differently. I swap out helmets often so they can never tell it's me. I'm Professor Mathilda," she said, offering her hand and smiling. "I specialize in training our officers in front-line tactics. I train bodyguards for the king and teach those who wield long swords or great swords."

Griselda's face lit up as she shook her hand, "You were Gunter's teacher, weren't you?"

"I was, finest student I ever had. So, are you looking for some lessons before the end of the world?"

"I mean . . . if you wouldn't mind—"

"Drop the pleasantries. I'm a professor. I teach. It's what I do. Whether or not you pay for the lessons is Dean Macbrick's problem. And since he, and everyone else, presumably fled, I don't see any issue."

Griselda had to forcibly restrain herself from squeaking with excitement, but there was one thing that was still nagging her. It felt wrong to be enjoying something at a time like this. "Before we start, there's something I'd like to ask. Since you said you train the king's guard, you might know something about what's going on inside the castle. Did you hear anything about a prisoner named Roran who escaped with his little brother Arno?"

Professor Mathilda drooped her head and exhaled. "You're Cormac's daughter, aren't you?"

"Yes, ma'am."

"And that sword on your back is . . ."

"Yes, ma'am."

She sighed and then smiled faintly. "I see. Well then," she clapped down her visor. "I'll have to be bringing you in." Professor Mathilda's body posture changed into a threatening, charging persona. She kicked up her great sword from its resting position and started swinging it in crisp, fluid motions as she pivoted and approached Griselda.

Griselda yelped as she barely dodged Mathilda's first swing. *You idiot, you're being hunted! You revealed too much!*

Griselda tried to escape the list, but Mathilda was startlingly fast in full plate and was at her side before Griselda could hop the wooden barricade.

Mathilda swung down from overhead, and though it was a blunted tournament weapon, the great sword still embedded itself in the wood.

"No running. Show me what a daughter of Cormac is made of!" Mathilda shouted through the holes in her visored bascinet.

Escaping the blow, Griselda threw herself backward to the ground. Panicking, she drew her side sword as she backed away on the sand and pointed it at Mathilda. Mathilda swatted it away, the momentum and mass of the great sword wrenching the side sword from Griselda's hands despite the hilt partially encasing them. The sword flew to the opposite side of the list.

"I won't have you fighting me with a kitchen knife! Show me the Cormac weapon!" Mathilda shouted as she continued her swings and stances, steadily approaching Griselda. Griselda scrambled to her feet and pulled End March from her back. She ripped the tarp off the blade, showing its vibrant blue-white, moonlight glow.

Mathilda paused in what Roran had called an ox guard, tip pointed at Griselda. She was taking in the awe of the blade yet maintaining a defensive stance. "So, they do glow . . . I'll have to try it out when I take it from you." Mathilda breathed in and launched a series of thrusts from ox guard making Griselda backpedal.

"Please—" Griselda said, ducking a strike. "I don't want to hurt you!"

"Well, I'm trying to hurt you! Fight me!"

"Fine!" Griselda shouted.

Griselda positioned herself in fool's guard, sword hanging lazily out in front of her, tip pointed at Mathilda's feet, trying to lure her in and strike.

Mathilda feinted left, then swept her great sword up, knocking the tip of End March skyward. A cold rush of air hit Griselda's face from the movement of the large blades. Now in close quarters, Mathilda gripped the blade of her sword with her left hand while keeping her right on the handle. She rammed the pommel of her sword into Griselda's cuirass, knocking her to the ground.

"Up!" Mathilda shouted as she made several overhead strikes at Griselda, who again found herself on the ground trying to get away. "Up! Get up!"

Griselda crawled over, threw her right gauntlet down,

grabbed her side sword, and stood up. *I can't continuously swing End March here without destroying the arena. So, I'll compromise*, she thought.

Griselda stood facing Mathilda, side sword in her right arm fully extended to ward off her attacker. In her left arm she held End March, ricasso resting on her shoulder as a six-foot threat. This way, she could use her agility and thrust with her side sword but easily pivot into a swing with End March to push back her opponent and keep her honest about the distance.

"Hmm, interesting. But your side sword," Mathilda said, sweeping her great sword up, threatening to knock Griselda's side sword out of her hand again, "it won't be able to clash with my weapon."

Got you, Griselda thought, pulling in her right arm and causing Mathilda to over swing when her sword connected with nothing but air. Griselda lunged and slapped her side sword down on Mathilda's helmet. She hadn't properly indexed the blade, so it hit the helmet with the flat. Her sword bounced off with a clang. Griselda jumped back just in time to evade Mathilda's pendulum swing back after she corrected from the initial over swing.

"Nice move, but that's why we wear helmets," Mathilda said. "Why aren't you wearing one?" Pointedly, Mathilda made several thrusts toward Griselda's face, which she evaded. Getting in closer, Mathilda switched her grip, left hand grabbing the ricasso and treating her great sword more like a spear with each thrust she made. The last thrust made it through Griselda's guard and skidded off one side of her cuirass, and again Mathilda tried to smack her in the face with the pommel now that she was in close. This time, however, Griselda was expecting the pommel strike, and so she pivoted away and brought down End March from on high off her left shoulder.

Griselda could have sworn she heard Mathilda stifle a yelp as the sword came dangerously close to smacking the side of her helmet.

"Doesn't matter if you're wearing a helmet," Griselda said. "You'll feel it if this thing hits you in the head at full swing." Griselda feigned confidence as Mathilda stumbled away from the swing. She had nearly lost her grip on End March trying to swing it with one hand. She positioned the massive glowing sword back on her shoulder. She could only swing it sparingly from this position and could really do nothing else than pivot and bring it down. Mathilda was clearly using her great sword with practiced grace despite its size while Griselda was treating End March like a bludgeon.

Mathilda positioned herself in what Roran had called roof guard. "You'll need to do more than just drop the great sword. Now that I know that's what you're doing, I can easily evade. But you did come very close, I'll give you that."

Unlike her opponent, who was cramped in her armor and breathing heavily, Griselda was still relatively fresh but frazzled. It was time to go on the offensive against her tired opponent. She lunged at her and thrust her side sword, which connected with Mathilda's gauntlets since she couldn't get her great sword out of roof stance to parry quick enough. Griselda retracted and slapped her side sword against one of Mathilda's pauldrons, the clang echoing around the arena and sending off sparks.

Mathilda got her great sword out in front of her in plow guard and warded off more of Griselda's thrusts with thrusts of her own. Mathilda batted away her side sword with a flick of the wrist, enough to send it off trajectory but not enough to throw it from Griselda's hands. Griselda flowed and lightly positioned herself behind where her side sword naturally wanted to go. Then she pivoted and spun, letting the momentum of the spin draw out her left arm, and ultimately, End March. At the end of the spin, the tip of End March was traveling incredibly fast, glowing dangerously.

Mathilda saw the move coming since the spin took too much time to execute. She braced herself, right hand on the handle pointing up, left hand bracing the blade tip down. End March collided with Mathilda's braced stance and the reverberation of the thunderous clang shook End March from Griselda's hand. Sparks, this time, the supernatural kind from the Cormac weapon, erupted and showered both combatants as End March fell to the sand. Mathilda held her great sword up to Griselda's neck.

"Yield. Though this is blunt, the tip can still do nasty things to an unarmored neck."

Griselda dropped her side sword.

Mathilda kicked the sword away and, still holding her sword pointing at Griselda's neck, picked up End March. She flipped up her visor, and the glow of the sword made her seem half her age.

"You know," Mathilda said, "you're better than half the delinquents in the program. Did you pick these things up on your own?"

"I sparred with my brother almost daily for years. I think being around my father inspired us to learn how to use the weapons he was making."

"I see. You have great instincts, and you're clearly fit from sparring, but you lack the basic fundamentals. Sure, you'll wipe the floor with any untrained lout, but you'll be bested by someone who knows what they're doing."

Griselda nodded. "You're not turning me in, are you?"

Mathilda smiled while still looking at End March. "I figured you'd see past that. But I needed the threat to be somewhat real so you would show me what you knew. Carrying something like this on your back is extremely dangerous. No wonder you thought to cover the blade and hide the glow."

"Can you teach me more?"

"I suppose. It's better than twiddling my thumbs waiting for Ewen to come."

Griselda paused. "You think he'll make it here and yet you don't flee?"

Mathilda shrugged. "I've lived here my whole life. I won't run. Though most scholars have packed up their work and books to flee for the other side of the lake, it's not in my nature to run. I'll accept what's coming and go down swinging while protecting the king. So, why are you still here?"

"I have to be ready for threats. I'll need to be skilled to protect myself while I look for my brothers."

Mathilda shook her head and rested her practice sword on top of the list. In her other hand, she held the edge of End March next to her face. "I can feel the warmth coming off this thing. And the edge still held even though you banged it against the flat of my blade. No rolls, nicks, chips, or nothing. I doubt I could say the same for your side sword. You'll need to sharpen it after slapping it against my plate."

Griselda nodded.

Mathilda walked over and handed End March back. "I see the legends about these weapons weren't exaggerated. Where are you currently staying?"

"At an inn."

Mathilda shook her head. "That won't do. If anyone hears what you're carrying, they'll slit your throat as you sleep. You can stay with me for the time being. I want to see the fabled flame lashes that these weapons produce." Mathilda offered out her hand for Griselda to shake. "You'll show me what this thing can do, and I'll show you what I can do. Deal?"

Griselda thought of the last time she saw the fires of End March. The headless man, the charred corpse, the neck pierced, the chest pinned to a tree, the warm blood she lay in. Would she want to do that again?

Griselda took Mathilda's hand and shook it. "Deal." It didn't matter if she wanted to. If she must, then she must. Whatever it took to reach her brothers.

CHAPTER 26
THE COST OF CHANGE

"You smell that?" asked Arno.

Roran nodded. For once, Arno wasn't complaining about Roran's own stench. The air was thick and laden with ash and smoke. It smelled like acres and acres of scorched land. The sky was engulfed in the grey haze, making the sun look orange. What they saw was not Verdin. Verdin did not have an orange sun, dark skies, barren expanses with no trees, and burning cities. Following the advice of Beans, they tried to stay away from the river. Easier said than done since the surrounding area was partially flooded.

There were no army encampments outside the city, signaling to Roran that they were already inside or had moved on. Either way, Stedtfest had broken, and Ewen would be moving on to his next target.

As they navigated the treacherous ground, careful to avoid sinking into the mire, the battlefield stretched before them—a wasteland of the dead. Hundreds of corpses lay strewn across the sodden land, their vacant eyes turned toward the dim sky. Swollen with river water and thick with mud, their pale, veined skin stretched taut, grotesque like overfilled wineskins on the verge of bursting. Black tunics, once proud, now drifted aimlessly in the dark water, their white mountain insignias barely visible beneath the filth clinging to the last traces of the fallen.

Arno put a hand to his mouth as Roran did his best to hop from dry patch to dry patch.

"Roran . . . please stop . . . I don't feel good."

Roran stopped on a higher patch of dirt and let Arno climb out of the harness. He tried to steady himself on his crutch but fell down and vomited.

"Arno!" shouted Roran, turning and trying to help his brother. He wanted to rest a hand on his back, but all he could manage was the cold steel cover where his hand used to be.

Some of the vomit splashed back up and got mixed into Arno's wavy auburn hair.

"I'm sorry you have to see this, Arno," Roran said, not feeling too well himself.

"You see now, right Roran?" Arno asked, wiping bile from his mouth. "Why it's so important to keep your promise?"

"I do . . ."

Arno nodded. "Can I drink some of the water?"

"You don't want to drink this. It's littered with corpses. Plus, Beans said we shouldn't touch anything the river touches."

Arno grimaced but nodded. He'd have to deal with the sour taste in his mouth until they could find clean water in Stedtfest.

Roran looked at the thin clouds of smoke as they swirled around the battlefield and town. These clouds didn't have the same fluffy substance as normal clouds. They felt more like wisps, spirits flailing about after being spurned from their bodies, looking for the next leg of the March. Though he wanted to give Arno as much time as he needed to recover, he felt incredibly anxious being in this ominous place, as if the combined dreadful fates of thousands could somehow influence his own.

Arno sat on his rear and hugged his knees to his chest. "You don't think we'll see one of *them* here, do you?"

With the field providing a plentiful bounty of dead bodies, Roran knew exactly what Arno was referring to and shivered. Corpse callers.

"I don't think we'd have to worry about them here, Arno," Roran said, trying to be as reassuring as he could standing amidst so much death. "They live mainly in the west. They'd be hunted if they were here. Even Ardhataz thinks they are vile."

Roran hoped that was true. Per Griselda's rendition of *The March Through the Mountain Pass*, the legend of corpse callers has them residing mainly in the massive mountains west of the Ardhataz plateau, where they live reclusively. Still, that doesn't mean frightening tales about them hadn't spread to Wilheim. In their paranoia, some people have accused their neighbors of being corpse callers in places outside the city proper. A heavy accusation like that outside of the city walls, outside of a set legal system, could mean exile or death for the accused. Even their name was a dirty word rarely spoken in Wilheim.

Arno climbed back into the harness. "I don't regret this."

"What do you mean?" asked Roran.

"This place is . . . it's bad. It hurts to see."

Roran nodded sympathetically as he pressed onwards to the main gates, which were now open. The outer walls of the city seemed relatively undamaged. The smoke was coming from inside.

"But," Arno continued, "we're still here for good reason. We can still help."

If anyone is still alive, Roran thought. Ewen was not known for leaving the land unscathed. According to rumors, there had never been a survivor in the villages he raided. Everyone had been captured or killed—the villages themselves resembled the gutted corpses they saw lying in the mud now.

372 • ANTON JONES

They were close enough to the city where they should have been able to hear signs of life. It would have been more hopeful if he heard screams. Hearing nothing but fire was not good. That, and the birds. Scavenger birds cawed raucously at Roran as he passed them, enjoying their found meals.

A mini river had formed in front of the gate, as if the city had tried to dig a moat before the siege started. It was wide enough that Roran knew he couldn't jump across it.

"How are we going to get over that?" asked Arno.

Roran bowed his head. "I have an idea. Neither of us is going to like it."

Arno looked down at the floating corpses. "Oh . . . no . . ."

"Can you unbuckle the harness?"

"Roran . . . maybe we can find another way in—"

"Just do it, Arno," Roran snapped a little harsher than he intended to. "Please."

Arno undid the harness. Roran shrugged off the straps and gently rotated his aching shoulders. Then he set to work. Carefully, he grabbed the corpses from the puddles and threw them into the moat in front of the gate. Without hands, this meant he would have to essentially hug each corpse he picked up and hold them tight against his body. He tried to grab the mostly intact corpses and held them feet up so he didn't have to look at their death masks as he carried them about.

They were heavy, wearing soaked gambesons; the bodies were waterlogged, too. It was grueling work, and Roran had to hold his breath each time he picked up one of the corpses. In the muddy killing field, the footing was hazardous, and Roran fell on top of the bodies he was carrying more than once.

Arno puked again at seeing his brother fall on top of one particularly bloated corpse, which then burst when Roran's full weight fell on top of it. The smell was unreal, like nothing in the world could feasibly smell that bad. Roran gagged and then rolled off the mess. He wanted so badly to scream, to writhe, to go feral and run into the woods. But he didn't.

You have to keep going, Roran thought to himself as he lie on his back in the mud and blood, staring into the unfamiliar sky. *For Arno. Bear the light, even if this is in vain, even if all that awaits us in Stedtfest is more corpses.*

Roran pushed upright, scrubbing filth from his face.

Next to him, Arno wiped his own mouth, eyes still glassy with sickness.

"We got this . . . together," Roran said, and moved on to the next corpse.

Soon, the bodies started to fill in the gaps. He heaved the bodies across, one on top of the other, to weigh the corpses down that naturally wanted to float to the surface. Thankfully, it did not look like the moat was very deep, probably waist-deep on Roran. There was no shortage of corpses, so Roran piled them high.

When the corpse bridge was completed, he leaned down, and Arno refastened the harness around his shoulders.

"Hold on tight, Arno," Roran said. "This will be unstable."

Roran bear crawled over the corpse bridge, his weight focused on the metal caps pressing nasty indents into the corpses, threatening to poke through and expose the rot inside. While Roran looked down and climbed through the death, Arno was on his back, looking up at the sky. *This is how it should be,* Roran thought.

As long as Arno was facing away from what Roran had to do, Arno could keep his dreams alive and constantly strive toward the endless blue. At least, that's what Roran hoped. In reality, Arno was looking at smoke and an orange sun. There was no blue visible in the sky over Stedtfest.

And then the bodies shifted under Roran's weight, splitting the bridge as the corpses floated off in either direction. Roran fell into the water face-first. He could hear Arno calling out for him, but something was very wrong with this water. It felt alien, like the water had a different texture, more slippery and slimy than it should be. And warm. He opened his eyes and saw tendrils of stars gathering around him. Roran quickly found his feet, pulled himself out of the water, and sloshed through the muck as fast as he could toward the gate. Then he was pulled down by something, something incredibly strong. All the while, Arno kept yelling.

Something grabbed his leg and was trying to hold him under. Roran's perception expanded. Suddenly, he was having all sorts of phantom sensations, not unlike the phantom sensation of still feeling his hands. But this was sensation for senses he didn't have. He was water flowing, trees growing, the worms in the dirt squirming. He was the stillness of rock, steady, stretching back beyond and without memory. For the first time, he felt pressure from the sky above as he realized that much air had a tangible weight. Everything the water touched, he could feel. Beyond that, he could feel the water's pervasiveness as it connected everything, stretching up to Wilheim to the north. He felt himself melt and gather and trickle down the Shatter Rock Range and through the walls of the city, felt himself be directed and diluted into irrigation channels and homes, felt himself exit the city. He felt the boats of Ardhataz as they rowed up the river toward the stone walls. And to the south . . . where it flowed all the way into Lake Verdin. There was something down there, way in the deep, dark body of water. Something massive.

It wanted to communicate. Roran felt it speak, but only heard gibberish. Then one clear word came through in his own language: *DOMINATE.*

Roran heard the voice, felt its emotion, its will to enslave and control and to cause suffering.

DOMINATE.

Another tendril tethered itself to his other leg, a third one went for his head. Then there was splashing as Arno beat the tendrils back with his crutch, freeing Roran. He scrambled to the safety of dry land near the gate beyond the moat.

The tendrils vanished, as if being retracted toward the river and farther beyond.

Roran coughed up the corpse water.

"Are you okay, Roran?"

Gathering his breath, Roran said, "Yes . . . I think. Did . . . did you see that?"

"Yes," Arno said. "Beans was right. There's a monster in the water. It doesn't seem like it can come out though."

"Good for that. Thank you," Roran said. "For saving me. Again."

"I don't need your strength to save, shooing things away with sticks works too sometimes."

Roran chuckled, but even chuckling felt unnatural in this place, after what he had seen and done to get inside. After some inexplicable force had almost drowned him in corpse water.

"We should avoid the water at all costs," Roran said.

Arno nodded solemnly, though Roran could tell this pained him. Arno was dehydrated, but Roran was unfazed since he escaped the ever-present pangs of human needs.

This place is dangerous, whether there are soldiers here or not, the air can kill us just as easily if we stay here too long, Roran thought.

Roran climbed to his feet and looked around. Like the rumors suggested, everyone was gone. No signs of any living person remained other than the structures themselves. The buildings in Stedtfest seemed mostly untouched, at least the ones on the outskirts, showing signs that soldiers had slept in them for a few days to recover after the siege. There was carelessly discarded refuse, food, tattered clothes. And for some reason, a lot of nasal helms laid in the streets, the helmets worn by many of the corpses Roran used to build the makeshift bridge. They weren't damaged; they were discarded.

"Hello!" Arno shouted.

"Shhh!" Roran hissed. "Arno, be quiet, we don't want to run into any soldiers."

"They've left," Arno responded. "At least that's what it looks like."

"There's nothing for you here," said Beans, materializing behind the two of them. "You almost got us all killed already, just get out of here now."

"And poof! It's Beans!" shouted Arno.

Roran couldn't help but smile every time Arno trivialized Beans' power as a "poof." He then turned around to look at the red man. Instead of looking condescending and uppity, he seemed much more distraught. He was pacing back and forth as if the ground was too hot for him to stand on in any one place for too long.

"This place has been overrun with something bad, not just humans," Beans continued.

Roran looked down at Arno who stood his ground, staring at Beans and holding his clenched fist to his chest. "If we can save even one person, then it's worth it."

Beans stooped down and drew his face close to Arno's, close enough that Arno recoiled from the heat emitting from the thousands of glowing tendrils that made up the thing's body. "And what if you can't save even one? Would it still be worth it? I'm telling you now. I've spied the place twice over," Beans paused, and then looked at Roran. "There's no one here you'll want to save."

Arno looked up into the sky and pondered on it. "I don't have the words for it like Henrietta does," Arno responded. "But I feel like it's still worth it. I don't know why, and I can't give you a good reason."

Again, both Beans and Roran sighed at the same time. Beans

wandered over to Roran and whispered, "You better put a leash on this kid. He's going to get us all killed."

Roran rolled his eyes and shooed Beans away. "He's my brother. I don't think you understand what that means."

Beans shrugged. "I'm trying, Ass-Face, but you humans don't always do things that are meant to be understood. And I really wish that my survival wasn't tied to yours."

Roran nodded. "Can I ask a favor?"

Beans raised an eyebrow.

"If you're already wandering around here, can you look for Griselda? We'll be able to get out of here faster, which should make you happy at least."

Beans chewed on it for a minute. "I'm not an errand boy, but I'll tell you this: there are only a handful of people left alive in this town, and they're all men. If she was here . . . you know."

Roran pressed his lips together into a hard line and then looked down at Arno. He wasn't listening but looking into the smoldering buildings for signs of life instead.

"Thank you," Roran said.

Beans nodded. "Well, if you two idiots are bent on getting us killed, then I'll see myself out. There are a few things I need to check on up north."

"Suit yourself," Roran said, his voice becoming hollower by the minute. Beans's implication was clear. If Griselda was here, and he's not sure, then she would have certainly been killed. *Don't think about it. Not now,* Roran thought.

Beans tipped his hat and vanished. Arno drifted back to Roran and pulled on his brother's pant leg. Roran nodded at Arno's urgency to move on and continue the search despite what Beans said.

They wandered through the town toward the pillar of smoke rising from the town center. All around them, buildings were beginning to collapse from the fires. At least the stone streets were not on fire. As they drew closer to the center, they heard noises. People noises. Signs of life.

"You hear that?" Arno said excitedly. "There might be some people still here!"

"Shhh, let's look first."

Roran crept around behind the buildings, staying off the open streets. The streets were filled with wagons and empty barrels, but no corpses. Compared to the graveyard outside the city, this seemed relatively fine. But the eerie absence of people was still enough to induce shivers in Roran. *If they weren't dead in the streets, then where were they? There are no Wilheim soldiers nor Stedtfest civilians.*

Roran approached the sounds of people talking and wheels clanking over the cobbled streets between the wooden houses. He hid behind a barrel in an alley and poked his head above to inspect what was happening. Arno craned his neck to check, too. Men not wearing Wilheim or Ardhataz colors were putting two people into a barred wagon.

They held spears and clubs menacingly, prodding two prisoners into the horse-drawn wagons.

"Slavers? In Wilheim?" Roran mumbled to himself. Was Ewen bringing slavers into the kingdom? Was that where all the people had gone?

"We have to help them," whispered Arno.

"Yeah," replied Roran, continuing to survey what was happening. The slavers were only moving two people into the wagon. By the looks of their clothes, they were nobility or public officials of Stedtfest or high-ranking officers in Wilheim's army. There were no civilians.

Why had fifteen slavers come all the way up here for just two people? Roran wondered. He crept a little closer and got a glimpse at their faces. One of them was Prince Zerebril being loaded into the wagon. His leg was fashioned to a splint, and he weakly hobbled into the wagon at spear point.

"What's going on over there?" Arno asked, struggling to twist his body and look behind him. "I can't really see."

Roran smiled. Imeel-Illin had brought forth justice. Zerebril was being imprisoned. This was possibly better than finding him dead since he would experience the same grief that Roran had, being imprisoned while everything he knew and loved was stripped away. Zerebril spotted Roran; recognition and confusion fell over his face.

"You," Zerebril whispered. "You! Are you with Ewen? Did you do this?" Though Zerebril looked incredibly fragile as he hobbled over and gripped the bars of the cage, Roran could see that a fire still burned inside him.

At his outburst, the slavers turned to try to find what he was yelling at. Roran ducked behind his cover.

"Change of plans," Roran said to Arno. "We're going to look for others."

"What?! Why?" demanded Arno.

Roran turned to walk back down the alley, which then gave Arno a clear view of what Roran had seen.

"The prince . . ." Arno said.

"Yeah. Let him rot," said Roran.

Arno shook his head vigorously enough to jostle the rest of the harness. "No, Roran. There's another person there too. Not just the prince. We have to save them, even still."

Roran snapped, forgetting to restrain himself from shouting at his brother. "What? You want to save *him*?! He branded your back. Twice! He tortured you. He gave the order to cut off your leg! He's the reason I don't have hands. He's the reason Griselda is missing. He is getting what he deserves for imprisoning us. This is retribution!"

"Slavery isn't right, Roran. It's banned. We have to help them."

"No!"

"Roran! You promised!"

Roran scoffed and continued walking down the alley, not looking back. "I promised I wouldn't kill anyone. I didn't promise I had to save them."

"Roran!" Arno cried. "I thought you were getting better! You're still muddy inside!"

Roran made no response and rounded the corner so that the wagons were out of Arno's sight. Arno started crying. "We came here to help—"

"Not those people. We can find others."

In between sobs, Arno yelled, "There are no others!"

Arno turned and started slapping Roran on the shoulders.

"Hey! Quit that!" Roran shouted.

"Turn back and help them!"

"No!"

Arno started hitting Roran in the back of the head. Roran winced and stooped down. He shook his shoulders, which rattled Arno around in his harness.

"Knock it off, Arno!"

Arno kept up the slaps. They didn't hurt as much physically as they did emotionally. Frustrated, Roran spun his shoulders and smacked the harness into the wooden building next to them.

Arno stopped his assault. Instead, he just whimpered. "We could have saved them."

"They don't deserve it."

"I thought you were changing. And you are, but you're changing for the worse," cried Arno.

Roran hardened his heart. He couldn't let himself succumb to every tantrum Arno threw. They would get themselves killed if he did. Arno was naïve. This was for the best. This was justice.

Roran rounded the corner. Smoke was billowing up from the

city center. It stung his eyes as he strained to see against the fierce brightness of the massive fire. It was easily as large as the Wilheim bonfires that they lit in the city squares during the night, likely bigger. The only difference was the fuel source for the fire.

In front of the fire was a cart with blood lettering painted on its side as a warning.

All traders with routes to Stedtfest or Wilheim should turn back and resume business in Ardhataz. After hundreds of years of exile and scarcity, true JUSTICE has come for Wilheim. EWEN, KING OF ALL VERDIN, MARCHES ON.

Bodies of Wilheim's soldiers were stacked higher than a house. The smell of burning flesh caused Roran to gag. Roran walked backward, strategically not turning. He didn't want Arno to see that.

Thankfully, Arno was still crying and didn't seem to notice what Roran had seen as he was facing the opposite direction in the harness. Then Roran had a terrible thought. *What if Griselda was here when the siege happened? What if her body was in that fire?*

The thought made him sit down. Arno continued to cry, not reacting to Roran. Should he check the corpses in the fire? But then Arno would have to see. They would be unrecognizable by this point anyway, and there were so many, countless would be buried and not visible. Roran squeezed his eyes shut and clenched his jaw, trying to hold it all in. Hearing his brother cry on his back because of his choice was like having Oros himself eating his insides. He knew this was all his fault, too, not just making Arno cry, but not saving his family from Zerebril in the first place. He should have known what was coming and run. It was his fault, he didn't know if Griselda was still alive or if she was on this massive, unceremonious pyre mocking the tradition of Wilheim. It all had a tremendous toll.

The bloody words on the cart mocked him. *JUSTICE*. Roran thought on that word over and over again. Griselda had used that word too. When they were younger and playing in the forest, she had stopped Roran from stepping on a frog. He didn't want to kill the frog initially, but it peed on him when he picked it up. Roran claimed the frog wronged him, and so the frog needed to be punished. That it was justice. She had said that real justice only protects and never seeks to harm. But where was her justice now? If she was in there, a mangled burning corpse amidst a multitude of bodies meant to depict "justice," then justice as he knew it did not exist. Roran shook his head. Bad to dwell on it. After all, how many more bodies would Ewen burn in Wilheim? They had to get going. The smoke would start hurting their lungs.

He hoped Griselda was smarter than someone who would stand in Ewen's path. She had to be.

"Are they going to make more slaves in Wilheim?" His brother asked.

"I . . . I don't know, Arno."

"Do you think everyone deserves that in Wilheim?"

Roran sighed. "No. Probably not."

"What . . . what if Griselda's there?"

What if Griselda was here?

Arno continued, "Is there any way to stop them?"

"Not without killing them."

"I'm not so sure . . . I don't think people want to kill. I think they do it because they think they have to. What if we told them they don't have to?"

Roran bowed his head. This world did not deserve his brother. "I doubt they'll listen."

"Well, could we at least help people get out of the city?"

"That will put us in great danger, Arno. They're already on their way there now. We might be too late."

"Even if you're getting worse—if you're dying inside—I still have to try. For Griselda. If you won't go, then leave me here and I'll crawl back to Wilheim."

Roran suppressed a choked noise, half-chuckle, half-sob. He believed his brother would crawl as far as he could to help people; he would wear his limbs down to nubs crawling miles and miles up rocky terrain toward Wilheim. No regard for himself or logic. That's why Roran needed to protect him. This world *really* did not deserve to have someone as good as Arno living in it. The only thing that mattered to Arno was doing the right thing, and Roran had the gall to interfere, to tell him "no," to stop him from saving people, even bad people. Roran now knew the worst option of the lose-lose scenario. It would be worse to watch Arno's spirit wither. It would be so much worse for this world to lose Arno's goodness, despite the world not deserving it in the first place. Not only would the world itself lose a vital source of light, but Roran might lose his will to live. As best he could, Roran would make sure his brother's soul stayed intact.

"No, Arno. I'm not letting you crawl to Wilheim."

Arno turned around and tried to unfasten the buckle.

"Hey! No need for that. I'll go with you. We'll go there and look for Griselda. We'll try to help however we can. And we won't kill anyone."

Arno huffed. "Are you lying? Are you going to refuse to help people again?"

"No, Arno."

"What if it's the king that needs help?"

"You want me to help the king?"

"If he needs help."

Roran exhaled. It felt like he had been holding his breath for years. "Fine."

"It's like you said, Roran. You want to use your talents to help people. You don't dream anymore of making weapons or wielding them. Don't let yourself become a weapon. You hear me, right?"

"Yes, Arno, I hear you."

"Good. Now say you're sorry."

Roran frowned. "For what?"

"For slamming me against the side of the building. That really hurt. I didn't deserve that, and Zerebril didn't deserve to be carted away to slavery."

"I'm sorry for hurting you."

Arno turned in the harness and poked Roran in the cheek. "And?"

"Zerebril got what he deserved. I'm not sorry for that."

Arno sat back in his harness and folded his arms. "People in progress," he said to himself. "Well, I'm taking away your ability to judge what people deserve and what they don't. From now on, I'll tell you what people do and don't deserve. You weren't trying to protect me from the prince; you were just angry. It wasn't right. So, you don't get to make decisions until you've grown enough to be better at judging."

The more good-natured Arno was, the more he had to fight to protect him, and the more he had to fight to protect his brother, the more Arno would scold him. There was no way to win with the little guy on his back. But that didn't mean he wasn't going to try and make him happy anyway. Even if what Arno demanded was impossible.

"Fine, Arno. I'll let you be my conscience until I start thinking more like you."

"Good. Now, off to Wilheim."

Roran sighed. "Sure, No-No. Off to Wilheim."

"Do you think you can run faster and catch up if you get big? We need to catch up."

That was an interesting question. How long could he maintain the form for? It seemed like it was for a short duration, for about as long as he could hold his breath. But could he sustain the form longer if he was drawing in energy from trees and other living things, like what he had done to push over the giant tree? Like what the thing in the water was doing?

"I . . . I don't know if that is a good idea," Roran said.

"If we don't try, all of the bonfires in Wilheim are going to be stacked with people."

Roran exhaled. "Loosen the straps all the way. They might snap if I grow in them when they are tight, and I don't want to carry you in my arms all the way there."

Arno nodded. "People in progress."

CHAPTER 27

GROUND OR SKY

THOSE TRAITORS ARE ALIVE! And they stood by and did nothing while their kingdom crumbled. They must have been all along, Zerebril thought.

Another bump jostled the cart, sending a wave of pain across his entire body. Ewen had his healers tend to Zerebril's wounds before selling him to slavery. His leg had been splinted and his broken ribs set into place. Ewen knew that selling him to slavers in the condition they found him after the fight would have been a death sentence. The slavers wouldn't pay for him if he couldn't move, even if he was a prince. His body had begun the process of mending, but it was still a long way out. Thankfully, Ardhataz was a week away by cart. It would help somewhat. The slaver had been kind enough, more likely business-savvy enough, to apply Life Nectar salve to help with the healing. Problem was, all his injuries were internal, so they had to cut him open at the places where breaks were detected and rub the Life Nectar into his wounds.

Connor groaned at the next bump. The same bleeding and nectaring processes were done to him. He stirred and sat up from his sleeping position. A little dazed, he looked around at the scenery: tall trees hundreds of years old, the scent of pine and tree tar in the moist air, and the occasional bird chirping, hoping to hear a response in the deep woods. They were still in the lowland forests outside of Stedtfest but had moved past the flooded zones.

Another bump, and they both groaned.

"You too, huh?" asked Zerebril.

"Yeah, Ewen gave me quite the beating. Thankfully, unlike you, I'm not a twig, and not as many of my bones were broken. But if I had a mirror, I would probably be appalled by what he did to my handsome face." It looked like it took a lot of effort for Connor to form an approximation of a half-smile since his left eye was swollen shut, nose was broken, and lip was very fat.

Of all the people to be sold into slavery with, Zerebril thought. *Why him?*

"I will say, though," Connor continued, "for a twig, you survived much longer than I would have thought. Oros's piss, you even got Ewen in a chokehold."

Zerebril shook his head. "It wasn't enough. Maybe if I hadn't focused on art, maybe if I had trained more with you and Gunter, I might have—"

"Saved the kingdom?" Connor said, raising an eyebrow. "No offense meant, Zerebril, but if I couldn't beat him, you were never going to. You're puny. And that's it. Nothing would have changed that. Don't bother beating yourself up over it. Ewen already did that for you."

Zerebril bowed his head. Had his father given him an impossible task? Shoulder the weight of a crumbling kingdom? It felt less like he was carrying Wilheim and more like he was standing at the bottom of a cliff while someone rolled a boulder over the edge and commanded him to catch it.

But now that Connor was awake, he could at least get some answers, not that it would do anything to better their situation. "What happened to the Vanguard? Why did the plan fail?"

Connor attempted to spit some blood out the side of the barred wagon. His lips, dumbly moving and puckering in the air like a rooting infant, did not have the dexterity to launch the projectile. Instead, he just blew bubbles of spit and blood before resolving to wipe it off with his tattered sleeve.

"How should I know?"

"What do you mean? You were there!"

"I was in *one* of the quadrants, not all of them. Arthur, Dale, Carl, and I all attacked from different sides. That way, we could locate the beasts and wouldn't get in each other's way. I don't know what happened to the other three. All I know is that I did my part. I torched the southern end of the camp real quick. Even took out a couple officers. Several beasts did come after me, and I kicked their asses too. Professor Mathilda is a remarkable weapon."

Zerebril groaned.

"Then a man in scholar robes showed up. He was dressed in the robes of the College of Observation. I thought he was on our side. Apparently not."

"Well, what did he do?"

"I tried to question him about the location of the beasts or why he was there, but he never spoke."

"So, how'd you get captured?"

Connor spat again, a little more successfully this time. "*He* captured me. The screw-turning scholar!"

"How?"

Connor raised his hands in protest. "Now, now, I wasn't expecting it. I would have won if I knew the bastard was a traitor. The man had powers without having a Cormac weapon. These weird tentacles came out of the river and slapped me around. Professor Mathilda could burn them, but with Ewen's troops jumping on my backside, there was too much, and they eventually had me by each limb. Then the scholar walked up and put his hand on my forehead, which apparently knocked me out.

390 · ANTON JONES

Next thing I knew, Ewen's fist was forming a very intimate relationship with my face."

Zerebril tried to take all this in. "Did you see which professor
it was? Did you recognize who was wearing the robes?"

"No. He had his hood up, covering most of his face."

"How did he end up in Ewen's army?"

"How should I know?"

Zerebril shook his head. "I'm just thinking out loud. If he
had powers and was an academic, I'm guessing he's responsible
for Ewen spontaneously getting these new bestial weapons."

"You're the smart one. I'll let you do the thinking. I'll just sit
here, be handsome, and use my connections."

Zerebril frowned. "What do you mean?"

Connor chuckled. "For getting out of this mess, of course. As
soon as they know who my father is, I'll be able to get us out of
here."

Zerebril slowly nodded. He had not even considered escape.
All he could think about was what would happen to Wilheim
without him there, what would happen to his increasingly
unstable father. Did he even want to escape? What would be left
of Wilheim by the time he returned from Ardhataz? Would it be
easier for him to just die in slavery? And when was the next time
he could have some poppy?

"Hey? You with me?" Connor snapped his bruised hands in
front of Zerebril's face.

"I guess, but why bother? What's left for me out there?"

Connor scoffed. "Well, I don't know about you, but my
father can set me up with something. Give me a bit to restart
with in Ardhataz or opposite Lake Verdin."

"Useless . . ." Zerebril whispered.

"Come again?" Connor said.

"It was all for nothing . . ." Zerebril mumbled.

"Alright, Prince, sure, feel sorry for yourself. See what good
it does you," Connor said, shaking his head. "And for a second

there, you almost earned my respect the way you stood up to Ewen. Sheesh, I should have bloody known better. Right now, you're no better than a cow. And you'll probably stay that way. Zerebril, prince of the cows! Pathetic."

Zerebril looked down, only partially registering the barrage of insults. He didn't care about the insults. All he cared about was . . . what? What did he care about now?

Another bump reminded him of his injuries, and he groaned again.

Connor exhaled. "You know you earned that pain, right? Not the stupid garbage in your head. But that blood and bruises. You earned that. Don't let it go to waste."

"Go to waste? Is this some nonsense warriors tell themselves so that they're more willing to throw their lives away?"

Connor huffed and looked into the sky still visible through the bars. "Forget it."

"Fine." Zerebril looked up at the sky, too. Once, it was his favorite thing to paint. Now it was a patchwork of iron and blue. Even the blue was partially covered as storm clouds began to gather overhead. The cage made it hard for Zerebril to distinguish whether he was the one behind bars or the sky was. Now he cursed it. If he hadn't spent so much time painting the horizon, he would have been able to help his kingdom more.

"You only make use of your pain because you know it's not the end," said Zerebril. "You know you still have dreams, a future, a way out of this. For me, it just hurts and will continue to hurt until I die."

Connor rolled his eyes. "You are aware I will die too, right? I just plan to party a little bit more before I get to that point."

"So," Zerebril scoffed. "You follow tenets from *The March of Joy*? Taking in as much pleasure as you can before you fizzle out?"

Connor looked flabbergasted. "What do those dusty books have to do with this? I don't know what kind of life your

392 • ANTON JONES

pampered ass had in the castle, but most people out here can live and live well without anyone telling them how."

"You know, I always wanted to fly," Zerebril said, voice distant, scarcely talking to Connor at all. "Maybe it's why I spent so much time painting clouds."

Connor's confusion grew more. "Are you hysterical? What are you even talking about?"

"I wanted to learn some way or invent something so I could fly. When I couldn't and gave up, I imitated it on a canvas."

Connor threw his hands up in the air. "You're hopeless."

"I think that's why I respected Carl more than the rest of my family did. He had a way to fly. Not really himself, but his falcon could. And he could take advantage of that. Even though he was sent to the Lichtfangrs, relegated to hiding Father's dirty work, and mostly ignored by all of us, he did have a window to the sky."

"I don't see why anyone would ever envy Carl. His face is permanently deformed from his ever-scowl, and he spent most days dealing with corpse callers—"

"What do you think death is like? Do we go into the ground or the sky?"

Connor sighed and shook his head. "He's losing it, and I'm stuck in here with him. Don't go catch Grief Sickness on me. I don't want to deal with that."

"I'm serious," Zerebril said. "Do you think we go into the ground or into the sky?"

"Fine, I'll play along and pass the time," Connor said, shrugging. "I guess the ground. It's where they bury us, at least in Wilheim. Only makes sense. But there's also the pyres for nobility—"

"That's where our bodies go. But what about our spirits?"

Connor raised an eyebrow. "I never would have pegged you for converting to religion because of desperation."

"I don't intend to. I don't follow the Marches. But this is

unwritten and unknowable. We can only postulate. So, I'm postulating. Ground or sky?"

"Postu—what?" Connor shook his head. "Well, anyway, in that case, I guess . . . I'm guessing it's the ground, but I'm hoping it's the sky."

"Why?" Zerebril asked.

"If we still have something like our senses in death. It would be a better view. Probably taste better too. I don't want to eat dirt. Ewen already gave me a four-course meal, treating me to different layers of soil."

This actually managed to get a chuckle out of Zerebril. "I do that a lot too," Zerebril said.

"What, eat dirt?"

Zerebril chuckled further, a smile threatening to unscrew his face. "No. Hoping in things. Or rather, I used to. Knowing one answer for certain but hoping I was wrong. Hoping the world was secretly a better place than I was giving it credit for. Like it was all some grand surprise, that one day I would come out the other side and realize it wasn't all for nothing. That it actually meant something grand, that it was infinitely enjoyable and infinitely good to enjoy it. I just couldn't see it yet. And one day, at the end of my life, I would be pleasantly surprised by what was always there, but I couldn't see. Something somewhere in that expanse of sky." He looked up but the blue was almost completely covered by clouds now as the cart headed farther into the growing storm.

"And you don't have that hope now?" Connor asked.

Zerebril shook his head. "Did you know our astronomers from the College of Observation theorize why the sky is blue?"

Connor rolled his eyes. "Great, a lecture. I think this is why I, and many women, avoided talking to you. Your stream of thought is all over the place, or at least, you don't clue in the rest of us on how you are connecting one idea to the next."

"They theorize that light gets fragmented into filaments—"

"Great, he's ignoring me—"

"Into filaments of different colors when the light from the sun reaches our planet and that the blue ones get trapped in the sky."

Connor frowned. "So . . . knowing why the sky is blue . . . is that what makes you mopey all the time? It makes you lose hope because it's explainable? Am I following your thoughts, Z?"

"There's nothing special about it. The sky. All that time I spent dreaming about it—it was just a trick of the light."

"Alright, Prince," Connor said. "Here's one of the only things I remember from our classes. The only naturally occurring blue color on the continent is from Verdin Stars and the sky. And the lake—well, sea or gulf, I remember that too—doesn't count since it just reflects the sky."

"Mmmhmm, clean water doesn't have a color," Zerebril said.

"Right, so even if your 'trick of the light' is explainable, it's still the only place where everyone on Verdin can see that color. There's still wonder in that."

Zerebril looked up as a raindrop fell on his forehead. "Not anymore . . ."

"Seriously?" Connor asked as the rain started to come down harder. "You do know that the clouds don't erase the sky, right? It's still there."

Zerebril shrugged. "But I can't see it, so it might as well not be."

"That's your problem, Prince. If something exists outside the confines of your oversized head, then one of two things happen. It crushes you or it inspires awe. How can the same thing create two different results? If you don't understand something and that lack of understanding causes you temporary pain, then you deny it or rationalize it or let it crush you or, worse yet, turn to poppy. Yeah, I've heard. If you don't understand something but it gives you joy, then you worship it. You're the problem. The sky is still the same one you loved in your childhood. Now, you're just fixating on the rain because you're wet. As for me," Connor said, standing up, using the bars to support and balance his weight. "I'm going to use it to wash some of the blood off my clothes and face." Tenderly, Connor started rubbing at the bloody stains on his clothes and skin.

Zerebril focused on the rain. Though it was cold, it had a numbing effect on his aches and pains. "Don't let the pain go to waste . . ." he murmured.

"What's that?" Connor asked.

"Nothing."

Despite being an unreliable hedonist, Connor was right about a couple of things. Behind the bars, behind the clouds, the blue sky was still there.

He could hear Gunter's words getting twisted into something new. *Though I'm in the ground, don't stop looking at the sky.*

Zerebril smiled as he watched the hilarious sight of Connor try to catch rainwater in his hands to splash on his swollen face.

He thought back on his task of trying to catch the boulder of Wilheim as his father rolled it off the cliff to him below. If it was his duty to catch the boulder, an impossible task, there was a benefit to it. As he waited for the boulder to fall, he would have to look up at the sky.

CHAPTER 28
PEOPLE IN PROGRESS

"CAN you at least give me . . . just a few minutes to catch my breath?" Griselda asked, gulping increasingly thinner patches of air. Her and Mathilda had taken a hike into the Shatter Rock Range behind Wilheim to truly test End March without the risk of burning down the town.

"No. You need to learn to fight when you are tired. If your form cannot hold up when you are tired, then you might as well welcome your new screws on the Ardhatazian torture table. You'd be dead if that wasn't clear. Very dead. Form and endurance will keep you alive more than strength or talent."

Griselda sighed and sat down on a rock. At least it was a good view. The rock she sat on overlooked Wilheim nestled in the valley below. The sun was rising in the west slowly above the fields and hills that stretched westward beyond the walls of Wilheim. She knew Lake Verdin was out there over the horizon, but the air was filled with dust and smoke, preventing clear sight.

"I get that . . . I really do," Griselda huffed. "But did we have to do the hike in our armor?"

Mathilda lifted up her visor. "Yes."

"Why?"

"If you can choose, would you rather fight in armor or street clothes?"

"Well, armor—"

"Then you learn to get exhausted in armor. You learn how heavy it can be. And you learn how fatigue affects your form. Now up, up, off the rock. Show me ox guard."

Griselda stood and pressed her hips forward, raised her hands over her head, and then bent to stretch her aching back, abs, and stabilizer muscles. There were so many muscles she took for granted and didn't even know she had until they were pushed by carrying fifty pounds of armor and weapons around on a hike. She rolled her head from side to side. Even though she wasn't wearing a helmet, Griselda's neck and shoulders burned from the weight of the breastplate.

To taunt Griselda's shabby display of physical shape, Mathilda started running in place in her full-plate armor. "Come on, come on! If I can do it, you can."

Griselda pulled End March off the hooks on her back plate. "Fine," she said. Griselda put herself in the steps. She had trained with Mathilda only a handful of times thus far, mostly practicing the basics of stances and footwork. She had an idea of the guards and stances one could use with a great sword, even if she wasn't really able to make her body naturally fall into each stance at will without concentrated effort.

Griselda started with End March tip down. She kicked the sword up like Mathilda had shown her, letting the momentum of the sword do more work than her shoulders. She let the sword swing in a large loop before she held her form with the handle by her head, the tip pointing out toward Mathilda so that the blade was parallel with the ground.

"Good, now hold it."

Griselda huffed but did as she was told. Mathilda started wandering around while Griselda held the stance. Mathilda walked out of Griselda's field of vision.

"Hey!" Griselda said. "You're not going to leave me up here in this stance, are you?"

"No," Mathilda said. Griselda could tell she had put her visor back down as her voice was muffled. "Show me plow guard, opposite side."

Without thinking, Griselda pivoted to face Mathilda as the sword swung. Good thing she did, too, as a rock came whizzing at her shoulder. Griselda yelped and pivoted again as End March continued its long, looping path to dodge the rock. She then let her arms hang out in front of her, tip pointing at a 45-degree angle between Mathilda and the sky.

"Good instincts," Mathilda said. "I wondered if you would naturally turn to face me. Holding a weapon like that makes you the biggest target on the field. You'll get strikes and projectiles coming at you from all sides. Seems like you already have that ingrained."

Griselda nodded, remembering the faces of the men who she still saw for a split second when she closed her eyes. She relaxed her guard, letting End March's tip dip toward the ground in fool's guard.

"Keep your plow guard. I didn't say to rest yet."

Griselda lifted the sword back up.

"No. Do the steps again until you reach plow guard."

Griselda exhaled loudly but repeated the motions. She moved, flowed, stepped, and swung the sword in the vertical loops until she had come to plow guard.

Mathilda was walking along the trail picking up and weighing different-sized sticks.

Is she going to throw a stick at me? Griselda thought.

Griselda held the guard and waited.

"Ahh, this is a good one," Mathilda said, picking up a stick a little shorter than she was.

Griselda focused on her breathing as she felt her arms begin to tremble from holding the great sword in the same position for

400 • ANTON JONES

so long. Mathilda, using her new treasure as a walking stick, leisurely strolled over while Griselda was pouring sweat.

"Good, now high guard."

Griselda sucked in air as she whirled End March until her hands were just above her head, tip pointing high and behind her.

"This is also known as wrath guard," Mathilda said. "As your blows will be devastating with the weight of the sword assisting you. However—"

Wham!

Griselda's wind was knocked out of her as Mathilda broke the stick over Griselda's breastplate. Griselda fell to her hands and knees.

"Well, at least you didn't drop the sword," Mathilda said. "Now up, back to your stance."

From the ground, Griselda coughed and shot Mathilda an evil eye. Mathilda lifted her visor to respond with a wicked grin.

"I hope you're having fun torturing me," Griselda wheezed as she stood back up and whirled back into high guard.

"Do you think I would be a teacher if I couldn't maliciously torture students for my own amusement?"

Griselda regained control of her breathing; her arms were still shaking, holding End March above her head.

"So . . . what have you learned about high guard?"

"It's," Griselda said, breathing heavily. "Tiring."

"Yeah. And?"

"I feel much more exposed. Why would anyone willingly hold their sword above their head like this? You can strike me easily without me being quick enough to respond."

"Not exactly," Mathilda said, grabbing another stick.

Griselda swallowed nervously. "This isn't really fair. I can't hit you, and you can hit me? How am I supposed to learn to defend myself?"

"Fair point. Trade?" Mathilda said, offering her the stick.

"Can I release the stance?"

"Good. And yes," Mathilda said as she took End March and gave Griselda the stick in return. She let her face feel the warmth of the glow for a second before dropping her visor back down. "You may hit me now."

"I feel like this is even less fair."

Mathilda chuckled behind her visor. "Don't worry, I'm not going to skewer you or light you on fire. Now, do your steps with the stick until you are in high guard." Mathilda paused as Griselda obeyed. "A great sword's greatest danger is not the edge or the weight but the way it intimidates opponents. It's a frightening thing to look at, let alone defend against, because of the reach. If you are in high guard, you better not be in it for long, because it is heavy to hold above your head, but at the same time . . ." Mathilda held End March in a high guard. "Watch how little effort and movement it takes for me to make a downward strike . . . there. See, I moved my wrist and elbows slightly, and the blade is now six feet in front of me, directly on my opponent's head."

Mathilda brought the blade back up and swung it down harder before letting the momentum carry the sword back up in a loop until it was in high guard again.

"It's an offensive stance," Mathilda said. "The threat of you bringing the sword down is also part of the defense. Your opponents will be hesitant to approach. You can also block from it by dropping the shoulder on one side . . . like so."

Dropping the left shoulder, Mathilda brought End March in a downward swing meant to ward off strikes from the left side and then flowed into ox guard as End March's handle naturally came to the right side of her helmet. "Now you try it."

With her stick, Griselda did as well from tip resting on the ground, to high guard, to ox guard.

"And hold it."

Griselda groaned.

"From here, I can continue to press the offensive with

402 • ANTON JONES

thrusts." Mathilda did a few quick thrusts. The blade started to glow more intensely. " If you can flow into your stances, this monster will naturally ignite and send the fire out without any need for unnecessary flourishes."

Griselda practiced the steps as well, bringing the stick down in a savage strike on an invisible enemy from high guard, looping it to ox guard, and then thrusting forward as if she were pursuing an opponent. She then resumed holding the stick in high guard above her head to strengthen her shoulders.

Mathilda set the tip down in the ground, and the sword cooled. "Armor, and a weapon like this, are equalizers."

"What do you mean?" asked Griselda.

Mathilda exhaled. "Though I am an experienced fighter, at the end of the day, I'm still a woman. I still have a strength, weight, and speed disadvantage when fighting most male opponents. At least, the men who train every day have that advantage. I'd thrash any blowhard man who thought he could best me without vigorous day-to-day training. But if I am fighting a hardened male warrior . . . I've learned a few things to balance the scales."

"Like what?"

"You're holding that steady in high guard, right? Endurance is one thing. Awareness of the environment is another. General intelligence of fighting is a third. None of that is barred from our sex. And this," she said, raising End March overhead. "This big-ass sword is the best equalizer. I may not be as large as my male opponents, but I don't need to be when I swing something like this around. Accidentally dropping this thing on your foot could do the same amount of damage as a male opponent with a short sword slapping it against armor. But you got to use it with endurance and intellect and awareness."

Griselda nodded. Though she did understand the value in the things Mathilda was saying before, she now understood the clear connection to hiking in armor, throwing rocks from her blind spot, drilling her—rather painfully—on the advantages and disadvantages of certain guards.

"So . . . now comes the fun part. Using this monster to its full intended purpose. You ready to light the sky on fire?"

Griselda froze as Mathilda traded her stick back for End March. She'd had the weapon for a few weeks now but still hadn't tried to use the infamous flame lashes out of fear of the things she'd burn down in the process. The damage the sword could do, had already done in her hands, could not be underestimated.

"I brought you up to the cliff for a reason. There's not much vegetation this high up. Still, I'd rather not add a forest fire to Wilheim's problems on top of Ewen's impending assault. So, try to aim it, as best you can, high in the air. Without a direct fuel source, the flames will eventually fizzle out as they fall across the valley. If you aim it at a target that can catch on fire, it will. Be careful."

Griselda swallowed and became aware of the burn scar on her arm. Though End March's grip in her hand was familiar by this point, her hands seemed repulsed by the handle, an antagonistic force blocking her from what she was being asked to do. She hesitated, standing there dumbly with the blade in her hand.

"Run your steps and stances."

Griselda blinked and saw the faces.

"What?" Mathilda asked. "You scared of lighting your hair on fire? Helmet would prevent that."

Whatever she tried, now that she was tasked with using End March *that* way, she couldn't make her body move. "I . . . I . . . could you do it first?"

"No."

"Why not?"

Mathilda shrugged, her pauldrons clanking as the motion was awkward to do in full plate. "It's your sword. Your family. Your brothers on the line. You need to do it."

"But . . . what if I hurt something or someone with it? Training is different. That's improving me. But this . . . the fire seems like it is only meant to be . . . wicked, cruel."

Griselda heard Mathilda sigh behind her visor. She flipped it up, and Griselda could see the disappointment in Mathilda's frown and furrowed brow.

"You know, I don't do stuff like this. The feeling stuff. We had other staff at the academies for that kind of thing. I just do ass-kicking stuff. Are you not ready to ass-kick? This *should* be exciting. Why is it not?"

Griselda swallowed. "I've burned someone alive with it. I still . . . I still see his burned face when I close my eyes. I've cut off the head of another. I see him too. I have a scar on my arm—"

Mathilda looked at the ground and rubbed her chin with her gauntlets. "I'm not asking you to kill anyone. I'm asking you to swing a sword."

"So that I can become better at killing."

Mathilda groaned. "Look. The hike back down is going to be really awkward if you don't swing that sword."

Griselda did so, but very slowly, so that it would not ignite.

"Okay, dirt-muncher, we both know you're just being petty, or silly, or stupid, or something else I don't know much about. I don't have that weakness in me, so I don't know how to deal with it in other people. Work that out yourself. I don't have any advice. Do it here while it's safe and I'm watching. That's the whole point of bringing you to the cliff!"

"I'm not stupid enough to believe that I'll hurt anyone here," Griselda said. "It's the idea of it. Of allowing myself to do it now, so that I can kill in the future. I don't want to collect more faces."

Mathilda slumped, more exasperated by dealing with an emotional issue than by hiking up a mountain wearing full plate. "I'm not asking you to like killing. I want you to be proficient at using your own tool. Not knowing how a weapon works is just as likely to get yourself killed as it is to kill someone else. If you don't want to hurt anyone else, fine. I get that. But as long as you have that thing on your back, you better know how it works, or you'll accidentally kill more people than you ever do intentionally. It's a tool, like your father's hammer. Wielding it with endurance, awareness, and intelligence will save more lives than it takes."

Griselda nodded, exhaled, and closed her eyes. She saw the faces that haunt her. She saw the faces, but . . . they did not *need* to haunt her.

Griselda began to move End March into the first of a series of steps.

They could be there without haunting. They could be something else. End March was a tool. It did not make her a monster. But at the same time, the faces served as a reminder to never let her kill without serious consideration of all other possible outcomes. *You are,* she thought, addressing the faces, *all at the same time: remembrance, deterrence, and consequence.*

Moving from stance to stance, more quickly now, the sword glowed brighter and brighter in her gauntleted hands. In her steps, Griselda flowed to the side of the cliff and the open horizon beyond. *Though I may be forced to add more to your number, I hope your faces never leave me.*

The blade started to hum as the heat from it radiated off the blade.

Though my body may swing this sword more easily, killing should never become easy, lest I become just as hollow-eyed as the faces looking at me now from the opposite side of the March.

With a final flourish, the air ignited, and flame flew off following the swing of the sword. Griselda swung the sword high in the air and the fire arced out into the open. The flame cut a horizontal line across the sky and outshined the sun for a moment until eventually dissipating, never hitting the stoney valley far below.

I will save more lives than I take.

Griselda whirled the blade again, making sure to increase the momentum as the sword flew in front of her and decreasing it as the sword flew in any other direction, so that the fire would only fling off in the desired directions. She couldn't keep the smile from her face as she created a new strange fire-burst with each swing, painting the sky with her family's legacy. The air got dry and harder to breathe, and the temperature all around her increased dramatically though it was the beginning of winter. Even the air *smelled* different with the intense heat.

"Woah, woah, woah! Okay! Okay! That's enough!" Mathilda shouted above the roar of the combusting air.

Griselda slowed the swinging and jammed the tip of the sword into the soil, sending out a very satisfying sizzling sound that capped her fiery accomplishment. She turned back at Mathilda, smile still unconsciously plastered on her face.

"What, are you trying to write your name in the sky?" Mathilda flipped her visor back up, struggling to keep the smile from her face too even if it looked like her eyes were bulging out of her head. "I hope we are far away enough that no one in Wilheim saw that. If they did, they might think Ewen tamed Oros and is riding him here to burn the city.

"One last thing," Mathilda said. "Now that you've shown me something important, I'll show you something too: the College of Combat salute."

Mathilda beat her chest over her heart with her left gauntleted fist and then slowly rose it to rest on the top of her helmet. "Repeat after me: I acknowledge your head and you heart. And I will remember you with mine."

Griselda repeated, holding End March with her right hand and mimicking the salute gesture with her left.

Mathilda nodded in approval. "Say it after each fight. Say it after each training session. You'll know why eventually. But, now comes the hike down. In armor, of course. Then after that, we need to clean the armor and treat it with oil to prevent rusting. You got that? More work to be done. Let's go."

Griselda kept smiling stupidly. She had no words for the experience. Yes, she had acknowledged the weight of the power she held in her hands. But she also permitted herself to enjoy the pure spectacle of it as well. Come what may, she would be proud to wield her father's last work of art and learn to master the power he spent years crafting.

Roran was on a deadline and did not have the time he wanted to master the power he now held. He pushed the form as fast as it could go, running and jumping through the forest, Arno bouncing on his back in the harness. Though there was a demanding urgency to get to Wilheim as soon as possible, he thought Arno would be enjoying the ride. He was not. He didn't say a word and almost seemed to be getting sicker.

Roran sucked in air and pushed it down to stoke the inner fire, but he needed more. He tried to breathe in deeper but coughed and sputtered.

"Are you getting sick," asked Arno.

"No, are you?" Roran replied.

"Maybe," sighed Arno.

Hang in there, little guy, Roran thought. *This will all be over soon.*

Rather than draw in too much air and risk coughing, he held out his arms as he ran and let them graze tree trunks when he passed by. Roran's awareness swelled to include the nearby trees in the forest, their past growth, current connections via the root systems to other trees, and their instinct to grow taller to reach toward the sun. And he took that future from them. Roran breathed in deeply again as he stole bits and pieces of the trees' life force and added it to his inner fire, allowing him to move even faster and jump even higher.

Trees began to wither and collapse in his wake. Birds fell out of the sky. Not even insects chirped in the same vicinity as Roran. It was . . . unsettling. But something stranger nagged at him as he reached out and stole the futures of the forest, a connection he couldn't quite make . . . but he would need to worry about that later. Now was the time for running, and come what may, he would need to use everything in his arsenal if he was going to stand a chance at helping the people of Wilheim and protect the place his father had learned to call home.

CHAPTER 29
COLONEL

THE MOST IMPORTANT moments of Urrem's life so far, thought the now freshly promoted colonel, all revolved around a tool striking the dirt.

A nine-year old Urrem helped his father dig the foundations for their first home in Ardhataz, the shovel hitting the unyielding rocky soil. He learned his father's trade of carpentry while building their home together.

When Urrem's father was assigned to build bridges high in the mountains for the new mines, a fourteen-year-old Urrem was there in the caves with a pick in hand, striking the ore.

When the blizzard came that cut off the supply lines to the mining town, a sixteen-year-old Urrem picked up the shovel again. His parents made sure he had the last of the food. He dug in the snow until he eventually hit dirt, not willing to give his parents shallow graves. He carved himself out of the blizzard and down the mountain—the only survivor of the mining town. Always the only survivor.

A twenty-two-year-old Urrem set new foundations in a new town, his parents' sacrifice making it possible for him to live a new life. And after another decade of honing his trade as a carpenter, he was ready to start a new life that included Jezerelle and the hope of raising a family of his own.

He had three good years with her before fate called him away.

A thirty-five-year-old Urrem met Gunter's sword, tip first, stabbed in the dirt.

And then a bearer's mace, thrown from a distance into his campfire that exploded on impact.

And then a log had collapsed his ladder, smashing his troops as it hit the muddy ground.

Sometimes looking into the past didn't keep him from looking too closely at the present. The good *thens* were being quickly overwritten by an onslaught of terribles *nows*.

But Urrem needed to keep moving, like the water beneath the boat he stood on. He could not afford to get lost in reflection, not now, especially as his superior officer was giving him an order.

"Can you manage that, Urrem?" asked the Siege Master.

Urrem stared at the river as they floated along on the boat. All of Urrem's old unit was dead, save for Briggs, ambushed by four bearers who had tried to defeat Ewen's army before the siege of Stedtfest had begun. They had taken heavy casualties in the assault. Perhaps the only reason they had survived at all was due to Ewen buying Sophia. The dozens of light beasts that came to help had also been destroyed by the bearers, which included the one with a mace, the slaver's boy, and the twins from the Pits. Only three light beasts had not been killed, but that was enough. They slaughtered the mounted troops, leaving Sophia untouched, and invaded the city. The Scholar had captured one of the bearers, the slaver's boy, and Ewen decided to keep the glowing great sword he wielded despite the Scholar being visibly distressed in its presence.

"Urrem?" asked the Siege Master.

Ewen had quickly ushered everyone in the chaos into an assault on Stedtfest. And Urrem had been used as bait. Again. He had to join another unit since his was the first victim of the mace wielder. Due to taking charge of a unit when its field captain fell, some quick thinking with using the logs as ladders, and since one of the siege colonels was killed in the initial ambush, Urrem had been promoted to colonel in another branch and put in charge of overseeing construction of siege camps and siege weapons.

He was currently on the boat with the Siege Master, General Macintosh. The Siege Master was talking, but Urrem wasn't there. Half of him was in the mud outside Stedtfest. The other half of him was trying to burrow so far into the past that he would never see another future, a future where violence was done to him and he ordered violence to be done to others.

"Urrem, ya dere?" asked the Siege Master, snapping his fingers in Urrem's face.

Urrem forced himself back into the present. "Yes, I can manage da reconstruction of da trebuchets wit da help of some of yer engineers."

"Ya sure?" Macintosh asked. "Dis conversation has been awfully one sided."

Urrem shook his head and smiled. "I'll be fine. I get to do tings my muscles will remember even if my mind is elsewhere. It's been a bit since I held a hammer."

Macintosh shrugged. "Alright . . . let me know if anyting's da matter. Imeel-Illin knows we're all going to see tings by the end of Ewen's bloody March. Anyway, we have detailed plans and illustrations for how dey operate. I'm sure ya'll do fine."

Despite the Siege Master's discomforting appearance—short, balding, beady eyed, nasally voice, mountain-sized forehead—he was much kinder than Urrem had been expecting. Like Ewen, he seemed to reserve all the possible kindness and respect for his own troops while leaving nothing for the rest of the world.

"Thank ya, sir. It will be done."

"Dismissed."

Urrem bowed his head curtly and walked away. Though it

was expected for him to be chipper at the promotion, the rise in rank had been the result of Ardhatazian deaths, not for his own merit. And he couldn't shake the feeling, despite all the tight-knit camaraderie of the officers, that underhanded games were being played.

Because it happened again. He'd been used as bait *again*. He had witnessed firsthand the slaughter. The thousands left to gurgle in the mud as the murky water slowly crept into the puncture wounds in their lungs. The horror of the traps and falling onto spikes. The agony of being trampled by friends, the very second one lost his footing. And they left all their dead to rot in the killing field! No Ardhatazian rites, no ceremony, nothing. Just discarded refuse to feed the war machine. To feed whatever was in the water. To facilitate whatever the Scholar was up to.

Never again. Now that he was partially in charge of the siege tactics, no Ardhatazian soldier would be used as bait under his watch. They were going to do the siege properly this time. Build a perimeter, choke the city of outside resources like food and water, and bombard the walls until one of the sections fell. Besides, according to the Siege Master, they would have to wait a while anyway for new beasts to be made.

They wouldn't have nearly as much as they had before the ambush, but, according to Sophia, there were only three bearers left in the employment of Wilheim, all of which were at the ambush and were now likely scattered. It was possible they had gone back to Wilheim, but it was equally possible, since they were mercs, that they would flee or turncoat too.

Ewen had sent one of the colonels in the sea branch back to Ardhataz to recruit and replenish ranks. Though they wouldn't take nearly as long since the countryside had already been decimated and the river undammed, that would still take a while as well. According to Sophia, Wilheim, the fabled City of Lights, was at one-third of its initial strength, having sent so much of the garrison to Stedtfest. They just needed enough soldiers for the perimeter and to wrestle control of the city once the walls were down or were breached by siege towers.

Urrem proceeded to the front of the boat and looked into the water. It was curious how some of the boats no longer needed row men, including the one Urrem was standing on, even though they were going upstream toward the base of the mountains encircling Verdin.

Something wet landed on Urrem's nose. Urrem looked up and saw that flakes of white were beginning to descend. Though winter was on its way, Wilheim was higher up in elevation and would feel the effects quicker than the lowlands near Stedtfest. Snow would not be good for morale once the siege began. It would also take away a few good siege tactics, such as tunneling under the walls to weaken them. Tunneling would be much harder in the rockier soil in Wilheim, the cold only hardening the ground further.

Urrem looked over the boat one more time to see if he could catch a glimpse of the things in the water. He had seen them more and more since the flooding: slightly glowing, semi-translucent tentacles moving the boats along up the river. They were related to the light beasts somehow, Urrem was reasonably sure of that. But they were also different. The tendrils were several times thicker than the light strands making up Ewen's otherworldly beasts. There was also no main body in sight, but Urrem was certain that all the tentacles belonged to the same thing based on how they acted in unison. They were hard to see; once Urrem first noticed them, he had been keeping tabs on the things. He was reasonably sure they were on his side and that would have to do for now.

Most of the soldiers were too disturbed to talk about the strange things that defied reason. They instead preferred to think of it as Ewen's divine endowment, that he really is the next leader of the March like he claims.

Scribes followed Ewen everywhere he went to write down

the things he said and did with the goal of compiling the Wilheim conquest into a book that may stand next to the old Marches.

Urrem shook himself away from staring at the water so that he could retire to his quarters and stare at the wooden ceiling instead. Being a colonel now, he slept on a boat rather than in the tent encampments. A portion of the siege components and parts were on this boat, so it only made sense. Despite being a carpenter, despite spending years cutting, crafting, and shaping wood, wood still did not speak to Urrem like his troops had. His troops could make conversation, jokes, and meals together. They made some of the brutality of war more bearable. He could rely on Malcom's calm reasoning and Briggs's dirty jokes. Though Briggs survived the ambush, he was no longer under Urrem's direct command. Urrem was alone.

The sky was getting darker as the sun set behind the clouds of snow. Urrem tried to fall asleep early, waiting for when they would make camp outside of Wilheim. It would not be long now.

He knew it would be pointless trying to sleep. All he would do is lie stiff as a floorboard and continue to stare at the ceiling. But he didn't have the energy to talk with anyone else. There were expectations for him to be happy with his new role and how closely it matched his trade before the war. There were expectations that he would be a good leader though none of his men ever survived. But was that really his fault? For both the Battle of the Highest Hill and the Siege of Stedtfest, he and his men were bait to distract while the beasts did their work.

He tossed in his bed, kicking his blanket off his body despite the chill in the air. He had confronted Ewen about this, too. Not in a war room meeting, but more informally, after winning Stedtfest and finally getting the troops into houses and out of the mud.

"You're a colonel now, Urrem," Ewen had said. "I can let you in on more of the overall plan. Men need to die for this to work. Not just the Willies, but our men too."

Urrem dared to ask why, and Ewen smiled. "The powers that be rely on suffering; they are strengthened by it. The trail of dead bodies we leave in our wake gives it stepping stones to follow us."

Ewen had downed his mug of ale and moved on to another conversation, leaving Urrem with many more questions than answers. The two most pressing being what exactly was the "it"? And why were they leading it to Wilheim? Or were they merely trying to keep whatever it was away from Ardhataz?

CHAPTER 30
THE RIGHT TO BE RECKLESS

GRISELDA SAT MUTELY, legs growing numb in the uncomfortable wooden chair that she suspected Mathilda had made herself, while contemplating the wisps of steam rising from a bowl of hot stew. With the immediate soil surrounding Wilheim being mostly rocky, the land wasn't known for its extravagant cuisine. Most food was imported so the people of Wilheim were used to eating foods sampled from all around the lake. Now that most traders and merchants had fled Wilheim or had erased it from their route, they were left with hard-times food: a warm, hearty stew with potatoes and carrots and whatever meat that could be found.

Though Professor Mathilda was certainly paid well, Griselda would not have been able to tell based on her living space. Griselda ate the stew out of a wooden bowl with a wooden spoon, which she gently blew on. Mathilda sat on her own sloppily assembled, unsanded chair with nails only partially beaten into the wood at a haphazardly constructed table that leaned and creaked whenever she set her elbows on its dirty, bumpy surface.

There was nothing on the walls: no ornaments, no awards, no trophies, not even books. Only cobwebs in the corners of the ceiling added anything to the bare walls. Griselda's feet had blackened from walking barefoot on the dusty, wooden floor. One thing was certain: her father would have hated how unkempt Mathilda preferred her living space.

Her house on the outskirts of the Wilheim Academies had four rooms: Mathilda's bedroom, a kitchen, a living space, and a large room that was locked off.

Mathilda herself was just as strange and lacking in decorum as her house. She did not take herself very seriously, nor did she clean up after herself, which Griselda might have expected from a life of solitary dedication to combat. She took some getting used to, but Griselda was thankful for the roof and food, even if that food included mushy carrots.

Despite them being in a stew, Griselda still didn't much care for carrots. Nevertheless, she stomached them down for the sake of politeness and knowing that food was going to start getting scarce. Mathilda, opposite Griselda her with her own bowl, ate voraciously, not seeming to notice the hot temperature.

After having spent time with Mathilda, Griselda had learned that conversation with her at the dinner table was futile. Mathilda seemed to put all her concentration into stuffing her face as if it was the first meal she had eaten in a week. Griselda didn't have to wait long with a question or topic if one popped into her head anyway since Mathilda would be finished with her food so fast.

Griselda's stew had just cooled to a reasonable temperature by the time Mathilda had finished. She seemed aware of her eating characteristics and how awkward it could be for guests, so she made up for it by talking up a storm once she was done eating while her guests were just getting started.

"Have you been to the other regions around Lake Verdin?" Mathilda asked.

Mouth full of stew, Griselda resolved to shake her head "no." After swallowing, Griselda said, "And you?"

"Oh, certainly," Mathilda said. "I've been everywhere, fighting in tournaments. I've even been to the Highland Pits in

Ardhataz to fight some special exhibition matches. I wasn't always some stuffy academic."

Griselda hardly considered Mathilda as either stuffy or an academic.

"After I graduated from the College of Combat, I was a mercenary in other regions."

Griselda nodded, dabbing at the corners of her mouth with her shirt where some broth had escaped. Mathilda had no napkins. In fact, Mathilda seemed confused that such a thing as napkins was a concept when Griselda had asked for one during their first dinner.

"I was never lucky enough to be a merc outfitted by a noble who had bought one of your father's weapons," Mathilda sighed. She crossed her arms in front of her. Even though she was out of her armor, she was still wearing a green gambeson as if that was her everyday attire. "Which is why, I think, I've been enjoying sparring with you so much, despite the world coming to an end. So, thank you for that, making the last days some good ones."

Griselda shrugged. "It's the least I can do for your hospitality. And besides, I think I'm getting more out of it than you are." Griselda rubbed the left side of her rib cage where a fresh bruise was purpling after that day's sparring session. Griselda was getting her fair share of nasty bumps, but she was learning exponentially. This was the first time she had a proper teacher for any subject.

"Do you really think Wilheim will fall? You seem to be pretty pessimistic about it anytime you bring it up," Griselda said.

Mathilda leaned her head from one shoulder to the other while considering the question. "I'll say this: while you were out asking about your brothers, I received a messenger from the king. As soon as Ewen shows up, he wants me to head through the inner wall, toward the keep. Anyone who is left capable of bearing arms is to make our stand in the keep. There's too few of us to guard the entire city perimeter. I'm guessing King Morgen thinks we can hold the keep long enough to frustrate Ewen into offering terms. You know, the kind of conditional surrender that doesn't end with Wilheim being turned to charcoal with all our severed heads rolling in the streets."

Griselda's eyes widened. Mathilda sure was blunt.

"What's the point of Ewen killing everyone? It seems unnecessarily cruel and even detrimental to his goals," Griselda asked.

Mathilda shrugged. "That's a good question, isn't it? By all accounts, it doesn't make much sense to burn the ground you're marching over and planning on reclaiming. But he has won battle after battle regardless of his seemingly thoughtless tactics."

"When you said 'anyone capable of bearing arms,' does that mean me as well?" Griselda asked with a gulp. She was here for her brothers, not to get mixed up in the war.

"If you wish," Mathilda said. "But I think you're a little young for a glorious last stand. You'd best sneak into the mountains as soon as Ewen gets here. You can follow the trails we took to the cliff the other day."

"But you're fine with it?" Griselda asked. Her pace of stew-eating was growing slower as the conversation continued.

Mathilda laughed. "I guess. I've been training King Morgen's men for over a decade now. I know the king and the company he keeps quite well and rather like the lot of them. Though it is duty for me to go, I do so willingly."

Griselda wrestled with this information in her head. Time was running out and she was no closer to finding any information about her brothers. If anyone did know, she bet that the best source of information was the king himself. To find her brothers, Griselda might have to get more involved than she wanted.

"I'll go with you," Griselda said.

Mathilda raised an eyebrow. "Ready to die already? Is that why you don't wear a helmet?"

Griselda shook her head. Mathilda had been relentlessly badgering her about getting a helmet. "If you are to form some kind of last stand, you'll want me and End March by your side. I can burn down anyone trying to get into the gatehouse."

"You know, I like you a lot," said Mathilda, smiling. "But I don't think you've earned the right to be reckless yet."

"And how do I?" Griselda asked.

"For one, you're too clever."

Griselda laughed. "And you're not? You're a teacher!"

"Oh, believe you me, just because I'm a teacher doesn't mean I'm the smartest person in the room. I'm just pretty good at one thing. You're far more clever than me, I can tell. You should be using that intellect to come up with a sound strategy rather than vainly making a last stand."

Griselda tapped her finger on the table. "Well, what if it is strategy? I think the only person who might know about my brothers is the king. And the only way I'm getting close to him is by being his guard."

Mathilda leaned back in her chair, which creaked, and clasped her hands across her stomach. She let her head roll back, and she stared at the ceiling, deep in thought.

"If the king finds out you have End March, you'll either be used as a weapon or it will be taken from you and given to me," Mathilda said finally. "Look, Griselda, if your brothers are as smart as you, they would have been out of here long ago."

Griselda chuckled. "That's what I'm worried about."

"What? That they're idiots?"

"Well . . ."

"Oh . . . hmm . . ."

Griselda corrected herself. "I mean, it's not like they can't think. It's just that Roran's impulsive and—"

"He's probably putting himself in as much danger looking for you as you are looking for him. I get it."

Griselda shrugged. "I'm half convinced I should climb up on

424 • ANTON JONES

the city wall and use End March like a signal fire, waving it around, launching fire into the sky visible for miles until Roran sees it."

"Reckless. Don't be reckless. The fire comes back down. Plus, the king will see you as a threat when fire starts raining down on his city."

Griselda sighed. "I guess that's why getting close enough to casually ask about the two without the king knowing who I am is the best course of action."

Mathilda rubbed her hand on her chin, a gesture that seemed oddly masculine to Griselda, like Mathilda was stroking some invisible beard. "You may be right," Mathilda huffed. "But you can't have the glowing monstrosity slung over your back. And we need to do something about your face."

Griselda frowned. "What's wrong with my face?"

"Nothing, cupcake. But I'm guessing they probably know what you look like. Come with me," Mathilda said, rising from the table.

Griselda followed as Mathilda walked over to the locked room. When she unlocked and opened the door, Griselda finally understood where all her money went. The room was lined wall to wall with different sets of armor. Some looked incredibly old, and some looked like they came from different regions. At the foot of each armor stand was a book penned in Mathilda's hand that detailed the different origins and uses for each armor component. The largest room in the house was dedicated to the collection and maintenance of her weaponry. Griselda should have been able to guess that. On the wall opposite the door stood several weapon racks holding swords, axes, maces, and polearms all organized by type and period.

"Wow . . ." Griselda murmured.

"You like?" Mathilda said, smiling, obviously proud of her collection and arrangement. "It's taken decades to assemble and maintain and catalog all of this. When Wilheim burns, I will most regret that this collection will be looted or destroyed."

Griselda nodded. This was her legacy and life's work. The study and cataloging of weapons and armor across time and region seemed to be the only kind of academic work Mathilda immersed herself in. It would be a shame to see it lost.

"So," Mathilda said, "I'm going to give you a helmet of your choice. Don't want anyone recognizing you. I can also make you a proper scabbard for End March. It will just go up to the parrying hooks and be thick and black to hide the glow. Great swords don't usually have scabbards, but I think it will be necessary in your case. It's better than a tent tarp. Use your side sword unless it's life or death to avoid any unwanted attention."

Griselda looked at her in surprise. "You're just giving me a helmet?"

"I've had them customized to fit me, they will most likely fit you. They probably won't properly fit any dirty giant Tazz grunt trying to loot it, so might as well give it to you."

"Thank you," Griselda mustered while walking from stand to stand. She eventually pointed at one helmet on a stand closest to the weapon shelf. "I'll take this one."

Mathilda started laughing.

"What? Is that one not good?"

"No, it's fine, it's that I am making you pick a helmet, and you pick one that's practically half a helmet," Mathilda said walking over and plucking the sallet off the stand.

It was visored, but the visor didn't extend down to cover the chin and mouth. The back of the helmet had a long, drawn-out tail to protect the neck.

"What's the deal with you and not wanting full head protection? I don't have a bevor for your lower face."

Griselda shrugged. "I don't like confined spaces all that much. I feel like I would get a headache or wouldn't be able to breathe in a fully enclosed helmet. This one will allow me to breathe at least."

Mathilda rolled her eyes. "Oh, cupcake, the suffocation and claustrophobia are part of the fun. Very well, it will cover enough of your face to work as a disguise."

Mathilda gave her a padded head cap to wear under the helmet. "If it's not snug, we can add more padding."

"No," said Griselda, trying it on. "It fits well." She hit herself on the sides of the head, and the helmet did not jostle about.

"Good. Now you have my permission to be reckless."

Griselda smiled, which was visible since the helmet only covered the top half of her face.

Griselda took it off, and they went back into the kitchen. She insisted on doing the dishes, which Mathilda seemed maybe a little too eager to let her do. When relieved of dish duty, Mathilda lay on the floor and stared up at the ceiling, almost looking like she was doing breathing exercises. Griselda smiled at the eccentricities. Mathilda reminded her more of her brothers than any man she had met, even though Mathilda physically resembled her mother. She scrubbed away at the food gunk left in the wooden bowls and hummed the Anvil Tune. It all reminded her of home.

———————————

As the sun was starting to set, Griselda decided to have one final walk around the city to inquire about her brothers. The next morning, she and Mathilda would be heading into the castle and likely staying there until the end.

The campus was as empty as ever. And eerily quiet. She left the campus grounds and headed toward the market district, the district that had still been fairly busy while everything else was going dark. She was wearing her armor minus the helmet, a habit she thought would stick for a long time if Mathilda had anything to say about it. Additionally, she was wearing a winter cloak with the College of Combat's insignia engraved on it that Mathilda had given her as the days got colder. Though it had melted quickly, the year's first snowfall had happened a couple days ago, and she needed to start making the transition to heavier clothes.

The College of Combat's insignia was a derivative of the Wilheim sun, just with two swords crossed in front of it, as if blocking access to the light. Griselda thought that was a poor choice. If she had designed it, the swords would be behind the sun. It seemed more in line with the goals of the college and the reputation of Wilheim being a beacon of light and progress to assist all of Verdin.

But that would soon be gone. Griselda found herself taking in the architecture, the immaculately cobbled streets despite the debris left by fleeing citizens, and even the trees kept pristinely trimmed to contrast with the white stone. Different sections of the city had diverse trees that would all flower in the spring. Depending on where you were, you could be walking down the streets while pink, white, or yellow petals drifted down from the budding trees. Hundreds of years of knowledge and progress were about to be erased from the map. The legacy of countless people, forgotten, a dirty smudge on the scroll of history.

As the sun set in the east behind the mountains, the polished white stones seemed to soak it in, absorbing the light and reflecting the golden hue. They matched the colors of the sun on rise or set. Even the stone of the city was intrinsically linked to the whims of the sun. No wonder Tazzes would mock them by calling them "sun worshippers." But that golden hue was getting darker and would soon be another color entirely.

Griselda entered the streets of the market to find that even this bustling space was nearly empty. In the district's center was the stone square where a bonfire would normally rage. By this time of day, the fire was usually built for each district, and they would light it as the sun set, so that the city may never know true night. Not today. Today would be the first time since the tradition began where the bonfires would not be lit.

Griselda sighed as she sat on a bench in front of the massive stone fire pit. The previous night's charcoal and ash stared back at her accusingly, wondering where the light was. There was no fire tender. In front of the bench stood a dedication stone naming the bonfire after one of Wilheim's Beacons, the people historically thought to play a role in founding or maintaining the great city.

This bonfire, if it ever were to be lit again, was dedicated to Amalie, the girl who escaped the caves and provided a food source to the village that would eventually grow into Wilheim. With training and getting intel on her brothers taking up most of her free time, she had neglected to continue reading Redaway's commentary on the Marches. She had not gone back to see if Rodrick had the story right.

It felt almost disheartening to try and read anything while Wilheim was in this state as the books and knowledge from the library and colleges had been shipped somewhere else, an attempt to avoid a complete reset of human progress. But instead of it being in a central hub, it would be scattered all over the land in the hands of scholars, former powerful nobles, and collectors. The books might as well join the ash as it will be all but inaccessible to those who normally could.

Griselda owed the library an incredible debt throughout her life as she taught herself most of the things she knew from its resources. Nevermore would a little girl be able to better herself with that public and sacred treasure.

Even the few beggars the city had would congregate around the bonfires to stay warm at night and exchange their stories for food, but they were gone too. All the leaves had fallen from the trees and the sun was out of sight, only a faint glow providing evidence that it was ever there at all to light and warm the continent.

"Goodbye and thanks," Griselda said to the empty pit. She stood and bowed to the former light source, to Amalie's beacon, and headed back before it got too dark for her to see.

As she got back onto campus, she heard hushed voices. Two were aggressive and gruff, while the third one was high-pitched, whiny, and had the distinct tone of mortal peril. They were just around the corner. Griselda positioned herself against the wall and listened.

"I swear this is useless, there's nothing still there," said the whiny man.

"Orders are orders," said one of the gruff men. "If the boss wants us to look, we look."

"Oh, fine, but you don't have to drag me there, do you?"

"Can't have you running off. Boss needs you to come back."

She heard the hurried footsteps scampering away over the stone. Griselda risked a peek around the corner and saw two men in blue brigandine and a scholar. On the scholar's back was the College of Observation's insignia, the sun surrounded by a ring of stars. She only saw their backs as they approached the entrance to the college's massive observatory building. The ruffians had their arms looped in the scholar's and were not so gently ushering him along.

Instead of gauntlets on their hands, they had some unusual gloves Griselda had never seen before. They were leather and mail but had spiked glowing crystals lining the knuckles and a large patch of missing material that exposed the skin on the back of the hand. This exposed skin seemed to be scarred on both men in brigandine, as if it had intentionally been cut many times.

Despite his whining, the man didn't seem to be in imminent danger, so Griselda decided to tail them. What could they be looking for that would risk staying in the city? What would be in that building? Could it win the war? Or were they looting the expensive scientific equipment?

The College of Observation had taken on several roles over the years as Griselda had learned from Mathilda. First and foremost, they were gazers. They gazed into the sky to initially determine weather patterns. As their lens technology and optics advanced, they gazed past the atmosphere to study the sun and stars. Then, they took on the metaphorical role of gazing, by taking historical records and accounts, gazing into the past. And eventually, some of the newer faculty started gazing into the future, trying to write philosophies and predictions using a variety of methods based on historical patterns, the Marches, and even the stars and weather. Professor Mathilda often joked about the future gazers being useless, that they were no better than those who were in a staring contest with the sun.

The scholar climbed the steps and then unlocked the large wooden double doors into the building. One of the ruffians lit a torch while the other kept his oddly gloved hand as a reminding presence on the scholar's shoulder.

"Alright, now, where would they keep birth records?" asked the one still holding the scholar's shoulder.

"Th-this way, if they weren't taken already," said the scholar.

They disappeared into the maw of the dark building. Griselda crept out from her hiding spot and followed them. They had closed the door, but as Griselda found out after testing it, they had not locked it. She opened the door and shut it behind her, casting her into complete darkness. There were no windows in this corridor. The three men were already far enough ahead into the building where Griselda could not see their torch. She could still hear their footfalls on the tile floor and faint voices not bothering to whisper since they believed they were alone.

Griselda unhooked End March from her back and held it in front of her which was covered by the scabbard Mathilda had made. Griselda slid the black scabbard slightly up the blade, letting a sliver of the perpetual glow escape, enough for her to see what's in front of her but not enough where it would be a noticeable light that the other three men would see unless they extinguished their torch.

As best as she could, Griselda tried to follow the sound of the men's voices, but this building was a maze, seemingly much larger than it had appeared from the outside. As she walked down the hallway, she would shine the splinter of light onto the name plates of closed rooms. Some were classrooms, some were offices of faculty, and some were archival rooms. Curious, she paid special attention to the rooms with names like "Historical Record of Ardhataz," "Legislation: Past and Present," "Extra-canonical Records of each March," "Spring Star Charts," "Mountain Geography and Known Mineral Deposits," and many more. The whole building had tons of historical and archived scholarly information about a wide array of topics. It was much like the library, but these records were written by scholars for scholars and not necessarily meant to be accessible or even understandable to anyone outside their field.

By this point, Griselda had gotten so turned around that the voices she was following were out of her earshot. Curiosity had gotten the best of her, and she merely explored to sate her own interest in the records kept here. Many of the archival rooms were left opened, but all the records had been removed from the shelves in a hurried manner, leaving scraps here and there and bookcases knocked over. Griselda didn't plan on reading anything in the darkness, but she did want to see what kinds of information, what kinds of secrets, were being guarded by this windowless building.

"For every fact the college made known to the public," Griselda muttered, "there were a thousand kept in the dark."

Then she came across an office door that had been barricaded shut with several warnings scrawled on the door for people not to enter—notices warning, "Do Not Enter Under Penalty of

Law" and "Under Investigation" and "Temporary Relocation." Maybe scholars would obey signage like that, but for Griselda, it was an invitation to break down the door and see what was boarded inside. She checked the name plate above the door, but the name of the room had been crossed out with several scours from a sharp point.

Griselda fully unsheathed End March. The sword was not designed to hack through wooden barricades, but she would have to make it work. Through a combined effort of loosening the boards with several strikes and then pulling the boards free, Griselda removed the barricade until she was just facing the locked door. Already heated from the chopping, End March was glowing brightly, maybe dangerously so. The heat it was giving off was enough to make the small corridor feel much warmer than it should have been. Griselda stuck the heated tip of the sword into the keyhole and jimmied it in place until End March started melting the mechanism on the inside. She could hear the odd noises of the metal reacting to the heat.

Satisfied, she tried to push the door open. Still, it wouldn't budge. *I really thought that would work,* Griselda thought. Even if the lock mechanism was still in place, it must have at least been severely weakened. Griselda propped End March's tip down on the tile floor and leaned it against the wall. She backed up and, with a running start, threw her shoulder into the door. The lock mechanism failed, and the door flew open. Griselda landed on the floor amongst hundreds of scattered papers.

She rubbed her shoulder, which would certainly be bruised from the impact, and then picked up one of the papers. With the hot glow of End March illuminating the room from the hallway, she could strain her eyes to make out the bulkier titles at the top of the pages if she could not read the actual writing below them. She retrieved End March so she could read more easily.

Each paper seemed to be a sheet of experimental predictions based on star observations. Some of them were predictions as tiny as how long it would take boiled water to cool based on constellations in the fall sky. Some of them were predictions on when King Morgen would die based on weather patterns. Nearly all the sheets had big red lettering written over the writing denoting "EXPERIMENT FAILURE: REVISE HYPOTHESIS."

There were some treatises on theories concerning Grief Sickness and who was prone to it. Griselda squinted harder and held End March closer to read some of the finer print.

"The disease does not affect everyone," Griselda read to herself. "Only about a sixth of subjects develop the illness . . . Experiments on the remains of victims denoted that susceptible persons had a distinct type of blood from other test subjects—"

Griselda leaped back as the proximity and heat of End March caused the old paper to ignite.

"Oros's below!" she exclaimed and stomped out the burning paper. She looked at End March and shook her head. She placed the still-glowing hot blade tip down in the hallway again. It was too dangerous to keep it in a room of scattered dry paper.

She went back into the room and let her eyes adjust to the deeper gloom. Apparently, whoever ransacked the place was looking for something and flung all of the failed experiments onto the floor. The room was lined with bookshelves that had also seemed heavily rummaged through. At the far end of the office was a desk that had even more papers on it. Griselda walked over and started to sift through them. These papers weren't results of past experiments but outlines of future plans.

One of the plans was a detailed expedition to Lake Verdin to determine its unique geological properties. There were drawings and schematics on some of these papers, too. The scholar had designed what looked to be a water-tight suit of armor with a long hose attached to the helmet.

Then Griselda heard the voices returning. Hastily, she scampered back to the hall and grabbed End March. Though it was glowing less now, it would still stand out if they walked by the corridor. Griselda tried to pull the sword up, but the heated tip had partially melted into the tile floor and had wedged itself tight.

Her eyes widened as the sword was stuck fast into the floor and could not be pulled out. She put both hands under the cross guard and heaved it up to no avail. They were close enough now that she could hear their footsteps, see the faint yellow glow of the torchlight from around the corner. She would not be able to get the sword out of the ground in time, especially not without making a ton of noise.

Thinking quickly, she unclasped the sun-shaped brooch on her winter cloak and draped the thick garment over the sword, shrouding her in darkness yet again. Griselda held her breath, hoping the three wouldn't bother to turn their heads to the left as they passed her corridor. And that End March wouldn't set her cloak on fire. Thankfully, nothing happened. The torchlight got bright and then started to dim again as they trailed into the distance.

"I can't believe they hadn't excavated the birth records yet," the whiny scholar said.

"Oh, stuff it, Sorenous," said one of his escorts. "You just prefer to skedaddle before Ewen gets here. I'm sure you knew exactly what records had been relocated and what still remained."

The whimpering scholar made no response as they made toward the exit.

Griselda released her held breath and walked back into the corridor. She removed the winter cloak and eyed End March. "You're just as much a detriment as you are useful," Griselda said to the sword.

Placing her hands on the long handle, she started to wiggle the blade in its trap as much as she could until the friction warmed the blade back up again. Soon, the blade was hot enough to remelt the clay tile it was lodged in until it cracked, and

Griselda pulled the sword free. She waited until the glow dulled before putting it back in the scabbard, having learned her lesson to not let the heated blade touch anything until it had cooled down.

Griselda walked back through the hallways toward where she had come, still following the noise of the three pairs of shoes up ahead so she didn't get lost again. Once they had exited the building, she opened the doors and was confronted with the sky-shaking sounds of horns. From the walls surrounding Wilheim, at each tower, was a watcher who had a massive horn to alert the city of danger. With the horns blowing around the city, she knew exactly what it meant. King Ewen had arrived.

CHAPTER 31
TWO MONARCHS IN THEIR GOLDEN HOURS

URREM, atop the Ardhatazian command post on a hill overlooking Wilheim, surveyed the siege encampment. They had spent the week reassembling the siege weapons and encircling the city as much as they could, barring the mountains the city was backed up against. More boats and troops from Ardhataz had arrived so they could make a fairly sizeable perimeter. There was no getting in or out unless it was through Ardhatazian defenses. Or the mountains. Though no doubt Wilheim had some exits into the mountains, they wouldn't be traversable by wagon. It was possible for some smugglers to bring in food on foot, but it would be nowhere near enough to feed a whole city. Besides, the walls would fail somewhere first.

Though Wilheim's walls were tall and imposing, Urrem observed that they appeared to have been built before siege weapons were designed and would not hold up long to continuous barrage. They had the same issue with the terrain that Urrem did: the rocky soil not allowing for deep foundations. The walls were built to discourage hordes of bandits. They were not thick or wide enough to mount their own anti-siege weapons on the wall to destroy the Ardhatazian ones below.

Macintosh and Urrem had ordered the Ardhatazian trebuchet bombardment to target the corners and the gatehouse. According to reports, Wilheim's walls were not two layers thick with rubble fill in between the walls. They were only one layer of stone which could be diminished with concentrated bombardment. From Urrem's viewpoint, it looked like Wilheim had built a gate-house around its original simple gate to provide more modern defenses and to discourage troops with battering rams. It would still not protect it from continuous trebuchet volley.

One benefit of the rocky terrain was that there were plenty of large stones to go around, an essentially endless supply of ammunition provided the Ardhatazians were willing to work with some shovels and picks. According to the Siege Master, the counterweight trebuchet would take a significant amount of time to rearm after each payload delivery, so traction trebuchets were constructed on either side of the larger one. The smaller ones would provide continuous cover and make it more hazardous to reinforce walls damaged by the larger trebuchet.

The trebuchets had been going nonstop during sunlight for two days now. It was unlikely they would knock a hole in the wall large enough for the whole army to enter, but it was possible to create an uneven and hard-to-defend rubble mound from which an Ardhatazian siege tower could deliver troops. Wilheim had seen so little fighting since the city had never been sieged; it seems they thought updating their walls to ward off siege weapons was unnecessary.

Urrem was shaken from his thoughts when a heavy hand clapped him on the shoulder.

"What do ya see?" asked Ewen.

"An inevitable countdown," Urrem replied.

Ewen smiled. "Good, good. Da Willies tink demselves so smart but somehow were not smart enough to build demselves a proper wall."

Urrem nodded. The weight of the king's hand was a little

uncomfortable, both from the sheer size of his thick arms but also from responsibility such a friendly gesture implied.

Urrem breathed in. "Yer majesty, can I ask a question?"

"Certainly!"

"Is dere any reason we are not using da . . . um, tings . . . to immediately breach da city? Can dey climb? Or go through da Shatter Rock River water gate like at Stedtfest?"

"Good. Glad yer tinking strategically to bring down da city faster. But it wouldn't work as well dis time around," Ewen said stroking his beard with the hand not on Urrem's shoulder. "Though he probably made a lot of weapons dat didn't glow, Sophia tells me dere's an estimated twenty to thirty glowing weapons old Cormac made throughout his lifetime."

Ewen took his hand off Urrem's shoulder to pull out the great sword strapped on his back. He displayed it in front of him proudly. Urrem shied away from its heat and glow.

"Dese tings are capable of killing the beasts fairly easily, as ya no doubt remember from when dey ambushed our camp. Our number of beasts has been drastically diminished since then. We only have three left. Sophia tells me dat da Willies put out a call to any suspected bearers to fight on deir side. Sophia's team were just da people who could respond fast enough. If others did respond and were waiting in the city, den our beasts would be killed witout support from our troops."

Urrem breathed out. "So, using our men is absolutely necessary, strategically? Dat being, our men have an immediate purpose while dey are *still alive*, and not just because da suffering helps the creatures?"

"In short, yes," replied Ewen. "Even if we did have enough of da beasties to take da city without using troops, dey would be in dere and we'd be left to sit out in the cold. Da Scholar tells me dey only understand simple instruction such as 'kill' or 'don't kill anyone wearing black.' Saying, 'open da bloody gate' may not get us any results."

"They can . . . see color?"

Ewen shrugged. "I prefer when daScholar is da quiet version of himself. Hasn't really volunteered to give me an anatomy lesson on da tings. He said dey will learn over time—become more capable of advanced instructions. We need to make sure dey're alive long enough to adapt."

Urrem chewed on the inside of his cheek. "That's another gripe, Yer Majesty. How are ya sure we can trust him, da Scholar? He still wears the Wilheim Academy robes. What rank is he in your command structure?"

The king blew a raspberry, a strange sight from the mouth of a king. "Oh, don't worry about him. We have an understanding. He's not helping us from da kindness of his heart and will be on our side as long as I hold da bargain. He's technically an advisor if ya want to know his rank. He'd never give any orders. He really only talks to me and wouldn't dare order ya about. He hasn't given ya any strange orders, has he? Hopefully, he hasn't opened his mouth at all. He's a . . . quirky fellow."

Urrem thought about his encounter with the ominous figure and the Shadows of the Mountain. "He has spoken to me once. I was washing da field after Stedtfest. He told me not to worry about it—dat he and yer Shadows were taking care of any survivors who might catch Grief Sickness."

For the briefest of moments, Urrem saw the king's unflappable composure shift, just a twitch of the eyebrows, before Ewen returned to his jovial self. But Urrem saw it and knew something was amiss.

"Don't ya worry about him. I've got a plan to deal wit him on good authority from my Lichtfangr mentor back in Ardhataz. Between ya and me, he's trouble and dangerous, and I don't want him around forever. Right now, his plans and my plans are mutually beneficial. Dey might not always be dat way. And if it ever comes to dat, I'll take care of him," Ewen said with a wink, another very casual gesture for the implications of the conversation.

"Tank ya, my lord," said Urrem. "For being so forthcoming about tings dat aren't my business."

"Yer family now. It's yer right," said Ewen. He admired the glowing sword once more before resting it back on his pauldron. "Now, if ya excuse me, I've got some arrangements to make for my boy heading back to Ardhataz. We're training more men dere as we speak for da next step."

Urrem frowned. "But Wilheim's gone with dis victory. What next step?"

"Haven't you heard?" The king said, turning and descending the steps down the observation platform. "Dey say it's my destiny. Da first to unite Verdin. Wilheim is da only realm capable of hassling us if we started liberating da other western realms, so it's why we take care of dem first. After dat, we make our way up da other side of da lake. I'll make an official statement or someting later. But before it can be written for generations after us to hear of our conquest, we first have to do da physical march worth writing about. So, ya focus on dose walls over dere, and I'll worry about what comes next."

Urrem bowed even though the king was no longer looking at him. "Yes, ya lordship. I look forward to fighting at yer side for what comes next."

"Attaboy." The king descended out of sight.

Urrem frowned. Everything Ewen said and did was executed with such a calm, casual demeanor that it frankly unnerved him to be around the king.

"It's like he knows dat he's invincible," Urrem mumbled to himself.

Urrem looked down toward the trebuchet and the hundred-pound boulder they were heaving at the walls. Potentially, this was the first of many walls Urrem would be hurling stones at if what Ewen said was true. Though the kingdom of Wilheim dominated the eastern half of the lake, there were many smaller and often at war countries on the western side. Though their numbers were fewer, they will likely be expecting a fight now that Wilheim was falling so swiftly. And they'll be much more accustomed to warfare from constantly squabbling. Ewen was smart to start with Wilheim. If they had started with the smaller countries, Wilheim would have intervened, and they would be fighting on both sides of Ardhataz and likely get squished in the middle. But by attacking Wilheim first and swiftly, the other countries that normally despised one another wouldn't band together until the threat was at their doorstep. That, and Oros's Pass guarded the route from Ardhataz to the rest of the western realms, and nobody in their right mind would go through that.

Urrem was learning a lot about warfare in a short amount of time. But as the king implied, he wouldn't have to know all of it. It was like Ewen was some great contractor assembling people from many backgrounds to each fill specialized project requirements. It was stereotypically true that Ardhatazians were great fighters, but Urrem would have never guessed their military was run so efficiently and by so many different types of people all banded together in their pseudo-family camaraderie. He would have guessed an Ardhatazian troop in a one-on-one fight would best any other infantry soldier on the continent, but he always assumed the military would be full of bickering brutes. Maybe that was the case before Ewen came along. Maybe that's why, despite Ardhataz having generally larger, stronger, more military-minded men, that Ardhataz would generally collapse any forward progress they made in invasions. Despite them having the best fighters without exception, no progress had been made at expanding the border of Ardhataz in centuries, even though they desperately needed the land and resources from their neighbors to feed their ever-growing nation, even though they were on exiled land and rightfully should have claimed some from Wilheim for their atrocities. The highlands were not an ideal place to live and prosper. But it seemed like Ewen was changing all of that, for better or worse.

Urrem, despite being Ardhatazian, never liked fighting. But no trade was spared when the army was called. Malcolm had made shoes. Briggs, though he often fought for fun in the pits, had been a sailor, or pirate depending on the source, and then retired to herd sheep. Many of Urrem's dead troops had been shepherds. Even still, many of them had the bloodlust Urrem did not despite their professions. And Urrem would be responsible for bringing that bloodlust directly into many cities. How many buildings would burn because of him? How many families would be torn apart? Urrem shook his head and blinked.

Best not tink 'bout it, Urrem reminded himself. *You are not here to tink. You are here to build and implement siege weapons. What dose weapons do is no concern to ya.*

———

Griselda was finally used to the weight of her weapons and armor, and after about a week of being posted with Mathilda on various guard shifts around the castle, today was the day she would stand guard in the throne room.

"You're a bit lucky, the king is desperate for guards at the moment. From what I hear, many of them volunteered to go die at Stedtfest," Mathilda said as they walked down the cavernous hall to the throne room with four other guards. Three pairs would be stationed near the king. Two on one side of the large double-door, two at the other, and two directly in front of the king if he was granting an audience. Before the siege started, there would have been more, but all available hands were called to help bolster any damage done to the walls while dodging trebuchet stone rain. Griselda had not had to do that yet, thankfully, though she did have to stay awake all night and watch Ewen's army, even though they didn't use the trebuchets at night.

444 • ANTON JONES

"Normally, you'd have to graduate from my program with top marks to be in the royal guard," Mathilda chirped. "You'd then be vetted by his advisors."

One of the guards in front of them turned his helmeted head over his shoulder as best he could to eye the person who had cheated the system. He recognized Mathilda's voice from under her helmet and made no other remark.

Their armor clinked around the hall as they arrived at the door to relieve the first six of their post. Few words were exchanged as they swapped out. Most people had understood what would be coming and did everything with solemn duty as the end approached.

Griselda moved into position on the side of the door in the throne room. It had vaulted ceilings and massive stained-glass windows that bathed the room in all kinds of interesting light patterns. Griselda noticed each stained-glass panel was dedicated to the Marches and would portray a climactic scene from each individual book. There was a prophet from the many stories in *The March of Joy* discovering the properties of Verdin Stars; there was the army fighting the glowing, massive beast Oros in *The March Through the Mountain Pass*; there was the prophesied volcanic apocalypse foretold in *The March from Pain*; and others.

Griselda looked across the room to see King Morgen II. Though the king sat on his throne in the large empty room with a weary slouch. He was atop a dais, something meant to elevate him above everyone else despite him sitting down, but it only made him look lonelier. King Morgen sat there, intermittently placing his head in his hands and then looking up over at the stained-glass windows, sun crown perched on his head precariously, as if it would fall off at any moment. He looked toward Griselda, nodded at the incoming new guards, and then returned his head to his hands, perhaps lost in thought. His radiant purple and blue Verdin Star–dyed robes seemed gloomy on his body.

The door where Griselda and Mathilda stood on either side was about a hundred feet away from the king, far enough away where they could quietly whisper without the king hearing.

"*That's* King Morgen II? Lord of the Peaceful Dawn?" Griselda whispered.

Mathilda shrugged while still facing forward, her helmet masking the fact that she was responding. "If I were in his position, I'd probably look like that too."

Great, Griselda thought, *he looked like he already accepted defeat. In fact, everyone other than Mathilda walked around looking like that.* Griselda shuffled in her armor to find a comfortable standing position. While on duty, she had End March on her back in its scabbard, her side sword at her hip, and she had been given a familiar halberd, the ones shaped like a sun with rays becoming the points of the hafted weapon. She had seen her father and her brother both making these for the royal guards, and now she was holding one as part of the city's defense. She wasn't sure how she felt about that.

Most of the royal guards while on post carried a short sword and a halberd while in matching plate sets. Griselda wondered if her and Mathilda's armor not matching the rest of the royal guards would draw any attention. Mathilda had assured her that the king would let her get away with anything she wanted.

The other two guards marched up to the king, turned, and faced the door with halberds pointed up to the ceiling. The king continued to stew in his throne.

"Doesn't he have more pressing things to do than sulk?" Griselda whispered.

"Normally, yes. However, his duties have been decimated as most of the population of Wilheim has fled. Also," she added, "he's not mentally what he used to be. He's done his best to relinquish some of the important things to his advisors."

"So," Griselda huffed, "he's sad and bored?"

446 • ANTON JONES

Mathilda tsked, a strange sound coming from behind a helmet. "You do realize both of his heirs are presumed dead."

Griselda shrugged. She did not feel pity for the king. He was, after all, partially (if not directly) responsible for her brothers' pain. She *tsked* Mathilda back. "He's a man. Even at his age, he can still grab his royal, misshapen jewels, find a new queen, and produce more heirs."

Mathilda's armor clanked as she rounded on Griselda in astonishment.

"What?" Griselda said. "You're blunt. Why can't I be?"

"Not just his heirs, but do you realize he is mentally declining with age, that his legacy of being trusted to safeguard a thousand years of progress is being actively sieged as we speak?" Mathilda sighed. "We'll discuss this later. Try not to talk too much, even whispering. Your choice of helmet doesn't cover your mouth, and anyone could see it moving."

Griselda adjusted her sallet and blew out some trapped, hot air. Though she was getting used to the weight, sometimes even breathing needed to be done intentionally while encumbered by armor.

Griselda held her tongue from further comment. She wasn't being paid to give her opinions, no matter how insightful they may be. On the walls, communication was valued; here, however, silence was paramount. And she was being paid well, too. Even as the city crumbles, there were still plenty of riches to go around. She was getting paid twenty silver coins per day, not as much as Rodrick's offer, but still considerably good wages. She would have enough to provide and protect her brothers as soon as she found them.

So then, Griselda thought, *how to approach the king about the topic when I'm way over here and he's way over there in a sad stupor.*

Just then, Griselda heard some raised voices at the door behind them. She looked over at Mathilda, who had turned and held her halberd pointed at the door. Griselda mimicked her stance and prepared for whatever would come bursting through. She braced herself and held her breath.

Rather than flying open, the doors opened normally, with the two outside guards slowly pushing in the doors to reveal a single man.

"Your Majesty," said one of the guards opening the door, "I would like to announce the presence of . . ."

"Shut it," said the man. "He knows who I am. I assume he isn't that far gone yet."

The king perked up. Mathilda sighed and reassumed her position. Griselda followed suit. She watched the man angrily stride toward the king. His gait was fierce and looked like he was covering much more ground than his legs suggested. He was wearing a dirty green brigandine and only one arm poked out at the shoulder. Despite only one arm, he still had a bow strung on his back and . . . *Wait, is that a glowing flanged mace? One of my father's?*

"You're alive?" the king breathed, shakily.

"So I am," the man said.

"And Zerebril? He too?"

"He would be here instead of me if he made it."

"And . . . and Zerebril?" the king repeated, as if not registering what the man said.

The man sighed loudly. "Do I have to say it? He's likely dead."

The king bowed his head. After a second, he regained his composure and nodded at the man. Though he seemed present, the king's eyes were hollower, and they kept darting to the stained glass depicting the volcanic explosion.

Impatient, the man spoke. "What now?"

"Carl . . . what do you mean?"

"Orders. What are my orders? I've returned from the field and need new instructions."

Griselda found herself nodding. Though Carl's demeanor could scare Oros himself, at least he was still acting like there was work to do.

"Umm . . . report. What happened at Stedtfest? We haven't heard anything definitive yet."

Carl grunted in acknowledgment. "We executed the plan as designed by Zerebril. However, Sophia, one of the members of the newly formed vanguard, betrayed us. Ewen suffered heavy casualties but avoided having his head chopped off when the cavalry never arrived, since Sophia instead led them into an ambush. As for the whereabouts of the others, I don't know. The king's creatures were nearly destroyed, but a few got away."

"How many are left?"

"Uncertain. I never found where he was keeping them or making them as they ran out to attack me. I destroyed all I could find and then assumed the others had done their part as well in different areas of the camp. I was overrun by infantry and arrows and needed to retreat." Carl paused to scowl. "So, what next?" It seemed that Carl was hinting at something that should have been obvious to the king, but the king was either too oblivious or was blatantly ignoring what Carl was prompting.

"What next?"

"The throne. Who is the heir?"

"Well . . . Zerebril . . ."

"Is certainly dead. Though I didn't see it myself, the rumors are true. Ewen kills everyone in his path."

"Genocide . . . that corpse caller," the king muttered. "He's killing off our entire population. But for what?"

"Does it matter," Carl stated. Though it should have been intoned like a question, Griselda noticed that Carl did not do so.

"I suppose not," the king said, bowing his head.

"So, the throne."

"Is yours . . . what's left of it, that is—"

"Good. As crowned prince, my first action will be to

assemble any more bearers that responded to your call and have them sling fire from the walls."

"No one else came."

Carl's scowl intensified. It seemed he was capable of only various grades of scowls. "The twins?"

"I thought you would know where they went," the king replied.

Carl ground his teeth together audibly. "That won't work then. I guess I have no choice but to stay posted here and wait for the beasts. I'll have a better chance of defeating them here where I can funnel them all into one place. This mace," Carl plucked it from his belt, "behaves differently than the swords. It doesn't have range, but it will annihilate anything close by."

The king nodded.

"But before it comes to that. I will investigate your remaining guards. I cannot have another Sophia kill us when we should have won."

Griselda's heart jumped in her throat. Even Mathilda was noticeably shaken in her armor, her posture imperfect. Two things were giving Griselda a cold sweat, the first being she just witnessed a man with no claim being made heir, and the second that he was going to investigate everyone.

"Is this bad?" Griselda whispered.

"Yeah," Mathilda whispered back. "Carl hates me for some reason."

"Honestly, he might not personally hate you. He looks like he hates the world, and you happen to live in it."

"Either way," Mathilda continued, "this may not end well."

Carl turned around and inspected the guards nearest to the king.

"Sir!" the two said, stomping their feet and bowing.

"Names," Carl demanded.

"Heinrick," said one.

"Gerald," said the other.

"So, it's you two under the helm. They're fine. They were in my class of knights," Carl turned back toward the door and stared with a quizzical scowl at Griselda and Mathilda, a combination of facial expressions that Griselda had not thought possible.

Carl walked impossibly fast up to Griselda. "You're outfitted differently than the guard."

"I-I have my own armor," Griselda said. "I figured I wouldn't bother asking for plate if I had my own. We could use that to armor someone else."

"Name."

Mathilda breathed in as if to speak. Carl maintained his scowl but did so while raising his eyebrow and looking at Mathilda.

"She's my pupil," Mathilda said, lifting her visor. "I can vouch for her."

"Ah . . . Professor. So, you're on the guard now."

Mathilda nodded.

"Great," he looked back at Griselda. "Take off your helmet."

"But—" Griselda stammered.

"I need to know what the guards look like. I can't have Tazzes taking your armor and fooling me simply because I didn't know what you looked like. Take it off."

"Is that necessary—"

Now both of his eyebrows were raised. "You have something to hide."

Griselda sighed and braced herself. "No, I won't hide." She removed her helmet.

Carl stepped back. "I know your face . . ." his astonished look returned to a scowl.

Oh no, Griselda thought.

"You're Cormac's daughter, aren't you?" This time his scowl almost became a sneer. "You look exactly like those two traitors. Drop your weapons!"

"She's not here to betray you, she's just trying to find information about her brothers," Mathilda said, arms in the air trying to defuse the situation.

"Her *brother* bit off my arm!" Carl yelled.

Griselda blinked. "He . . . *bit* off your arm?"

Carl drew his mace from his belt.

Griselda desperately looked to Mathilda, who shrugged. She sighed and then dropped her halberd. It clanged against the stone floor. The king had stood up from his throne to get a better look, but made no further moves and said nothing.

"Turn," Carl demanded,

Griselda did as she was told.

Carl sheathed his mace so he could use his remaining arm to slide the scabbard down from End March, which dangled on its hooks. The glow lit up his face. "I knew it. You have Gunter's sword—Connor's sword, Professor Mathilda."

"What?" Mathilda asked in response.

"No, it's not theirs," Griselda said through gritted teeth. "Cormac made twin swords. This one stayed in our family. I swear it. I did not steal Gunter's sword, and I would never do anything to harm Wilheim! I just want my brothers back."

Carl grunted as he spun Griselda back around to face him. "And what if finding your brothers dooms this city. They don't have what's best for Wilheim in mind. Your brother is a monster who ran in Ewen's direction last I saw him."

"I don't believe that," Griselda said. "But while I'm uncovering the truth, you might as well use me. I can fight with this sword, right? I can even the odds."

Carl scoffed. "I could give a child that sword and turn him into a human weapon. I'll just take it from you and give it to Heinrick or Gerald over there."

This man had insulted both her and her brothers. A fierce anger was quickly getting hotter and burning away the fear. Griselda, who was just as tall as Carl, leaned in and said, "I'd like to see you try and take it from my family. I can lop off that other arm for you."

For the first time since he entered the room, Carl smiled. It was a challenging, sinister smile that looked out of place on his face. "You want to talk hacking off limbs. Do you know what I did to your little—"

"CARL! ENOUGH!" the king bellowed. His voice echoed around the throne room. A voice so powerful seemed even louder when it came from the withering king. "You are not lord here—not yet. I trust her if Mathilda vouches for her. If she wanted to kill me, she would have already done it. No one would have been able to stop her," the king breathed in sharply, as if shouting and speaking took great effort. "And she's right. If we still want to resist the setting sun, we'll need her help."

Carl's smile was quickly replaced by the familiar scowl as he stood aside. The king had stepped down from the dais and was slowly making his way towards Griselda. Though his stride was short and his motions slow, his actions were deliberate.

"I owe your family," King Morgen spoke, his face a little brighter as if the blood was returning to it despite being out of breath from the walk. "For the sword Cormac made for Gunter and for the mace Carl now has and for the sword on your back and for other things too. We have mistreated you out of desperation, and because I was foolish," the king placed his hand on Griselda's armored shoulder, "but I must make amends. I'm not always myself . . . and I'm getting worse. But while I have my strength and some clarity, I vow to you I will set things right. Name your price to fight for Wilheim on the walls against the siege."

Griselda searched the king's eyes, as he was uncomfortably close. They were cloudy and struggled to focus on anything for more than a few moments at a time. They were sincere yet grief-stricken; eyes that wanted the best yet were cursed with madness as he grew in years. Even still, he held her gaze. The rumors had been spreading about the king's health even before Ardhataz attacked. She wanted to believe with all she had in the version of the king who was currently standing in front of her and not the sad, skeletal figure she couldn't even muster pity for.

"Your Majesty," Griselda began. "I'll fight for my home without anyone commanding me to do so. It's what's right. Even if we're bound to lose, stubbornness runs in my family. Always has. But I want to be stubborn alongside my two equally stubborn brothers. If there's anything you could do to locate them or tell me where they are, that's all I ask."

"Like I said," Carl muttered out of the corner of his mouth, "the two of them ran south, heading straight for Ewen. They either joined his cause or were killed by his army. I certainly didn't see any big, red monsters fighting on our side while down there."

The king shot Carl a murderous glance, seemingly already regretting the position he's been put into in naming him heir to the throne.

"Yes, well, I think I can spare a few scouts to verify that," said King Morgen.

"Thank you, Your Majesty," Griselda said, bowing. "I appreciate any help I can get. They are all I have left of my home."

Carl scoffed, "So you've seen what they did to the forge."

The King fully turned himself on Carl, swelling to his full height. Standing up straight, the king had a much more intimidating manner and was several inches taller than Carl. "Enough! Don't forget your place in all of this. I am still here! You are not to speak to this young lady unless absolutely necessary. *That* is your order. Talking to people does not suit you."

"Yeah," Mathilda whispered. "Go chat up your bird."

Carl didn't seem to hear Mathilda and instead held the king's gaze. He did not cower like Griselda thought he might. Nevertheless, Carl gave a curt nod and exited the throne room. "Only days now," he mumbled.

454 • ANTON JONES

The king glowered at him until he was out of sight. He looked back at Griselda, and the pleasantness and warmth he was once known for returned to his face. "Mathilda," he said, still looking at Griselda.

"Yes, Your Majesty?"

Gesturing to Griselda, he asked, "Where would you recommend we put our best weapon, our last chance?"

CHAPTER 32
THE DAY THE SUN STOPPED SHINING

"IF RAINFALL IS MYTHOLOGIZED as the tears of God," Griselda quoted from *The March Through the Mountain Pass*, "then what is snow?" She stared up into the afternoon sky as a gentle snow began to fall, flakes landing and then melting on her sallet helmet. One of the benefits of fighting in so many layers of armor was it did keep her warm. Snow could be an environmental element she might be able to use to her advantage. She would need all the help she could get.

Oddly, though the sounds of arrows loosing, trebuchet slinging, men yelling, and men dying rang all around her, it was the quietness of snow that was mesmerizing. Unlike rain, snowfall was nearly imperceptible. It was a gentle, soundless death—a death that could sneak like a panther but take like venom in someone's sleep. The snow dotted her breastplate, and soon little rivers trickled down to her chausses.

Griselda sat behind the remaining stone wall near the breach. The crenellations had been knocked down, and parts of the wall had been laid low. It was a mound of rubble about ten feet lower than the unbroken section she sat on. It was low enough for them to send a siege tower. And Griselda was waiting.

For fear of hitting their own tower, they had stopped launching the siege weapons, but their archers were still peppering the area in case Wilheim decided to station troops where the siege tower was approaching. Griselda risked glancing around the crenellation to see how close it was. The tower moved at a glacial pace, which made her anxiety worse. The remaining Wilheim archers took up position in the towers on either side of the lowered wall and were doing their best to take out the men pushing the tower and then the men who replaced the fallen. Eventually, tower shield holders were sent out and made a shield wall around the men pushing the towers after they kept getting picked off. Though Wilheim's remaining garrisoned archers were making a dent, they just didn't have enough soldiers left to hold a continuous volley and pressure to dissuade Ewen from approaching.

Griselda breathed in. If this section of the wall fell, Ewen would rush in and Wilheim, the City of Lights, would see one last great fire, a fire that consumed it entirely instead of providing light to the world.

Griselda remembered the faces of the men she had killed at her camp, the smell and feel of their blood, the noises the body makes as it is cleaved through. She closed her eyes tight and tried to push the memory away. She was defending herself then, and she was defending herself now. She breathed out and gave herself permission to fully use End March. *They are aggressors,* she thought. *This will save more lives than it takes.*

She unsheathed the weapon, which glowed in response, lighting up the stone around her. She started spinning the weapon through the air, the friction making it hum and glow brighter. Once sparks started to appear near the tip, she stepped from behind her cover and swung the sword down toward the siege tower. A wide arc of flame following the path of the sword lashed down and collided with the siege tower in an explosion. The tower shook but did not fall. It didn't catch fire either.

Vapors rose from the wood. Apparently, Ewen was planning on a bearer to try to set the tower on fire and soak it before they sent it to the wall. Unfortunately, the snow didn't help either.

Even still, Griselda heard the frightened yelps of the men inside the tower. She yelped herself as a volley of arrows flew at her head. She ducked back behind the crenellation as the arrows bounced and splintered off the stone around her. The archers were not going to let her keep lashing at the siege tower. Griselda crouched and moved behind the wall toward the tower on her left. Inside, garrisoned men were loosing arrows through narrow slits in the wall, but they only had enough soldiers to occupy half of the defensive openings. Griselda climbed the steps in a hurry, feeling the weight of her armor as gravity tried to slow her pace. Once on top of the high tower, she could more clearly see the line of archers near the tree line who were loosing volley after volley on the wall curtain between the two towers, regardless of if anyone was there to defend it.

On top of the tower, five men were raining down arrows themselves into Ewen's line. But five men would not make a dent, especially from that far away. Griselda ordered the men to go under and shoot from the arrow slits.

"It's about to get very dangerous up here," she said. "Take shelter and loose arrows from underneath."

The men looked at her quizzically but obeyed once she started swinging the glowing sword over her head. Still heated, the blade took less time to start sparking. When it did, she heaved the blade from right to left, launching a wave of fire 50 feet wide that came down upon the tree line where the archers were taking shelter. It didn't look like she hit any of them directly, but their cover was quickly going up in smoke, and they moved into the open. Once there, the men loosing from the slits hit the exposed archers with more accuracy.

She let out her breath. Snow landed on End March and sizzled as it immediately evaporated off the searing hot blade.

Griselda's booted feet crunched on the tower surface as the snow started to make a slushy carpet, quickly liquifying anywhere near Griselda thanks to the heat.

Griselda turned her attention back to the siege tower, which was nearly to the broken wall. With everything she had, she swung End March down several times in quick succession, sending down multiple lashes of fire. It rattled as each lash slammed against the side of it but refused to catch fire.

Breathing heavily from the effort of swinging such a massive sword, pouring sweat into her gambeson underneath her armor from the heat radiating off the glowing blade, Griselda gritted her teeth and kept swinging harder and harder. Each impact from the fire shower shoved the tower, even if it didn't break or ignite it. *If I can't break it,* Griselda thought, *I can knock it over.* Swing after swing, the tower started to rock and lilt until one massive swipe sent it tipping over to one side and crashing against the ground.

Griselda collapsed to the stone floor, gulping in air greedily as her shoulders burned almost as hot as End March. As tired as her arms were, she made sure she kept the white-hot blade pointing in the air lest it melt and get wedged in the stone she rested it on.

Rising to a knee, she peeked over the crenulations and saw men pouring out of the fallen tower and running back to the shelter of the tree line, running in unpredictable zigzags to avoid the arrows from Wilheim's archers. They looked more like scurrying ants from this height than men. But their screams when an arrow hit their mark, or when they emerged on fire, made Griselda feel ashamed for even comparing them to insects. They were people. True, they were trying to take her home, but they had every right to live as Griselda did.

Griselda gritted her teeth. *Don't think about it! You don't have that luxury.*

It didn't help. The screams were louder than her internal scolding. Closing her eyes brought the faces back.

Would they turn back now that their siege tower had fallen? She thought. *Would this at least grant me some more time? How many must I kill? How many will this save?*

She rose to her feet, holding End March, trying to keep the superheated sword far away from her body in plow guard. She was close to catching her breath, then it was stolen again as three more siege towers broke through the tree line.

From the observation deck overlooking the battlefield, Urrem winced as the first siege tower fell sending up a swirl of snow and fire. Though it was strategic to send in one first to see how the defending army would respond, it still felt like he was using those troops as bait. But he did need to see if Wilheim would show if they had any Cormac weapon bearers, and they had. Unfortunately, this meant Ewen would not be sending in the three remaining light beasts to cause havoc and distract away from the siege towers.

Ewen sighed, standing next to him. "How long do dose take to make?"

Urrem looked over at the king. Ewen didn't seem angry at all. If anything, Ewen looked slightly annoyed but still had his jovial aurora about him.

"Depends," Urrem answered. "Have to factor in how many men ya task to build it and whether or not we already have da parts made."

The king blew air out through his clenched teeth, "Da nerve of dose Willies, breaking our toys like dat." Ewen looked over to the soldier next to him. "Sound da horn, send in da other three."

Urrem's voice seemed to jump from his throat without him

fully being aware of it. "But . . . but what about our men? We need to deal with da bearer or dey'll all be on fire."

Ewen turned to Urrem and raised an eyebrow. "I know. I've got a plan. I'll match deir bearer with my own if dey want to play it dat way. Come below with me, I've got a surprise for ya, though I hope ya don't mind me commandeering one of yer trebuchet."

Urrem looked at the king, baffled. "For what? We can't launch projectiles while our siege towers approach. Plus, it'd take too long to calibrate and position one to follow wherever deir bearer was moving."

The king smiled mischievously, "Oh, we're not launching projectiles."

Urrem stewed as they descended the wooden observation post, steps slippery with snow, and walked over to a trebuchet that had been aimed at the tower. The mercenary and bearer, Sophia, stood nearby, eyeing it with disdain.

"You better pay me double for this!" Sophia yelled, slapping down the visor on her helmet.

Urrem looked from the laughing king to Sophia as she positioned herself in the trebuchet sling.

"No—you can't be serious; she'll get smashed by da impact when she lands! It doesn't matter dat she's wearing armor or dat she has a fancy sword," Urrem said incredulously. He was getting used to speaking his mind more and more in front of the king.

"Already thought of dat problem," said a nasally voice. The Siege Master appeared and began fastening a backpack to Sophia. He then helped her into the sling.

Urrem looked at the Siege Master dumbfounded. "Not ya too! I can't be da only voice of reason here!"

"I've been tinkering with dis idea since before Stedtfest." The Siege Master's congested voice was hard to hear as the siege towers rolled by them into the open field between the Wilheim wall and their encampment in the tree line. "I wanted to launch our bright bestial friends into enemy lines, but unfortunately, dey burn through da sling. So, I put da idea on hold until we acquired an asset just as good, if not better, dan one of our light beasties."

Sophia huffed as she sat down and yelled through her visor, "I am NOT an asset!"

The Siege Master blushed, "I apologize, my lady, but ya have nothing to fear. I've experimented with this device several times. Just pull da cord here when ya are at da height of da arc and yer fall will be slowed."

"If ya be so confident," yelled Sophia in a mock Ardhatazian accent. "Den why is it my ass in da sling? If you Tazz idiots get me killed, I will haunt you all on the next leg of the March!"

Urrem shook his head and stared at his feet, eyes blinking rapidly as if they had nothing better to do. "If dis doesn't work, we kill our best weapon and hand over another Cormac weapon to dem. That would—"

"If dis *does* work, it will change warfare!" Ewen said, clapping Urrem on the back in what was supposed to be a reassuring way. Ewen looked down at Sophia, who was sitting in the sling with her plated arms folded. "And don't ya worry about pay. Ya can name yer price when ya take care of deir bearer. Da Willies got plenty to plunder in dere. I'll pay ya in whole kingdoms of land if we can use ya as a siege assault weapon in da upcoming battles."

The Siege Master made his final checks on the trebuchet and the sling. "She's good to go," he called over to the men working the latch. "Let her loose!"

"Tazz assho—" Sophia's voice trailed away as she was launched into the sky. Once in the air, a large plume of cloth erupted from her backpack and slowed her descent.

"Bearer versus bearer," the king murmured to himself as he watched her fall toward the tower. "I don't know if a Cormac weapon has ever faced another. This will be a sight to see."

Griselda braced herself. She was the only one who could prevent the siege towers from reaching the wall. *The good news,* Griselda thought, *is that if I knock these ones over too, the area will be clogged with broken towers, and they won't be able to attack this wall until they remove the debris.*

Griselda frowned as she heard a scream, not of pain, but one of terror. Or was that excitement? Was that a woman's scream? Griselda looked away from the siege towers to see a plated knight flying toward her, with what looked like bedsheet wings.

The knight, despite being slowed by the "wings," smashed onto the tower floor, rolled with the fall, and tangled with the white sheets. She stood up and slashed herself out of the sheets with a glowing sword before finding her bearings and assuming an athletic position, facing Griselda.

"God above, those idiots!" the female knight said. "That really hurt! That hardly slowed me down at all!"

Griselda ignored her comments. "You have one of my father's swords."

The knight huffed. "I do," she said. "So, you're his daughter, huh?"

"I am," Griselda said. "And, noting your lack of accent, you must be the bearer who betrayed Zerebril."

"I am. Name's Sophia. If we're going to do this. Let's have a proper duel," Sophia swiveled her shield, which was latched around her back, and placed it on her left arm. In her right, she held a glowing hand-and-a-half sword. She held up the glowing weapon as a gesture of salute and respect toward Griselda.

"I'm Griselda," she said, raising End March in response. *I have to finish this quickly,* Griselda thought. *She's here to take my attention away from the siege towers.* Griselda spared a glance over her shoulder and saw that they were already halfway to the wall.

The top of the stone tower they stood on was a circle about twenty feet in diameter, which would favor End March. Griselda recalled her training with both Mathilda and Roran. She would need to press her reach advantage, destroy the shield, and see if she could back up her opponent into the tower wall. But something Carl said nagged at her, about where her brothers were heading last time they were seen. She figured Sophia wouldn't mind talking if her goal was to slow Griselda.

"Hey, you haven't seen my brothers, have you? Carl said they ran off toward Stedtfest?"

Sophia chuckled under her visor. "Oh, you mean the red rage monster that ripped off Carl's arm? Unfortunately, no, I haven't seen him for myself."

"Thank you for your honesty," Griselda said. At least she knew they weren't killed by Ewen or in his army. "Now, if you don't mind, let's begin."

Griselda spun End March into motion, sending the tip up through the air. She made a series of sweeping upward cuts as she approached and tried to press Sophia into the wall. With a long weapon like this, she couldn't make downward cuts without the momentum carrying the blade into the stone floor.

As she hoped, the sheer size of End March was intimidating enough for Sophia to back up, whether she was aware of losing ground or not. Since End March was still hot from taking down the siege tower, Griselda flung a cascade of fire down on Sophia. Griselda would blow her off the side of the Wilheim tower and then resume attacking the siege towers.

Rather than raising her shield to block the fire, she instead pivoted her shield out of the way and held up her own glowing sword. The sword *absorbed* the fire, sending it from its calmly glowing, cooled state into its own white-hot state that matched Griselda's sword without Sophia needing to take the time to flourish it.

"Oh," Griselda breathed out. "Shit."

Sophia thrust her blade forward, sending a bolt of fire from the tip directly at Griselda's breastplate. Out of panic, Griselda stepped to the side and tried to deflect the fire with End March. The sword's edge passed through the fire and absorbed some of it as the bolt continued through the air and off the side of the tower.

That's a useful trick, Griselda thought. *So, there's little point in a bearer using the flame lashes against another bearer. She'll just absorb it and fire it back. I'll have to use the weapon conventionally until I can create an opening.*

But, as Griselda found out, End March was already too hot, and the weapon was going to shoot fire whether she liked it or not. Flame wave after flame wave flew through the air as Griselda assumed her sweeping swings toward her opponent. Thankfully, the stone floor wouldn't catch fire, and the flames that were not being absorbed by either blade dissipated into cold, open sky. The flames interacted with the falling snow, causing steaming vapors to whirl around the tower in a haunting haze.

Though Griselda's sword was effective at keeping targets away, the sweeping cuts were meant to hold back multiple targets. They were less effective against a nimble, individual opponent. Sophia lunged through a fire wave, sword absorbing the flames that would have hit her, and aimed her own white-hot sword at Griselda's arm. Griselda pivoted, and the sword barely missed her splint-armored bicep, a place she had been burned once before. Though her armor could deflect blows from normal cutting weapons, a direct hit from this weapon would cause intense burns as the best-case scenario.

Griselda backed up and decided to change tactics. Apparently, so did Sophia. Sophia threw down her wooden shield, which had caught a lick of flame. Griselda decided to turn her great sword into a spear as one hand choked up to the ricasso, effectively making End March into a thrusting weapon. She could feel the heat of the weapon through her gauntlet.

Sophia held her glowing sword hilt up near her helmet, now with both hands, settling into ox guard with the tip point toward Griselda's head. Like Griselda, Sophia was preparing to focus on mainly thrusting attacks.

Sophia lunged and the dance of sparks resumed.

Urrem watched as waves of fire poured off the side of the tower and either cascaded down the sides or vanished into whirls of flame in the heated air. He shuttered. Those things were monstrosities.

Ewen clapped loudly, his face changing colors as the flames came into and out of existence, illuminating the sky despite the fact the afternoon sun was certainly starting to dip toward the eastern horizon behind the snow clouds. Ewen pulled his great sword off his back and held it in front of him. "So dat's what ya can do. I can't wait to try ya out myself."

Urrem eyed the wickedly glowing sword, Gunter's sword, the sword that had claimed the lives of nearly three hundred people in mere minutes. He took a step back as if he could feel an evil force pushing him away from the weapon. In any case, he did not want to be anywhere near Ewen if he started swinging it.

"Hey, you!" someone shouted from the forest behind them.

Both Urrem and Ewen turned around and peered into the trees. They looked at each other, eyebrows raised.

"Did we raise a perimeter to prevent reinforcements?" asked Urrem.

"Didn't tink we needed to," said Ewen, "no one's coming to deir aide. We took care of dem all on our way here."

The voice continued. "That doesn't belong to you! I'm taking it back!"

"What, da sword?" Ewen called into the trees, trying to get

the person to speak so he could locate where the voice was coming from.

"Yeah," it responded. "It's mine."

"And who are ya to have such claim?"

The voice paused and then said, "I'm Roran, son of Cormac, and that blade was given to me."

"Roran!" Arno whispered. "Don't do this! There's too many of them. You'll get killed!"

Roran was in no mood to listen to reason. That beefy, bearded man wearing a lordly plate was waving around *Roran's* inheritance. And he would be punished for daring to touch the blade. Roran set Arno and the harness down, letting the straps slide off his shoulders.

"You stay here, Arno, you'll be safe in this cubby," Roran said, motioning to the trunks and brush. If he kept quiet, there's no way anyone would be able to find him unless they were looking for him.

"Roran! You're not listening to me!"

"I'll be back for you, just you wait."

"No! I'll be alone, I'll be scared, and you'll get captured or killed."

Roran gritted his teeth, "I'd like to see them try."

The bearded man's voice came booming into the forest. "Well, Roran, son of Cormac, I respect yer claim, but I won dis sword fair and square and haven't even used it yet. How about ya win it from me in da same manner? A good ole fistfight. The Ardhatazian way. Yer father's way. Come on out and I'll let ya fight for it honorably."

"You won't send arrows at me as soon as I come out?" Roran called back. It seemed too good to be true.

"I will not. Ya have my word as King Ewen, ruler of

Ardhataz, soon-to-be ruler of Wilheim, and leader of the next March."

"King Ewen," Arno whispered.

Roran smiled. "This just gets better and better. See, Arno. I'll stop the war right here and now. He's challenging me to a fist-fight, I'll crush him for sure!"

"Roran, please, we can still run."

"No. This is a problem I can finally hit back," he stood up from his hiding place and walked to the king. In the distance, he could see Wilheim under full siege as three towers moved toward the wall, a wall that seemed constantly engulfed in flame.

As Roran approached the string of armed men, Ewen had begun to take off his plate.

"I really don't tink ya should be unarmored near a battlefield, yer lordship," one of his attendants said.

"Oh, stuff it, Urrem," the king said. "Live a little. I'm divinely ordained and, by all accounts, invincible. I'll finish dis whelp quick and get back to it. Ya know I can't resist a little Tazzian brawl."

Whelp? Roran thought. Roran had never met anyone who seemed to be more physically imposing than himself. But Ewen was the exception and probably could call Roran "whelp" and mean it.

Much like Roran, Ewen, now shirtless, was enormous and didn't seem to mind the elements. Snow gently fell on his massive, wide-set shoulders before melting or being whisked away by the wind that was starting to pick up.

One of the soldiers noticed the metal caps at the end of Roran's arms and elbowed the king to look as well.

"Are those gauntlets?" the king asked.

"No," Roran said. "I lost my hands."

"Lost dem? How da ya misplace yer hands?" Ewen chuckled. "Very well, I'll let ya keep the caps on. It's been a while since I had a proper challenge."

"My king, I really don't—"

"Urrem! Get out of my ear. If ya keep challenging my authority, I'll be brawling ya next."

Urrem bowed and stepped back into the gathering troops. Ewen's elite troops, fully armored in black plate and standing nearly as tall as Ewen, surrounded the pair, creating a box made of men, the arena for the match.

Roran eyed Ewen up and down. Though Roran was larger than most men, Ewen made him look like Arno. But that wouldn't matter for long. Once he stoked the fire, Roran would be much stronger and larger than any normal man could ever be.

Ewen looked at Roran oddly and sniffed. "Hmmm. Ya have da scent of one of dem on ya. Yer like da Scholar."

The one called Urrem opened his mouth to speak, but one of the black plated soldiers next to him elbowed him hard in the stomach.

Ewen smiled. "Dis fight hopped to da top of my priorities."

Roran had no idea what the king was talking about and didn't acknowledge it. Instead, he spoke on the terms, "If I remember correctly from my Pops, an Ardhatazian fight is one of strikes and grapples confined to the arena. It is until surrender or incapacitation, right?"

"I'm glad good ole Cormac raised ya in our ways," the king said.

"Then if I win, I get the sword."

"On my honor," the king nodded.

"Then what do you want?" Roran asked.

The king smiled, "Oh, ya've already given me what I want. Dis will be a fight for da ages. Urrem? Go get da scribes."

Urrem, recovering his breath from the elbow blow, nodded and ran off.

"Good, we'll add it to da March. Let it be known dat King Ewen faces a monster."

Roran frowned. *He knows? And still wants to fight?*

"So, you don't mind if I use my advantage?" asked Roran.

The king's grin broadened, revealing his large teeth. Everything about the man was large. "Oh, I'm counting on ya using it," said the king. "I'd be insulted if ya held back. I need to show my men what we're up against. I am proving my destiny, and I won't even need Lichtfangr gauntlets to do it!"

Roran shrugged. He breathed in deep and stoked the fire in his diaphragm. He grew taller and wider, even larger than Ewen. His veins emitted light, letting his body glow in the growing dusk. Strands of glowing filaments trailed off his skin, and his eyes began to glow. And his shirt shredded.

Oros's blood, Roran thought. *I forgot to take off my shirt first again.*

The line of men surrounding the two yelped in terror and stepped back.

"Not to fear! Hold yer ground men!" Ewen barked. "This is a host. He houses a filament in him. In da west, once we're finished with Wilheim, we will fight more of his ilk. Men who acquired dis ability through corpse calling, men who are a danger to our world." Ewen looked around the square of troops and nodded at Urrem who had returned with the scribes. "Dis is da kind of threat we must stop. It's why I've been called to lead da March!"

Roran raised his arms to his chin in challenge.

Ewen traced a triangle over his chest. "Tank ya for fighting me wit all ya have, Roran, son of Cormac. I've been waiting for a fight like dis!"

Roran charged him, closing the distance quickly. He brought his club of an arm down toward Ewen's head.

And Ewen caught the metal cap.

The king used both hands and grunted loudly at the impact. The ground seemed to shake as the king dissipated the shock of the blow all the way down his body, through his arms, shoulders, core, bent knees, and feet. The king's feet were indented into the soft forest floor and a puff of snow flew up around both of their legs.

The king blinked and shook his head, the blow seemingly taking a lot out of him. "Wow, son of Cormac, dat strength's nothing to sniff at."

Roran's jaw hung open in disbelief. "How?" he said, his voice deeper and louder in the form.

Ewen smiled. "I don't need to cheat to match yer strength," the king said. "I've been training my whole life to fight monsters."

The king kicked Roran in the stomach to create some distance. Roran actually *felt* that kick. It was clear Roran was still far superior to Ewen in strength and durability, but Ewen fighting unafraid was very concerning. But there would be no way Ewen could block one of his blows at full strength. Roran planted himself, pulled back his right arm, and then launched it toward Ewen's head with all his might.

"Got you," Ewen smiled.

Ewen ducked the punch and followed it up with a full-body uppercut smashing the stumbling Roran in the solar plexus.

And all the breath left Roran's body. Roran gasped and found he couldn't properly engage his diaphragm. With his breath gone, his fire fizzled out. Roran struggled to breathe as he fell to one knee and reverted down to his normal human form. He looked up at the approaching king with wide-eyed terror. This was a man who could do the impossible, a force of nature, seemingly more of a monster himself; with one punch, he took down Roran without any advantage, and there was nothing Roran could do to stop Ewen from coming. Ewen's soldiers were cheering, heralding him as the conqueror of monsters. The king seemed not to notice their shouts, his gaze was locked in on Roran as he steadily marched forward.

Roran's whole body trembled, partly from the shot to the solar plexus, partly from the terror. Never had anything scared him more in his life than this mountain man who had so easily taken away all of Roran's unstoppable strength. Even this problem he couldn't punch. As soon as Roran regained his ability to breathe, he jumped to his feet, turned, and ran at the line of soldiers. He broke through their lines and fled to where Arno was hiding.

"I wasn't finished!" the king shouted. "Why can't anyone give me a proper contest?! Look, men! Not only do we fight monsters, but we fight cowards who only fight when dey have da upper hand, no pun intended!"

Arno's head poked above a log and watched as Roran sprinted toward him. "Hurry, Arno," Roran said, "buckle the harness. We've got to go!"

Arno nodded and hastily buckled the straps around Roran. Roran stood up and immediately ducked down as a wide arch of flame blasted by overhead.

"I will not let monsters run amok in my kingdom!" Ewen shouted. "I gave ya yer chance to fight me like a man, but ya refused. Now I hunt ya like a beast!"

———

Griselda heard an explosion of fire in the woods in the enemy camp. She was pretty sure she didn't do that one. *Focus!* she thought as a thrust flew by her head. Fire shot from the tip of Sophia's hand-and-a-half sword after each thrust, effectively increasing the reach of the weapon by tenfold.

The siege towers had made it to the wall, and Ardhatazians were stumbling over the rubble and climbing into Wilheim. Griselda had failed. But she still needed to fight if she wanted to continue living. Sophia seemed determined to kill her, even though her main mission was already accomplished. She probably wanted End March.

Griselda gritted her teeth and tangled the tip of her sword

with Sophia's. The weapons locked themselves in a bind where both warriors fought for leverage and an opening, dangerous heat pouring off from the blades. In the bind, Griselda had the advantage. She locked Sophia's sword in place against her Oros-head parrying hook. Griselda twisted her sword and wrenched Sophia forward as she clung to her weapon. Off balance, Griselda pivoted out of the bind and smacked the pommel of End March into the back of Sophia's helmet. Mathilda would have been proud if she were watching.

Sophia slipped on the water accumulating on the tower and fell forward, but as she fell, she wildly swung her blade back, shooting flames out and preventing Griselda from advancing to take advantage of her downed opponent. Griselda absorbed the flames with End March and continued to press. She trapped Sophia's sword again with her parrying hooks and fell on top of Sophia, wrestling her to the ground and trying to pin her arms. The stone floor was hot and cracking from the intense flames constantly dancing off the surface during their fight. From this position, all End March was good for was blunt force, the cold taking away its lethal heat quickly when it wasn't rapidly moving. She repeatedly bashed the rings on the cross guard into Sophia's helmeted head, which bounced against the cracked stone.

According to Matilda, this was how most fights between fully armored opponents would end if it was to the death. They would go to the ground and try to stab at weak points with a dagger. Griselda did not have a dagger, but she could maneuver one of End March's pointed quillons into the eye gap in the visor. But did she want to do that? Did she really want to stab this woman in the eye socket as those terrified, dazed eyes looked into her own?

And that hesitation was enough for Sophia to roll Griselda off her into a warm puddle. Though End March was still separating the two warriors, now Sophia had the leverage and could maneuver the quillons into Griselda's eyes. Griselda pressed End March with all her might up into the air to resist the quillon from closing in on her visor gap. Breathing heavily as the fight wore on, sweat and spit dripped out of the visor air holes around Sophia's mouth and landed on Griselda's helmet.

Griselda managed to angle the quillons to the sides away from her helmet but did not escape getting bashed in the head with the rings on the cross guard. It did not feel good. Her head bounced off the stone, rattling inside her helmet. The tail on the back of her sallet forced Griselda's head up into an awkward angle, prominently displaying her neck. If she couldn't manage the eye holes, Sophia would try to stab the quillons into the vulnerable, soft flesh of her neck.

But before she could, she needed to daze Griselda more. She continuously shoved the rings into the helmet, over and over again. Griselda was starting to see stars and thought she was hearing cracks too. Her head started to pound fiercely; her thinking slowed to an abysmal crawl. No longer could she use her intellect to protect her against a much more experienced opponent. With the pain in her head distracting her, the weight of her armor bogging down her limbs, and Sophia on top of her, she felt like she was moving through a hot, thick stew. She would be dead soon. Either from the blows to the head or a punctured neck, it didn't matter.

Her eyes began to close. And there they were. The cold, dead faces, welcoming her to the next leg of the March.

Another smack from the rings made even her inner vision fuzzy. The faces shifted, replaced by others. *Father, Mother*, she thought, as she was greeted by Cormac's smiling face, his large, dirt-stained arms draped around Gretchen's shoulders. Gretchen smiled too, as if to say it would be all fine, whatever happened.

Another smack and Griselda's head bounced off the stone. She saw Roran and Arno, fighting for their lives, but still together. And she wanted to be there with them.

These are the faces I want to see when I close my eyes. These are the faces I will fight to save.

The only good thing about being underneath Sophia was that it allowed Griselda to catch her breath in return for the severe damage to her head. Sophia, on the other hand, was getting noticeably weaker and more exhausted.

Reaching deep and flailing like a trapped animal, Griselda managed to roll right with Sophia in tow. To her surprise, she kept rolling as they bounced and clanged down the spiral staircase into the tower. Sophia's longsword fell down ahead of them and then off the side of the wooden circular staircase toward the base of the tower.

They landed on a platform and scrambled apart from each other, Griselda retaining control of End March. They both stood shakily, dazed and tired beyond what felt possible. They breathed slowly, each taking their time to rejuvenate. Sucking in all the air she could, Griselda threw End March unto the hooks on her back and pulled out her swept-hilt side sword, which would work better in the narrower quarters of the flammable staircase, wooden railing on her left and stone wall to her right.

Weaponless, Sophia held up her metal mittens, ready to deflect Griselda's side sword or wrestle it away from her. Griselda lunged and thrusted at the opening in the plates near Sophia's groin. Sophia sidestepped the blow and planted a heavy punch right into Griselda's helmet. Still dazed from before, Griselda stepped backward, found that there was no ground to step on, and tumbled down the remaining stairs. Her helmet strap broke free as she hit the bottom.

Sophia, looking undaunted, came down the staircase after Griselda, rolling her head and cracking her neck, which was audible even under her helmet. "You know," Sophia said, breathing heavily. "You're putting up more of a fight than I expected."

The helmetless Griselda rose shakily to her feet. She sighed and held up her sword to ward against the next onslaught.

Roran sprinted through the tree line as flames exploded in the branches overhead. Snow crunched under his feet, slowing his steps and making the flames seem like they were gaining on him.

"How long can that big of a guy run?" yelled Arno.

"No idea!" Roran yelled back.

Roran evaded a vertical fire lash that cleaved a tree in half. He jumped through the splitting tree as either side fell.

"He's still chasing!" yelled Arno.

"I know!"

From behind them, Ewen was bellowing, likely for the sake of his troops and scribes. "I fought my way through da Pits, I was trained by a Lichtfangr, and I have never lost a battle! Ya will not escape my wrath!"

A high flame flashed into the tree above Roran and exploded, leaving a puff of smoke and falling branches in its wake that Roran barely dodged.

Roran was starting to get tired. Sprinting with Arno on his back was much more tiring than jogging with him, and that was on normal terrain. The snow doubled his fatigue. With his breath seemingly stolen from him with Ewen's blow to his solar plexus, his stamina no longer felt infinite as his diaphragm was paralyzed. He would run out of air soon, and then Arno would once again be hurt by a blade Roran made.

No, Roran gritted his teeth. *Never again. Kings will topple before I let anyone else hurt Arno.*

"Roran," Arno said, snapping Roran out of his thoughts. "I think I know how we can shake him."

"How's that?"

"You can jump the wall, right?"

Roran sucked in air. "Yeah, but I'll need to . . . catch my breath first . . . to transform. I can't do it . . . while I'm sprinting."

Another fire lash nearly clipped his right shoulder.

"I don't think he's going to let you," said Arno. "But I don't think Ewen would be stupid enough to run toward the walls while Wilheim still has archers. Plus, he took off his armor too."

"We'll find out!" Roran turned sharply to the left and sprinted into the clearing between the tree line and the wall.

"Yer a slippery little bugger!" bellowed Ewen behind them when he realized Roran had turned.

Roran broke through the tree line and looked up at the walls. With any luck, hopefully the archers wouldn't shoot at a hand-less man carrying a child on his back.

Roran yelped and ducked an incoming arrow, causing him to almost fall. Luck was not on his side.

Roran took shelter behind the fallen siege tower. He tried to catch his breath as he heard arrows pelt the wooden structure around him. He sucked in the air and pushed down into his diaphragm, stoking his fire.

"Arno, loosen the straps. I think I got my wind back."

Arno did as asked. The straps slackened but soon stretched taut once again as Roran grew. He looked up as a bright flash came from the Ardhatazian camp. Another wave of fire spewed at him as Ewen kept swinging the great sword. Roran jumped over the sideways siege tower just as the flames hit.

Roran turned and sprinted toward the wall. Three siege towers had docked alongside each other, and dozens of Ewen's forces were climbing the rubble and infiltrating the walls. Roran could hear the clanging as the soldiers clashed with the last of the Wilheim garrison. They weren't much of a match. Ewen's troops were now as well-armed by this point with scavenged gear, and their numbers and battle prowess quickly overwhelmed the few Wilheim fighters.

Can't think about that right now, Roran thought. *If I fight, I'll risk hurting Arno.*

With his enhanced strength, Roran leaped high enough to land on the rubbled wall. He stumbled with the forward momentum, slipped on the snowy, bloody slop covering an exposed brick, and smacked his head against the stone.

"Roran! You okay?"

Roran shook his enlarged head. "Yeah," he responded, though his vision was blurry. He looked up, and three men became two men became one who was lunging at Roran with a poleax. He was wearing the green of Wilheim, too. Roran grunted, dodged the thrust, and then jumped over the soldier.

Roran landed in the city streets. The buildings had seen better days. Trebuchet boulders had smashed through the structures closest to the walls during bombardment and calibration. The amount of rubble made navigating the street incredibly hazardous, let alone fighting on the uneven footing. But of course, being the big glowing red monster, both Ardhatazian and Wilheim troops stopped fighting to attack Roran, at least the brave ones who didn't flee as soon as they saw him.

Roran shouldered past a Wilheim shield bearer, who then flew into the wall.

"Sorry!" Arno cried from behind Roran in his harness.

Roran scrambled around two soldiers locked in the bind and then two more who were wrestling on the ground. The streets were in chaos as it looked like no one was in command or in any kind of formation.

"Roran, look!" Arno yelled.

Roran turned around to see where Arno was pointing. A girl, helmetless and in bloodied armor, stumbled backward out of a tower. She was being pursued by a knight who had picked up a glowing hand-and-a-half sword. On her back was the glowing great sword that Roran and Cormac had made together.

"It's Ellie!" Arno shouted.

"Griselda!" Roran shouted, but it was no use. She was still on the other side of a warzone, and no one would be able to discern individual yells.

The Wilheim soldiers were pulling back, Griselda with them, as they backed their way toward the large keep, the keep where Roran and Arno had been imprisoned.

Roran could just make out yells for Wilheim's retreat. Roran sighed as he noticed the one calling the retreat: a scowling, one-armed man in green brigandine. He waved a glowing mace over his head in his remaining arm.

"Really, Pops," Roran mumbled. "Just how many of those weapons did you make? And why do they end up in the hands of everyone trying to kill me?"

Griselda turned to run back to the keep as soon as the knight with the glowing sword turned her attention to Carl. And then Carl turned his attention to Roran.

"You!" Carl barked.

"Hi . . ." Roran said.

"I'm guessing you're thrilled to see *me,* too," the knight with the glowing sword directed at Carl, a woman's voice behind the helmet. She walked up next to Roran and looked him up and down. Arno waved from the back of the harness at the knight. The knight awkwardly waved back.

Carl smiled, a demonic-looking thing on the usually grouchy man's face. "Great! I can kill two traitors at the same time!"

The three of them faced off in a triangle, the knight holding her glowing sword in plow guard, Carl holding his glowing mace with the flanged head resting on his shoulder, and Roran, who just shrugged. Arno craned his neck to get a view of the others.

"Well, hate to go, but I'll let you two settle whatever lover's quarrel you have—" Roran said, making a break for the gap between the two fighters so he could follow after Griselda.

"You're going nowhere!" Carl yelled.

Roran felt a burning sensation as something wrapped around

his leg. He looked down to see blue tendrils of light latched and burning into his calf, which was promptly yanked out from under him.

"Damn, you're heavy!" Carl said. He had tried to throw Roran, but Carl didn't weigh enough to move something Roran's size and could only trip him up.

Roran yelled, beating his metal caps against the stone. He sprang back up just as Carl, who had blue light streaming from where his right arm used to be, used the tendrils to latch onto the wall and propel himself forward, putting him between the keep and Roran.

I told you he was pregnant, the red man's voice said in Roran's head. *You definitely should have killed him.*

"Since when can you do that?!" the knight yelled.

"That's not all, Sophia," Carl said, still with his wicked grin. "Want to see something even more impressive?"

"N-no, not really," she said as she stepped up next to Roran's side. She turned to him and whispered, "I've got no beef with you if you've got no beef with me. It looks like Wilheim doesn't like you very much either."

Roran nodded at the knight, apparently named Sophia. "Truce," he said, not taking his eyes off Carl.

"Truce," said Sophia.

"Did you make a friend?" Arno asked, delighted. "Woe-Woe, I'm so proud of you!"

Roran rolled his eyes, and Sophia chuckled.

Carl huffed and sprang into action, his light arm grabbing the glowing mace. He took the bow off his back with his real left arm and held it out in front of him, aiming it at Roran and Sophia.

"I thought I'd never wield my bow again when you took my arm," Carl said. "In reality, you made me deadlier." Carl's light arm split into multiple writhing strands. Some of the strands coiled around his own legs, strengthening them. Others kept holding the mace, which snaked up higher and higher into the air. The last strand formed a bow string and nocked the arrows from Carl's quiver.

The remaining soldiers looked between the combatants in the street, the steaming red giant, and the knight with a Cormac weapon. And then they saw Carl the Falconer, the former Licht-fangr, corpse-caller hunter, and assassin, wielding powers none of them had ever seen. The troops saw the three and fled, no matter what colors were on their tunic.

Roran really needed to have a talk with his brother about the no-killing rule, especially if the people he spared came back ten times stronger. He started to approach Carl, knowing he would have to get through him to get to Griselda. Sophia stayed behind and bent her knees, both hands on the glowing hand-and-a-half sword.

The mace, which had climbed high into the sky with the support of the blue tendrils, swung down at Roran as arrows started raining down at Sophia, speed enhanced by the blue light bow string.

Roran yelped and jumped into the air as the mace collided with the stone in front of him. The collision created a massive explosion that shot rubble everywhere and leveled the nearest house. Roran felt a shock wave push him even higher into the air and send him over to his left off the street.

"Whoa!" Arno yelled.

"Hang on!" Roran cried.

Sophia held her blade up in front of her to fend off the blast, which charged her blade with the flames from Carl's explosive mace. She then readied herself to deal with the incoming arrows by swinging her own storm of fire with an upward sweep of her sword, disintegrating the projectiles coming her way.

"Thank you, Connor," she said.

Roran landed on a roof and tried to get his bearings. Carl could threaten him from several different angles with snakelike arms carrying an explosive mace. He couldn't afford to lose sight of it, which he already did.

"Behind you!" Arno yelled.

Instinctively, Roran jumped from the roof of the house back onto the wall, landing among fighting soldiers. The house he was standing on was flattened by the mace.

"Sorry!" Arno said again to the soldiers Roran shoved out of the way.

Sophia inched closer and closer to Carl with each upward sweep. His arrows, despite being loosed from his bow at an incredible rate with several working tendrils drawing and nocking multiple arrows, were being eaten by Sophia's flames.

Carl frowned. "Let's switch it up."

Still watching the mace, Roran spotted it climb back into the air over Sophia's head. "Shit," he muttered. He jumped from the wall and swooped Sophia off the ground in the crook of his arm just before the mace would have landed on her head.

You do realize, echoed Beans, *that now he doesn't have to divide his attention.*

"Double shit," said Roran as several arrows flew past his head. One arrow narrowly missed Arno and pierced into Roran's rear right shoulder. He cried out and dropped Sophia.

Carl gave chase with his enhanced legs while also using his tendrils to help him maneuver at speed through the collapsing city. Sophia darted off in another direction, but Carl seemed to decide he was fully committed to hunting down Roran.

"Why me?" Roran yelled, exasperated. With all this sprinting, he was going to run out of breath soon, and his fire would fizzle out. Worst of all, the terrain was lifeless white stone. Beautiful though it may be, he could not draw any life force out of the stone like he could when he was running in the forest toward Wilheim. "Instead of griping in my head, you could try to help!"

Bring him toward the Shatter Rock River, said Beans.

Roran sprinted as fast as he could through the crumbling city streets as Ewen's troops flooded in on all sides. In hot pursuit, Carl was sweeping the troops aside with his light arms or outright annihilating them with his mace while his arrows maintained their target on Roran.

"No, no, no, no," Arno whimpered behind Roran. "There's so much death."

Roran winced. Feeling Arno's sorrow hurt worse than the arrow in his shoulder. That pain was amplified as another arrow found it's mark in his hamstring. Roran stumbled and, unable to keep his footing with his unnatural speed, fell and skidded across the stone on his face. He came to a halt at the base of the Shatter Rock River.

Roran scrambled to his feet as best as he could and jumped over to the other side, but he collapsed in a heap of snow as his leg gave out on the landing. Roran backed up against a wall— Arno sheltered at the very least—and watched as Carl approached him. It seemed like Roran had nothing left. He tried to dig deeper. There was nothing there. But then, suddenly, he did find something, something small, frail, gentle, and . . . and he pulled on it. With his last ounce of strength, Roran pushed the two arrows out of his skin. Steaming blood began to heal the wounds, but that was all Roran could do in this state. Out of breath, Roran reverted down to his human form.

No longer seeing Roran as a threat, Carl laughed as he landed, the Shatter Rock River dividing the two opponents. He strung his bow over his back and then moved the glowing mace to his real arm. He pointed it at Roran from across the river. "I've been thinking about how I was going to do this."

Roran scooted back until the harness was pressed up against the wall.

"I haven't decided if it would be more rewarding to ground you to paste with your own weaponry," Carl said, holding the mace aloft, "or if it would be poetic ripping you limb from limb with these things I got because of you." He nodded to the bright blue tendrils floating in the air.

Carl almost stepped into the river, but frowned. He could tell something was wrong.

Oros's big, burly ass! Beans swore in Roran's head. *His fledgling filament is communicating with him now inside his head. It's learning quickly. Soon, it'll be like me.*

"So, now what?" Roran asked.

This.

Beans jumped out of the ground behind Carl and shoved him into the river.

Carl fell in, surfaced, and turned to see the glowing, aristocratic red man smiling devilishly.

"You!" Carl shouted.

"Ah, yes, Carl, was it?" said Beans. "I do mean this sincerely, but I am really impressed with how quickly you're catching onto things. Ass-face and pipsqueak over here are making agonizingly slow progress."

Carl scowled and raised his mace to launch it after Beans, but he was dragged under the surface of the river.

Beans waved, "Let me know what's down there if you come back up."

Roran shivered at the memory of the force lurking in the water and its draw toward people who carried the filaments. Whatever was down there had now officially stretched all the way from Lake Verdin, up the Shatter Rock, through Stedtfest, and made it to the walled city of Wilheim—a distance Roran couldn't even fathom. The long-reaching hand of death itself had emerged from the lake and taken hold. What would that mean for everyone living on the continent? What did it want?

DOMINATE.

After a few splashes and muffled cries, the river returned to being eerily peaceful. Carl never resurfaced and vanished into the murky river.

Roran looked up at the snow as it fell and burned away on his heated skin. He let himself breathe out and relax his tensed muscles. "Good thing I had you when I fell into the water back in Stedtfest, huh, Arno?"

Silence.

Roran twisted his neck around, trying to glimpse Arno. He wasn't moving. Roran's heart jumped into his throat as the weight of it all jumped back on his chest.

"Oh . . ." Beans said from across the river, seemingly aware of what was happening. "Oh no."

"Arno?" Roran yelled. "Arno!"

CHAPTER 33

THE OLD RED KING

GRISELDA COULDN'T HEAR MUCH other than the pounding of her heartbeat in her skull. Though she had escaped Sophia, she endured terrible, maybe irreparable, damage to her head, and now all forms of sensation drifted into the abstract, rendering the world around her inexplicable and hazy. She tenderly touched the back of her head to find that her hair was coated in her own blood. This, on top of the painful headaches she regularly gets, compounded until all noise became so loud yet so indistinct she felt like she was in a whirlwind. She was aware of the screaming, the barricading, the slamming doors, brisk commands, and clanging metal, but it all seemed to sync with the thunderous pulsing of pain in her temples.

Griselda grimaced as she helped Mathilda block the throne room's doors with furniture they pulled from other rooms.

They had planned to hold fast at the keep's gatehouse, but Sophia had reappeared after Griselda escaped her. She had used her Cormac sword to annihilate the gate and lead Ewen's troops into the king's castle proper.

Few of the royal guards remained, as Sophia had overwhelmed them, and Mathilda forced Griselda back to her prime duty, the safekeeping of the king. There were about twenty of the royal guards, halberds at the ready, pointing their remaining strength at the freshly barricaded door.

Their resolve was impressive, bracing themselves even though their shaking limbs could be heard gently clanking in their armor; however, the royal guards' last stand would be fruitless. It was over. Wilheim was burning, the castle was overwhelmed, and they were all trapped in the throne room.

Exhausted from the previous fighting, Griselda sat against the wall. She could smell the ends of her hair had been singed. She could feel the leftover salt caking her face after the sweat evaporated. She let out a long breath, and with it, she let acceptance flood in.

None of them were getting out of this room alive. Death had it out for her, and she could only escape it so many times in a single day. Though she had let herself hope and used that hope as motivation in her previous skirmish with Sophia, she knew for certain she would never get to see her brothers again. There was only one hope she didn't relent to the easy darkness of surrender: she could still believe that they somehow made it out alive, even if she never got to see them herself. She gave herself permission to have that one seed—that one small, pathetic seed of faith. Despite the world crumbling, her head working against her, despite all evidence to the contrary, this was the hope she would take with her to the next leg of the March.

A shadow crossed her face. Griselda looked up.

"You lost my helmet, I see," Mathilda said, looking down at her, still wearing her own helmet.

"Yeah. Sorry about that. That knight, she was strong," said Griselda.

"I figured that much. Want mine?" Mathilda asked, tapping her gauntlet against her visored bascinet helmet.

Griselda shook her head and lowered her eyes back down to the floor. The pounding in her head intensified and she gritted her teeth.

"What's with the face?" asked Mathilda.

"Wha—oh, nothing," Griselda said. "Nothing important."

Mathilda sighed and set her great sword tip down in front of the sitting girl. Mathilda stood there, resolute, hands clasped over the pommel, ready for whatever would come next. The sight of her standing like that somehow made Griselda's head hurt worse. She stood there staring, like she wanted something.

"It was . . . nice . . . spending these last few days with you," Griselda managed. Though she said it to fill the silence, it wasn't untrue. For the first time since her mother died, Griselda had a female figure who was encouraging and supportive—at least sometimes—mentoring her and providing things she didn't know she craved.

"It's just . . ." Griselda continued despite the headache making it hard to think. "I wish we had more time—that it didn't have to end like this. Oh, listen to me prattle," Griselda forced a smile. "I'm guessing this isn't what anyone wants to hear in their last moments."

Mathilda said nothing; whatever expression was on her face was masked behind her helmet. She merely listened and seemed to take everything into full consideration.

"I should have . . ." Griselda continued. Might as well fill the quiet, for the throne room was eerily silent, other than the pounding noise in Griselda's head. "Maybe I should have left when I had the chance . . ."

"I agree," Mathilda said. Her sudden voice startled Griselda.

Griselda reluctantly nodded.

"Then again," Mathilda continued. "Would you have really been satisfied if you didn't try to locate your brothers?"

Griselda shrugged, her vision almost getting foggy from the

pain. Her breaths seemed to sync with the stabs of pain that came with each beat of her heart.

"So," Mathilda said. "Are you done doing whatever it is you're doing? The self-pitying? We have settled that you should have left, but you didn't. Tough shit. You're here now. What are you going to do?"

An enormous thud, this time not just in her head, crashed into the other side of the door. Griselda almost jumped to her feet in fright at the sudden break from the environmental silence, but it was much easier to stay seated against the wall, much easier to let the weight of her armor tether her to the floor, much easier to surrender to the pounding and let it all wash over her.

The other soldiers lowered themselves into an athletic stance and braced the tips of their sun-like halberds at the door in defensive formation, waiting for whatever came through to skewer themselves on the harsh steel. The door shook again and again, rhythmically, one concussive shock after the next, like the thunder in her temples. The door rattled but held firm. For now.

"What are you going to do?" Mathilda said, unimpeded by whatever was battering on the other side of the door.

Everything was just too *loud*. Griselda couldn't think and let her frustration and agony burst out. "What do you mean, 'what am I going to do?' I'm going to sit here, and we're all going to die." She gently rested her head back against the wall, hair wet with blood squelching as it made contact with the cold stone. "There. I said it."

Thud.

"You're not going to join the defensive formation?" asked Mathilda.

Thud.

"Why would I? It's twenty versus thousands. Even with End March—"

Thud.

Griselda shook her head. "I mean, I can hardly move my arms anymore. I'll give out eventually. All so I could retain some pride and kill dozens more? Is that what you want?"

Thud.

"I don't think so," Griselda continued, angered that she was being pressed for so hopeless a cause. "Even if we hold, all they have to do is wait until we starve."

Thud.

Mathilda released her breath, the air flowing through the holes in her faceplate. "Well, if that's your choice. I told you before: I don't deal with the weak shit. Go keep the king company."

Mathilda stepped aside and pointed her thumb at the king.

Griselda stood to move.

"I taught you the salute!" Mathilda yelled, fury well and known even behind the visor. "Do you know what it means?"

Griselda looked at her feet.

Mathilda performed the salute, beating her left hand against her heart and then resting it on top of her helmet. "'I acknowledge your head and your heart. And I will remember you with mine.' We look at a person's whole life, all the effort and sweat they put in to make it to their last moments. We acknowledge that it mattered! And we respect the unseen years of work making themselves who they were before they lost in battle. That's why we do it! They will remember me, remember my fighting spirit, even if I die today."

Mathilda calmed herself down, slowing her breathing behind the visor.

"Get out of the way. Sit back with the king if you won't fight."

Griselda closed her eyes as Mathilda's words bounced around in her pounding head, unable to fully comprehend the weight of Mathilda's scolding. She turned toward the king, anything to look at something other than the fuming Mathilda.

Griselda had forgotten he was there at all. He was so quiet, sitting on his throne, staring at the stained-glass windows, like an animate corpse curiously watching the living. He didn't seem distraught, even at the collapse of his kingdom. He seemed *serene* somehow?

Though her head still pounded, though the door still pounded, and though it took great effort to move her exhausted body in armor over to the king, she was already standing and might as well make use of her legs. She walked past each depiction of the Marches on the glass until she made it to the king's side at his throne.

He stirred and looked Griselda up and down. He smiled. "Hoping I have a secret exit under my chair?"

Griselda smiled back weakly and shook her head. She winced as even the slightest jostling of her head caused a spike of pain.

The king sighed and returned to looking at the stained glass. "You know," he said. "Though this castle was here long before me, I must say that whoever built it thought like I do. Too fascinated with the beauty and grandeur to plan for the worst-case scenario. This room is situated high above the courtyard so others can see the glass from outside the castle. Thankfully, we're so high up that they can't break the glass to get in. When all else crumbles and fades, I hope this glass remains."

Griselda shuffled uncomfortably. She was pretty sure the king was aware of what was happening, but his demeanor suggested he was somewhere else, perhaps far away on a boat sailing across Lake Verdin, wind in his beard, light on his face, his cares behind him.

"Why the glass?" she finally asked.

"Hmmm, why indeed," the king mused. "I think more than anything else, this glass is who we are. What Wilheim stood for. The glass holds it all: our important stories, our accumulated knowledge, and it does so by preserving it in art, art that makes full use of the sun. When the sun hits the glass just right, I see colors I could have sworn didn't exist dancing in patterns on my stone floor. You know, I remember my young son Zerebril trying his hand at paint for the first time. He must have been . . . what? Five years old?"

Griselda chuckled. "He tried to copy the stained glass in his paints?"

"Actually," the king chuckled too. "He had little interest in the glass itself. He tried to paint what the glass did to the floor. The swirling colors, the shimmering light creating a haze in the dust of this old room. But the light kept moving while his paint could not. He got so fed up he couldn't produce the same effect that he dumped his paints on the floor," the king laughed harder. "He was inconsolable, the little brat."

Griselda raised an eyebrow.

"What? I loved him, but he was a brat. Sometimes. His tantrum didn't subside until Gunter came in singing and put the crying child on his shoulders."

At this, Griselda smiled too, Arno coming to mind. Though Arno was generally well-behaved, there were definitely times where she had to soothe his frustration with games or distraction. Griselda looked behind her back toward the barricade as the thuds from the door stopped temporarily.

"But the thing was," the king said, "putting Zerebril on Gunter's shoulders didn't make him stop crying. So, Gunter tried another tactic. He feigned back pain from carrying Zerebril, set Zerebril down, and comically squirmed on the floor. You see, children have to learn empathy. It takes time. 'People in progress' I once heard it called. But you should have seen how quickly Zerebril refocused on his brother's pain. He dismissed all his petty frustration to kneel next to his brother and ask what was wrong."

Griselda smiled, but shed a tear at the same time. She found it a tad bit manipulative, but she also saw Roran and Arno in the story, too. There was good in this world. She wished she would be around for a little longer to see it.

The king suddenly became sterner, more focused. He stared into Griselda's eyes with his regal intensity. "Do you think I tell you this in vain? That I'm just biding my time with one last story before I die?"

"I-I don't know," Griselda said, rubbing her forehead.

"What does it mean to do something in vain?"

"I guess . . . when you work for no result. When you work knowing it won't accomplish anything or get you closer to your goals."

The king's kindly face returned to its old glory before the age set back in. "Young lady, there is always a result. You just might not have the light around you to see it. It might be tiny, imperceptible. It might be something only you know or feel. But those tiny results add up—they make a person into who they are. You are not who you are because of this war. You are thousands of unseen interactions and conversations with your friends and family, moments seemingly in vain when held up against this world's violence. But our deaths will not erase those moments. Try as Ewen might to remove us from this world," the king sighed and looked over to the glass again. "We were still here, we still lived well, we still made art. The fabric of the world depends on countless people, all living the best they can. Like threads that make a tapestry, drops that make an ocean, stars that make the night sky."

Griselda squeezed her eyes hard and did her best to listen.

The king returned his gaze to her and smiled despite the pain evident on Griselda's face. "We are all filaments in some grand cosmic web, and whether you find that comforting or not, the fact remains that death does not make living a vanity."

Griselda tried to take it all in but resisted. She shook her head. "So, this conversation too, then, this is supposed to make me who I am. Convince me to take up my arms and make a last stand? Do you think we'll win because of your speech?"

The king chuckled. "No, you're too smart to be manipulated. This conversation only happened because I, like my sons, saw someone who was hurt and forgot myself. I saw someone in need and dismissed my problems for a moment so I could help."

Still, Griselda resisted. "Well, it didn't work. It was in vain."

"Young lady, I wasn't talking about you. I was trying to convince myself," the king smiled brightly. "And it worked. I can die as myself and not as the shadow I was becoming."

Griselda sighed. "I feel like . . . like I am becoming something else too. Each day away from my brothers. Each day, wielding this sword," she held End March up in front of her, the glow illuminating her dour features. "Each time I'm forced to kill. I'm fading away. I thought this was supposed to make me stronger, like Roran. Good thing I'll die before I can't recognize myself too."

The king nodded sympathetically. He sat and thought for several moments. "Are you familiar with *The March from Pain*?"

Griselda nodded. "Parts of it. I haven't had the time to read it myself, but I've heard some stories." She looked at the stained glass depicting the prophesied volcanic disaster.

The king shook his head. "No, not that part. It's what everyone fixates on, but I'm more concerned with how it begins."

Griselda tried to wrack her memory for the stories, but that made her head hurt more. However, hearing the king talk, even if it was nonsense, was soothing. "I don't remember. Please tell me."

The king stood up, to Griselda's surprise. He walked over to the window depicting the volcanic scenery. Griselda followed him over.

"*The March from Pain* is thought to be the oldest of the Marches," the king said.

"I remember," Griselda replied.

"Indeed," the king said, stroking his beard, eyes staying on the glass. "It starts with the unnamed prophet trying to save his world. He had been told by a monster that if the prophet wasn't always in pain, then his world would fade away, sucked into the void by the monster. So, the prophet isolated himself, starved himself, whipped himself, and stayed awake every hour of every day. For years. The world depended on the pain he inflicted on himself. Though he wanted to give up, he couldn't."

Griselda nodded. It was starting to come back to her.

"In the book, the prophet lives in a land with a red sky covered in clouds. The clouds were heavy, hot, and always present. He never got to see what was behind them. He lived with a stifling red ceiling. So, the author took to calling the prophet the Red King for how his self-inflicted bloody acts were meant to sustain the red world he lived in."

"But he couldn't live like that forever, right?"

The king shook his head. "No, and what was worse, his world was still fading anyway. His red sky began to disappear in long strands, like it was being pulled into fine lines and off into the unknown. Then it happened to the things on the ground, too. Rocks and soil were stretched thin and pulled away. His world was ending, though he had spent years in agony trying to keep it alive. In vain, you might say. This is what broke him. He developed Grief Sickness. First known record of it being mentioned. He experienced pain worse than anything he had already inflicted on himself."

Griselda winced and then frowned. This was not how the story ended. But she couldn't remember the details of how this problem resolved.

The king walked over to the stained-glass window prior to the volcanic one. In the top of the frame, it depicted deep red clouds being pulled and stretched in lines beyond the sky, like it was dripping up. In the lower portion of the frame, the ground was rocky and barren and dark, almost devoid of the light from the red hues in the sky. The ground, too, was being pulled into the air. In the center of the frame, on the vanishing ground, were two figures. The first was a man curled up on the ground in bloody armor. The second was a glowing feminine figure holding the armored man, her blue light in stark contrast to everything else. Lines sprang out in loops from her back, making her look like she had glowing bird wings without feathers.

"Is the bloody man the Red King?" Griselda asked.

The king nodded.

"Then who is the blue woman?"

"The author was unclear. She never had a name. But she took him away from his dying land and brought him to Verdin. From there, the text doesn't mention her again. The rest of the book depicts the Red King forming a community and then trying and failing to help people with Grief Sickness. The book ends abruptly without any resolution. One scholar thinks the final section, the most famous section, was an add-on by a later scribe. The book changes to the first-person perspective, as if the Red King were writing to us, and he talks about witnessing an explosion so massive that nothing could have survived it. Interpreters take this as a prophetic dream rather than something that happened to him. He wouldn't have survived the explosion if it did."

Griselda shook her head gingerly. "No wonder why I didn't bother to remember it. Though it's called *The March from Pain*, it never seems like he fully escapes it. It stays with him, and he constantly fails, and he seemingly witnesses the world end twice because of his failure."

The king laughed, still looking at the blue woman in the glass. "I once knew a woman who thought nothing could be done in vain. She tried to convince me of it for a long time, too. Said we needed to be a light no matter the darkness." The king rolled his eyes. "What a Wilheimian thing to say! She said we shouldn't live as if we were expecting rewards or consequences, that we should be light regardless, since it was simply right to do so. Didn't matter if we worked toward our dreams or not. And you know what?"

"What?" asked Griselda.

"Of all the learned people in the Wilheim Academies, none of them could hold a candle to her. None of their philosophizing could ever touch that simple truth. She was one of the many strings that made me, and she was a chambermaid!" The king smiled. His demeanor then changed as sorrow passed over his face; his head drooped low enough that his crown almost slipped from his head.

"I have many regrets," the king continued. "And though it is selfish of me, I regret more of what I did as a man than what I didn't do as a king. There is always so much pain and failure, so much that it seems like my failure has caused our world to end. Like my predecessor, that pain never made me a smidge stronger or more capable of enduring it."

"Then why?" Griselda asked. "Why keep going?"

"Our pain doesn't sustain this world. Our pain doesn't make us grow. It's the battlefield itself, not our weapon. It's merely a proving ground for us to test our true weapon. The Red King's pain didn't sustain his world; it was his love for the world and what he was willing to do to keep it around for even a fraction longer. The supposed second author of *The March from Pain* seems to think that whoever survives the fire cataclysm will be stronger because of it, equating us to being tempered like swords in the flame of pain. This is why I think the last part of this book is fraudulent. It has the wrong conclusion the real Red King would have drawn from everything. He would have said that if we survived, it was because our love was stronger than our pain. That we found something to love—love worth it all, despite everything else. That's the real miracle of the story. Not that he was somehow whisked away from his dying land, but that he loved enough to keep going despite witnessing the death of two worlds."

The king paused, breathed in deeply, as if bracing himself, and then continued. "Apathy and hope are equally infectious. Some people take comfort in their lack of agency, that the world has already ended twice before we were even born, and will continue to end over and over again until all becomes dust. This attitude removes accountability for personal action. But a hopeful person could hear that same story and be amazed that somehow we persist. The hopeful person will take action to make sure we keep persisting." He said, nodding at Griselda and then looking down, seemingly in a concentrated effort to get the words out while he was still cognizant. "If you decide not to care, you just made it easier for those around you to give up, too. But if you hope and dream and strive, there's no telling how many worlds you will save. Our language has evolved from the first recorded copy of *The March from Pain,* and I think there has been a critical error in the translation of the preposition. I don't think it should be called *The March from Pain,* but rather 'The March Through Pain,' or better yet, the March *despite* it."

The king picked his head back up and looked at Griselda. "I'm not asking you to kill any more people with that sword. You don't need to fight what brings you pain. Only to protect what you love, only to have belief in something. This army coming through our doors, what do they love? Are they fighting to protect anything?"

"How . . . how could I possibly know the answer to that?"

He nodded in response. "I suppose we can't. But you know what you love. And I know what I love. Even if my sons are dead, even if I am already half gone, half mad, I will still protect their memory," the king said, gesturing to the glass. "If my age robs me of my memory and sanity, then I will at least have the glass and the Marches, Gunter's singing, and Zerebril's silly, little paintings." He then tapped his finger to his temple. "Belief in nothing is worse than madness."

Griselda looked back to the blue woman in the stained glass and then to the king. She had nothing to say, and her headache was preventing her from fully contemplating her thoughts. But the pain had faded slightly as they talked.

And it came roaring back as the doors and barricade were blasted away.

CHAPTER 34
THE ANGRIEST MAN IN THE WORLD

"CALM DOWN!" Beans yelled at Roran from across the river.

Roran was frantically trying to unlatch the straps but could not without the use of his hands. "Arno! Arno! Tell me he's just sick or tired. Tell me there's not an arrow in him!" Roran could not get the harness off and was flailing about trying to get a glimpse of little Arno. He tried to unlatch them with his teeth but that failed too.

Beans vanished and then reappeared next to Roran on his side of the river. Beans slapped Roran across the face with enough force to nearly knock him over.

"I said calm down! Get ahold of yourself. Let me see," Beans walked behind Roran and examined Arno. "Good news. He's not dead. Now quit your tantrum."

Roran fell to his knees, allowing himself to catch his breath. "He's . . . okay?"

"I didn't say he was okay. I said he's not dead."

"*Will* he be okay?"

Beans stroked his scraggly beard made of thousands of strands of light floating in various directions. "I don't know how to break this to you. But he might not be. It looks like you started pulling his lifeforce from him to feed your form. You've been doing it subconsciously for a while now, but that last effort hurt him. He's alive, but he's not here, if you get my meaning."

Roran stared into the murky, fast-flowing river. "I've . . . I've been draining him? I did this to him? I hurt him? Again?"

Beans shrugged his shoulders. "Like I said, I don't know how to tell you this. I knew you wouldn't take it well. Since Arno is in close proximity to you, you pull on him a little every time you stoke the flame, even if you don't know it. As long as he's close to you, he might remain in this state."

"Take it off."

Beans blinked, not used to being ordered. "Excuse me?"

"I said take it off! Get the harness off me!"

Beans wound up to slap Roran again, but this time Roran caught it on his forearm. He stared down the Filament of God, a dark anger burning under his skin. "If you hit me one more time, I'll throw myself in the river. Whatever happens to me, I don't care, but I'll make sure you die."

Beans removed his hand from Roran's forearm. Roran's skin was sizzling from the burns sustained from Beans's strike, but his skin quickly healed.

"No . . . no, no, no!" Roran yelled as he forced his body to not heal, to not draw on the power. The act of trying to prevent the healing hurt more than the burn wound itself, feeling like all of his blood vessels in his arm constricted around chunks of ice. He had to refuse it if he wanted to keep Arno safe. But he had to use it if he wanted to save Griselda, who was trapped in the keep with Ewen's army smashing through the doors as they spoke. He looked up at the keep, the tall, white stone walls surrounding the fortress. He saw the buttresses and décor and stained glass Wilheim was so proud of and how soon they would be destroyed. He was actively killing Arno to save Griselda.

Roran let out a guttural howl, an animalistic, monstrous

sound. He smashed his metal caps into the stone, cracking the stone even without the transformation.

"Behold!" Beans mocked. "The angriest man in the world, that's what he called you, right?"

Roran ignored Beans and smashed the ground beneath him again,

"It's so often frowned upon in the academic circles I frequented. But I disagree. I do think it's necessary for motivation. It's only a bad thing when it's uncontrolled. When it's not being put to good use."

"By that," Roran sneered. "You mean *your* use."

"Well, you're not wrong. I am always right."

"I am not an arrow for you to direct!"

Beans shrugged. "If you don't have an archer pulling the string, the arrow never flies."

"I think Griselda would say that's bad wordplay."

"And she'd probably be right. But she's not here. So, I am currently the smartest person—thing—in the conversation. You want a more apt comparison? Fine. I'll give you a simile. Your anger is like a river. The water is going to flow somewhere, and it doesn't take much to redirect its course. Think of the flooding at Stedtfest. If you don't get a grip on yourself, anyone can redirect you and use your anger. Not just me."

Roran looked up from the stone he broke. "What can I do?"

"You can pull it together. You can't lose it on a battlefield. You'll make everything worse."

"And Arno?" Roran asked. "I can't leave him here, asleep, alone in a warzone. I can't take him with me and transform without hurting him further."

Beans shook his head. "Look, you're not going to want to hear my advice, so I won't even say it."

Roran looked up at the red man, eyes burning. "Please, tell me anyway."

Beans sighed. "Forget the girl. She's done for. Leave now

while you can. Lick your wounds, get Arno back to health, and find a new place to live out your lives."

Roran looked back down at the ground and answered Beans with silence.

Beans couldn't help but chuckle. "See. I told you. You're a very predictable kind of Ass-face. You're going to try to save Griselda even if it gets you killed. I know you. I know that means I'm likely next on the chopping block, too, if that happens. But what in Oros's name am I going to do about it? I can't control you. The river has long since jumped its banks. I can't even slap you anymore. Go do what you have to do. I'm going to try and enjoy my last moments before you get us all killed."

Beans shook his head and disappeared in a puff of snow.

"Poof . . ." Roran said quietly, bowing his head. Arno's weight somehow became much more present and cumbersome, forcing a forward curve into his spine.

Roran stood up, Arno loosely jostling on his back with each movement. His tiny head was drooping forward, with only the straps keeping him fastened to Roran. Even Beans had given up on Roran. His situation was hopeless. He had become what he had despised in Zerebril, Carl, and the king: someone who hurt children. Now, all he could do was listen to the keep fall in the distance and imagine what that meant for Griselda.

"I'm sorry," Roran choked. "I'm sorry, Arno. I'm sorry, Griselda. I'm sorry, Pops. I still wasn't strong enough to save them. I was useless in the dungeon; I'm useless outside of it."

Maybe the best option he had was giving up and just saving Arno like Beans had said. But would he be able to live with himself if he gave up on Griselda? Would he be able to look Arno in the eyes when he woke back up—if he woke back up— and tell him that he had abandoned Griselda?

Tears mixed with snow blurred Roran's eyes. There was no good option, and there never had been. There was no point to any of it. All of it would lead to him and his family dying. What did he do when there was no good option?

What you can regardless of reward or punishment. Do what you can.

Henrietta's words brought more tears to his eyes, but at the same time, they also moved his legs out of the snow that had been collecting in piles around his bare feet. Time was running out. So, he'd do what he could with what time he had left, regardless if it led to any good. He'd have to be content with the fight itself, being able to fight right there and then, that he still could, that he still willed himself forward, and that he had plenty of anger to spare. That would have to be enough. And if it all came to an end, perhaps he could try it all again on the next leg of the March.

An unconscious Arno in tow, Roran set his jaw and made his way toward the keep.

CHAPTER 35
TO BE A MONSTER

GRISELDA WOKE up to find herself pinned under a plank of wood. The explosion had destroyed the blockaded furniture and sent debris everywhere. Being knocked around did not help the state of her throbbing head. How long had she been out?

Sound slowly became discernible to her ears again when the ringing subsided. Even more slowly, her vision unblurred and refocused. She was staring at the ceiling, lying on her back, but she could hear metal footsteps on the far side of the room.

With tremendous effort, she propped up her head to look toward the entrance to the throne room. Arhatazian troops were placing the Wilheim royal guard in shackles and leading them out of the room. Griselda watched with horror as Mathilda was heaved up from the ground—helmet nowhere to be found, blood leaking from the corners of her mouth—also placed in shackles.

"I've heard of dis one," said the man from behind his scavenged great helm as he hoisted Mathilda's arm. "This ole lot will make good show in da Pits."

"Fine by me," Mathilda growled. "If it means I stay alive and kill more of you in the Pits, you won't hear a single complaint from me."

"See!" he exclaimed to another soldier, grabbing her other arm. "What I tell ya? Damn, good shows in da Pits for at least a few months. Maybe even more of a good show than—"

"Stuff it Briggs, not the time," said the other soldier.

But Mathilda had stopped paying the soldiers any mind. Her eyes were fixed on the figure that just walked in.

A scholar from the College of Observation, his large hood up to shadow his face, slowly and deliberately, with almost stiff movements, stepped into the throne room. Behind him, some sort of tendril of gelatinous material, like a contained river made of stars, emerged from under the long robes and was dragging a soaked, unconscious Carl by the ankle.

Even unconscious, Carl was still scowling, his remaining hand gripping the handle of his glowing mace in a vengeful deadlock.

King Morgen to Griselda's left, who seemed to have taken minimum damage from whatever blew in the doors, suddenly came to life. "No . . . him too? Even him? Is there nothing you won't take from me?"

As the Scholar approached the throne, the soldiers shied away, some of them almost stumbling as they backpedaled in haste. They hurriedly escorted the remaining royal guard and Mathilda out of the room, leaving just the king, the Scholar, the unconscious Carl, and Griselda buried under broken furniture. Mathilda gave one last mournful look at the king, seeming to know how the next few moments were going to play out, before she was shoved out of the throne room.

"Why do you wear our colors? Why wear our prestigious robes if you mean to burn down everything those garments stand for?" The king yelled.

The Scholar stopped a few steps away from the king and removed his hood. The figure underneath could hardly be described as human, more like a corpse. His hair had fallen out, even his eyebrows were gone. His skin seemed too tight, showing ugly green veins under the surface, and it was ashen and pale, with what looked like unhealed bruises. But his most frightening feature was his eyes. They glowed with the same eerie starry night as the tendril trailing him. Instead of having one pupil per eye, each of the many glowing stars in his eyes all behaved like individual pupils, all acting in dissonance as they swirled and looked in many directions around the room, all at the same time.

"Y-you!" the king stuttered.

The Scholar smiled, revealing gums that had receded from his teeth. His eyes stopped glowing and returned to a somewhat human semblance: brown irises and normal pupils. He gasped and gluttonously breathed in air like a man who had been drowning.

"I'm surprised you remember me, given your . . . condition," the Scholar croaked initially, like he hadn't spoken in a while and needed to remember what his own voice sounded like: something sinister and high-pitched.. "You remember my face, but do you remember my name?"

The king merely stared back at the Scholar, growing more agitated by the moment.

"No, do you even remember the name of your own flesh and blood by this point?" The Scholar mocked, and the tendril raised Carl into the air, letting him dangle upside down by the foot.

"Y-you're—you're a corpse caller!" the king shouted.

The Scholar's eyes narrowed. "That's not my name. That's not even what I am, not anymore."

"The Falconer was supposed to have killed you. He cut off your legs—"

"He failed," the Scholar said, pointing to Carl. "He let me get to the lake and then assumed I died when I didn't resurface," he laughed. "But I'll give him this, he did put an end to my research and forced my hand into . . . alternative options."

The king's eyes were wide with fear. He seemed to squirm on

his throne, as if under tremendous unseen pressure from a heavy weight in his lap.

"Now," the Scholar said, bringing Carl's dangling body close to the king's face. "I have an alternative option for him."

The candles illuminating the throne room flashed out. The room was cast into darkness; only the feeble sunlight of a dying day, obscured by clouds, made it into the room through the stained glass. The tendril tightened around Carl's leg. Though his eyes remained closed, Carl's mouth dropped open and let loose an otherworldly, metallic howl. Then his mouth closed, and his eyes snapped open. They were the same terrifying, many-starred pupil eyes the Scholar had before, all darting wildly around the room and taking in the scenery and situation, like a collective swarm of glowing flies.

The tendril slackened and dropped Carl to the floor. Slowly, Carl picked himself up; most of the pupils now homed in on the king writhing in his throne. Carl looked down at his hand holding the mace and cringed in pain. He dropped the mace, which flashed and bounced on impact with the ground, cracking the stone floor.

"What's my name, king?" the Scholar laughed.

"R-ruf—"

The Scholar smiled that grizzly, partial gum smile. "Rufus Redaway."

Griselda gasped. *The writer of the March commentary? Was this also the man whose office was blocked shut in the College of Observation?*

"Though I am now part of something else," Redaway continued. "Something much larger than your small kingdom, it doesn't mean I won't enjoy this."

The king's nails dug into the throne's armrests. "What have you done to my boy? To Gunter . . . n-no, Zere—no. To my—"

"Bastard," Carl said, his eyes returning to normal. His remaining arm shot out with incredible speed, fingers clenched around the king's throat. Carl raised the king into the air and squeezed, seemingly attaining fierce, inhuman strength. The king clawed at Carl's hand as his eyes bulged and legs kicked frantically in the open air.

"What . . . what's happening?" Carl mumbled, his eyes darting between his arm and the strangling king. He turned his head toward Redaway. "Are you controlling me?"

"Please," laughed Redaway. "You've wanted to do this your whole life, my influence or otherwise."

Carl breathed in and refocused his attention on the king. "You're right." Carl gritted his teeth and then heaved the king across the room and into the stained glass of the Red King, shattering it as the king's old, broken body flew out into the darkness below.

"No!" Griselda whimpered.

"So ends the long reign of Morgen II, King of the Peaceful Dawn, cast out into the coming night," said the Scholar. He walked up and placed a hand on Carl's shoulder. "So begins the reign of Carl the Falconer. Long live the king."

"Long live the king," Carl scowled in return.

Griselda shouted, a near animalistic, primal shout without words, all the while prying herself free of the debris. She drew End March from off her back. "Your reign will be very short. This night, you bastards die by my blade!"

Carl rolled his eyes.

"Interesting," the Scholar said. "A bearer, still alive?"

"Roaches—her entire family; very hard to kill," Carl muttered.

Griselda wasted no time flourishing End March and stepping toward the two monsters. Was this the smartest thing she had ever done? No, it was not. But she no longer cared, seeing that all she had was continuously being stripped away from her. The king's death, Mathilda's capture, Wilheim's fall . . . it could not be in vain. She refused to let it all end. No matter what the king said, it would still all be vanity in her eyes if she lost.

But what she did take to heart: *belief in nothing is worse than madness.* So, she believed, despite reason, that she would win. She had to win.

With all her fury and speed while swinging End March, the blade heated to white-hot in a few strokes, she shot a wave of flame at her two enemies.

Both jumped up in different directions, dodging the flame and sending out tendrils of the starry material to the vaulted ceilings. They swung around the room by their tendrils, each one lashing itself to the ceiling and propelling them along to the next attached tendril, evading each shock of fireburst Griselda sent their way. Fire collided with the arched ceilings, missing their targets each time, then rippled and whirled with the stone contours and architecture. The noise of the fire waves in the confined space caused a roaring, oppressive soundscape that drowned out everything besides the Scholar's laughter as he swung around the room.

The pair of flying monsters split up as another wave narrowly missed them. Now they were flying in opposite directions, and Griselda was not quick enough in her exhausted state to send flame lashes at both of them simultaneously. She dropped out of her stance as she was forced to duck and pivot away from a tendril Carl swung at her.

As soon as she ducked Carl, the Scholar swiped at her with his own tendril from behind her. Instead of evading, Griselda let the momentum of End March sweep up and slash at the tendril. Though End March passed through the tendril as if it were immaterial, the tendril stiffened on contact and sent a jolt of pain running up to the Scholar. He stifled his laughter with a cry of agony and fell from the ceiling, hitting the floor hard.

As the sword passed through the tendril, Griselda heard a voice like a thunderclap in her head: *DOMINATE.*

Before she could react, Carl tried to swipe at her legs. She jumped back and landed near Carl's glowing mace.

"You don't like this weapon anymore, do you?" she mocked.

Keeping her left hand gripping End March, she swooped up the mace in her right and hurled it at Carl. Though it missed hitting him directly, it collided with the portion of the ceiling his tendril was clinging to. The explosion shook the throne room as portions of the stone ceiling cascaded to the floor along with Carl. He landed hard on his left leg, which buckled and snapped. He howled in pain before it shifted to laughter.

Carl slowly got back up to his feet, a bone protruding from the side of his leg. He scowled down at the white spear that had erupted from his skin, but he didn't seem altogether too concerned. On the other side of the room, the Scholar got to his feet with an even uglier scowl. Livid, he flashed his teeth and receding gums as his eyes blinked in and out of the glowing state. He slapped his hands on the floor, and dozens of tendrils burst out from underneath his robes.

Griselda yelped and jumped back, swinging End March in front of her to ward off the tendrils. They halted whenever End March swung near, but eventually they encircled her. One snatched her up by the leg with such force that she dropped End March. She felt the tendril giving off heat through her pant leg. Panicking, she unsheathed her side sword and swiped at the tendril holding her upside down by the leg. Though it did connect, unlike End March, it didn't seem to have any effect. She could hear the moisture on her side sword left over from her fight with Sophia in the snow, sizzling as it made contact with the hot tendril. She continued to whack away at it, but it wouldn't cut.

"No, no, no!" Griselda screamed with each hack.

Though the Scholar seemed to resume his laughing, an audible sigh rang out from the other side of the room.

"Really? You too!" Carl yelled.

Griselda looked over and beheld yet another impossible sight. A red Roran, steaming and rapidly shrinking down to his normal size, was perched in the broken window, metal caps where his hands should be bracing himself in the frame. His bare feet were bloody on the broken stained glass. A sleeping Arno hung loosely in a wooden contraption that was fastened around Roran's shoulders and chest.

"Roran!" Griselda yelled. "Arno! You're alive!"

Griselda knew her brother had been forced down a hard path these last few months, but that did not prepare her for the sight of him. With patchy beard covering a face that would frighten Oros himself, Roran returned Carl's scowl a thousandfold. "Let her go," Roran said, the full force of his menace and ill will barely contained in his voice quivering with rage. "Let her go before I rip you to pieces!"

CHAPTER 36
REUNION

IT DIDN'T MATTER that Roran had lost his hands. It didn't matter that Roran couldn't use anything other than his own human strength. It didn't matter that they were all going to die. Roran was going to wield that sword anyway. He and Cormac had made that sword. Arno and Griselda had named it. End March was, collectively, their whole family's legacy, and he was going to wield it, hands or not. Even if he was up against Carl and some other filament monstrosity in scholar robes, Roran would do whatever it took to keep his siblings safe.

Roran ran to the center of the room, beneath the dangling Griselda, while the scholar figure was still confused, and picked up End March. With his teeth. His jaw clamped down on the long handle, feeling the immense heat of the white-hot blade with his face so close to the steel. Using all the muscles in his back and neck, Roran rapidly spun himself, which was all that End March needed to send a wave of flame in a circle around him. The momentum of the sword swing was so great that the sword was wrenched from his teeth, but not without first burning the tendrils surrounding Griselda and sending the Scholar flying into the wall. End March flew through the air and embedded itself into the wooden throne on the dais. The throne burst into flames.

Though it was not the time to dwell on it, Roran did get some small level of satisfaction from stealing the last breaths of the shattered king to make the jump up to the window and then burning his throne.

The tendrils dropped Griselda, who landed on Roran's shoulder. Roran heard her groan. The impact between his shoulder and her stomach could not have been pleasant.

"Sorry," Roran said. "Hard to catch without hands. Good to see you. I've got more to say, but—"

"It's . . . okay," she wheezed.

Roran bent over, and she slid off his shoulder and down to her feet. She looked down at Roran's own feet, which had left bloody prints from the window frame all the way to where he currently stood.

"Don't worry about it," Roran said, noticing her eyes looking down. "Worry about them."

Carl placed his hand on the protruding bone and shoved it back in with a grunt of pain. He then smiled as the wound started to steam and heal itself. Likewise, the Scholar, who had taken massive burns to his face and hands, looked at them and smiled too, the upper half of his face nearly invisible from all of the steam.

"Shit," Griselda said.

"Yeah," Roran replied. "It's so much worse being on this end of it."

"How is Arno sleeping through this?"

"Don't ask. Just focus. Who do you want?"

"I'll take the scholar," Griselda said.

"I've got one arm."

"Carl?"

"You know his name?" asked Roran.

"Don't ask. Just focus."

Roran nodded. "Right. Any brilliant plans? Or just brute force?"

"I'll let you know if I think of something," Griselda responded.

"Got it."

Roran raised his metal caps to his chin in a hand-to-hand guard. *Hey Beans?* Roran thought.

That's not my name, the red man replied in Roran's head.

I know you may not be too happy with me at the moment, but how dead are we? Roran asked.

Very.

Oh. Shit. Can you, I don't know, power up my metal caps like one of Pop's weapons?

Beans sighed in Roran's head. *It's not a bad idea, but it won't work. Doing that would continuously burn your arms, and you would have to constantly siphon from everyone around you to fight it.*

Well, can I siphon from these guys?

Siphoning from another host won't work either. The bond prevents energy from being stolen as only the filament can take from the host. However, they can still siphon from Griselda or Arno if they know how.

Double shit, Roran thought. *Well, can you help in any other—*

Fully healed, Carl charged at Roran.

You can still do some things without the form drawing on Arno. You can still heal somewhat, and you still won't get tired.

Roran found that out very quickly, as he blocked a tendril whip with his forearms. The skin sizzled but healed. He could apparently heal without hurting anything, yet he still *felt* the hurt himself. What puzzled him, however, was that the tendrils Carl sent to lash him had changed color. They were a bright blue earlier. Now, they looked like the night sky.

Roran ducked another swipe and stepped closer. Out of the

corner of Roran's eye, he saw Griselda grab End March, take up plow guard, and walk toward the Scholar, making sweeping upward cuts with each step. He knew all along she wasn't really spending all her time cooking growing up. She had to be practicing her swordplay when he wasn't looking, trying to best him without making it look like she was pushing herself that hard. Roran couldn't help but feel an immense sense of pride . . . that he couldn't afford to think about as he jumped a swipe aimed at his legs.

He continued to press Carl's position, next to rubble from a partially collapsed ceiling. Next to . . . was that Carl's mace?

That moment of distraction let Carl land a blow square in Roran's chest. He was pushed five feet back but remained standing. Chest healing from the burns already, Roran resumed his guard and continued to walk Carl down.

He heard Griselda behind him start launching waves of flame, feeling the glow and heat from each fireburst. She would be fine. He on the other hand . . .

"What's wrong, son of Cormac? Why stay puny?" Carl mocked.

Roran breathed in. Dodged a swipe. Breathed out. Blocked another on his sizzling forearm. Stepped closer.

"The little one in the back seems awfully quiet, too. Don't tell me he's dead?"

Carl had misjudged how quickly Roran could close the distance, even while in his human form. Roran took advantage of an overswing from the tendril and sprinted in, launching a metal-plated right upper-cut into Carl's solar plexus.

Carl gasped for air as his tendrils retreated inside his body. He fell to one knee, his remaining arm clutching at his ribcage.

"Learned that trick from Ewen," Roran spat. With his left arm, Roran cocked back and punched Carl's head directly into the stone floor. Though he was motionless, his face, currently halfway embedded in the stone floor, started to steam.

"There," Roran said, "Not dead. Happy Arno?"

"Roran, look out!"

Now that she only had to focus on one opponent, Griselda felt like she could handle Redaway. Moving through her steps, she launched fireburst after fireburst into the air, both as an offensive tactic and as a defensive countermeasure, as the tendrils would not try to attack her through the waves of flame. Though she would be fine, her brother, on the other hand, with the lack of hands, had no means of protection.

She risked a look over her shoulder. There Roran was, in the same stance he always used when beating up Griselda and Arno's bullies, marching toward Carl despite being whipped numerous times. Like that, Roran was an angry wall of stone threatening to fall on whoever was mean to his siblings. He would be fine.

Some things never change, she thought. *And I'm glad that he's one of them.*

She refocused on Redaway, who was once again trying to encircle her. Griselda went into high guard and spun End March around her head, showering the stone floor in a ring of fire. Redaway hissed and pulled back his tendrils that were licked by the flames.

"What happened to you?" Griselda asked. "You seemed so dedicated to your craft, to the Marches!"

"I'm *still* dedicated to the Marches," he said. "You just don't yet know *who* we are all marching for and toward."

Griselda heard a hard metallic clank. She risked another glance over her shoulder and saw Roran bury Carl's face into the stone floor. Then she also saw a stray tendril Redaway sent sneaking behind Roran.

"Roran, look out!"

But it was too late. The tendril wrapped around Roran's foot and tripped him. Roran fell hard, face-first into the stone rubble. The tendril then whipped him at incredible speed into the air and toward Redaway. Upside down, Arno's unconscious body slipped out and was flung from the harness. Griselda rushed over to him. She hooked End March on her back and barely had enough time to catch poor, little Arno's weak body. He was noticeably smaller than she had last seen him. And his leg . . . just the sight of the suffering he must have endured was enough to bring tears to her eyes.

"It's okay, Arno," she said, rubbing some dirt from his cheek, "Ellie's got you."

She looked up, helpless to stop Roran from being smashed into the wall and ceiling as the tendril snapped him back and forth. The harness on Roran's back was splintered and crushed to pieces, bits of wood and leather being scattered around the throne room. But then . . . wait . . . what was that in his mouth?

Griselda gasped as she saw Carl's mace clenched in Roran's teeth. As Redaway whipped Roran toward himself, Roran let go of the mace right as Redaway brought his body in close. The carried momentum launched the mace directly at the floor underneath Redaway. Griselda was blinded by a flash of light and a blast that set her ears ringing. The ground shook as the mace impacted with the stone, causing the throne room floor to collapse in and fall. Roran and Redaway disappeared in a cloud of dust as the floor fell to the grand hall below.

The portion of the floor Griselda was on slanted down toward the hole. She cradled Arno as they both slid down into the darkness.

———————

Roran's body was utterly shattered. He hurt in so many places that he lost track of his other senses. He could tell that his legs were broken, his ribs were broken, his arms, even his spine. Slowly, sight and sound came back to his perception. It was all he could do to prop his body up against a stone chunk of floor. As the dust cleared, he realized where he was. He was in the grand hall, below the throne room. This was the place where he had first killed those people, where he had dropped Arno in their blood. The first time he became a monster.

His body was erupting in steam from all the various breaks and cuts covering every square inch of his skin. So much effort was needed to just turn his head to the left and right, looking for Griselda and Arno. Were they okay? Or had they been caught up in the blast and floor collapse? Had he hurt them again?

"That—that was a clever trick!"

Roran groaned as the Scholar came strolling out of the cloud of dust. Eyes glowing like his tendrils, the scholar's right hand pushed his dislocated jaw back into place. That same hand then set his broken left shoulder. He moved his jaw in a casual circle and then smiled, showing his ugly mouth. The glow in his eyes diminished as he saw Roran's steaming body, crumpled up against a rock on the red carpet.

"You're a host too, aren't you?" the Scholar asked.

Roran couldn't speak; he had bitten partially through his tongue and vapor steamed from his mouth whenever he tried to breathe. Since he couldn't speak, he thought. *Beans?*

I told you, that's not my name.

"He can assimilate two hosts in one day!" the Scholar said enthusiastically. "First the man with one arm, then the man with no hands."

"Roran?" Griselda shouted out of the dust.

"No . . ." Roran mumbled. "Run . . ."

The Scholar looked in the direction of Griselda's voice and sent five tendrils her way. She screamed as both she and Arno were dragged into view and held in the air.

I don't care what your name is, Roran thought at Beans. *We need your help!*

Griselda, still holding Arno, though trapped in the burning tendrils, did her best to sing to her little, unconscious brother. "O-over mountains—" she then cried out, feeling the tendril's pressure and heat, "over . . . hill. Over r-river, lake so . . . still . . ."

Beans materialized next to Roran. "There's nothing to be done," he patted Roran on the shoulder. "We had a good run, Ass-face."

"Poof . . ." Roran said more clearly as his tongue healed.

"Interesting," the Scholar mused. He relaxed his tendril's grip on Griselda and Arno. "Your filament, it's very far along for someone as young as you are. So many strands! So much power, knowledge, and experience contained in that. Would you like to see mine? Well, more like . . . ours."

The room grew colder as if the air had come down from the highest mountains, or even higher still. Or maybe the heat was being sucked out of the room. The clouds of dust stopped moving, like time itself had come to a standstill. The stone walls began to shake as an enormous presence made itself known to physical world. The wall behind the Scholar changed to a massive eye that mirrored the night sky. The starry pupils, moving everywhere at once, looking at everything.

"We're too far from the river, so this is only a fraction, but soon, there will be enough suffering where it can manifest all over this land."

Beans yelped and disappeared as soon as the many glowing pupils focused on him.

DOMINATE, the thing said in Roran's head before the wall returned to normal. Apparently, Griselda had heard it too as she looked around the room, still clutched in the night tendrils.

I think I have an idea, Roran thought at Beans.

Good, whatever it takes. I do not want to be eaten by that thing.

You know how you can poof into thin air?

Yeah?

Could you do that to a person . . . or three?

Kid, I'm not exactly what the academics call fully corporeal. I'm not trapped in a physical body, so I can do it. You're physical matter. It's something I've never tried. Anything could happen. And it would take an exceptional amount of lifeforce. And before you say it, I can't just drain you dry and kill you to save your siblings. That would kill me too.

Roran swallowed a mouthful of steam as the Scholar looked at Arno and Griselda.

"Did you know this little one's nearly drained?" the Scholar asked. "Fascinating! So that's what happens if we pull from humans instead."

Dreams . . . dreams and future intent. You can drain those, right? That is just as powerful a force.

Yeah . . . but you only have one right now. One dream left. I don't think you want that—

"Just do it!" Roran shouted out loud. He fixed his eyes on Arno and Griselda. His unconscious—no, sleeping—baby brother. Precious and pure, hopeful and righteous. His brilliant, strong sister. A warrior and scholar in her own right. A great leader and caretaker. The world did not deserve them. He did not deserve them. They would only continue to get hurt if they were around him. Tears began to streak down his face.

The Scholar looked over at Roran. "Do what?"

"Griselda . . ." Roran croaked through his tears. "Take care of Arno for me."

Griselda cocked her head and furrowed her brows, confused by what Roran was trying to say.

If you do this, I doubt you'll like what you become on the other side. A man without dreams, without hope, barely alive, hardly enough to even feed on. How can you continue living without anything left to hope for?

"Regardless of rewards or consequences," he said to himself, to Griselda, and even to Beans. "Do what you can to bear the light in this dark."

A tear came down Griselda's cheek as well. She nodded.

The Scholar cocked his head in amusement. "Oh, he's in so much pain that he's delirious. I've heard about this. Good thing you can't get Grief Sickness twice," he paused and then put his hand to his chin. "Or can you?"

"I love you both. This is for the best," Roran said.

"We love you too," Griselda replied.

The Scholar frowned but didn't further interrupt. He seemed to be studying the whole interaction.

Roran gritted his teeth. "I'll think about the two of you . . . every day. A-and maybe," he stammered, fully losing himself to grief. "One day, I'll see you again, on the next leg of the March."

Beans sighed audibly in his head. *Roran, you have to say it.*

"I give up my dream," Roran choked. "Of keeping our family together. Save Arno and Griselda, even if it means I won't get to see them again."

I'll do what I can.

The stone rubble in the room began to vibrate.

"What are you doing?" the Scholar asked.

Griselda and Arno's skin began to glow and shimmer. "We the sun," she continued to sing. "We shine on all."

The Scholar yelped in pain and released his hold on them, the strange light seeming to react negatively to his own. "Are you doing what I think you're doing? Is that even possible?"

"Morn to rise and night to fall. Morn to rise and night to fall."

Their glowing skin became brighter and brighter, lighting up the grand hall as if the sun was still shining. On carpeted ground, holding Arno in her lap, Griselda looked at her hands and Arno's face. The glow was so bright Roran had to look away, his eyes couldn't take it to look at such a light. But he looked down and noticed that he was glowing with the same immaculate light. The three of them, shining like new Beacons of Wilheim, glowed so intensely that their skin became translucent. Glowing vapor poured off their skin and swirled around them. Then Roran realized that the vapor *was* his skin, his whole body was being broken down into liquid light. Roran wondered if this is what it was like to be Arno all the time, to be someone's sunshine. Roran wondered if he could ever be the sun for someone else, what it would take to care and nurture and help so many people. And above all else, he wondered where the warmth of the sun came from, how far it traveled in the darkness to reach them, how diligent it was in its ever-long journey into the hungry, starry pitch of night, how the warmth felt the same whether he was happy or sad, whether he was with them or not. Even when the sun had set, its warmth never truly left; some heat would always remain. If Roran could become like the sun, would Arno and Griselda still feel him as he knew he would feel them? Would they be able to feel the warmth of the sun in the palm of their hand and know that it was him, that he sent that warmth from wherever he was, just for them?

Before his mouth became intangible, he wanted to say one last thing to his brother and sister. "You both, you make me proud. You make the world proud. It doesn't deserve you, but you make it better all the same."

The room became nothing but light in a flash of white-hot heat that lit the carpet on fire. And the three children of Cormac —Arno, Griselda, and Roran—vanished into the unknown.

EPILOGUE

"WHAT DO you mean you threw him out the window?!" Ewen exclaimed.

Carl shrugged. "I mean what I say. I defenestrated King Morgen II."

"Ya defen—what? Dat's-dat's not a real word!" Ewen shouted.

Urrem, Ewen, and Carl were standing over the king's body. Urrem expected the body to be grisly and broken from a roughly 60-foot fall. But he didn't expect the king's body would be black and rotting after a day's worth of decay.

"Look Willie, I ain't no scientist from ya fancy academies, but I've seen a lot of death. Dis is not da body of a man dat fell from a window! Not only are ya lying to me, but ya denied me da Ardhatazian right of conquest. I should've been beating da daisies out of da old coot as is my right. Dis is not the greatest start of our relationship as lord and king."

Carl scowled.

Ewen scowled back much harder, looming into Carl's personal space. "Titles mean piss water, ya hear? King Carl?

534 • ANTON JONES

Sure. But know it straight, bird whisperer. Ya serve me and Ardhataz, got it?"

Carl held his ground and looked up unflinching into the eyes of the massive Blood-Red King.

Ewen stepped back and looked Carl up and down. "Ya smell funny, ya know that? Like da Scholar and da Cormac pup. Ya got something to hide?"

"You want me to oversee the reconstruction and integration of Wilheim into Ardhataz. Do you not?"

Ewen stroked his beard. "Fine, be dat way, but just so ya know, it would take me very little effort to march back in here and depose yer bastard hide all over again. As long as both me and mine get access to dem caves and crystals under dis peninsula, I won't have to beat yer face in."

Carl's eyes seemed to almost flash with recognition, but he quickly hid behind a stoic mask and shrugged.

Urrem guessed the uneasy threat would have to do.

Urrem followed Ewen into the keep proper. The grand hall was strewn with rubble from the floor of the throne room that had collapsed above. Not only that, but in the center of the rubble were scorch marks. Not just any scorch marks, but the stone itself was blackened as if it had been struck by lightning.

"Da black marks created a ring of shadows dat outline da rest of da rubble from da epicenter of whatever unholy, Imeel-Illin-forsaking happening took place here," Urrem mused to himself.

"Where'd ya learn a word like that?" Ewen asked.

"What?"

"Epi-whose-it?"

"Epicenter: da center of an earthquake. I needed to know a smidge about earthquakes for carpentry and mining so we could be prepared for 'em. Dad had a Willie scholar shipped in just to brief us on da bridge building and mining process."

Ewen blinked and shrugged. "Sure ya did. Ya and the stumpy, one-armed brick can write each other fancy letters using yer fancy made-up words. Anyway, it don't smell right. Nothing 'bout dis smells right. Da Scholar isn't talking again. Our new lord and savior Carl's just as stone walled as da Scholar. Dey're hiding something. I don't like it. Keep an eye on 'em would ya?"

Urrem nodded. Ewen clapped him on the shoulder and clanked away in his white-and-black plate.

"Dese Willies be crazy," a familiar voice laughed behind him. "First of all, dey have no sheep. Second, half da houses I've inspected have suicided Willies. Bunch o' morons drinking themselves silly on Life Nectar. Dey have no brains in deir heads."

Urrem turned around. "Briggs!"

As Urrem went for a hug, Briggs walked up and lightly tapped Urrem in the groin.

Urrem bent over and wheezed, "Ya wily bastard."

"Yer not da only one with a shiny new promotion. Ya moved up, and so someone needed to replace ya. Guess who."

"Con-congratulations," Urrem responded, catching his breath and righting himself, "Captain Briggs."

Zerebril and Connor were led into the cave system. Both were given merely burlap clothing to combat the harsh Ardhatazian winter. Zerebril was already chilled to the bone. Connor's teeth were chattering, though he would never admit he was cold. The shackles clicked together as the whole chain gang was led to the Highland Pits, the most barbaric place in the world.

The cave systems couldn't truly be called caves. More like blackened holes in the ground with many interconnecting tunnels that connected warrior quarters, prisoner quarters, and audience quarters together. The tunnels all led to the massive pits in the center of the complex, where multiple fights could be happening and bet on at once.

536 • ANTON JONES

Small windows were carved in the tunnels and filled with iron bars, so that both audience members and workers could stick various objects into the pits to create additional obstacles.

"Ya hear? We getting a large batch of fresh pit meat come soon," one of the slavers said to the other as they guided the chain gang on either side of Zerebril and Connor.

"Yeah, I did. All da top-crop Willies. We'll see how top crop dey are compared to da Tazzian veterans. Very few Willies can claim lordship over da Pits, but's still fun to watch anyway."

Zerebril looked to his right into one of the iron-barred windows between his tunnel and one of the pits. On the other side of the tunnel stood a harrowing sight. A man with his head encased in rough iron stood in the center of the pit with five spearmen surrounding him. His iron-head prison only had small holes for breathing, and two punctures for eye slots, which looked like they had been added haphazardly after the fact. He was wearing a cloth for his waist, but nothing else. And all over his body were hundreds of screws.

"I give you the Tazzian Tiger Tamers versus a newcomer, the Screw-Turned Man!" the announcer bellowed to the audience's cheers.

The man didn't even have a weapon, Zerebril thought. *Where was the honor in that? How was he going to . . . oh.*

It happened very quickly. One spearman made a thrust at the Screw-Turned Man, who turned sideways and caught the spear haft in between the screws lining his rib cage and the screws lining his biceps. With a swift motion the man snapped the haft and caught the spear-tipped end. He then flung it right through the throat of the man who attempted to stab him. The screws, which Zerebril could *hear* cranking in the man's skin and muscles, turned as if the man was willing them to rotate his limbs and store vast amounts of kinetic force. His limbs snapped in motion as the countless screws turned and released his muscles, like a large tree branch that would snap back into place after being pulled too far back. The cranking and snapping was heard over the crowd, his skin like stretching leather straps, his muscles like a cracking bull whip.

Another tried to stab him, but the spear point was deflected off the host of screws covering his back, though the blow still tore at his skin from which he bled sickly, greenish, red blood from his jaundiced, slack skin. The man may as well have been wearing the world's most painful plate armor as each and every thrust was either caught and trapped by the screw heads or outright deflected off the metal. One by one, each spearman's haft was splintered or taken and used against them with expert precision. In mere moments, four of them were dead. The final one dropped his spear and cried out for mercy. The Screw-Turned Man didn't seem to understand the gesture. Instead, the screws turned his right arm back, released, and snapped his arm forward, sending an inhumanly strong punch into the man's jaw. The man flew into the side of the pit, which shook the wall.

The force of the impact shattered—which Zerebril could also hear—not only the punched man's skull, but also the bones in the Screw-Turned Man's knuckles, hand, wrist, and forearm. The Screw-Turned man held up his right arm in front of his dark eye holes to examine it as his whole foremost part of his right arm dangled unnaturally, screws knocking against each other as the skin that seemed not wholly attached to the man's body jostled and bunched together. The structure entire of his arm jounced and bobbed at the fulcrum of his elbow. He seemed to feel no pain, and, like a child, was delighted at the sight of his arm bouncing as all of the ligaments, muscles, and bones had been snapped, broken, or knocked loose.

The whole audience was silent. Even the announcer was flabbergasted and didn't offer any commentary. The doors opened behind the Screw-Turned Man as he stiffly walked out of the arena, mumbling some tune under his breathe that was muffled by the iron casing.

538 • ANTON JONES

"Oros's shit," Connor said. "I sure hope we don't have to fight whatever monster that guy is. I think I prefer Ewen over that thing."

Zerebril nodded. Supposedly, all kinds of horrors were lurking in the Pits creating the wide-appeal spectacle that attracted gamblers, slavers, and blood-thirsty rabble from all around Verdin. Soon, Zerebril would have to fight something like *that* thing. And he was not ready.

ACKNOWLEDGMENTS

This effort was brought to you by many people. I would like to thank my editor and publisher, Jill Carlyle, as well as Concordia University Chicago. Both made it possible for me to involve my students in the creative process, which has always been one of my biggest dreams. I was allowed to provide students and alumni a competition for creating the cover art and maps. I wish to thank Meghan Cummings, Patryk Dabrowski, Ronnalynn Fleming, William C. Foellmer, Cesar Hernandez Gonzalez, Joshua McCoy, Guadalupe Patino, August Penaloza, Jazmine Pittman, Annika Wassilak, Alexis Wommack, and our winner, Caleb Egland. Students Rayna Wagner and Dominick Jolley modeled for the cover art while Nathaniel Clayton photographed the reference images of the models. I would also like to thank Professor Nikkole Huss and Professor Angela Dieffenbach for assisting with the creation of this competition. I was a very, very lost puppy without their expertise.

In the same way, I was also able to enlist Concordia students and alumni to be a part of the beta reading process. I am grateful for the help of Evalynn Berg, Maxine Bittner, Caleb Egland, Isabella Gentile, Eduardo Hinds, Harry Mueller, Eric Perry, Abigail Porter, and Maggie Shasko. These students were enlisted from the Concordia creatives group I run that workshops a variety of creative work such as visual art, poetry, fiction, drama, songs, hymns, and instrumentals. They are all very talented, dedicated, and insightful. Watch out for their names in a few years. They teach me as much as I teach them. Other beta readers include Mike Curtis, author of *Around the World in 80 Sandwiches;* Malachi Allgood, coach of cross country; and Josiah Hahn, teacher of middle school. They all deserve the highest praise in maximizing the potential for this work.

Because AI is the bane of my existence, Caleb Egland was also commissioned for the creation of the book trailer, which featured interviews of some of the mentioned beta readers. In addition to beta reading, Abby Porter also helped with social media promotion, something I notoriously hate to do and am very grateful to have help with. God willing, I will be able to work with these great people again on the next book in the series.

ABOUT THE AUTHOR

Anton Jones is a tenure-track professor at Concordia University Chicago, where he teaches English and creative writing, mentors the track team, and plays pranks on his students. In his spare time, he puts on armor and fights in the great sport of buhurt under the banner of the Chicago Hydras. He wallops and is walloped by swords, maces, and axes, all in the name of glorious research.

ALSO BY ANTON JONES

Explore the depths of *This is Not A Death Sentence: A Memoir in Verse* where poetry meets the raw truths of living on the schizophrenic spectrum.

Jones crafts a poignant narrative that weaves together the threads of depression, mania, boxing, door-to-door sales, delusional crushes, poverty, haunted houses, suicide, healthcare challenges, homelessness, fatherhood, and the backdrop of the Pacific Northwest. His poetry captures the essence of this lived experience, depicting the suffocation of coherent thought through a cascade of movements, associations, and vivid hallucinogenic imagery. Despite years of decline and what seems like an endless fight, Jones finds the strength to confront his illness, refusing to surrender to despair.